Borrowed Heart

Book One of the Evie Sanders Series

a novel by
Linda Lamberson

BORROWED HEART
by
Linda Lamberson

ISBN: 978-0-615-49876-8

To my husband—
Thank you for making it possible for me
to spend more time with our family and
for keeping your grumblings to a minimum
while I ventured down the path of writing fiction.
You are the love of my life.

And to my children—
I'm the luckiest mom *ever* because I have
the two best boys in the whole entire universe!
I will always love *you* more—no backs!

Acknowledgements:

Kim "Kimmy" Perez, you're an awesome sounding board!
Thanks for willingly coming along with me on this ride
and for loving the characters as much as I do.

Maggie Vandermeer, thank you for taking on this editing
project. You asked the important questions and
helped me strengthen and polish part one of this story.
I love the book more for it!

Patrick Uranin, amazing cover! The website you
designed is terrific too. Thanks for all your hard work
—and the Twitter crash course!

Prologue

"Eve, how much of the accident do you remember?" Peter began.

"Not much." I strained to remember anything about it, but I couldn't. The chain of events was all so hazy. I looked down at the floor as if it could provide me with the clarity I sought. "I was driving ... there was another car—two cars, I think. One of the drivers was ... drunk. But there was someone else ... something else happened." I was mumbling, trying to talk myself through the accident. And then a memory flashed through my mind; I saw two bright lights barreling towards me as I was standing in the middle of the highway. Instantly, the accident, or at least the very last part of it, became crystal clear.

No one could have survived that, I told myself. I gasped and looked at Peter in terror.

"How ... how long have I been ... dead?" My words were barely audible, choked back by the fear and anguish of my horrifying realization. Peter glanced down at his watch.

"Nearly five days," he said apologetically.

Nearly five days. I repeated Peter's words in my head, not really knowing how to process this information.

"Am ... am I in Heaven?" I asked in shock.

"It's a little complicated," Peter answered.

Borrowed Heart

1. Starstruck

"I've never seen an aura like this before," she said in her thick Eastern-European accent, shifting her gaze from my hands to my eyes. "It's so strange ..."

"I don't understand. What's so strange?" I asked. I had been there for all of two minutes and already thought this was some sort of a scam. I tried to pull my hands away from the woman sitting across the table from me, but she only tightened her grip. Her almond-shaped black eyes looked almost sinister with the thick layers of black eyeliner and mascara around them. She pulled me in closer.

"It seems as though your fate is shifting—*changing*—right before my very eyes." She looked down at my hands again and began mumbling to herself in her native language. Then she glanced back up at me in alarm.

"Listen to me very carefully. What I'm about to say is important," she warned gravely. "Bad things always happen in threes. You will have two near-death experiences, and then the third ... I'm sorry ..." Her voice trailed off.

Wait a minute—did she really just tell me that I was going to die? I was beyond shocked. I was beyond offended. I was downright pissed off. This was supposed to be some fun, harmless psychic reading. Some "oh-you-have-a-boyfriend-who-loves-you-and-will-be-with-you-forever" type of crap—not some "I-hate-to-be-the-one-to-tell-you-but-you're-on-death's-door" cryptic voodoo message from beyond. Who was she anyway? A psychic? Yeah, right! More like a *psycho*—a twisted, sick fraud who got off dressing like a gypsy and preying on the fears of others.

"Look," I began, "I don't know who the hell you think you are or what you think you're doing, but if you think I believe one word of this psychic *babble*, you're crazy." I tried to stand up, but I couldn't. Her long fingers were still clutched

3

around my wrists like a hawk's talons around its next meal. "Psychic babble, hmm? Let's see." Still grasping both of my wrists, she closed her eyes and began spewing out various facts about me. "My dear, you traveled from Michigan to be here today. Your parents—they are lawyers. In fact, the two of them met in law school and are still together. And you—you're very smart," she opened her eyes and studied my face, "but skeptical. And you trust your own judgment above everyone else's, even that of your parents."

Okay, so she was dead on, I thought. But I was still convinced the psychic was a fraud. Emma could've told her this stuff about me. It was my best friend's idea to come here today, and she had met with the psychic first.

"You could have pumped my friend for most of that information," I said suspiciously. "And judging from my reaction to your *reading*, you easily could have guessed the rest."

"You have been through a lot in your young life," the psychic continued, ignoring me. "When you were younger, someone close to you was very sick." She suddenly looked at me like she knew my deepest, darkest secrets. "Your mother … she almost died."

"What? How … how did you know about that?" Now I genuinely was surprised. Very few people, of whom Emma was not one, had known about my mom's battle with cancer. It was the main reason why my dad retired from practicing law at a large firm in downtown Chicago to do legal consulting. It was also why we moved to Sawyer, Michigan when I was nine to spend more time together as a family.

"Trust me, dear," the psychic responded, "I know more about you than I would like to. And I'm very sorry to tell you this, but you have been marked with the Curse of Three. I've only ever heard of the Curse. I have never before met anyone who was stricken with it." She paused, inhaling deeply. "I'm

4

sorry, my dear … but you will not see your nineteenth birthday."

My mind, my soul, my entire body exploded with rage. I tore my hands away from the psychic's grip only to lurch forward in my bed startled and confused. Beads of sweat formed on my brow as a wave of panic swept over me. I looked around and laughed nervously. I was in my dorm room. It was just a dream. It was only a bad dream.

I took a deep breath and sighed in relief before groaning and falling back into bed. My face was buried under a blanket of my long brown hair, which helped block out some of the morning light beaming through my dorm windows. I knew I had to get up, but I was exhausted. My hand blindly wandered over to my bedside table, grabbed my alarm clock, and brought it inches from my face. Eight fifteen. *Crap!* It was later than I thought.

A new type of panic washed over me; I was going to be late for my psychology class—again. I grabbed my glasses and flew out of bed. The winter chill hit me as soon as I stood up. I groaned once more. It was nearly a month into the second semester of my freshman year at Indiana University, and Bloomington was a pretty cold and miserable place to be in the dead of winter.

My roommate, Lisa, was nowhere to be found. She was probably already eating breakfast. Shivering, I scanned the floor on my side of the room for anything that resembled clean clothes. I spotted my favorite grey IU sweatshirt, already worn through around the neck and sleeves from overuse, and quickly threw it over the T-shirt I had slept in the previous night. On the other side of my bed, I found a pair of jeans and my boots and pulled them on. Usually I wouldn't be caught dead wearing my glasses out in public, but I was running so late I didn't have time to mess with my contacts. I gathered my hair into a makeshift bun at the nape of my neck and hid the rest of it under an off-white knit hat. No make-up other than a little bit of clear lip gloss, but that was standard protocol for me. I only wore makeup when I went out at night. I popped a stick of gum in my mouth and threw on my winter coat. Then I grabbed my backpack, my mittens, and my roommate's scarf, which I absolutely adored, and bolted out the door praying I could still catch the campus bus.

Not a chance. I ran out of my dorm building just in time to watch the bus pull away from the stop. *Great.*

I really hated Wednesdays. It was bad enough that I had four classes and my biology lab today, but on Wednesdays my psychology class started at eight thirty in the morning. Apparently, Professor Swain already had some prior commitment this weekday morning. And rather than reschedule the entire three-day-a-week class, he forced his students to show up an hour earlier than the regularly scheduled lecture once a week. Unfortunately, Swain's seminar was a prerequisite for my major, so I sucked it up and registered for it anyway, knowing I would regret it someday.

As luck would have it, today would be the day of several regrets, including this class. Out of breath, I ran into the lecture hall later than usual. Swain stopped mid-sentence and glared at me. The room fell completely silent; I could feel every pair of eyes on me. Blood started rushing to my face, and I was thankful that my cheeks were already flushed from the brisk walk to class in below freezing temperatures.

"I'm glad you decided to grace us with your presence this morning," Swain said condescendingly while he peered at me over the top rims of his bifocals.

"Um, sorry ... rough morning." Mortified, I slinked into the first open chair I spotted and removed my jacket and mittens as quickly and inconspicuously as possible.

Swain's lecture was on Erikson's developmental stages of the human psyche, but I couldn't pay attention to a word he was saying. I was still rattled by my nightmare. It had been a while since I had even thought about the psychic. So why now? As I sat there in class, I mentally rehashed the day I met Madame Sasha.

It was nearly two years ago during my junior year of high school that Emma had overheard one of her mom's friends talking about a "truly gifted" psychic in Chicago that everyone should see at least once in their lives. Emma loved that sort of stuff. The next thing I knew, we were ditching school and driving the hour-and-a-half to Chicago so we could pay this woman to tell us about our futures.

I remembered standing outside the small wood-sided house built next to the El tracks, which loomed above. The two-story structure was painted a pale, buttercup yellow with white trim. A rusted-chain link fence surrounded the house, separating it from its grim surroundings. It was a charming little home in a not-so-charming urban neighborhood. Emma and I giggled anxiously as we slowly made our way up the stairs of the house to the small front porch. Before we even had a chance to ring the bell, however, a middle-aged woman opened the door.

"Good afternoon," she said in her thick accent. "I am Madame Sasha."

Emma and I giggled again like little kids. Emma was excited to be there. I, on the other hand, felt downright foolish. I didn't believe in any of this nonsense, but Emma swore up and down that this woman was the real deal. And as Emma's best friend, it was my duty to be her partner in crime that day to go see this so-called real deal. Besides, it had been a beautiful spring day in April, and I didn't feel like wasting it away sitting in class.

I remembered cringing at the thought of how my boyfriend Ryan would react if he knew I had ditched school to go see a psychic. He would have been disappointed to say the least. It was the one time I was glad we had gone to separate schools. For the most part, I was a good student. I certainly hadn't made a habit of skipping class. But Ryan had taken high school much more seriously than I had. He had graduated near the top of his class and never ditched, especially for something this asinine. No, I wouldn't ever tell him about this little adventure. In fact, if I had my say, this trip would be one of life's little moments I wouldn't recount to anyone.

"Come in, come in." Madame Sasha smiled as she waved us into her home. Her long dark hair was pulled severely away from her face and tied back with a multi-colored silk sash. She had dark, olive-toned skin, which I suspected would have looked more youthful and attractive if she hadn't used so much makeup. She wore a garnet-colored button-down silk blouse tucked into a billowy, black skirt that ended just above her ankles. She was barefoot; her toenails were painted a dark plum color, the same color as on her long, manicured fingernails. Large, gold hoops hung from her ears, and several gold bangles were stacked on each wrist. Her fingers were adorned with gold rings inset with oversized, semi-precious stones of every color—amethysts, yellow and blue topazes, garnets, and a huge black onyx. Around her neck, however, she wore an understated, small, silver charm on a thin, silver chain; it looked out of place compared to the rest of her ornate jewelry.

I remembered the smell of Madame Sasha's strong, musky perfume as Emma and I followed the psychic into her living room. The room's décor seemed to be at odds with the exotic-looking woman standing in the middle of it. The overwhelming scent of sweet floral incense and Pine-Sol soon filled my nose. The room itself was surprisingly pink—the carpet, the drapes—even the armchairs were all a dusty rose color. Only the sofa differed in motif; it was covered in white, satin polyester that was ambushed by an explosion of bold pink and green floral patterns. What was even more remarkable was that *all* of the upholstered furniture was protected underneath thick, translucent plastic sheaths. Plastic runners also covered large sections of the carpet. The room could only be described as tacky-retro-granny-chic run amuck.

"Okay, I see that Erikson's infant and toddler stages are not moving us this morning," Professor Swain barked loudly and abruptly. His voice jolted me back into reality. Was he singling me out again? Anxiety began creeping up the back of my throat, making it difficult for me to breathe. I peered up at Swain out of the corner of my eye and then quickly scanned the lecture hall. Thankfully, I was far from the only person whose head seemed to be in the clouds this morning. Relieved, I looked down at my notebook and tried not to call any additional attention to myself.

"Let's end class early today," Swain announced in frustration. "We'll pick up on Friday where we left off today. And everyone, please bring a little more enthusiasm with you to the next class. This information could appear on your midterm exam." He gathered his lecture notes and walked swiftly out the door.

Thank you, Professor Swain, I said to myself. Now I didn't have to race across campus to make my bio lab. Still somewhat preoccupied with my dream, I absentmindedly began packing up my stuff.

"Hey, would you mind giving me your notes from last Friday's class?"

Startled, I looked up to see who was asking. My jaw dropped open. It was *him.*

"That is if you were here last Friday," he added.

Painfully aware of how ridiculous I must have looked, I snapped my mouth shut, stood up, and put on my jacket. I had noticed him the first day of class. In fact, I was pretty sure that every girl in the class had noticed him. He was stunning. Standing next to me, he towered over my five-foot-seven-inch frame. His thick, black, wavy hair ended just below his ears. He had the deepest blue eyes I'd ever seen; they looked like dark blue sapphires against his golden skin. His black parka was unzipped, and I could see traces of his chest and stomach muscles beneath his white T-shirt.

I must have been standing there for a while, utterly star-struck, because he leaned down towards me and picked up my backpack. As he did, his right shoulder brushed up against my arm and my skin tingled at the point of contact. I gasped.

Get a grip, I told myself. I took a deep breath to calm myself and was hit by the smell of mint, citrus, and a hint of something else—what was it? Chlorine? Whatever the combination, he smelled amazing. I felt a wave of heat begin to creep up my face. Knowing full well that my cheeks were turning red, I turned my head away from him slightly.

My reaction to him surprised me. Yes, he was hot as hell; but it wasn't like he was the only attractive guy I had met at IU. So why was I acting like a complete idiot around him? It was probably because I was still flustered from the unwanted attention I'd received when I walked into class so late. The fact that I looked like something the cat had dragged in from the back woods certainly didn't help matters any. Of all the days this guy had to ask me for my notes, why *this* one? I suddenly was annoyed with myself for not even putting in my contacts that morning.

"Sorry, I didn't mean to startle you. I guess I should've introduced myself before I tried to snag your notes. I'm Quinn." His voice was soft, velvety, and deep; it was like music to my ears, but it still paled in comparison to his appearance. There was no need for introductions. I definitely knew who Quinn was—just not by name ... not until now anyway. Trying to regain my composure, I glanced over at his two friends waiting for him in the wings.

"What, Larry and Curly don't come to class either?" I asked. I desperately wanted to run out of the lecture hall—away from Quinn and his friends—before I made an even bigger fool of myself. I zipped up my jacket, adjusted the scarf around my neck, and grabbed my mittens before motioning towards the front door of class. But Quinn just stood there, unfazed by my gesture.

"Would you trust the likes of them for class notes?" He smiled at me, and I felt more heat surge through my face. Quinn's smile was captivating; it made him even more attractive and charming, if that were at all possible. Even if he hadn't been blocking my escape route, I would have been afraid to move for fear that my knees would buckle under me with my first step.

This is totally ridiculous, I snapped at myself. *Stop acting like a bumbling idiot; grab your stuff and walk out of here.* I took a deep breath and looked directly into Quinn's eyes.

"And you would trust me? A perfect stranger that you randomly picked out of the class?"

"You tell me. Should I not trust you? I mean, you certainly look smarter than those two heathens ... and a bit more attractive I might add," Quinn said without missing a beat.

"Great, so I'm a step above a heathen. Thanks," I responded, taking another mental inventory of my appearance and shuddering. Totally cute guy talking to a seriously gnarly-looking girl—and he knew it. *Could this morning get any worse?*

"Let me ask you something," I continued. "Do you always make a point of being so nice to someone you're asking for help?" The flippant edge in my voice was not overlooked by Quinn's friends. I swore I heard "Mayday" calls coming from their general direction as they tried to stifle their laughter.

"Let me ask *you* something." His voice remained calm as

he ignored his friends. "Do you always make a point of being so difficult when someone asks for your help? Hmm … I bet Professor Swain would have something to say about that." He flashed me a playful little grin. Heat surged into my face again. It wasn't like me to be this rude. A twinge of guilt rippled through me for acting so callously towards Quinn. I just couldn't remember the last time a guy made me feel so self-conscious, and it bothered me. In fact, I couldn't remember the last time I even cared about what some random guy thought about me. I momentarily set aside my foul mood and forced myself to return Quinn's smile.

"Didn't he already say enough about me this morning?" I asked as I rolled my eyes.

Quinn laughed. The sound of his laughter drew me in further. I wanted to hear it again, but he simply handed me my backpack instead.

"Oh, thanks." I took my bag from his outstretched hand and threw it over my shoulder. "Look, I'm sorry. It's just that good moods and early mornings don't really go hand-in-hand with me—especially when I'm running late for my next class. Speaking of which," I looked down at my watch, "I really have to run. Excuse me." I gently pushed by Quinn and walked out the lecture hall.

I opened the double doors of the psychology building, keenly aware that Quinn was right behind me. A rush of cold winter air hit my face. I welcomed it. I took a deep breath, letting the frosty air fill my lungs. Exhaling slowly, I watched as a thick cloud of steam escaped my mouth and quickly dissipated before my eyes. I had to admit, there was something beautiful about the fresh-fallen snow on this sunny winter's morning. Everything was white and pure, covered in a blanket of snow. Every limb of every tree looked like it had been frosted with a layer of vanilla buttercream at least an inch or two thick. Icicles were glistening like crystals in the sunlight, hanging from the branches like Christmas ornaments. Even the crisp air smelled fresh and inviting.

As if my feet were on autopilot, I started walking towards my next class, being careful to avoid patches of ice. Quinn walked alongside me, talking the entire way. *Maybe his next class is across campus, too*, I thought.

As we walked, I couldn't help but wonder what everyone we passed was thinking when they saw what an odd pair he and I made.

Quinn mentioned he was from somewhere just outside of Chicago. He also mentioned he was a sophomore and was attending IU on a swim scholarship.

Figures, I said to myself.

"So what about you? What's your story?" Quinn asked, just as we arrived in front of the building that housed my biology lab. I honestly couldn't figure out why this guy was suddenly so interested in getting to know me—or why I was suddenly so interested in getting to know him.

"Ah, just in the nick of time." I let out a quick sigh of relief followed by a little laugh. "Here's my next stop ... I guess I'll see you in class on Friday."

"Yeah, um, speaking of this Friday ... what are you doing that night?" Quinn took a step forward, closing the distance between us. I could feel the warmth of his breath kiss my face.

"Friday night? Why?" I asked hesitantly. *He* couldn't possibly be asking *me* out.

"Well, there's going to be this huge party at a friend's fraternity—invitation only. I could get you on the list if you wanted to stop by—you know, to show my appreciation for letting me borrow your notes."

Not a date, I told myself.

"Oh thanks, but that's not really necessary." Did I detect

a hint of disappointment in my voice? What was going on with me?

"I know, but it'll be fun—lots of people, live music, the whole deal. You really should come. Bring some friends if you want."

"Sounds great," I blurted out without thinking. *Why did I just say that?* I lashed out at myself. "But … uh, I'm not sure I can go." I was backtracking. "My friends and I already have plans that night." I tried to sound nonchalant, but my words were forced and my throat was parched, making my voice sound raspy. I felt the blood rushing to my cheeks, no doubt turning them deep crimson. My body was betraying me, and I was sure that Quinn could see it. I dropped my head slightly, masking my embarrassment by paying an undue amount of attention to the task of taking off my mittens.

Quinn lifted my face up towards his and held it there for a moment until my eyes reluctantly caught up. When our eyes met, he gently brushed the tip of my nose with his finger.

"You should come." He smiled at me. His perfect full lips parted so that I could see his pearly white teeth. His smile was so seductive; it was like a secret weapon, rendering me utterly defenseless against his charms. I felt my heart skip a beat.

"Thanks again for your notes," he added as he turned and walked away. Unable to move, I just stood there and watched him leave.

It dawned on me that I hadn't even agreed to give Quinn my psych notes. He just presumed I would hand them over. And he was right—I would. Nevertheless, that still didn't excuse his arrogance. Irritated, I frowned.

Quinn suddenly turned towards me again, catching me off guard. *Crap!* He probably thought my expression was due to his leaving.

"That's just great, Evie. Just great," I mumbled under my

breath. "Way to look like even more of an idiot."

"Hey," Quinn called out to me. "What's your name?"

"Eve—but most people call me Evie," I managed.

"Well, *Ee-vee*," he said, drawing out each syllable of my name, "I hope to see you Friday night." He winked at me, turned back around, and continued to walk away.

It wasn't until Quinn was almost out of sight that my heart jumpstarted itself and began pounding in my ears. This was nothing—nothing at all, I assured myself. I wasn't acting like myself today. My reaction to Quinn was just par for the course for the strange morning I was having. It was just bad timing that he chose today of all days to flirt with me to get his hands on my psych notes. I'm sure he used his God-given "talents" all the time to get what he wanted. He probably suspected I was still rattled by walking into class late, and he used it to his advantage, knowing exactly how I'd react to his little performance. And I was sure I did not disappoint. I cringed, realizing what a predictable and easy target I'd been.

Out of nowhere, Ryan's face popped into my head. He hadn't crossed my mind once since Quinn had approached me after class. I cringed again, even more disgusted with my-self. *What in the world was wrong with me today?* I pulled out my cell phone and called Ryan, only to get his voice mail.

"Hey there, it's me," I said. "I was just thinking of you." *Ugh.* I prayed Ryan couldn't hear the guilt in my voice. "I wanted to tell you that I love you and I miss you. Talk to you later." I ended the call wishing more than ever that Ryan and I attended the same school.

I looked at my watch and realized that my lab had already begun. I was late to yet another class.

Great. Just great, I said to myself as I bolted up the steps and inside the building.

* * *

15

I was distracted the rest of the day Wednesday and most of Thursday. To my surprise, I found myself daydreaming of all the different ways I could devise future "serendipitous" meetings between Quinn and me after our psych lecture in hopes that we could walk to our next classes together again. Maybe I could be waiting casually outside the psych building on my cell phone. Or I could be looking for something in my bag as he happened to walk past. Maybe I could catch up with him one morning and pretend like I had to ask him a question. But I spent the majority of the last two days trying to figure out how Quinn managed to get under my skin—and I was totally annoyed at myself for having had let him.

Late Thursday afternoon, I was sitting at an empty table in the student union waiting for Lisa and our friend, Rachel, who lived across the hall from us. The three of us had planned to grab a quick bite to eat and then head off to the main library to study. For once I was early, so I decided to try to get a hold of Ryan. He had yet to return my call from yesterday. His phone went straight to voice mail again. I just shrugged it off, assuming he was busy studying, and left another message for him to call me. As I ended the call, I heard a strangely familiar voice over my shoulder.

"Who was that? Anyone *interesting?*" The voice was deep and smooth. I could smell hints of citrus and mint, overpowered by the strong smell of chlorine. *Quinn.* I froze. Tiny, little shocks bombarded my body. My pulse started racing. I didn't dare turn around to look at him as I felt the heat of my blood rushing into my face. Even my ears were burning.

"Who wants to know?" My voice sounded surprisingly calm and playful. I took a deep breath. *You can do this!* My mind reassured me.

"Still being difficult are we, Evie?"

He remembered my name. Another battery of shock waves hit me. *Breathe. Just breathe,* I repeated in my head. I

16

knew the last thing I needed to do was waste my time with Quinn, but there was something about him I couldn't shake. What was it about this guy that made me react this way? I mean, even in the extremely unlikely event that he was interested in me, I was already in love with someone else—Ryan. *Ryan. Ryan. Ryan.*

"What, cat got your tongue? Or is it *still* too early in the day for you?" Quinn teased.

He's just flirting with me to get my psych notes, I reminded myself. *Well, two can play at this game.* I took another deep breath, this time with more confidence. I could feel my face cooling down, so I turned around to see him standing behind me, his deep blue eyes twinkling.

"Maybe it's just the present company," I replied. I tried to look serious, but a devilish smirk escaped me despite my efforts.

"Sorry, not buying it." He matched my grin with that dangerous smile of his, but I was prepared for it. I refused to be that easily flustered by Quinn this round.

"Well, I have news for you—nothing about me is for sale."

"What—not on the market?" he asked, looking down at the cell phone still in my hand.

Huh, I thought, *he wants to know if I have a boyfriend.*

"Let's just say that I don't make a habit of discussing my personal life with people I barely know." *Why did I just evade Quinn's question?* I could have kicked myself. Here was the perfect opportunity for me to tell him about Ryan, but for some reason I held back.

"Okay, good to know. Well, now that we're setting the ground rules ..." He pulled out one of the empty chairs next to me and sat down.

"Ground rules?"

"Yeah, well, I seemed to have offended you yesterday,

17

and I have a sneaking suspicion I'm on the verge of doing so again right now. So before I say something I'll regret later, is there anything else I should know about you? You know, any personal mantras, pet peeves, wild sides, tattoos, piercings, or addictions of which I should be aware?"

"Wow!" I laughed, completely taken aback. "That's quite an interesting list you've compiled. I hope these aren't the standard questions you ask all the girls. Because if so, I could give you a few pointers." *Right, Evie, like he needs a few pointers on how to pick up girls.*

Now it was Quinn's turn to laugh. That laugh. That intoxicating laugh. My head started to swim as a tingling sensation ran from my head to my toes. *Addictions? Yeah, I could name one,* I almost said aloud … only half-joking.

"You are pretty feisty, aren't you?" Quinn asked.

"So I've been told." I smiled at him again. *Am I really flirting with this guy?*

"What else do people say about you?" His voice was calm, but his eyes were flickering wildly with curiosity.

"You expect me to just open up and reveal all my secrets to you? Come on, that would be *way* too easy. Besides, where's the fun in that?" I smiled again, but I felt oddly unsettled as I stared into his eyes. Maybe I felt uneasy because this was the last thing I expected. Quinn could get any girl he wanted—so why me? My mind couldn't quite wrap itself around the idea. Or maybe I felt anxious because I was playing along with this risky little game even though I had a boyfriend. Maybe it was because I was hiding the fact that I had a boyfriend—or because I *wanted* to hide that fact from Quinn. I would never do anything to jeopardize my relationship with Ryan—or so I had thought. So why not just come out and tell Quinn about him?

"Full of surprises, are we?" Quinn looked at me even more intently.

"I guess that's for me to know—"

"And for me to find out," he said, finishing my sentence. He leaned in towards me so his face was mere inches away from mine, our eyes still locked. "I look forward to the challenge."

My heart skipped a beat or two and then began pounding at a deafeningly loud volume; I was sure Quinn could hear it. It was so loud I couldn't even hear myself think. All I could do was stare into his eyes. I was mesmerized by them. They reminded me of the ocean—clear around the shallow edges, but darker and more mysterious closer to center. His eyes seemed to be hiding something of their own. I wondered what kinds of secrets Quinn had locked away.

"Well, I should get out of here while we're still on good terms." He smiled and stood up to leave. "I'll see you tomorrow night, Evie."

"Maybe," I mumbled as I looked down at the table. The truth was that I hadn't yet decided if I was going to the party. I knew I shouldn't go, but part of me definitely wanted to.

Quinn stepped behind me, put his hands on my shoulders, and gave them a quick squeeze. A shiver ran down my spine, making me jump a little in my seat. He chuckled. He'd obviously gotten the response from me he wanted. As if to torture me further, Quinn leaned in so close to me I could feel his breath dance on the back of my neck. I shut my eyes, taking in his scent wafting in the air all around me.

"Well, then I *hope* to see you tomorrow night," he practically whispered in my ear. My head started to spin; I felt dizzy. I was thankful to be sitting down. Quinn squeezed my shoulders once more before letting go, and then he was gone. I opened my eyes just in time to see him walking down the corridor of the union. I would bet money that he was grinning triumphantly from ear to ear.

This was the *second* time my body had betrayed me in front of him. *There will not be a third*, I told myself. But deep down I knew better—bad things always happen in threes.

* * *

"*Who* was that?" Lisa exclaimed as she and Rachel sat down at the table.

"Who was who?" I asked, still dazed.

"What do you mean, '*Who was who?*' That amazingly hot guy that was just *massaging* your shoulders! That's who!" Rachel prodded. "Hey, have you been holding out on us? Is there something going on between Ryan and you—you two break up or something?"

"No ... Ryan and I are ... fine," I stammered. I was totally unprepared to deal with Rachel's twenty questions. "Quinn is just a guy from my psych class—we met yesterday. He was just ... thanking me for some lecture notes." *Notes that I had yet to agree to give him*, I reminded myself.

"Some thank you. I wouldn't mind if he thanked *me* for something." Lisa looked like she was already mentally undressing Quinn.

"No, you don't understand. He wants me—us—to go to some frat party tomorrow night. *That's* his way of saying thank you."

"*Us?* So, is he available?" Rachel asked. Her eyes lit up with possibility. I could only imagine what she was picturing in her head.

"I don't know," I snapped. "Why do you care, anyway?"

"Relax, Evie," Lisa chimed in.

"Yeah—I'm just asking. I mean, you did get a look at him, right?" Rachel said.

"Yeah, so?" The truth was I didn't want Lisa or Rachel, or any other girl for that matter, to be interested in Quinn. If I couldn't have him, I didn't want anyone else to have him either—most certainly not one of my friends. I couldn't believe it; I was actually jealous over some guy I had met *yesterday*. I sighed in frustration.

Okay, Quinn, you've definitely got my attention. I was interested in him. Now the real question was what to do about it? *Do not go to that party tomorrow night. That's what you do about it.*

"So, we *are* going to the party tomorrow night, right?" Lisa asked.

"Maybe," was all I could manage. I knew this would be a losing battle. I knew Lisa and Rachel wanted to go to the party. And I knew it wouldn't take much effort on their part to convince me to go. I sighed again hopelessly, already in the throes of defeat.

"You sure you're okay, Evie?" Lisa sounded concerned.

"Yeah, I'm fine." I forced myself to sound more upbeat. I could tell Lisa and Rachel were not convinced. "Really, it's nothing." I faked a smile and stood up. "It's getting late. Let's grab something to eat and head to the library."

* * *

I woke up Friday morning in plenty of time to put in my contacts, clean myself up, and dress in something other than the first thing that was readily accessible on my dorm floor. I hated to admit it, but I was anxious to see Quinn. And for that very reason, I was going to do the right thing. I was going to tell him I couldn't make it to the party tonight.

Unfortunately, Quinn didn't show up to class that day. For the first few minutes of Professor Swain's lecture, I kept glancing at the door to see if he would walk in late, but he didn't. Swain's forty-five minute monologue seemed tortuously long and tedious. As I gathered up my stuff at the end of class, one of Quinn's friends walked up to me. I recognized him as the one I had nicknamed "Larry" the other day.

"Hey, you're Evie, right?" he asked.

I nodded.

"I'm Adam. Adam Shaw. Quinn's friend. He mentioned you'd be stopping by the party tonight."

"Oh." I tried to sound indifferent, but the butterflies in my stomach began to flutter. *Tell him you can't go!* My mind shouted. *Just make up some excuse! Anything to get yourself out of this!*

"So, uh, can you tell me your last name and if you're planning on bringing any friends? You know ... so I can put you on the list?" Adam asked.

"Um ..." I was straining to make up some excuse, but I couldn't think of any. My mind was completely blank. "Sure," I managed. "My last name is Sanders. Evie Sanders. And it'll probably just be me and two friends."

"No problem. I'll see to it personally that you guys are on the list." Adam winked at me. "See you tonight," he threw in as he walked away.

"Thanks," I muttered, but Adam was already out of earshot.

Way to go, Evie, I told myself. *That's really taking the bull by the horns. You* cannot *go to this party tonight. Nothing good can come from it.*

But another nagging voice in my head was getting louder and more obnoxious. *You want to go to the party. You want to go to the party*—like a little kid chanting "nanny-nanny-boo-boo" over and over. And like a broken alarm clock, I couldn't shut it off.

I immediately called Ryan on my cell; it went straight to voice mail, but I just hung up. I was sick of hearing that he was unavailable. Other than a couple random texts telling me how stressed out he was studying for a huge exam at the end of the week, I hadn't heard from Ryan for days. In fact, it had been nearly a week since we last spoke, and right now I really needed to talk to him, to hear his voice.

The rest of the day was a blur. Unsure of myself and of the situation I was getting myself into with Quinn, I struggled to figure out what to do about tonight. I pictured his face— his deep blue eyes; his thick, black, wavy hair; and his seductive smile. I heard his laugh. I was reminded of his intoxicating scent. My mind started wandering off to places it definitely shouldn't have gone. I thought about Quinn's breath on my neck and his hands on my shoulders. A tingling sensation ran down my spine. I shook my head, trying to empty it of these images. I didn't trust myself with him. I hadn't felt such a strong physical attraction towards someone since I'd met Ryan.

I pictured Ryan's face. I could see every detail of his boyishly handsome, all-American good looks. I pictured the way his brown eyes sparkled when he looked at me. I thought about how he brushed my hair out of my face just before he kissed me and how he always kissed the top of my head when we embraced. I loved that Ryan knew exactly what to say to make me feel better when I was upset and that I could trust him with my most intimate secrets. I smiled as my heart filled with warmth and joy. Ryan was my first love, and I still loved him.

I love Ryan. I'm meant to be with Ryan. I suddenly realized how ridiculously stupid I'd been acting. I was overanalyzing this Quinn situation to death and was just confusing myself. Of course I was meant to be with Ryan. How could I have second-guessed the one thing I'd always been so sure of? One guy, even one as charming as Quinn, wasn't going to change how I felt about Ryan. I felt like a fool for not recognizing this for what it really was—a test. Quinn was simply a test of my feelings for Ryan and of the strength of our relationship.

I would go to the party tonight and tell Quinn about Ryan. Quinn would get over whatever inexplicable fascination he had with me, and I would put him out of my mind for good. Feeling ten times more self-assured, I went to go find Lisa and Rachel and tell them to get ready.

2. Baby, It's Cold Outside

Lisa, Rachel, and I descended the stairs into the fraternity's basement a little after eleven. It was dark, stiflingly hot, and incredibly loud. The only sources of light were from the makeshift stage lights—a dozen or so black lights placed strategically around the room and a few strobe lights pulsing in the background. The room was packed full of people. I took another few steps and was assaulted by the smell of stale beer and cigarettes. I began to feel claustrophobic.

I scanned the room, assuming I'd never find Quinn in the sea of people before me. But just as I finished my thought, I spotted him in the midst of the crowd. He looked beautiful. His hair was tucked behind his ears, but one loose curl had escaped and was hanging by his temple. I quickly averted my eyes, hoping he hadn't caught me looking at him. No such luck. A huge smile stretched across his face as our eyes crossed paths.

"Damn it!" I muttered under my breath as my body shivered with excitement.

"Evie!" Quinn yelled over the music.

I was still cursing myself as Quinn made his way across the room towards me. The rhythm of the pulsing strobe lights mirrored the pounding of my heart. *Coming here was a mistake*, I thought. *I should leave.* I looked around for Lisa and Rachel—my support network—but they were nowhere to be found. I assumed they had maneuvered themselves closer to the stage to dance. Weaving through the crowd, Quinn was getting nearer. Butterflies fluttered wildly in my stomach. *Walk away!* my mind screamed. But I couldn't.

"Evie! You made it!" Quinn made it sound like we were longtime friends. He picked me up and gave me a huge bear hug.

"Um, yeah," I croaked, trying to catch my breath when he

released me.

"For a while there I thought you wouldn't show," he yelled loudly over the band.

"For a while there, neither did I," I responded, my voice equally as loud. The song ended and there was a noticeable drop in the volume of the room while the band was in between songs.

"Well," Quinn said more softly, "I guess my wishful thinking paid off." He took a step back, gave me a quick once-over and smiled. His pearly white teeth looked fluorescent under the black lights. "Not in your *usual* attire, I see. Dress up for anyone special?"

"Yes, *me*." Thankfully, the room was dark because I felt heat radiate across my face and perspiration bead up around my hairline. I realized I was nervous.

Usually, I didn't care about what I looked like at a party. I wasn't model material, but I was confident and secure enough in the way I looked that a fitted T-shirt and jeans always seemed to do just fine. Besides, I wasn't ever looking for anyone; I had Ryan.

That said, I'd decided that if I was going through the trouble of subjecting myself to this test, I was going to make it worth my while. So I *did* pay special attention to how I looked. I kept my outfit simple, but it was definitely designed to show off some of my better assets. A thin, black, plunging V-neck cashmere sweater clung to my body and accentuated my full chest. I wore my favorite pair of boot-cut jeans pulled over black, high-heeled, patent leather boots, which added a couple of inches to my height. My hair was flat-ironed to look straight and sleek, ending just above the middle of my back. Makeup-wise, I kept my eyes simple and fresh; I didn't want to take away from their color, which was a strange mix of green and gold. A touch of blush on my cheeks, some cranberry-colored lip gloss, and a little perfume, and I was ready.

"Well, Evie Sanders, you look beautiful." Quinn stared at me more intensely. I hadn't been there for more than a few minutes and already warning bells were going off in my head like sirens. *I have a boyfriend!* I wanted to scream out loud. But I didn't. I thought about holding up my fingers in the shape of a cross to ward off Quinn, but I kept my composure. *There's no rush,* I told myself. I would pass this test. I would weave Ryan into the conversation—eventually.

"Thanks." I smiled.

"Want something to drink?"

"No, thanks. I'm fine."

"Want to dance?"

I noticed the band had begun to play another song, the tempo of which was considerably slower. I watched as bodies moved closer to each other on the dance floor.

"Maybe later," I replied. Honestly, I didn't think I could handle having Quinn standing that close to me, having his hands touching me and holding me as we moved together to the seductive rhythm of the music.

"Well, then, maybe we should get some fresh air," he offered. "It's quieter out there."

"Sure." It was unseasonably warm that evening, and the air would do me good. Quinn took my hand in his. As our fingers intertwined I felt a spark of electricity surge through my fingertips. It was as if a low-voltage current was coursing through our hands. He glanced down at our hands and then back up at me and smiled. He must have felt it too.

Quinn led me through the crowd, up a different staircase, and outside into the snow-filled courtyard of the fraternity. We found a spot just off to the right of a security light, and I could see him more clearly.

We stood there gazing silently into each other's eyes for a moment. If his eyes were like the ocean, his long lashes curled around them like waves breaking on the surf. I wondered what he was thinking. I stood there for a moment or two before realizing I was holding my breath. *Breathe.* I exhaled deeply, allowing a rush of warm steam to escape my lips.

"You're cold," Quinn observed, breaking the silence between us.

Actually, I was shivering, but I couldn't tell what was making my body react more—the brisk night air or standing there with Quinn. He stepped behind me and rubbed my arms up and down with his hands to create some friction. Then, without warning, he wrapped his arms around me and pulled me in closer to him.

Very smooth, I thought. I wondered how many times he had used this move before.

We huddled so closely together that I was beginning to question whether dancing with him would've been the safer choice. But I could still hear the sultry rhythm of the song the band was playing inside and thought I would be far better off out here. Besides, I did feel a little warmer; and I wasn't ready to go back inside where it was so loud and stuffy, so I didn't object to being in his arms.

His embrace was different from what I was used to experiencing. After all, these weren't Ryan's arms around me. But somehow, Quinn's arms felt familiar. In fact, his embrace felt safe … natural, even. I couldn't really explain it. It was as if he'd held me in his arms a hundred times before.

Quinn edged closer to me, eliminating what little space there was left between us. I could feel the entire length of his body against mine. His arms closed around me a little tighter. His breathing got a little heavier and the muscles in his body tensed up slightly.

I froze. *Now what, genius?* I asked myself. But before I could think of a response, Quinn reached up with one hand and swept all of my hair to one side, exposing my neck. He leaned in, and I could feel his breath on my skin. I heard him slowly inhale as he took in the scent of my perfume. Electricity shot through my body like lightning, leaving me trembling in its wake. Without thinking, I leaned back into him and pulled his arms tighter around me in hopes that I'd stop shaking. He obliged all too willingly.

Nice, Evie. Way to be up front and honest. My mind continued on its warpath. *Why don't you send him a few more mixed signals?* I knew my actions were not helping matters, and I let out a little disapproving laugh, which was enough to interrupt the moment.

"What?" Quinn asked curiously.

Tell him the truth, my mind urged. But I didn't want to yet. I wasn't ready for this evening—for this game—to end. So I raced to come up with some bogus explanation for my laughter.

"I just realized I never actually gave you my psych notes," I blurted out.

"Uh, yeah," Quinn chuckled awkwardly. "I guess I should fess up about that … I don't really need your notes. I just used them as an excuse to talk to you."

"And to get me to come here?"

"That too," he conceded. "Is that so wrong?"

Yes, it's wrong! my mind shouted. *Being here with you is very wrong!* But I bit my tongue. I wanted to pretend that Ryan didn't exist—if only for a few more minutes. I wanted to feel Quinn's arms wrapped around me for a few moments longer. I knew I wouldn't let things go too far; it wasn't my nature to do so—regardless of whether or not I had a boyfriend. Still, I was in unchartered territory. I'd never so much as thought about cheating on Ryan before. But then again, I had never been so interested in anyone else since meeting Ryan either. I wondered just how much further I was willing to let this go. Where would I draw the line?

"So the psych notes were part of your master plan to get me here tonight … standing outside with you in the freezing cold."

"Well, I don't know if *outside* was the exact place I had in mind." Quinn chuckled. "But things have worked out pretty well so far," he said in a rather self-congratulatory tone as he pulled me in even closer to him.

"I have another confession to make," he added more hesitantly.

"What's that?" I asked curiously.

"I noticed you the first day of Swain's class."

I flashed back to my disheveled appearance in class a few days ago and mentally cringed, realizing that it wasn't the first time I'd gone to class dressed like a zombie.

"Yeah, I'm sure you did." Sarcasm dripped from my every word. "Night of the walking dead is a hard look to miss."

"I wouldn't go *that* far," he laughed. "I think you come to class looking more … real. It's like you don't care what people think about you. You're comfortable just being you … doing your own thing. Most of the girls around here seem to have one goal in mind—to be part of the college version of *Next Top Model* or something. I mean, don't get me wrong, they're pretty and all—but not one of them can hold a candle to you … especially tonight." He turned me around to face him.

I was convinced he was just trying to flatter me, but I blushed anyway. *Hook, line—and sinking.*

"Evie, you're different … You stand apart from the rest like you're above all that superficial stuff. I just kinda get the sense that you know what's really important, and I like that about you."

"Wow. Hmm. I have to admit I wasn't expecting that." I sighed and took a step backwards. "Look, Quinn, you just met me; and you obviously know nothing about me. I'm really not all that carefree about my appearance. I come to class dressed the way I do because I don't have time to care about the way I look. I'm *always* running late. I roll out of bed in the morning with barely enough time to make it to class. If I had my crap together, don't you think I'd wake up early enough to at least find something to wear from my closet instead of my floor?

"In fact, if I had my priorities straight," I continued, on a rampage now, "I wouldn't even be here with you tonight having this conversation with you right now. And I certainly wouldn't have allowed myself to be here in your arms flirting with you ... wondering how far I might let this little game go—And, trust me, if your master plan included sleeping with me tonight, you're going to be sorely disappointed. I have a *boyfriend* ... and I *don't* cheat.

"And I also wouldn't be worrying about trivial things like psych notes or boyfriends ... or *you* for that matter, when I don't even have the luxury of time on my side—" I stopped mid-sentence and winced. I had said too much.

I waited for Quinn's reaction, but he seemed completely unaffected by my last declaration. In fact, I didn't even think he'd heard it. He was distracted by something else.

"So," he began slowly, "if you have a *boyfriend*, why *are* you here with me tonight?" The tone in his voice was a combination of intrigue and mischief.

"I ... I don't know," I admitted sheepishly, looking down at my boots. Quinn put his fingers under my chin and gently lifted up my head so he could see my eyes.

"Well, don't worry, it was never my intent to get you to sleep with me tonight," he said sincerely. "Although," he added, flashing me a playful smile, "if it had been *your* intent to do so ... well, I can't say I would've objected."

"I'm sure you wouldn't have." I rolled my eyes at him.

"Evie, when I saw you that first day of class, I just wanted to get to know you better—I still do." He picked up the silver charm hanging from my neck, rolled it between his fingers, and then let it drop back down onto my chest. He looked into my eyes again.

"I can't explain it—there's something about you. I can't stop thinking about you." He studied my reaction. I didn't know how to react. How could someone like Quinn be interested in someone like me?

"Quinn, we've spoken twice before tonight. Other than that, you've seen me—what—a handful of times in class?" I paused, took a deep breath. "Even if what you're saying is true," I continued after exhaling, "it can't happen … it just can't." I shook my head in disapproval and closed my eyes. "I shouldn't even be here right now—"

"And yet you are," Quinn interjected.

I opened my eyes to look at him.

"Yes, but only to confirm for myself that this isn't right—that this isn't what I want."

He sighed. "Are you *at all* interested in me?"

"Whether or not I'm interested in you is irrelevant. I'm not available—"

Quinn didn't let me finish my sentence. Maybe he didn't want to hear what I had to say. Or maybe he didn't trust the words about to come out my mouth. Instead, he pulled me into him. His eyes grew darker, smokier. As he lowered his head towards mine, I pulled back slightly in a pathetic attempt to resist his advances, which only made him draw me in closer. He gently brushed his lips against mine; they felt so warm and soft, I couldn't refuse them. That was all he needed. He kissed me again, this time more intensely, and a moan escaped his throat. Quinn's mouth traveled down my neck, and I didn't even try to stop him. Rather, I instinctively tilted my head backwards, giving him free reign. I heard a gasp, but this time it came from me.

He stopped suddenly. Confused, I lifted my head to find out why. He was smiling triumphantly. He looked so damn arrogant—although I guess he had every right to be. *I* was the hypocrite. *I* was the one who was guilty as sin. But right now, I didn't care.

I pulled him back towards me, kissing him with such fervor I surprised myself. I had never wanted someone so much before. I could feel Quinn's body pressing into mine, and it made me even more excited. As his hands wandered down my back, his mouth moved down the nape of my neck. He kissed the length of my collarbone, tracing it with his tongue before returning to my mouth. Quinn's kisses made me quiver. I had goose bumps over every inch of my body. My knees went weak, and I wrapped my arms around Quinn, clutching onto him as if he were my lifeline.

It was as if the rest of the world had melted away. I could no longer hear the song that had so perfectly set the stage for this moment. I could no longer hear anyone's voices. I didn't even feel cold anymore. In fact, I felt like a bonfire was blazing inside of me. My head spun out of control while my body was calling all the shots.

Quinn pulled back again only to kiss my lips gently once more. I kept my eyes closed, feeling his breath lingering on my face, still smelling him ... tasting him. Even with my eyes closed, I knew he was smiling. I could *feel* him smiling. My body had betrayed me a third time. He undoubtedly knew I was interested in him. I opened my eyes and looked at him, only to verify what I already knew to be true.

I could've been embarrassed, and maybe I should've been. After all, I was the one who only moments ago had told Quinn that this—that *we*—couldn't happen. But I wasn't embarrassed. His eyes, his words, and his body had also given away a lot. He was interested in me too.

"Evie," Quinn managed in a hoarse whisper. I buried my face in his chest, and I could feel his heartbeat pounding loudly against my cheek.

"I know," I whispered, still dazed and swept up in what had just happened. There was something more going on than just this intense kiss we'd shared. Talking to Quinn, being with him—it was all so effortless, so natural. It felt so strange and so normal at the same time. I couldn't begin to explain it even if I wanted to.

My cell phone buzzed in my back pocket. *Ryan! Oh crap!* Reality hit me hard, and my heart seized with a sharp pain like someone—correction, like *I*—had just stuck a knife into my chest. I gasped, feeling overwhelmed with guilt. Nausea consumed me, and I couldn't catch my breath. I felt like I was going to be sick. Utterly disgusted with myself, I ripped myself away from Quinn. I had failed the test—*my* test— miserably.

"I'm ... I'm sorry ... I have to leave." I couldn't even look at Quinn. I took a few steps backwards, turned around, and ran back inside.

"Evie! Wait! Please!" I could hear Quinn shout.

I didn't dare look back.

3. A Guilty Conscience

I was awoken by the sunlight pouring through my dorm windows. I had no idea what time it was nor did I care. I lay in bed for a few minutes wondering if last night was all a dream. I put on my glasses and scanned my room only to see the clothes I'd worn last night draped over my desk chair. Nope, no chance it was a dream. I saw my cell phone sitting on my desk. I hadn't had the nerve to check my voice mail last night when I'd returned home.

I walked over and picked up my phone to check my messages. *Crap.* Ryan had not only called me last night while I was with Quinn, but he'd texted me too:

"LUV U. MISS U. SWEET DREAMS ANGEL."

I read the words on the screen and my stomach immediately twisted itself into knots. Tears sprung into my eyes as I reluctantly checked my voice mail.

"Hey, angel," Ryan said sweetly. "It's me. Got your voice mails—so sorry I didn't call you back sooner. I got caught up studying for an exam I had this afternoon. Hey, are you okay? You sounded upset. I hope everything's all right. I'm worried about you … Man, it sucks being so far away from you. I'd feel a lot better if I could see you—know that you're all right. Call me when you get home—no matter what time. Love you. Miss you."

"That's great. That's just perfect," I squeaked as tears streamed down my cheeks. The back of my throat and lungs burned with the pain that was overflowing from my heart. I tossed my phone back onto my desk and fell back into bed. I couldn't call Ryan right now; I felt too ashamed.

A month ago, Ryan and I were spending our winter breaks happily together in Michigan, but I hadn't seen him since. And, up until last night, I had been faithful to Ryan the entire two years we were together. Honesty, loyalty, and fidelity were of the utmost importance to me—or at least they used to be. I would've rather broken up with Ryan than betray him by cheating, and I knew he felt the same way. It had been simple: Ryan was in love with me, and I with him. We respected each other. I trusted him completely ... obviously more than he should have trusted me.

What a stupid idea it had been to test my relationship with him. I flipped over on my back and slammed my fists into the mattress. I didn't even *try* to resist Quinn last night. I *wanted* him to kiss me! My stomach churned again with self-loathing nausea. If I'd been honest with myself from the get-go, I would've admitted that I had wanted him to kiss me since the first day we met—probably since the first day I saw him in class. And last night he did. He kissed me, and it was amazing. It was wrong, but it was still amazing.

I couldn't understand how I could feel so comfortable with Quinn. I barely knew the guy and here I was telling him things about me that I would never tell anyone. I mean, did I really admit to him that my daily wardrobe was decided in large part by what I found on my dorm room *floor? Nice going, Evie. Really nice.*

And even more disturbing, I had been about to reveal something to Quinn that I hadn't revealed to anyone. What in the world would possess me to open my mouth about how much time I thought I had or didn't have left? It was crazy enough that I'd driven close to a hundred miles to see Madame Sasha, but to actually breathe a word to anyone about what she'd said made me sound completely certifiable. I clearly hadn't been thinking straight last night.

And what was Quinn's deal anyway? Why would he still want to kiss me after I told him I had a boyfriend? And why did I give in to him without a fight? The only reasonable explanation I could come up with was that Quinn was gorgeous and charismatic, and I was weak. I had fallen for his charms. I had made a mistake.

Now I feared that last night would change everything between Ryan and me. I didn't know what to do. At the moment, all I knew was that I missed Ryan more than ever.

Lisa barged through the door, and I quickly wiped my tears away. She was in her robe, hair wrapped up in a towel, shower caddy in hand.

"Good morning, sleepyhead," she said cheerfully. "I had to take a shower first thing when I woke up. I can't stand the smell of frat party in the morning." She smiled at me, hoping that I would partake in the morning pleasantries, but I didn't. She shrugged it off and walked over to her closet to find something to wear.

"So what happened to you last night?" she asked. "One minute you were in the party room and the next, that totally hot guy was leading you off somewhere." Lisa peered around her closet door, her eyebrows raised and her eyes burning with curiosity.

"Nothing. I ... Ryan called ... and I left." I was fumbling my words so miserably; I knew I wasn't fooling Lisa.

"You hooked up with him, didn't you?" Lisa exclaimed excitedly as she leaped onto my bed. "Details! I want details!"

"Lisa, it wasn't like that—really." I couldn't even look her in the face.

"You are so busted, Evie Sanders!" Lisa squealed, bouncing up and down on my mattress. "I know you too well. You can't hide something like this from me, so don't even try."

I knew she'd get the truth out of me sooner or later. I looked her in the eyes and sighed.

"Fine," I began. "We kissed. That's *all* that happened. But Ryan called during it, and I totally freaked and ran out of there. Happy now?"

"Well, that's not exactly what I would call *details*." The disappointment in Lisa's voice was palpable.

"Lisa!" I shoved her with my hand, jokingly. "C'mon, I've got a serious mess on my hands here."

"Not necessarily," Lisa said as she repositioned herself beside me.

"What do you mean?"

"Well, do you like this guy? What's his name again?"

"Quinn."

"Quinn. Right. Do you like him?"

"I *can't* like him. I'm with Ryan."

"Evie, I'm not asking if you *could* like him, I'm asking if you *do*."

Leave it to Lisa to call me out for dodging her question. I thought about her question for a moment. It reminded me of Quinn's right before he kissed me.

"Last night, Quinn asked me if I was interested in him."

"And?" Lisa asked in anticipation.

"I told him that his question was irrelevant because I have a boyfriend."

"And what'd he do?"

"He kissed me anyway."

"*And?*" Lisa was literally on the edge of her seat.

"And I kissed him back," I responded hesitantly. I looked up at Lisa, who was wide-eyed, clenching her teeth, and miming a strangle hold around my neck. Despite my particularly glum mood, I had to laugh. I was having fun stringing Lisa along about last night. I sighed and paused melodramatically.

"Good Lord!" Lisa exclaimed. "This is like pulling teeth! *And?*"

"And ... it was pretty amazing," I confessed.

"I knew it!" Lisa shoved me so hard that I fell over onto my side, laughing. "So you *are* interested in Quinn."

"I don't know, Lisa. Maybe that's all last night was supposed to be—a perfect kiss—never to be repeated so it can never be spoiled." I replayed the kiss in my mind, and a shiver rippled through me from head to toe.

"Besides," I continued, trying to rationalize last night, "I barely know Quinn. I just met him a few days ago and that's hardly enough time to justify throwing away two years with Ryan."

"Look," she began. "I can't tell you what to do. But it seems to me that if you're *sure* that last night was just one perfect little kiss, and if you're *sure* that it won't ever happen again, then I wouldn't worry about it. And I *certainly* wouldn't tell Ryan. If you're *sure*, then it was just an innocent mistake.

"But," Lisa went on, "if last night *wasn't* so innocent, and this Quinn guy *does* interest you, then that's a completely different story. Evie, if you like this guy, you're gonna end up making another *pretty amazing* mistake." Lisa flashed me a wicked grin.

"What—you don't think I can control myself?"

"Oh, like you did last night? Come on! Don't you have to see this guy like two to three times every week for the rest of the semester? Not to mention that you *told* him you had a boyfriend, and he pursued you anyway. Do you really believe he's just going to give up now that you kissed him? Trust me, if you are the slightest bit interested in this guy, you'll end up kissing him again—or doing something else."

I looked down at my fingers and watched as they nervously fidgeted like they had minds of their own. I flashed back to Quinn taking my hand in his last night and felt the energy surge though my fingertips again. I shook my left hand a little.

"Crap." I looked up at Lisa. "I can't get last night out of my head."

"Good!" she said excitedly. "Then you can tell me every

last detail! How did it happen?"

"Lisa!"

"I know, I know." Lisa looked disappointed again. "Back to the issue at hand—what are you going to do about Ryan?"

"I'm not sure. I have to think about it." Actually, I knew what I *should* do—I should tell Ryan what happened, beg him for his forgiveness, and prepare myself to let the chips fall where they may. I just wasn't ready to say it out loud yet. It would make it all too real, and I wasn't ready to be slapped with any more reality this morning.

"You should take time to mull it over. It's not every day that you have to choose between Ryan and *the* hottest guy on campus." Lisa winked at me in jest, but it didn't make me feel any better. "But in the meantime, my dear, spill it. I want the *un*abridged version."

"You're relentless!" I laughed. I knew Lisa wouldn't give up until her curiosity was satisfied. But living with her had also taught me that I could confide in her; she wasn't a gossip. So I would give in and feed her curiosity—not all of it, but enough of it—and hope she'd stop asking me questions.

"At least let me get something to eat first!" I insisted.

"Absolutely." A wide smile spread across Lisa's face.

* * *

I managed to avoid Ryan's phone calls all Saturday and Sunday. From his voice mails I knew he was still worried about me, and it only made me feel worse.

Ryan liked to work out in the morning, so I called him early Monday. The call went straight to voice mail and, for once, I was relieved I couldn't reach him. Trying to sound as calm and collected as possible, I left him a message saying I was sick all weekend and slept most of it away. I added that he shouldn't worry about me and that I'd call him again when I was feeling better. My heart ached; I hated lying to Ryan. In fact, I could only recall one other occasion in which I'd hidden the truth from him outright … my visit to Madame Sasha.

I ditched my psych class on Monday. I couldn't handle seeing Quinn. I didn't know what to say to him. I wanted to forget the whole evening ever happened. I wanted to forget about him, but I wasn't fooling myself. Quinn was very much stuck in my mind.

On Wednesday, I purposely walked into class late. Professor Swain looked at me disapprovingly, but I didn't care. Out of the corner of my eye, I saw Quinn in his usual seat in back, and I quickly grabbed a seat in the first row. I could *feel* his eyes on me, burning into me, the entire class. Goose bumps formed on the back of my neck. My chest was pounding so loudly I swore Quinn could hear it from where he was sitting. I tried to pay attention to Swain's lecture, but it was no use; I didn't hear one word of it. When class ended, I quickly gathered up my stuff and ran out of the building.

Please don't follow me. Please don't follow me, I begged silently. To my relief, Quinn didn't.

I stepped outside after my bio lab only to discover that any relief I'd felt was to be short-lived. Quinn was waiting for me on the stairs outside of the building. There was no avoiding him now. I tried to take a deep breath, but the cold air felt like shards of glass piercing my lungs. I walked over to him slowly.

"So you mind telling me what that was all about?" Quinn asked.

"What was what all about?" I asked, trying to sound nonchalant.

"You. Not showing up to class on Monday. Showing up late today. Skipping out the second it's over. Are you avoiding me?"

I knew he wouldn't like my answer, so I just stood there

staring at him.

"Okay, so now you're not talking to me?" he asked, confused.

"What's there to talk about?" I countered.

"What's there to talk about?" He chuckled wryly. "So that's it, huh? We had this … this … whatever it was on Friday night, and you can just walk away? You can just leave it at that?"

"Yes," I replied bluntly. I didn't need Quinn to complicate things even more than he—even more than *I*—already had. I had to make a clean break with him as soon as possible.

"Why? Because of some other guy? A guy that you obviously have doubts about anyway?"

"That's not fair," I snapped angrily. "First of all, *Ryan* is not just some other guy. We've been together for two years. And second, why do you even care how I feel or what I think about him—or anyone else for that matter? You've known me for all of one week and you think you have me all figured out? You know, you're one misguided, arrogant—" I stopped myself from finishing my thought out loud. I couldn't believe how quickly Quinn could get me worked up. I turned towards the campus bus stop, but he caught me by the arm before I could walk away.

"*Let—go—of—me,*" I hissed, as I unsuccessfully attempted to wrench my arm free from his grasp.

"Evie, I don't want to argue with you," Quinn said apologetically as he loosened his grip. "And I'm not saying that I have you all figured out. But last Friday was more than just some random kiss." He drew me close enough into him that I could smell the chlorine on his skin. His dark blue eyes were burning into mine, making my insides ache—not out of anger or guilt for cheating on Ryan, but because I wanted Quinn.

Be strong, I told myself.

42

"And," he continued, "I realize that we only met last week, but I also know enough to realize that there's something between us, whether you want to admit it or not."

I didn't want to admit it, but I knew he was right. I knew my attraction to him surpassed anything I'd ever felt before—even with Ryan. I also realized that Quinn clearly didn't shy away from pursuing whatever it was that he wanted. And right now, he wanted me.

But knowing any of that didn't help me. None of it mattered. I still loved Ryan, and I couldn't hurt him. I respected him too much to do that. And I respected the relationship we had built together.

"Look," I said curtly as I pulled my arm free from Quinn's grip, "I don't know what you think happened between us last Friday night, but let me assure you that you caught me in a weak moment and nothing more. *It was a mistake*—one that will *not* be repeated."

"Go ahead," Quinn said. "Keep telling yourself that if you think it'll help you sleep better at night. But we both know better." He took a step towards me, eliminating virtually all of the space between us. "I can't stop thinking about you." He tucked my hair back behind my ear and leaned in even closer. "And I know you can't stop thinking about me," he whispered into my ear.

I could feel the heat building between us like trapped steam ready to explode. I could almost taste his lips on mine, and I had a sudden urge to kiss him. But I didn't, and neither did he. Instead, he smiled at me smugly, turned, and walked away without even looking back.

My desire for Quinn immediately turned to rage. I was furious with him for being so pretentious as to dare make these presumptions about me. And I was furious with myself because he was right.

"Just because you *think* you know how to get me worked

up doesn't mean that I have feelings for you!" I shouted as he walked away.

Everyone stopped and turned to look at me, but I was too angry to care. Quinn stopped and turned around as well.

"Like I said, whatever helps you sleep at night, Evie," he called out. "Look, I'll tell you what. I'll stay out of your way if that's what you want. But just do me a favor—don't avoid me in class. I didn't do anything to deserve being treated like a leper." He turned back around and walked away.

* * *

That night, I dreamt of Quinn and myself at the party. I dreamt of him kissing me, but the dream didn't end there. Quinn and I were suddenly in my bedroom back home in Michigan and things got pretty heated pretty quickly. Then, out of nowhere, my dream switched gears. I was back in Madame Sasha's living room, sitting across the table from her.

"Okay, look, this has gone far enough," I protested. Even for a bad practical joke, she was taking things way too far. "Why don't you just give up on the act and let me get out of here." Still, Madame Sasha wouldn't release my hands.

"This is no act, Eve Sanders, or should I say *Evie*," Madame Sasha replied, her eyebrows raised.

I was caught off guard. I hadn't told her my name. Or had I? No, I could swear I hadn't. In fact, Emma and I were careful *not* to say our names because we wanted to test Madame Sasha's *psychic abilities*. And we paid in cash, so no identifying information exchanged hands. Maybe Emma let my first name slip, but she certainly wouldn't have said my last name. I started to get this strange, sick feeling in the pit of my stomach.

"Look, I don't know how you got my name or who paid you to say all of this stuff, but it's not funny. It's just twisted and wrong." My voice started to quiver nervously.

"The only thing that is twisted and wrong, my dear, is your fate."

"And just what is that supposed to mean?"

"Like I told you, I know more about your future than I want to. And, knowing what I know, it wouldn't be right for me to let you walk out of my home completely unaware of your ill-fated future if there is even the smallest chance that I can help you break the chain—the Curse.

"What I do," Madame Sasha continued, "is not an exact science. I can only see what I see. And right now, I can't see the third incident. I don't know when it will occur, other than that it will happen some time before your nineteenth birthday … right around the time you meet your true love."

"My true love? Well that's just ridiculous," I scoffed. "I've already met my true love." Ryan was everything to me.

"No, my dear, you haven't," Madame Sasha said matter-of-factly.

I woke up startled, in a cold and clammy sweat. I tried to go back to sleep, but it was no use. I just tossed and turned in bed the rest of the night. I knew what I had to do. I had to go see Ryan.

4. Road Trip

Because I had gotten a 3.7 grade point average my first semester of college, my parents decided to reward me by allowing me to bring my car back to Bloomington for the remainder of my freshman year. Not surprisingly, as a trade-off for their so-called newfound trust in me, I had to agree to a bunch of new "car rules," the main one being that I had to ask my parents for permission every time I wanted to drive more than fifty miles outside of Bloomington. Not so coincidentally, Ryan was 175 miles away at the University of Illinois in Champaign-Urbana.

Bottom line, my parents knew I'd be more than just a little tempted to visit Ryan every chance I got, and they were not about to make it easy for me. They thought Ryan and I were way too serious as it was. They never said it, but I knew they were happy that we had gotten into separate schools. I could still hear my parents' muffled sighs of relief when they heard the news.

"Relax, Evie. This is not the end of the world," my mom had said in a patronizing tone. "Besides, you know what they say: 'absence makes the heart grow fonder.'"

"Mom's right, Evie," my dad interjected. "If you two really are meant to be together, spending some time apart won't matter."

But what did they know about long-distance relationships? They had never spent more than a few weeks apart since they met in law school.

Still, it was pretty decent of my parents to let me take my car back to school; I had to respect them for that. So I decided to play fair for once and try to follow their rules. I'd ask them if I could take the car to Champaign for the weekend, despite my suspicions that they wouldn't like the idea of my spontaneously planned road trip.

Borrowed Heart

* * *

It was eight o'clock, Thursday evening. Nearly a full week had passed since the infamous evening when I had kissed Quinn at the party. Lisa was out on a date with someone she had met at that very party, so I had some privacy. It was now or never. I called my parents. While the phone rang, I mentally ran through my list of arguments and rebuttals in support of my trip to visit Ryan, hoping I had all of my bases covered. I could hear the tension rising on the other end of the line as soon as I mentioned that I wanted to drive to Champaign the following day.

"Mom," I started in defensively. "I know what you're thinking, but I won't be skipping any classes. I'll wait to leave until after my last class tomorrow afternoon." But before I could get another word out, she exploded.

"Eve. Olivia. Sanders," my mom said in as stern a voice as she could muster. "How could you think for one minute that your father and I would support such nonsense?"

How typical, I thought resentfully.

"The idea of you taking a road trip—*alone*—in the middle of winter, no less—to Champaign. It's ludicrous! It'll be dark before you get halfway there! It's just too dangerous. And what about your schoolwork?"

"Mom," I blurted out, "I'll be home by Sunday afternoon, leaving me plenty of time to review for my Monday classes. Plus, Rachel is going with me, so I won't be driving alone." Okay, that was a little white lie. Rachel had been planning to go with me to visit some high school friends that were attending U of I, but she came down with strep throat and had to cancel on me at the last minute. Rachel was now destined to stay in bed all weekend.

"Evie," my dad started in. "When Mom and I agreed to let you bring the car down to Bloomington, it was for the sole purpose of helping you get around town more easily. It was *not* so you could traipse around the Midwest and neglect your studies."

Crap. I didn't realize he was also on the line. I cringed. *Great, there's nothing like being double-teamed by lawyers.*

"If we had thought for even a second that you had different ideas brewing in that head of yours, we would never have allowed you to take the car back with you to IU," my dad continued. "Don't make us regret our decision." I could tell that he was annoyed, but his voice remained calm and steady; he was good at that.

"Mom, Dad, don't you think you're overreacting just a little? I haven't seen Ryan in a month. In fact, I haven't done anything but study since the semester began!" Okay, so that was another little white lie. School was never all that difficult for me, and it didn't take much effort for me to maintain my GPA. But I was losing ground quickly and was grasping at straws.

"Look, I'm eighteen," I continued. "Legally, I'm an adult. I'm getting good grades, I'm not behind in my schoolwork, and … and I shouldn't have to justify myself to you two when it comes to me wanting to visit my boyfriend. What is *so wrong* with me wanting to see Ryan?" I heard my voice crack as my temper began to flare.

My efforts were futile. My parents' decision had been final the second I'd opened my mouth. They forbade me to drive to Champaign, reiterating that it was unsafe for two young women to take a road trip at night in the dead of winter. Then they reminded me that it was still *their* car. For added impact, my parents threw in several not-so-subtle threats to personally come down to Bloomington and repossess and sell my beloved car if I disobeyed them.

"Thanks for being so understanding!" I was fuming. "You know what? I don't really care what you say! I'm going anyway!" I shouted into the phone right before I hung up on them. My hands were trembling out of sheer anger.

"Nice going. Way to deliver an argument, Evie. Very effective," I muttered to myself. I'm sure my mother and father were just as happy with me. In fact, I'm sure they were so thrilled they were probably heading to Bloomington right then to prove that their threats were by no means idle.

The phone rang a few times, but I didn't pick it up. Then my cell phone rang, but I didn't bother to check the caller ID. I knew my parents were calling to make some last-ditch effort to try to reason with me and talk me out of going to Champaign. But my mind was made up. I would smooth over this episode with them later. Somehow, I always managed to do so.

I had no idea why I felt the need to go through the stupid charade of asking them for their permission in the first place. Sure, they were my parents. I didn't always agree with them, but part of me felt like I should at least try to listen to their advice once in a while—in bits and pieces anyway.

Still, I was an adult now. I didn't live under their roof anymore. It was time I started paying more attention to my own advice. I should've just driven to Champaign without telling my parents. They never would've been the wiser. I knew how to cover my tracks well enough. And if my parents had found out about the trip after the fact, I would have dealt with it then. As was often the case with them, it was better to ask them for their forgiveness than for their permission.

But there was something else about this trip that was gnawing at me—I could feel it in the pit of my stomach. I *wanted* my parents to know I was going to Champaign. I had felt anxious the minute I'd decided to take this road trip, and it had nothing to do with my need to come clean with Ryan. Something else was amiss; I just couldn't put my finger on it.

I was used to paying close attention to the uncomfortable

feeling I'd occasionally get deep within the recesses of my stomach, lurking like a monster in the shadows. I learned to be careful whenever this monster reared its ugly head. But, this time, I chose to ignore the nausea that was slowly creeping up into my chest, making the hair on my arms and neck stand up on end. Instinctively, my fingers found their way to the silver chain around my neck, tracing down the length of it until I felt the charm hanging at the bottom.

I made up my mind. I am *going to see Ryan tomorrow.*

* * *

I woke up the next morning with a renewed sense of purpose. I would get through the day and leave for Champaign that afternoon. Initially, I'd debated skipping psych class, but I knew that would only serve to feed Quinn's already-inflated ego, and I wasn't about to let that happen. No, I had something else special in mind for him this morning.

I walked into class with barely a minute to spare. Quinn and his friends were seated in their usual spots. As always, the seat next to Quinn was empty.

Perfect, I thought. I climbed the center aisle stairs towards the back of the lecture hall and sat down in the available seat next to him.

"Good morning," I said cheerfully. The look on Quinn's face was priceless. He was surprised at my bold gesture— pleasantly so—but surprised nonetheless.

It's my turn to catch you off guard, I laughed to myself.

"Good morning," he said hesitantly, his eyes full of suspicion.

I scanned the room. I usually sat in the first or second row, and sitting back another couple dozen rows gave me a completely different vantage point of the large room, one that I wasn't particularly fond of at the moment. *All* of the girls, and several of the guys, had turned around to stare at me, wondering why the sudden change of classroom geography from my seat up front to a seat next to *him*.

"So what did I do to deserve the honor of your visit way up here in the nosebleed section this morning?" Quinn asked, as if reading everyone's minds.

"As I recall," I noted, "you recently accused me of avoiding you, so I'm making it clear that I'm not."

"Well," Quinn chuckled, "I had no idea I would be in for the VIP treatment." I could tell he still had no idea what I was up to, but he seemed more than willing to go along for the ride.

"I could move back to my old seat if my sitting here makes you uncomfortable."

"No, no," he responded quickly. "This is fine. So, tell me, does this change of attitude of yours include seeing me *outside* of class too—like this weekend?" Quinn was testing me.

"Afraid not," I replied. "I'm going to Champaign this afternoon to spend the weekend with Ryan." *That is, if he'll still have me.* My stomach rolled over, and I fought off a wave of anxiety.

"Oh, the *boyfriend*." He sounded thoroughly amused—not exactly the reaction I was expecting. "Are you going to tell him about *us*?"

"Quinn, there is no *us*."

"Ah, so you're *not* going to tell him." He grinned.

"Draw whatever conclusions you like, but I'm not about to tell you what I plan to say or *do* with Ryan this weekend."

Quinn's body stiffened; he grimaced slightly. I could only imagine the images of me with another guy running through his head.

"Is something bothering you?" I asked, feigning sympathy.

"No," he said through gritted teeth, "why would the thought of you with some other guy bother me?" He kept looking straight ahead with his jaw clenched. He was jealous … And much to my surprise, I liked it.

Professor Swain entered the lecture hall late and a little winded; he must have been running. He started the lecture immediately, but that didn't stop Quinn from continuing our conversation.

"So how are you getting to Champaign?" He asked quietly, keeping his eyes forward.

"I'm driving," I whispered.

"Alone?"

"Yes."

"Evie," Quinn turned to look at me, "I don't think that's such a good idea—you on the road alone. What if the roads are icy? What if something happens to you?" I wasn't sure if he was genuinely concerned about my safety or merely trying to rattle me so I'd think twice about going on my trip.

"I think I'll be okay, *Dad.*" I rolled my eyes.

"I'm serious, Evie," he said with a furrowed brow.

"Look, my car is reliable, I'm not driving at night, I have a cell phone, and—" I shook my head and smiled foolishly, "and, quite frankly, I don't really know why I'm explaining any of this to *you.*"

"If you two are finished, I'd like to be able to continue my lecture *uninterrupted*," Swain barked. I immediately looked at our professor and then around the lecture hall to discover that all eyes were on us. I felt the blood flooding my cheeks; my ears were burning. Larry and Curly were cracking up on the other side of Quinn.

"Sorry," Quinn and I mumbled in unison.

Even though we'd stopped talking, I could see out of the corner of my eye that Quinn was itching to continue with his line of twenty questions. Not wanting to get in trouble again, I tried to concentrate on the lecture, taking notes to distract me. It only took about two minutes for Quinn to lean in towards me and pick up where we left off.

"Can this guy really make you feel the way *I* made you feel the other night?" he whispered.

"What does that have to do with anything?" I replied, flustered.

"So he doesn't," he declared victoriously in a little louder voice, smiling from ear-to-ear. Someone a few rows ahead of us shushed him.

"That's not what I said," I whispered angrily.

"You didn't have to."

Quinn had an irritating way of twisting my words, interpreting them to hear only what he wanted to hear.

"Ryan and I have been together for a long time. We have more than just a physical connection. We *love* each other. We *respect* each other. We're best friends. And, FYI, Ryan makes me *feel* just fine."

"I'm pretty sure I made you feel *better* than *just fine* last Friday night."

"Has anyone ever told you that you're impossible? Do you always hear only what you want to hear?"

"Give me one good reason why I should listen to anything you're saying when your actions speak volumes to the contrary?"

"What are you talking about?" It was a stupid question. I already knew what he was going to say. My body had betrayed me on at least three occasions with Quinn, and I knew it was just a matter of time before he would throw it in my face. And, truthfully, today of all days I couldn't have cared less if he did. The ball of nerves that spun violently in the pit of my stomach each time I thought about confessing my indiscretion to Ryan was more than enough to keep me clear-headed and focused.

"You say you love this guy," Quinn went on. "You say

he's your best friend and whatever. But you're here sitting next to *me*—talking to *me*. You went to the party last week to meet *me* ... and you were the one *kissing me*."

"Your point?" I asked impatiently.

"Evie, the point is that *things change*. *People* change. *Relationships* change. And, I think that deep down you're freaking out because you've found someone else who interests you more than this boyfriend of yours."

"And I suppose this *someone else* is you?" I shot back. He just smiled at me, radiating total confidence and charisma. "You're looking through rose-colored glasses," I said, rebuffing his charms.

"How do you mean?" he asked, still smiling.

"You refuse to see things as they really are. Tell me, Quinn, when you're forced to take off your glasses someday and see the world in the same colors as everyone else, what will you think then?"

"Well, at least I'm looking. I'm not the one with tunnel vision. You only see the future you created for yourself back in high school."

"Excuse me," Swain's voice boomed towards the back of the auditorium where we were sitting. Quinn and I instantly stopped talking and jerked our heads towards the front of class. Swain was staring straight at us.

Crap.

"If you two can't postpone your lovers' quarrel until after my class, I'm going to have to ask you to leave."

I looked down, thoroughly embarrassed—mostly because of Swain's characterization of us. But Swain's scolding didn't stop Quinn from getting in the last word.

"You're stuck in the past," he whispered a minute later, "and I think you like it that way. It's safe. It's easy. That way you don't have to ask the difficult questions. You don't have to take any risks." He paused to take a deep breath and then exhaled. "Open your eyes, Evie, and take a good look around; or you're going to miss something great sitting right next to you." This time his voice lacked a single trace of the arrogance I was used to hearing.

Quinn's words haunted me for the rest of Swain's lecture. I wasn't stuck in some high school fantasy because I was afraid to take risks. I was hanging onto the fantasy because it was all I had. It was a hell of a lot easier for me to be with Ryan than worry about whether or not I had a future. So for the past couple of years, I'd just gotten used to not thinking about my future. And I never really gave much thought to the present either. I just wanted to maintain the status quo long enough to reach my nineteenth birthday at the end of the summer—that was until Quinn came along.

I began to wonder if Quinn might be right. Could my feelings for Ryan have changed without me even realizing it? Still engrossed in my thoughts, I didn't even notice everyone packing up their bags to leave when class ended. Quinn nudged me.

"Evie," Quinn called out softly.

"Hmm," I responded, dazed.

"Class is over."

"Oh." I snapped back to reality and scanned the room. The lecture hall was nearly empty. I started cramming my stuff into my backpack.

"So when are you leaving?" Quinn asked reluctantly.

"Why do you want to know?" I asked, walking down the stairs of the lecture hall behind him.

"You know," Quinn said, shaking his head as he stopped and turned to face me, "you're not exactly the easiest person to have a conversation with. It's like you have a natural talent for deflecting every question I ask. Why is it that you never answer me directly?"

Feeling a little braver than I probably should have at the

moment, I decided to take on his challenge and prove him wrong.

"You want me to be direct? Okay, go ahead. Ask me anything. You get *one* question." I regretted the words the second I uttered them, and I was right to do so. As soon as Quinn smiled, I knew he was going to take full advantage of my offer.

"Are you in love with him?" His gaze was so intense. I could feel his eyes probing mine like he was trying to see inside me—like he was searching my soul.

"What?" I asked, taken aback.

"You heard me. *Are you in love with him?*" Quinn wanted the truth, but for the first time I wasn't even sure of it myself.

"A week ago," I began, taking a moment to collect my thoughts, "I would have said 'yes,' without a doubt. Now … I'm not so sure. I'm confused. But that *doesn't* mean I've fallen out of love with Ryan. It just means I have to figure a few things out—on my own."

"So if you have to figure things out on your own, why are you driving a hundred-and-some miles to see him?"

"Nice try. You had your one question, and I answered it. Don't go trying to sneak another one in there." It figured Quinn would try to drink from the well twice.

"Oh please." He sounded so irritated. "You couldn't have been more ambiguous. A simple 'yes' or 'no' would have sufficed. But instead you handed me a load of BS. You tell me that you don't know how you feel about this guy, that you have to figure it out *on your own*. But you're driving off to Champaign this weekend to be with him." He sighed. "Just be honest with me—why go and see this guy one week after I kissed you?"

I thought about his question. I *really* thought about it. And while I firmly believed that the details and status of my relationship with Ryan were none of Quinn's business, I had to admit that Quinn had everything to do with the reason for my visit to Champaign. So I decided to be as truthful as I could with him.

"I have to see Ryan. I need to find out if things between us really have changed or if I screwed up for some other reason."

"So you're considering that things between the two of you might have changed," Quinn said with a hint of optimism. "Good." He smiled devilishly.

"Hey, don't go getting your hopes up," I replied.

"Why not? I like my odds."

"Your *odds*? You don't even know the first thing about Ryan. What if he's *ten times* the guy you are?"

"Evie, if that were really the case, you would have just come out and *told me* that he's ten times the guy I am—not asked me. You also would've been up front about him when we first met or, at the very least, after you called him that day I ran into you in the Union."

So he'd known about Ryan since before the party. I mentally winced.

"And you never would've allowed things to go this far between us." He tucked some stray wisps of my hair behind my ear, brushing my face as he pulled his hand away.

Quinn may have had a point, but that didn't mean I liked hearing it. I definitely didn't need to hear '*I told you so*' from him. Exasperated, I turned on my heels and briskly walked out of the classroom and then out of the building. He followed close behind me. The cold winter air hit my face. I experienced *déjà vu*, like it was the first day Quinn and I met. When things were different. When I at least felt like I had a decent grasp on what was going on with my life.

"I hate to break it to you, but you still don't know everything about me," I asserted.

"True. But I know I'd rather be with you this weekend than without you. So why don't you just hang out here instead and give us a chance? Maybe that's all you need to figure things out." Quinn's confidence seemed to evaporate right before my eyes; he suddenly looked so vulnerable. His eyes were pleading with me to give him something I couldn't because my heart already belonged to someone else. He was throwing it all out on the line; he wanted me to know how he felt about me.

I planned on doing the same thing today—only with my boyfriend. My conscience grappled with the guilt I felt over two different people: Ryan and Quinn. What could I say? I mean, how could I tell Quinn that I was going to Champaign to fight for my relationship with Ryan.

"Well, I should get going," I said awkwardly.

"Evie, promise me you'll be careful."

I looked into Quinn's eyes; they were dark and muddled like an ocean during a storm. He was genuinely worried about me.

"I promise."

"I'm serious." He still looked concerned.

"I know."

"And, hey, I'll save a seat for you in class on Monday," Quinn added, forcing a smile in an effort to lighten the mood.

"I'm not so sure Swain will like that," I replied, smiling, also trying to cut through the tension in the air.

Quinn's smile broadened. He leaned in towards me and kissed me on the cheek. I inhaled his scent, memorizing it. Our gaze lingered for a moment before he turned and walked away. I wanted to call out to him, but I fought the urge. Instead, I just stood there and watched him walk away until he was nearly out of sight. The back of my throat ached. My heart throbbed. I suddenly felt like this was the last conversation I would ever have with Quinn, like it was the last time I'd ever see him. My eyes stung as I fought back the tears.

5. Blindsided

I decided to surprise Ryan and not tell him I was coming to Champaign. The last thing I wanted him to do was question why I'd planned such a spontaneous visit to see him or whether my parents knew of the trip—sore subjects to be sure. I also knew Ryan would've voiced his own concerns about me driving to Champaign alone. And, under the circumstances, I figured the less communication I had with Ryan before I saw him the better. So I'd kept my contact with him during the past week to a bare minimum. Basically, I texted him every so often to let him know I was feeling better but was afraid of falling behind in my classes and would be busy studying the entire weekend.

Before leaving, I stopped by a convenience store and bought throat lozenges, a six-pack of Gatorade, a few packages of Ramen noodles, and the latest gossip mags for Rachel. I felt bad deserting her when she was sick, but she insisted she would be fine. Besides, Lisa was around; I knew she would stop by and look in on Rachel. After giving Lisa strict instructions not to tell Ryan where I was this weekend should he call, I grabbed my overnight bag and headed out the door.

It was three o'clock on Friday afternoon by the time I hit the road. There was still a chance I would miss rush hour traffic in Indianapolis. The drive started off slowly; in fact, the first fifty miles to Indy seemed to take forever. But I also welcomed the solitude. I pondered whether it was at all possible to be in love with two guys at the same time or if this kind of love was truly an exclusive state of the heart. Did being in love with one person necessarily mean you couldn't be in love with another? Was falling in love with one person a sign that you were falling out of love with someone else? The more relevant and frightening question for me was whether I was actually falling for Quinn or just infatuated with him.

I thought of Ryan, of our love, our history, and our friendship. Could all of that really be erased the minute I gave into the slightest temptation? Extinguished by some guy with deep blue eyes that just happened to walk into my life one day and turn it upside down? No way. In my heart I knew that whatever was going on between Ryan and me started well before I met Quinn.

I suspected Quinn was only a symptom of the problems between us. Quinn was merely a distraction—someone to help me pass the time so I didn't have to feel so lonely about being alone at school. I had missed having someone there for me on a daily basis. *Someone?* Didn't I mean *Ryan?* And what would possess me to even risk allowing Quinn to be Ryan's proxy? I was practically defenseless against Quinn's charms, his looks, his scent, his touch, his lips …

Ugh! Stop it! I was pathetic. Here I was on my way to see Ryan, and thoughts of Quinn were invading my head. I quickly pushed Quinn from my mind. I had to think clearly. I had to focus on how I was going to explain to Ryan what had happened a week ago. I had racked my brain for the past couple days trying to find the right words, rehearsing various monologues, but nothing sounded right.

I thought of trying the beg-for-forgiveness approach: *Ryan, I have to tell you something. Last week I went to a party and kissed a guy. It went no further. I'm so very sorry. I don't know what happened, but I promise it meant nothing. And it won't happen again. I think I was just lonely and confused—but I'm not anymore. Being here with you now, my head has never been clearer. I know that I love you and want to be with you. I made a mistake, and I hope you have it in your heart to forgive me.*

Or the desperate, more pathetic version of the same: *I'm so sorry, Ryan. I know what I did was inexcusable, and I shouldn't even have the right to ask for your forgiveness. Please know that I miss you so much. I never meant to hurt you. It was a stupid and selfish thing to do—a moment of weakness that will never happen again. It's just that sometimes it's so difficult with me being in Bloomington and you all the way here in Champaign. I don't know what I can do to make it up to you, but I'm willing to do anything if you'll just forgive me. Please say that you'll forgive me.*

The somewhat open and honest approach was along the lines of: *Ryan, we need to talk. I met someone last week and we kissed. It didn't go any further, but it did happen. I'm so sorry. I don't know if I'm just stressed out about our long-distance relationship or confused about us, but I feel like my whole world has been turned upside down. That's why I had to come see you tonight. I need to see if we're still okay. I need to know if you're willing to forgive my mistake. I still want to fight for us, but I need to know if, after hearing what I did, you still think we're worth fighting for.*

The more brutally honest approach had also crossed my mind: *Ryan, I met someone who seems to be really interested in me. And since meeting him, I've been confused about us. I don't know if I just like the attention that I'm getting from him or if there's something more to it than that. We kissed last week. It didn't go any further, but it wasn't exactly the most innocent of kisses either. I'm sorry. I never meant to hurt or betray you in any way. I felt like I had to come down here and tell you in person—that you deserved at least that much. I need to hear what you're thinking. I need to know where we go from here.*

Brutal honesty was the one approach I seemed to shy away from the most, although I wasn't too crazy about the somewhat honest approach either. Ryan was going to be so hurt and angry with me, I didn't feel the need to rub salt into the wounds I was about to inflict upon him. Seeing Ryan that night was going to be one of the most difficult and unpleasant things I would ever experience, of that I was sure.

When I saw the exits for Champaign-Urbana, my hands grew cold and clammy and my head began to throb. What if Ryan didn't forgive me? What if he ended our relationship? Broke up with me on the spot? Were we destined to be yet another doomed high-school romance? Yet another long distance casualty?

I began to rethink whether it was such a good idea to tell Ryan about Quinn. Maybe Lisa was right. Perhaps the best thing to do was put Quinn and the kiss behind me and bury it in the closet for good. But I knew the solution to my problem wasn't that straightforward. For one thing, my guilty conscience was eating me alive. Not to mention, I couldn't get Quinn out of my head. Even worse, however, I wasn't sure I wanted him out of my head.

You have to be honest with Ryan, I told myself. *You owe it to him to tell him the truth.*

I pulled into Ryan's complex and found a parking space directly in front of his apartment door. I remembered Ryan mentioning that his two roommates planned to go to Louisville that weekend, but Ryan couldn't go for some reason. The living room lights were off, but I could see the flickering lights of the new flat-screen TV his parents had given him for Christmas. Ryan was home. My chest started pounding. I felt like I was going to be sick.

Calm down. Take a deep breath, I told myself as I flipped down the sun visor and checked my appearance in the illuminated mirror embedded within. I brushed my hair, reapplied some lip gloss, and flipped the visor back up.

"Ready or not, here I go," I muttered. I took another deep breath and opened the car door. The cold air whipped my hair around as I stepped outside. Fearing the worst, I left my bags in the car. I would get them later ... that is, if Ryan wanted me to stay. A short stabbing pain ripped through my chest at the possibility that he wouldn't. Anxiety and panic overwhelmed me, and my hands began to tremble. *Please let me survive this. Please let him forgive me. I swear I will never cheat on Ryan again.*

Using the spare key Ryan had given me, I slowly and quietly unlocked his front door. This was supposed to be a surprise after all. But, when I stepped inside, *I* was the one who received the shock of a lifetime. Ryan wasn't alone. Stunned, I had to blink twice to believe what I was seeing. He was naked on his couch on top of some ... *slut.* As my brain slowly began to register what was going on, my emotions rapidly imploded and rage began to seethe inside of me.

"Damn you, Ryan Walker! Damn you!" I screamed. Startled, Ryan looked up at me, his eyes immediately filled with horror.

"Evie!" He leaped off of the girl, who now turned around to see who had dared interrupt her evening. She looked at me, but her face showed no iota of surprise, remorse, shame, anger—nothing. I didn't know which was worse, seeing his face or hers.

"Evie!" Ryan croaked frantically, his eyes still wide with alarm as he stood there naked, using his hands as a makeshift fig leaf.

I couldn't stand to see the picture in front of me, so I shut my eyes. I had to get out of there. I spun around and bolted out of the apartment, leaving the front door wide open, my spare key still in the lock. Tears began streaming down my face as I ran for my car.

Stop crying! my mind ordered. *Whatever you do,* don't *let him see you crying!* I choked back the tears as best I could. I refused to let Ryan see how much he had hurt me—how much he had crushed me. I jumped into my car and slammed the door shut, locking it immediately.

"C'mon! C'mon!" I shouted at myself as I fumbled with my keys. "Damn it! Start the car!" I could barely see through the tears that were welling up uncontrollably in my eyes. When I finally found the right key, I shoved it into the ignition and started my car, revving the engine as loudly as I could before throwing the car into reverse. Ryan, who had somehow managed to put on his pants, ran after me bare-chested and barefoot in the snow.

"Evie! Please don't go!" Ryan begged.

I couldn't help but notice the irony of the moment. This was the second time in a span of a week that a guy had cried out to me, pleading for me to stay. In another context, in an ideal world, I should have felt like I was floating in Heaven; but, at that moment, I felt like I had crash-landed in Hell. I punched the accelerator and barreled out of the parking space backwards before Ryan could reach my car.

"Evie! Please! I can explain! Just give me a chance to explain!" Ryan had positioned himself about fifteen feet or so in front of me, blocking my only exit route. His hands were raised defensively out in front of him as if he could stop my car from hitting him should I choose to ignore his pleas. I rolled the window down a crack.

"Get out of my way, Ryan, before I run you over! I swear I will!" I revved the engine again purely for effect. The power of the engine rumbling under me felt good; it felt like the only thing in my control. Ryan stood his ground, not budging an inch. I certainly wasn't going to let this son of a bitch stop me from leaving. I wanted to put as many miles as I could between Ryan Walker and me as fast as possible. I looked at him with daggers in my eyes. *The bastard!*

The vengeful part of me wished I could hit Ryan with my car. I surveyed the asphalt—it wasn't icy. I indulged myself a bit and popped the clutch, letting the car jerk forward about ten feet before I slammed on the brakes. It was enough to make Ryan jump out of the way. He looked scared, which only made me laugh out loud. I must have seemed completely deranged, but I didn't care. Once Ryan was safely out of harm's way, I punched the accelerator and peeled out of his apartment complex. I couldn't drive away quickly enough.

"And to think I drove to Champaign to confess *my* sins!" I shouted. I bit my bottom lip so hard I could taste blood. I was furious. I slammed my fists into the steering wheel to release some of the anger churning inside me, but I found no relief. I slammed my fists down again and screamed. I could feel the steering wheel vibrate from the blows. Never in a million years did I think that Ryan would do this to me. How long had this been going on? Were there other girls? Did he screw around in high school too? Had I been too blind to see him for what he really was—a liar and a cheat?

So much for forgiveness. Ryan and I were one hundred percent *over*. I knew I was being hypocritical, but based on the Fujita scale, my mistake was an F-1, at most an F-2. Ryan's mistake, on the other hand, was a full-blown F-5.

My cell phone was going nuts. I turned it off and tossed it into my bag. I couldn't deal with *anyone* right now, let alone Ryan. I just wanted to be alone for the trip back to Bloomington.

It started snowing shortly after I hit I-74. I hadn't even thought to check the weather report before leaving Bloomington that afternoon. Large wet snowflakes started to pummel my windshield as I sped down the highway. It was an understatement to say that my mom's hand-me-down car didn't handle snow well. And despite my overwhelming desire to get as far away from Ryan as I could, I still had enough common sense left to slow down.

It wasn't until halfway home that I realized I'd gone emotionally numb. I couldn't feel anything. The rhythmic sound and motion of the windshield wipers had me in some sort of trance. *Swish-swish. Swish-swish. Swish-swish.*

Emotionally anesthetized, I felt safe enough to begin running through the past couple of years, searching for some evidence, some clue or sign, something ... *anything* that would make sense of what I had just witnessed. I couldn't figure it out. How could Ryan do this to me? If there had been one person I thought I could always trust and count on, it was him. How could I have been so wrong?

I replayed the scene in Ryan's apartment and felt queasy. Well, at least now I knew what had caused that unsettling feeling in the pit of my stomach when I first decided to go to Champaign. It was fate trying to tell me what I'd find when I got there. If only I had listened. I could've been spared the ugly details now coursing nonstop through my head.

I eased up on the death grip I had maintained on the steering wheel for the last hour-and-a-half and stretched out my stiff fingers. I took a deep breath. Oddly enough, when I exhaled I felt like a huge weight had been lifted from my chest.

"Open your eyes, Evie, and take a good look around; or you're going to miss something great sitting right next to you." I heard Quinn's words echo in my head. I pictured his blue eyes. I smiled and stepped on the gas. I was suddenly anxious to get back to Bloomington.

6. Head On

Headed southbound on the local highway between Indianapolis and Bloomington, I was twenty-five miles north of
campus when I slowed down for the red stoplight ahead of
me. The light turned green before I reached the intersection,
so I sped up. Twenty yards or so from the light, a pickup
truck coming from the other direction unexpectedly swerved
and made a left turn in front of me. I reacted immediately,
preparing to slam on the brakes at a moment's notice if necessary, and watched the truck clear my path.

That was a little too close for comfort, I said to myself as I
glared at the truck angrily. I turned my attention back to the
intersection only to gasp in terror. A car had followed the
pickup truck and was turning left in front of me as I entered
the intersection.

No! This can't be happening! my mind screamed in alarm. I
slammed on the brakes with both feet, but it was of no use.
There was no way to avoid the car. It was almost as if the
driver was aiming straight for me.

"*NO!*" I shrieked, clutching the steering wheel, bracing
myself for the impact. In that moment it was as if everything
was moving in slow motion. I became hyper-aware of everything that was happening to me—and of everything that was
about to happen. I could feel every muscle in my body tense
up. I could hear the screeching of my tires on the pavement
and smell burning rubber. My heart was pounding in my ears.
My chest ached like my heart was trying to beat its way out of
my body and save itself.

Memories of my life flashed before my eyes. I saw my
parents. *Mom, Dad—I'm so sorry! I love you!* Random images of
me at various stages of my life raced through my head. I saw
my friends. *Thank you, God, for giving Rachel strep throat.* I
thought about the schoolwork I'd never do, the dorm room

I'd never again see, and the classes I'd never take. And ... I saw Quinn's deep blue eyes. *"Promise me you'll be careful,"* I heard him say.

SLAM! I heard the metal of my car being crushed inward as I collided head on into the side of the car that had so recklessly and perilously positioned itself in my direct path. I was thrown forward. I could feel my seatbelt lock and the pressure of the belt against my ribs.

SNAP! Part of my plastic seatbelt buckle broke, and I was catapulted forward a few inches while the intact portion of the buckle strained to hold me back. I heard more metal crunching and scraping. I smelled smoke and gasoline fumes. My front windshield shattered, and glass fragments rained down on me. All the while, my hands gripped the steering wheel of my car and both of my feet were firmly planted on the brake. My car swerved out of control and started careening into the right lane.

CRASH!

What was that? I spun my head to the right just in time to look out my passenger window before it shattered.

"What the—?" I shouted in fear. Another car had come up from behind, slammed into the right side of my car, and somehow fused itself to my passenger side. Both cars began spinning out of control together. I saw a shower of sparks fly between us as our cars were grinding together. Then I heard the sound of sheet metal tearing as our cars were ripped apart by sheer momentum. My car was flung into the median, and finally, miracle of all miracles, it stopped. Only then did my driver's side airbag deploy, which did nothing except fry what little nerves I had left.

It took me a minute to realize I'd survived the crash. I was still alive. I grabbed the charm hanging around my neck, reveling in my good fortune. *Thank you! Thank you! Not today. It was not meant to be today.*

Everything seemed eerily quiet. My mind went on autopilot as the urge for self-preservation kicked in. It was as if a voice in my head began walking me through a mental checklist of what I needed to do.

I smell smoke; something could be burning, the voice whispered urgently. *Turn off the car.*

"Okay," I responded out loud as I turned off the car and removed my keys from the ignition.

Are you hurt? the voice asked.

"Not too bad, I think," I said as I conducted a mental inventory of my body.

Can you move? the voice continued.

"Yes," I replied numbly.

Get out of the car—it could explode.

"Okay." My hands trembled as I fumbled to open the door.

Walk away from the car.

"Okay." I slowly stepped out of the car, carefully finding my balance and assessing my body for any injuries.

Don't look back; you'll only freak out, the voice continued.

I was sure my car was totaled, and I knew looking at it would only make me realize just how close to death I had come this time. I shuddered at the thought.

I spotted the third car involved in the accident, which was not more than fifteen yards behind me in the median. The driver, a middle-aged man in a dark grey suit, was standing beside his car talking on his cell phone. He had a nasty gash in his forehead, but it didn't seem to faze him much. I assumed he was going into shock. The front of his car was smashed in and most, if not all, of the sheet metal on the driver's side was ripped off.

"You all right?" I called out shakily.

"Yeah," the man responded. "You?"

"Yeah ... I think so." I still couldn't believe it myself. I had survived! Not only that, I was actually *walking.*

"What in the hell was that asshole thinking?" The man scowled, looking at the old-beater sedan that had caused the accident. I followed the man's eyes across the highway to the shoulder on the opposite side of the southbound lanes. Without so much as glancing to see if there was any oncoming traffic, I bolted across the road, determined to get the answer to that very question. What kind of a person would pull such a stupid stunt?

The "asshole" was still in his car. He was hunched over his steering wheel, groaning.

"What in the hell is wrong with you? You could've killed us!" I screamed, but nothing was registering with the driver. It sounded like he was gasping for breath. No, that wasn't it. He was dry-heaving. He was going to throw up! The driver looked up at me, but his eyes couldn't focus on anything. He tried to say something, but he was slurring incomprehensibly. I took a few steps closer to the car and was overcome by the smell of alcohol.

"*You're drunk!*" I yelled, enraged. That was the last straw. Whatever emotional numbness I had been fortunate enough to feel on the way home from Champaign was instantly gone. I could no longer contain my wrath, my fear, my anguish, my disgust, my guilt—any of it. I looked at my car across the median; it was almost unrecognizable—a smashed-in, crumpled-up heap of scrap metal. Horrified, I looked away. The magnitude of what had just happened began to hit me. I started to shake uncontrollably; I was losing it fast.

Not knowing what to do, I started backing away from the drunken idiot hunched over in his car. I had to get away from him. I had to get away from everyone and everything. I took another step backwards and then another.

"Stop! Get out of the way!" someone hollered.

"Hey, little lady, what do ya think you're doing?" another voice shouted.

Were they talking to me? I looked around, but my head was spinning. My ears were buzzing. I couldn't focus. Nothing was making sense.

I snapped out of my haze when I heard the loud horn and the sound of screeching brakes. My eyes darted over my right shoulder. But by the time I realized I was in trouble, it was too late. I saw a pair of lights rushing towards me. Like a deer in the headlights, I was frozen in the middle of the highway, absolutely terrified. There was no time to run. There was no place to go. I was acutely aware that I wasn't going to get out of this unscathed. Not this time.

"Bad things always happen in threes ... I'm sorry." Madame Sasha's words rang like a death knell in my ears.

I heard screaming—my screaming. The headlights were so intense and bright, they blinded me. Still, I couldn't turn away.

The impact of the pickup truck launched my frail body into the air. It felt like I'd been struck by a semi moving at warp speed. Instantly, an agonizing tidal wave of pain slammed into me. I felt like every bone, every organ, every part of me had just ruptured into thousands of tiny pieces. I thought I felt myself hit the pavement, but I couldn't be sure. My lungs burned, desperate for air, but no matter how hard I gasped for breath, they remained empty. And then everything went black.

7. Rude Awakening

I awoke to the smell of a wood-burning fire. The faint scent of pine trees and cedar welcomed me next. Something else was familiar, too … the smell of my sheets, my blanket, my room. Not my dorm room, but my bedroom at home. I opened my eyes to discover that I was back in Sawyer.

What am I doing here? I asked myself, thoroughly confused. Then I vaguely remembered the car accident. I stirred slightly, waiting for the unbearable pain of my injuries to sweep over my body at any second. But nothing happened; I felt fine. In fact, I felt better than fine. I felt oddly refreshed and well rested.

I turned my head to let the sun streaming in through my bedroom windows beam across my face; it felt so warm and welcoming. I looked around and saw the white beadboard on the walls and vaulted ceiling of my room. The floor was made from reclaimed wood—a feature that my parents were not shy about sharing with their guests. *"All of the wood was dredged up from the bottom of the Mississippi River; each plank is well over one hundred years old,"* my parents would announce proudly to their friends when we first moved into the house.

My full-sized bed took up most of the room, but there was still space enough for a small desk and chair, a bookshelf, a narrow dresser, and my bedside table. All of the furniture was white. Most everything was white. Even my bed linens were varying shades of white, accentuated by muted stone, taupe, and straw-colored throw pillows. I never realized how sterile my room must have appeared to an outsider. My alarm clock was across the room on my dresser; it was just after two o'clock in the afternoon.

I heard someone rustling around downstairs. I pictured my mom in the kitchen slaving away, making my favorite comfort foods. She did it every time I was sick … or hurt.

"*Ugh.*" I cringed at the thought of what I had put my parents through. They must have been so worried when they found out about the accident. How long had I been unconscious? Days? Weeks? Longer? I looked out my bedroom window and saw the thick blanket of snow that covered the backyard and the partially frozen lake in the background. It was still the dead of winter. Relief washed over me as I realized I couldn't have been unconscious for all that long.

I wanted to let my parents know I was awake. Feeling up to the challenge, I decided to test my strength and walk downstairs to the kitchen rather than call out for them to come up to my room. I sat up gradually. A dizzy spell hit me almost immediately and I paused. When the spell passed, I grabbed my bedpost for support and slowly and carefully stood up. I didn't dare let go until I knew I had my balance. Once assured that I wouldn't fall flat on my face, I tentatively took a small step forward, not yet trusting my legs. I let go of the bedpost and looked down at my feet as I took two more baby steps.

"Okay. So far so good," I mumbled to myself. I lifted my head to see how much progress I had made towards my bedroom door.

"What?" I muttered in disbelief. I was no longer in my bedroom. In those few steps, I somehow had made it all the way downstairs and was now standing in the kitchen doorway. Shocked, I did a double take from where I was standing to the staircase I'd apparently just descended. I had no memory of walking out of my room, much less walking down a flight of stairs and through the living room to the kitchen. Panic and nausea hit me simultaneously. Maybe I wasn't feeling as well as I thought.

Blackouts are a common occurrence among trauma victims—right? I asked myself nervously. I didn't know the answer to my own question. The monster lurking in the pit of my stomach began to growl uneasily.

"Mom?" I called out anxiously. My throat was so dry; I felt like I had swallowed a handful of sand.

No one answered. Maybe no one had heard me.

"Mom? Dad?" I tried to muster more strength in my voice. "Are you here?"

"Your parents aren't here, Eve," responded an unfamiliar male voice from the family room off the far side of the kitchen.

Startled, I took a step backwards, partially concealing myself behind the doorway of the kitchen and the living room.

"Who's there?" I asked hesitantly, my voice barely audible. It wasn't like my parents to leave me alone with a complete stranger without any warning. It was even more unlikely that they would have done so while I was unconscious. In fact, I wouldn't have been surprised if, after the accident, my mom had camped out in my room the entire time I was home until she knew I was in the clear. She was probably so worried that she insisted my doctor do daily house calls.

"Are you my doctor?" I called out to the stranger.

"Not quite," the stranger chuckled. "But I am here to help you." The man stepped around the corner into the kitchen so I could see him. If I had to guess, I would have said he was in his late-twenties, maybe early thirties. He was quite attractive, but not particularly striking. Every feature of his face fit well together, but not one feature stood out. He had short dark brown hair and hazel-brown eyes, which had a certain warmth and sincerity about them. He smiled at me, which somehow eased my tension. He was wearing a thin, pale-blue crewneck sweater over a white T-shirt, a pair of khaki pants, and brown loafers.

"Help me with what?" I asked cautiously.

"My name is Peter," the man offered, unsolicited. "And I've been sent here to help you with your *transition*." He emphasized the last word slowly and carefully, so that I was sure to hear it.

"Transition," I repeated. I looked at the stranger standing in front of me. "Transition? I ... I don't understand. Transition from what?" Had my injuries from the accident been so bad that my parents had to pull me out of IU for the rest of the semester? How could that be? I felt just fine.

"Where are my parents?" I demanded. "Just how long have I been unconscious?" I looked desperately around the room for answers. I began to panic. My lungs felt heavy; it was hard for me to breathe.

"Eve," Peter said calmly as he walked over towards me. When I didn't respond, he repeated my name more loudly. "Eve."

Startled, I looked at him and nervously took a step backwards into the living room.

"Take a deep breath, Eve. Everything is fine ... in a manner of speaking. Here—please sit down." Peter gestured to one of the two blue-and-white striped lounge chairs that flanked the matching sofa in the living room. I didn't move.

"Please," he said sincerely, "sit down and I'll do my best to explain everything."

"Okay," I managed. I took a deep breath, attempting to calm myself. My throat was still parched. As if Peter could read my mind, he walked over to the kitchen cabinet to the left of the stove and grabbed a glass. He filled it up with water from the pitcher in the fridge, the same one my mom always kept in there, and handed me the glass. He seemed to know his way around my parents' house well enough. I began to feel slightly more at ease. I gulped the water down.

"More?" Peter asked.

"Yes ... please."

* * *

Still holding the glass of water, I followed Peter into the living room and sat down in the lounge chair he'd originally singled out. He sat in the chair opposite me, allowing for plenty of space between us.

"Eve, how much of the accident do you remember?" Peter began.

"Not much." I strained to remember anything about it, but I couldn't. The chain of events was all so hazy. I looked down at the floor as if it could provide me with the clarity I sought.

"I was driving ... there was another car—two cars, I think. One of the drivers was ... drunk. But there was someone else ... something else happened." I was mumbling, trying to talk myself through the accident. And then a memory flashed through my mind; I saw two bright lights barreling towards me as I was standing in the middle of the highway. Instantly, the accident, or at least the very last part of it, became crystal clear.

No one could have survived that, I told myself. I gasped and looked at Peter in terror.

"How ... how long have I been ... dead?" My words were barely audible, choked back by the fear and anguish of my horrifying realization. Peter glanced down at his watch.

"Nearly five days," he said apologetically.

Nearly five days. I repeated Peter's words in my head, not really knowing how to process this information.

"Am ... am I in Heaven?" I asked in shock.

"It's a little complicated," Peter answered.

"It's a little complicated," I repeated.

"Yes."

"Okay, so you tell me that I've been dead for nearly five days, but you won't do me the courtesy of telling me where I am ... Unless ..." I shot Peter an alarmed glare.

Oh crap! my mind exclaimed. *Just how much had I sinned in my short life?* I winced at my own question.

"Am … am I in … Hell?" I asked in a soft whisper.

"No," he responded calmly.

"Purgatory?" The word just slipped out of my mouth.

"No. Eve, allow me to explain. You could have gone to Heaven … What I mean by that is you conducted yourself—your life—in a manner that made you were eligible to go to Heaven. But your path was *diverted,* so to speak." He paused. "Eve, you have been chosen to be one of the select few whose purpose is to guard other humans who also inadvertently end up in your position."

"My *position?* … You mean *dead?* Doesn't everyone end up in my *position* someday?" I asked defensively. What was I? Some type of pariah in death?

"Yes and no. Everyone dies … someday." Peter's voice remained calm. "But, as fate would have it, not everyone is given the same type of foresight to know when their lives will end. Your experience with death is a little bit different in that respect, wouldn't you agree?"

Without even thinking, I reached up to grasp the charm around my neck, only to discover it was gone.

"Do you really feel the need to have your patron saint looking after you anymore?" I could hear the slightest hint of mockery in Peter's voice.

"No, I guess not," I conceded. "All the same, I feel better with it nearby."

"It's not gone," Peter reassured me. "It's in that keepsake box." He pointed to a small, unadorned wooden box on the end table just to the left of the sofa. I didn't recognize it. My parents probably had picked it up from some local antique store while I was away at school.

"The box and its contents are yours," Peter explained.

"Oh." I reached over and picked up the box, opening it

to find my silver charm and chain lying on top of a red velvet cushion.

My whole life is in this box, and this is all I have to show for it, I thought. I forced a little smile as I picked up the charm and rubbed it between my fingers. *Some guardian angel you turned out to be.* The thought reminded me of something that Peter had mentioned a moment before. Still holding the charm, I looked at him.

"You said I was *chosen* ... to *guard* people? So what am I? A guardian angel or something?" I snickered. Who in their right mind would be crazy enough to make *me* a guardian angel?

"Not exactly. We're a little different ... We're known as Shepherds."

"Excuse me? *What?*" Okay, this was too much. I wondered if all of this was some sick joke, if someone was going to jump out from around the corner and tell me that I'd been punked.

"You're not being *punked*, Eve—whatever that means."

Did I say that out loud? I asked myself, caught off guard by Peter's response.

"No," he said aloud, responding to my thought again. "But you new ones are so easy to hear. You haven't yet developed the ability to control your thoughts—to keep them private and separate from the communal group. Don't worry; you'll learn to do it in time. We all do.

"And for your information, this keepsake box is not meant to represent your life; its purpose is not that symbolic. Shepherds do not live in the past—we can't. The keepsake box is just that—something in which to store a few personal items and trinkets. You'll forget all about it soon enough."

"Right ... no living in the past," I repeated calmly, like I was speaking to a mentally unstable person that could freak out on me at any second. Peter just looked at me, expression-less.

"Look, I'm sorry," I said skeptically, "but do you really expect me to just sit here and believe that what you're telling me is the truth? On blind faith? That I died and now I'm some type of guardian angel, but not exactly because actually I'm some sort of ... sheep herder—"

"Shepherd," Peter corrected.

"—Shepherd ... whatever ... who is supposed to protect people somehow?" I asked in disbelief.

"Yes."

"So what if I don't believe you?"

"You can choose to believe me or not, but sooner or later, Eve, you are going to have to accept the fact that your life as you knew it is over." Peter sounded so nonchalant that his words stung.

My life is ... over.

8. My Life Examined

"Okay, let's suppose for a minute that I am ... dead. Then why bring me back here? Why bring me back to my parents' house?"

"Eve, do you really think you're back in Michigan?" Peter's voice was tranquil and kind, but his eyes looked troubled. He had the look of someone who'd drawn the short straw and now had to be the bearer of bad news. Like a father who was about to tell his child there was no such thing as Santa Claus.

"This is not my parents' house?" I asked apprehensively.

"No, Eve, this is not your parents' house. It's a replica—a movie set of sorts—except that nothing here is real. It's all a construct of your mind."

"Wait a minute," I blurted out. "Are you telling me that I'm hallucinating? That this house, this chair—that *you* are not real? That I'm just trapped in some kind of wicked nightmare?"

Of course! That explains everything! I'm just having a bad dream, I thought to myself. Elation and relief washed over me from head to toe. I felt like I had just solved the riddle and won the grand prize. *Oh, thank God.* I could hardly contain the smile that beamed across my face.

"I'm sorry to disappoint you, Eve, but this is *not* a dream. Although, I suppose you could describe the house and everything you see here as a hallucination ... but not me. I am as real as ... well, as you are. I realize that may not seem like the most comforting answer at the moment, but being a Shepherd soon will feel as natural to you as it felt being a human."

Peter's response did little to help me understand what was happening. In fact, all it did was make me feel even more baffled and overwhelmed.

"Look, I know that this is a lot for you to handle right

now," Peter continued. "And I don't want to confuse you further by overloading you with more information than you need to deal with at the moment. But I can help alleviate some of the uncertainty you're experiencing if you're willing to listen to what I have to say." He paused, waiting for some acknowledgement on my part. He took my silence as confirmation that I would hear him out.

"Eve, you recently experienced a trauma from which your *body* did not recover. But a part of you *did* survive—*your mind*. And right now, your mind still needs to process what has happened. It is trying to come to terms with your death, and it needs a safe place to do it. So your mind created certain illusions, or hallucinations, as you put it, to create that safe harbor. You believe you're sitting in your parents' house because your mind *wants* you to be here. This house, *your home*, is your safe place. But since you physically couldn't go home after your death, your mind recreated your safe harbor up here." Peter pointed to his head.

"Wait … I don't understand," I stammered. Millions of thoughts were racing through my head but not one of them made sense. "Part of me actually *lived?*"

"In *your* case, Eve, *yes*—a part of you survived the accident," Peter responded calmly.

"But … how can that be? I mean, I thought the whole thing about being *dead* was that it was an all-or-nothing deal," I remarked, bewildered. I felt like I was treading water in a sea of my own ignorance. The extent of my religious education could be boiled down to a few simple sound bites, namely, believe in God and Heaven and Hell, treat others the way you want to be treated, and be kind to all living creatures … well, almost all—I did have a few bug issues.

"Eve, it's important for you to understand that a human's spirit, soul, and body are independent entities, each of which exist separate and apart from the other. Nonetheless, a human being cannot be complete—cannot *be*—without all three," Peter explained.

"When life begins, a human spirit and soul are anchored to a new body," he continued. "Once bound, the spirit and soul operate in tandem with each other—together they form a human's conscious mind. The human spirit can be best described as a human's *id*, or pure instinct—the raw life force that seeks pleasure and survival over pain and fear at any price. The human soul is best described as a human's *superego*, or conscience; it is the "inner voice" that acts as a constant reminder of the highest ideals of moral behavior and human compassion. When combined, the human spirit and soul shape an individual human's belief systems, values, and personality, or what one might call a human's *ego*.

"Of course," Peter added, "free will ultimately governs humans' behavior and the choices they make along the road of life. Fate plays a significant role, too, since there is a predetermined roadmap that each human can walk. So in the end, the strength of the human spirit and the purity of the human soul will vary depending on a particular human's reactions to the obstacles and hardships thrown at him or her by fate. Are you with me so far?"

"I ... I think so."

"Typically, when a human body dies, so does the mind," he went on to say. "You see, the connection between the spirit and soul is designed to break once the human physical form expires. When the body dies, the human spirit and soul are no longer anchored to anything, and they separate and drift apart from each other. Once separated, the human spirit finds its way back to the collective pool of living energy, or lifeblood, for lack of a better term, to be recycled. And the human soul often goes up ... or down," Peter's eyes followed the direction of his words, "depending on its purity.

"But I digress." He cleared his throat. "The point is that

once the spirit-soul connection is broken, the conscious mind is extinguished. Or at least that's the way it works the majority of the time. *Your* case, however, is a little different." He paused momentarily, as if to let me process the full weight of his words.

"Eve, *your* spirit and soul became inextricably fused at some point during your life—forever bound together. It happens from time to time, but only very rarely. So, when you died, your spirit and soul were abruptly ripped away from your body, *but they remained permanently intertwined.* The connection between your spirit and soul was never broken, which means that your conscious mind still exists." Peter paused again and studied my expression. I just stared at him blankly.

"What I'm trying to tell you, Eve, is that even though your human body is gone, *your mind is still very much alive;* it is, after all, still complete. And, right now, your mind hasn't fully realized that the physical world no longer exists for you— well, not in the same way, at least. So, according to your mind, you are still the exact same person you were before the accident. You still act like you did when you were alive; your mind even thinks you *look* like you did while alive.

"And it is true that the very essence of who you are has been undisturbed. However, as you are fundamentally no longer a corporeal being, you technically no longer have an actual need for any tangible earthly possessions or objects— such as this house, the furniture in it, or that necklace." He looked at the chain dangling from my hand. "This twist—this fly in the ointment, so to speak—is the enigma your mind is currently grappling with. You see, your mind was not designed to deal with your death, much less survive it. Nonetheless, here it is. For your mind, the entire game has changed— not just the rules—and it doesn't like that.

"But fear not, your mind will figure it out. Until then, though, you get to enjoy all of this while your mind is fighting to hang onto your former mortal life." Peter held both hands up in the air as he scanned the room with his eyes.

"Once your mind realizes that there is no human *life* to which it can return, that it is only recreating the *illusion* of the physical creature comforts that you loved and clung to while you were alive, your mind will accept your death—*you* will accept your death.

"My role," he continued, "is to help you with this life-to-death transition so that your mind adjusts more smoothly and quickly. Once your transition is complete, you can undergo your transformation and begin your training, at which time you will learn the history, the rules, the skills, and the limitations of being a Shepherd. And, in the end, you will only know yourself to be one thing—a Shepherd. The Eve that you know—that you *were*—will be gone forever."

Peter's tutorial ended. He sat there quietly, patiently, like he was waiting for me to say or to do something. I didn't know how he expected me to react. Quite frankly, I didn't know how to begin digesting the information he had just unloaded on me.

"Eve, this is definitely complicated. Feelings of fear, confusion, and frustration are to be expected." Peter must have read the apprehension on my face—or he simply read my mind. "You are bound to have numerous questions, many of which may not be easy to answer at this stage of your transition. Just take comfort in knowing that we do not expect you to understand or accept all of this overnight. I'm merely giving you the simplified version for now. You will have plenty of time to figure out what all of this means."

"Figure out what all of *what* means? Which part am I to understand first? I still can't wrap my mind around the part where I'm dead!" I snapped.

Peter sighed. "For now, why don't you try looking at it this way—this illusion of home represents the one place you know best. Your home is where you grew up, and it's where your parents still live. You have memorized every nook and cranny, every creak of every floorboard, and every smell of every room. Even when you were away from home, you always maintained the ability to mentally draw on these images, sounds, and scents when you wanted these things around you but couldn't have them.

"Right now, you still want to be in this house. You still want to be wearing your favorite clothes and drinking water from your mother's water pitcher in the refrigerator. So your mind took the reins and recreated the illusion of what comforts you most. The only difference being that you no longer have the same physical limitations that you once did—that is, you no longer have your human body—so your mind has virtually no boundaries in terms of what it is capable of creating. The result is that you are now experiencing full-blown, life-sized hallucinations of your creature comforts rather than just fond memories locked inside your head."

I looked at Peter, still puzzled.

"Eve," he continued with more enthusiasm, "do you recall what time it was when you woke up this afternoon?"

"Yeah, it was a little after two o'clock."

"The alarm clock was clear across the room from your bed. How did you see what time it was without your glasses or your contact lenses? How are you seeing things so clearly right now?"

"I … I don't know." *Huh.* Until that moment, I hadn't noticed I wasn't wearing my contacts.

"And how did you get from your bedroom to the kitchen?"

"I don't know … I just assumed I must have … blacked out or something while walking down the stairs," I mumbled.

"Eve," Peter said, smiling as if he was about to reveal the secret behind his trick. "You don't need glasses anymore because you're no longer handicapped by any of the physical limitations of your former human body. Likewise, you don't need to walk down the stairs—or anywhere for that matter—because you are no longer bound by human legs. You were in your bedroom because that's where you wanted to be. When you wanted to go to the kitchen, your mind simply created the illusion of your kitchen and, like magic, you were there. Allow me to demonstrate."

He turned his attention to the wood-burning fireplace at the east end of the living room. I followed his gaze. It wasn't long before I saw something flicker. Then, the entire east wall started to fade into the night sky; it was actually disappearing right before my eyes. I blinked a few times in disbelief.

"How are you doing that?" I asked in awe.

"It's quite easy, really." He looked thoroughly amused and pleased with himself. I could tell these parlor tricks never got old for him. "I am simply interfering with your thoughts by adding one of my own, thereby altering your illusion. We all can do it. We can block these intrusions from happening as well, as you soon will learn. For the time being, however, you've been inadvertently allowing me to interfere with your thoughts all afternoon. That's why I can be … well, sitting here in this room talking to you. But this place," Peter explained, holding his arms out for emphasis, "is all in *your* mind. I'm just freeloading, as it were, on your journey."

"So let me get this straight … I'm not in Michigan?" The words slowly tumbled out of my mouth. I already knew the answer to my question, but I needed to hear Peter say it again.

"Technically, you're not even on *Earth*," he clarified. I began to feel a little lightheaded, but, glutton for punishment that I was, I pressed on with my questions.

"And … I'm not sitting in this chair right now?"

"No. That chair doesn't really exist."

"And I'm not really drinking this water?" I muttered, holding up my glass of water. I remembered how thirsty I was earlier.

"You no longer need to drink."

"And," I inhaled deeply, "I'm not really … breathing this air?"

"Eve, you no longer need to breathe." As I heard Peter say the words, I instinctively inhaled again. It certainly felt real. It felt like my lungs were filling up with air. He laughed at my reaction, and I shot him a grimacing look, which only made him laugh harder.

"And you don't *need* this house because you don't need to have a roof over your head any longer," he threw in. "Just like you don't *need* water or air because you no longer have a human body that requires these things."

Peter glanced down at his watch and smiled at me curiously.

"Eve, how much time do you think has passed since I introduced myself to you?"

"I don't know—forty-five minutes, an hour, tops."

"It's been exactly sixty-two minutes, which on Earth is just over twenty-four hours."

"Excuse me?" I looked at Peter, stunned. "Are you seriously telling me that we've been talking for an *entire day*?"

"On Earth—yes."

I've been dead for nearly a week. I cringed at the thought. My mind was on overload; it started spinning out of control. I felt the cup of water slip out of my hand and heard the sound of glass breaking as it hit the floor.

* * *

When I came to, I was lying on my back, stretched out on the sofa in the living room. Peter was still sitting in the same chair.

"Did I faint?" I asked embarrassed.

"Well, your mind certainly made you think you did," he said, trying to fight back a smile.

"How long was I out?" I was worried that I had been out for another hour or so.

"Not long."

"According to whom?" I asked alarmed. "Has another day passed on Earth?"

"No—just over an hour has passed down there," Peter clarified, trying his best not to chuckle as I attempted the math in my head.

"Don't worry, Eve, it will all be explained to you during your training." He extended his hand to help me sit up, and I accepted his assistance.

I looked around the room. The same white beadboard in my bedroom covered the living room walls too. Wide wood planks, also painted white, created an arched ceiling more than two stories up. The east wall of the living room was now intact; it was no longer the image of the starry night that Peter had conjured. The artwork, the photos, all of it was there. Peter was right—everything was in its place, right down to the last detail.

My mind created all of this? I thought, mystified.

"Why would my mind go through all the trouble if none of this is real?" I asked. "I mean, isn't there an easier way for someone to transition into the afterlife?"

"Not really," Peter responded. "In fact, over time we have realized that those of us who keep our spirits and our souls in the afterlife make the transition from life to death much more smoothly if our minds are grounded in a comfortable, familiar setting while the transition occurs. Your mind has employed its self-defense mechanisms by creating a mental and visual buffer that it will continue to use until it has had enough time to absorb the shock of your demise. The need for such defenses is particularly strong for those who have been ripped so suddenly and prematurely from their lives—like you."

"So why no people?" I asked. "If my mind can recreate every detail of my parents' home, why aren't my parents here?"

"That is a question I cannot answer," he replied.

"*Cannot* or *will not?*" I didn't try to hide my frustration.

"I *cannot* answer your question because, quite frankly, I don't know the answer to it," Peter stated humbly. "We simply do not understand all of the detailed inner workings of the human mind. I will say that it is highly unusual for others like us to create, in death, the illusions of those humans to whom they were the closest during their lives. I suspect it's because human relationships are so complex and multi-faceted that the mind would quickly realize any misstep or mistake in its own re-creation. The mind can fool itself only so far before it realizes its own trickery. And, right now, your mind wants to remain ignorant for as long as it needs to so it can process your untimely death."

"Ignorance is bliss," I mumbled under my breath.

"When you fully accept your death," he continued, interrupting my train of thought, "your transition will be complete, and you won't need the illusion of your home anymore. You'll be ready to put it behind you. You'll be ready to put *everything* in your past behind you. And, once you complete your transformation, you will no longer remember your family and friends—or your life. Even your face will be new to you."

Whoa! Back up. What did he just say? My mind did a double take.

"I won't remember my life?" I asked out loud, aghast.

"No," Peter confirmed. "Of course, you will retain the essence of who you are—the sum of your personality, emotions, values, knowledge, and so on. But your actual experiences and the relationships you formed during your life will be erased. You would likely compare it to a state of amnesia."

"Why?" I demanded in alarm. "Why must my mind be erased?" I didn't want to forget my life. My memories were the only thing I had left, and now they were going to be taken away from me too.

"Eve, it's necessary. It's easier on you ... and on them." Peter eyed a framed photo hanging on the wall of my mom, my dad, and me. It was taken last year at the top of the Warren Dunes. It was a family tradition ever since we moved to Michigan—our annual family picture.

"I know it might seem unfair, and even extreme, but as Shepherds we have a crucial function. We cannot be distracted by our pasts. We cannot afford to make a single mistake when we are protecting humans from harm. Mistakes made by us cost mortals their lives," Peter said soberly.

"So what about my parents? Can ... can I at least *see* them ... you know ... before I forget them?" I asked Peter, choking back the anguish welling up inside me. The thought of no longer being able to see or remember my parents made me miss them even more.

"I'm afraid that's impossible," he replied. "Your parents are grieving over your death, which they need to do—something that *you* have yet to do, I might add. Watching them, seeing them, will not help you; it will only make things harder on you. You will only be reminded of things left unsaid and undone. Your transition will be delayed because you will be stuck in the past."

Stuck in the past. The words echoed in my ears. I was reminded of my last conversation with Quinn, and I swallowed hard.

"Did my parents already have a funeral for me?" I asked, trying to shift the focus of my thoughts. A chill ran through me as the word "funeral" left my mouth.

"Yes." Peter offered no other information.

That's it? Just a generic "yes"? That's all I get? I wanted to know more about my funeral, but what was I supposed to ask? *"So, did it go well?" "Was there a big turnout?" "Nice eulogy?" "Were people crying?"* Each question seemed more ridiculous and inappropriate than the last—like I was trying to satisfy some morbidly narcissistic curiosity of mine.

What did it really matter anyway? Peter was probably right. What good would it do me to think about people I'd never see again, a life I would never have again, or a situation I could do nothing about? Still, there was one thing I had to know.

"How are my parents handling all of this? ... Will they be okay?"

"Your parents will be fine; they will get through this. Understandably, no parent wants to outlive his or her children. And they will need time to deal with their loss, but they will rely on each other for support. Eventually, they will grow stronger together as a result of the tragedy of your death."

Despite the reassuring tone in Peter's voice, his response gave me neither the closure I needed, nor did it put me at ease. In fact, it made me feel quite the opposite. I felt horrible leaving my parents.

No! my mind cried out. I refused to allow myself to feel guilty. I didn't leave my parents; I was *stolen* from them. How could this have happened to them? How could their only daughter—their only child—be taken away from them? I was growing angrier and angrier by the minute, thinking about the pain and suffering my death had caused them.

Not to mention *me*. How could this have happened to me? I would never see my parents again. I'd never be able to apologize for disobeying them and driving to Champaign. I'd never again be able to hug them or tell them that I loved them. I'd never see my friends again. I would never fall in love again. I would never get married or have children. I was robbed of my life. I was robbed of my future.

Suddenly, I was back in my bedroom—by myself.

"Screw you!" I shouted as loudly as I could up into the air.

I fell forward onto my bed and buried my face in my pillow to muffle my tortured screams. I wanted to cry. I wanted to sob uncontrollably. But I couldn't. No tears would come.

That's just great! I can't even cry! I slammed my fists into my mattress. Rage filled me. I jumped off my bed, ripped all the linens off of it, and threw them in a pile on the floor. It felt good. I looked around my room and leaped over the pile to my desk, which I summarily flipped over. Then I turned over my bedside table. It wasn't enough. I was still fuming. I stormed over to my dresser and launched the drawers across the room, welcoming the sound of the splitting wood as they hit the opposite wall.

I paused for a moment to survey the damage; it looked like a tornado had whipped through my room. I laughed. If only my mom could see this, she would have a fit of epic proportions.

My mom. My dad. I would've given anything to be with them right now, but I had already given my life, and there wasn't anything left. An unbelievable sadness washed over me. I had never felt so alone in all my life. I sank to the floor shaking.

I was dead.

9. Hindsight is Twenty-Twenty

I opened my eyes to see the light of the full moon casting shadows across the walls of my room. I was curled up on the floor in a pile of blankets, sheets, and pillows from my bed. I rolled over, only to bump into the side of my flipped-over desk. *Ouch.* My body was aching all over; I felt like I'd gone ten rounds in a boxing match—or like I'd been in an awful car accident.

Could it have all been a bad dream?

I slowly sat up and scanned my room. It was trashed. I closed my eyes hoping for the best but fearing the worst. When I reopened them, I knew I was in serious trouble. My room was now in perfect order—not a thing out of place.

And, instead of moonlight streaming through my windows, I saw the early morning rays of the sun. I heard the birds outside chirping excitedly. I blinked a few times in hopes that my eyes were playing tricks on me, but each time I opened them, my room was still clean, and, apparently, it was now morning.

I was too exhausted, too confused, and too upset to try to figure it all out right then. All I wanted was a nice, long, hot shower. I stood up and dragged myself into the bathroom, closed the door and turned on the water. It wasn't long before the bathroom was filled with steam, making it difficult to see anything clearly. I sighed with relief. I didn't want any more clarity today.

I peeled off my clothes and stepped into the shower. I closed my eyes and let the jet stream of hot water massage my sore muscles—or at least, it felt like my muscles were sore. Whatever the case, the water felt good. I opened my mouth and let the water overfill it, run back out of my mouth and down my chin. I leaned back against the shower wall and sunk down to the shower floor as I watched the steam rise up to the ceiling; it reminded me of my breath on a cold winter's day.

I desperately wanted to go back in time. I wanted to be back in Bloomington. I wished I had changed my mind about driving to Champaign. I wished I could go back to the evening of the party with Quinn. I pictured him kissing me. Then I thought about Ryan, and rage stirred within me. Knowing then what I knew now, I wondered if I would've said or done anything differently that night with Quinn at the party or in the days that followed.

Random scenes from my fatal accident began flooding my mind against my will. I saw flashes of the car crash with the drunk driver, followed by the bright lights of the pickup truck that slammed into me. The accident had taken my life. I didn't want to believe it, but I had to accept the truth.

I took a deep breath, sighed. *The dead breathing.* If that wasn't an oxymoron, I didn't know what was. My mind started firing off question after question as I slowly began to accept the reality of my new "existence." I had to get some answers. I had to find Peter.

* * *

Instantly, I found myself back in the blue-and-white striped chair I had sat in earlier that day, dressed in the same white T-shirt and jeans I'd been wearing then. Peter was sitting in the chair opposite me. It was as if mere seconds had passed—like I had never left the living room.

If Peter had overheard my little episode upstairs in my room, he didn't mention it. And for that I was grateful. I was feeling more than a little self-conscious about my tantrum, and I didn't want to have to explain myself.

"So let me get this straight," I began. "I died and ended up ... *here*, wherever here is, because I am now one of *you*? A *Shepherd*?

"In the oversimplified version, yes," Peter responded.

"Why me?"

"Truthfully, Eve, I'm not sure why you were selected to become a Shepherd—we rarely ever are. I suspect it's because you met certain criteria. The first of which," Peter noted, "is something that I mentioned to you already. You are one of a very small group of humans whose spirits and souls have been fused. This condition is a prerequisite that must be met in order for any mortal to be considered eligible to become one of us. It's a job requirement, so to speak."

"This ... spirit-soul fusion thing—how does it happen?" I inquired.

"Again, we're not really sure how or even why it happens. We do know that some humans are born with a fused spirit and soul—they are the true '*old souls*' of the world, wise well beyond their years, even at birth. These humans are blessed and burdened with the secrets, the insights, and the wisdom of the many generations that have come before them. The term "old soul" has lost some credibility over time as it has been casually tossed around and overused to describe people. But, trust me, you will know immediately when you meet a true *old soul*. You can see it in their eyes—there's something deep, almost haunting about them.

"As for most other mortals who meet this prerequisite, their spirits and souls are fused permanently after a near-death experience. As the body begins to die, the spirit and the soul begin to stretch away from the body like stones in a slingshot, ready to be propelled outwards with the last physical breath. But then something happens to jolt these humans' bodies back to life and their spirits and souls are catapulted back into their bodies with such force that they are irreversibly intertwined and bound along the way.

"And then there are those rare humans whose spirits and souls are fused together through some type of external interference. These humans' fates have been manipulated or changed at some point during their lives."

Instantly, I heard Madame Sasha's words resonate in my head: *"I've never seen an aura like this before … It's so strange … It seems as though your fate is shifting—changing—right before my very eyes."*

"Your fate was forever changed about the same time you met Madame Sasha," Peter offered, obviously having read my mind.

* * *

"Please, listen to me." Madame Sasha's words resonated in my memory. I could still see the pity in her eyes. "I might be of some help," she said in her thick accent.

"What? Are you going to tell me that if I give you more money you can show me how to prevent this … this … so-called *Curse* from happening?" I sneered.

"No—I'm sorry. I don't know how to stop the Curse of Three. But I can tell you what I see. Maybe that will help you. Please … sit down."

I don't know what came over me, but I did as Madame Sasha requested.

"The first incident will happen due to an illness—in a hospital perhaps—some time before your eighteenth birthday. The second incident will involve an accident—wait, yes—a car accident. You will survive both … barely. But the third incident …" Madame Sasha strained with closed eyes, rubbing her temples. "I don't know. I see a bright flash of light, but I cannot see its point of origin. All I can tell you is that the third incident will be sudden and unexpected." She opened her eyes and solemnly dropped her hands to her sides. "That's it. That is the last thing I can make out. I'm sorry, but I see no future for you after that."

"*You're wrong*," I snarled. She *had* to be wrong. I refused to believe what I was hearing.

"My readings may not always be exact, but I'm rarely wrong," she announced proudly.

"Being *rarely* wrong is a far cry from being *never* wrong," I criticized. "How could you possibly know what fate has in store for me? I could get hit by a bus tomorrow or I could live to be one hundred. Nothing is written in stone," I hissed between gritted teeth. I wasn't about to listen to any more of this crap. Glaring at Madame Sasha, I bolted up out of my seat and grabbed my bag, but she caught me by the arm before I could storm out of the room.

"I'm sorry to have upset you so, my dear. Really, I am. Please understand—I just couldn't let you leave without knowing your destiny. I wish I could have given you better news. Here ... please take this." She held out the necklace she had been wearing around her neck. "The charm—it is of the patron saint Andrew Avellino; he will help protect you."

Her offering enraged me further. I snubbed her gift, but Madame Sasha pushed the necklace into the palm of my hand and curled my fingers around it anyway.

"Please ... take it. I insist. Wear it always," she added. "And good luck to you, Eve."

I just stood there, stunned, as she opened the door for me to leave. And, just like that, it was over.

I followed Emma outside of the house, still in shock. I stared blankly at the charm in my hand and shoved it in my pocket before Emma spotted it. She was beaming from ear to ear. Clearly, Madame Sasha had told Emma something very different about her destiny than what the psychic had told me about mine.

The entire drive home I was silent. Emma, however, went on and on about how she and her boyfriend Derek were destined to be a part of each other's lives forever. Madame Sasha had also told Emma that she and Derek would be living together in Michigan some time within the next two years. I laughed at the idea in my head. I knew Derek had no intention of staying in Michigan when he graduated in a couple of months; he had said it a thousand times. In fact, Derek had received a scholarship to a college out East. Emma, on the other hand, was a hometown girl through and through. She never imagined living more than twenty minutes away from her family. I was convinced that Emma's reading was just further evidence that Madame Sasha was a full of it. Only a miracle would keep Emma and Derek together.

* * *

"A miracle, indeed," Peter said.

"Yeah, some miracle," I scoffed. "Emma and Derek got pregnant three months later—almost to the day." I looked up at Peter. "You know, the strangest thing about going to see Madame Sasha was that after a week or so, I never thought about her or my reading again—not until Emma got pregnant. I mean, when someone tells you that you have less than three years to live—joking or not—that should bother you for a while, right?" I looked at Peter for confirmation, but his face was devoid of any expression.

"But it didn't," I continued. "A week after my reading, it was like I had never heard of Madame Sasha. Emma was the same way, and she was the one who had the fairy-tale reading ... or so she originally thought."

I flashed back to the day Emma brought up Madame Sasha's name. It was a couple of weeks after she found out she was pregnant and just a few days after Derek did the "responsible" thing and asked Emma to marry him. I wasn't at all surprised when Emma accepted his proposal. With a wife and a baby on the way, college would have to wait. Derek joined his family's local business, indefinitely postponing his dreams to move to the East Coast.

"When Madame Sasha said Derek and I would be together," I remembered Emma saying, "I didn't imagine it would turn out like this. Some Cinderella story, huh?" Her voice was riddled with self-pity, but I couldn't comfort her. The instant I heard Emma mention Madame Sasha's name, my mind was ambushed by the psychic's tale of what was in store for my future.

Six weeks later, I was rushed to the hospital for an emergency appendectomy. I slipped into a coma after having an adverse reaction to the general anesthesia, only to wake up a few days later to find my parents hovering over me with tear-stained faces. When they explained what had happened, the smell of floral incense and Pine-Sol hit me like a ton of bricks.

"The first incident will happen due to an illness—in a hospital perhaps—some time before your eighteenth birthday." I remembered the fear creeping into my body as I heard Madame Sasha's thick accent in my head. Never before had I considered wearing the silver charm that she had insisted I take. But the same day I was discharged from the hospital, I dug the necklace out of the bottom of my jewelry box and put it around my neck. I'd never been a day without it since—that was until now. The day I came home from the hospital was also the first day I began to give credence to the inner voice warning me of bad things to come … the monster that lurked deep within the pit of my stomach.

* * *

"Did Madame Sasha change my fate?" I asked Peter.

"No. She just noticed that your destiny was altered. We believe that you threatened the Servants, or more appropriately, their plans, so they manipulated your fate in order to eliminate you."

"The Servants?" I asked, confused.

"Demons. A sect of very powerful demons."

"Demons?" I burst out laughing. "You expect me to believe that *demons* changed my fate? That *demons* are responsible for my death?" This truly was the icing on the cake.

"Eve, make no mistake about it. Demons walk amongst the humans—as do we. We maintain a truce with most clans in a mutual effort to maintain the balance between the greater good and evil. In other words, we stay out of their way and they stay out of ours. But we have been and will remain eternal enemies with one particular clan, the Servants. In fact, our very existence came about because of them. When they were created eight centuries ago, so were we. The Servants' purpose is to tip the balance of evil in their favor, and our purpose is to help stop them from achieving that goal. They've since grown in strength and number, making them increasingly problematic for us all."

"So just how did the … Servants," I had trouble uttering the word without snickering, "change my fate?"

"We're still trying to piece that together. Whenever we learn that the Servants have targeted a mortal by manipulating his or her destiny, the process of untangling that human's twisted threads of fate begins immediately. But it's a long and complex procedure, during which time the human is vulnerable and can become the victim of his or her redirected destiny at any moment. That's where we come in; Shepherds protect those humans whose fates have been altered by the Servants. By guarding these targeted humans, we buy them more time, hopefully during which the Servants' meddlesome misdeeds can be discovered and reversed. Most of the time we are successful, but sometimes … sometimes we are not." Peter shifted uncomfortably in his seat.

They didn't save me in time, I realized.

"Which brings us back to your original question," Peter said, changing the subject. "Why were you chosen to be a

Shepherd?" Peter cleared his throat. "Well, just because a mortal has met the first prerequisite of becoming a Shepherd doesn't mean he or she has what it takes to be a Shepherd. But those in the Order of the Realms, the ultimate 'Powers-That-Be' so to speak, were curious about you. It's not often we encounter a case like yours where the fate of a human has been manipulated so radically in such a short period of time. The Servants can mask subtle changes to a human's fate, making it difficult to find their signs of interference. But when your destiny was changed, sirens and alarms went off—metaphorically speaking, of course. We don't ... really ... have sirens and alarms."

"Of course," I said in a mocking tone.

"Anyway," Peter continued, ignoring me, "you were unfortunate enough to be given a death sentence in just under two years. Such a drastic change in a human's fate is nearly impossible to hide. We suspected you must have presented quite a credible threat to the Servants for them to risk so much exposure. So I suppose the Order of the Realms wanted to keep you close by after you died to see if they could figure out just how formidable a threat you posed to the Servants.

"I also suspect that the Order believed you could handle the job. At age sixteen, you were given this strange *gift*—this knowledge about your ill-fated future. And you handled the news quite well under the circumstances, even when you realized what Madame Sasha told you was more likely true than not. Even when you believed your days were numbered, you faced your future head on; you maintained your focus, your direction, and your inner-strength."

Yeah, right, I thought, *I hadn't faced my destiny as much as I tried to ignore it.*

"Eve, you give yourself too little credit." Peter paused for a moment, looked at his watch and then up at me. "Well, I'm sure you have many more questions, but the time has come for you to undergo your transformation and begin your formal training. Rest assured, your questions about your future as an immortal will be answered then. But now the time has come to say good-bye to the old you. It's time to forget your past and accept your new existence as a Shepherd ... Congratulations, Eve, your transition is over."

I was overwhelmed by feelings of dread, grief, and anxiety. I wasn't ready. How could I ever be ready to forget my life? Although it wasn't really my *life* anymore, was it? I took a deep breath and sighed.

"Peter, can I have a few minutes first—to collect my thoughts? You know, to make peace with my past—with myself?"

"Of course," he replied without hesitation.

Instantly, I found myself walking on the beach just outside my house. It was my favorite place to be. The blustery cold wind whipped through my hair and it felt good. I took a few deep breaths, taking in the fresh air. The sound of the waves crashing into the peaks and valleys of frozen water that lined the shore for miles on either side of me, the smell of the beach in winter, the feel of the cold sand and ice crunching under my feet—it all felt so real. It was my home, and I would miss it.

I thought about summers on the beach with my parents. My dad taught me how to swim in this water. We would build huge sand castles together, complete with moats and bridges. My mom and I would sit under a huge beach umbrella for hours, playing checkers and reading books. She'd always wear the same wide-brimmed straw hat and huge old-Hollywood sunglasses.

When I was older, I hung out on this beach with my friends. We would have bonfires at night, roast marshmallows, sing songs, take late night dips in the lake, and just goof around. I met Ryan on this beach …

Ryan. I wondered how he felt about my death? Did he feel responsible? Part of me wanted him to feel guilty. After all, I wouldn't have been on the road that night if I hadn't caught him cheating on me.

I shook my head in self-disgust. It was wrong of me to blame Ryan for my death or to even hope he blamed himself. In all fairness, I wouldn't have been on the road that night if *I* hadn't kissed another guy. Besides, even if the events of that horrid evening had unfolded differently, even if I had left on Sunday like I originally had hoped, I knew the outcome would've been the same. I was never supposed to make it back to Bloomington. My time had come. It was as simple as that.

I was dead … and soon I was going to forget everything about myself—my parents, my friends—every memory I ever had … gone. Refusing to waste my last few minutes on Ryan, I turned my attention to the expansive landscape before me.

The sky was perfectly clear and the sun was just beginning to set. The seasons had changed and now the fresh smell of spring permeated the air. I could make out parts of the Chicago skyline across Lake Michigan. I watched the sky ignite with fiery yellows, oranges, and reds as the sun slowly dipped below the horizon, just behind the dark outlines of the buildings so far away. The skyscrapers looked like tiny fingers reaching out towards the giant ball of fire, hoping to grasp one last bit of warmth before the moon and the stars came out to play. It was truly an amazing sight, and I was glad I got to see it one more time as me.

I suddenly realized I was no longer alone.

"Beautiful isn't it?" I asked Peter.

"Always," he responded. Standing side-by-side, we silently watched the last traces of the sun drop below the horizon.

I took a huge breath and sighed. "Okay, I'm ready," I said shakily. Peter grabbed my hand and squeezed it reassuringly.

"Don't worry, Eve," he said. "Once you wake up, you will feel completely at ease. In fact, you'll never question why you're a Shepherd. It won't occur to you to do so, just like it never occurred to you to question why you were a human."

I tried to relax, but inside I felt far from calm. The beach, the lake, the horizon—all of it started to fade away before my very eyes like a sidewalk chalk drawing in the rain. I took another deep breath.

"Let's do this," I said unsurely.

"Go ahead, Eve—close your eyes."

10. Time Keeps Moving On

"Eve?" I heard my name being called.

"Eve?" the voice called out again.

I groaned. I felt groggy, as if I was coming out of a deep slumber.

"Eve." I felt someone nudging me gently. "It's Peter."

I slowly opened my eyes and saw a blurry figure hovering over me. As my eyes gradually began to focus, I recognized Peter. I looked around. I was in a huge library of sorts, and I was lying on top of a long wooden reading table. I didn't think I'd ever been here before, but I couldn't be sure.

"Where am I?" I asked, still dazed. "How did I get here?" I was struggling to remember, but I couldn't. Actually, I could remember only three things. First, my name was Eve. Just Eve. If I had a last name, I couldn't recall it. Second, I was a Shepherd—not that I knew what that entailed exactly. And third, I knew Peter. He was here to teach me what I needed to know about being a Shepherd. Despite the fact that I was armed with only these few tidbits of information, and that I had absolutely no idea where I was, I was peculiarly at ease with my circumstances.

"Welcome to the Archives. This is where we *live* when we're not on assignment." Peter chuckled at his own joke.

"On assignment?" I asked.

"We're on assignment when we are protecting a mortal whose fate has been—"

"Manipulated," I said, completing Peter's explanation. My mind began filtering in more and more information.

"Yes, that's right. Very good," he said, smiling. "I hoped I had been careful enough when completing your transformation to leave in place at least some of the fundamentals we had discussed." Peter seemed very pleased with himself. "Tell me, what else do you remember?"

"About what?"

"Well, about whatever comes to mind."

"I remember little bits and pieces of information, but it's all jumbled." I crinkled up my forehead, straining to make sense of whatever I could. "I know my name is Eve, and I'm a Shepherd."

"Okay—good. And what do you know about Shepherds?" Peter inquired.

"Well, I know you're a Shepherd. I know that I died recently—suddenly, I think—and then I became a Shepherd. And our job is to guard humans whose destinies have been manipulated ... by the ... the ..." I was struggling to remember the wrongdoers' names.

"The clan of demons called the Servants," Peter assisted.

"Right—the Servants." My mind was trying to wrap itself around all of this. *Servants and Shepherds. Demons and ...*

"So," I asked, "what are we exactly? I mean, why are we called Shepherds? Why not just call us guardian angels?" I asked the question and then wondered if maybe there were no such things as guardian angels. Maybe we were the only protectors out there.

"Guardian angels are different. Every human is assigned one at birth. Guardian angels watch over their humans, or their *charges*, throughout the course of the humans' lives, subtly guiding their charges with respect to their beliefs, choices, and other matters relating their humans' physical, emotional, and spiritual health and well-being.

"Shepherds, on the other hand, are assigned to watch over humans only if and when we realize they have been targeted by the Servants."

"Okay, so once you realized that my fate had been manipulated by the Servants, you—what—stepped in and took over for my guardian angel? He wasn't up for the job anymore?" I asked.

"No, I'm sure *she* was quite good. That said, it's not part of the guardian angels' job description to intervene and save their charges if they need rescuing," Peter continued. "Guardian angels advise their charges, they are not there to protect them the way we protect ours. They do not possess our special skills and they cannot take certain … liberties that we can; liberties that come in handy when protecting humans who have been touched by demons."

"What skills? What liberties?" I was intrigued.

"You'll find out soon enough," Peter responded, flashing a knowing grin.

"Okay, so let me get this straight. I *had* a guardian angel, but she was replaced by one of you—one of *us*," I corrected myself, "when it was discovered that the Servants had altered my destiny. I was assigned a Shepherd because he or she supposedly could protect me better. So what happened? I mean, why then did I die?" I strained to remember my life. And my death.

"Unfortunately, we couldn't save you." He looked at me solemnly and sighed. "It all happened too fast."

"I feel like I should remember something, anything, about my life, but I can't. It's all very strange, like I'm staring into the murky water of a marsh pond."

"You do realize you're not supposed to remember anything about your past, don't you?"

"Yes, but that doesn't mean I like having a black hole where all of the memories of my life should be." I looked at Peter as innocently and as sweetly as I could. "Can't I at least know *how* I died?"

"You were involved in a car accident," he replied bluntly.

"Oh." Somehow, I hadn't expected Peter to be so forthcoming. *A car accident, huh?* I repeated in my head. I looked down at this body—my body—expecting to see some evidence that I had been harmed in some way, but I was fine.

My hands, my arms, my legs—everything seemed so familiar and yet so foreign at the same time. I was completely comfortable in this body; I just wasn't sure that it was mine.

"Give it a few days and you'll feel right at home with your new body and appearance, which I will tell you are identical to how you looked previously, that is, before the accident."

"Oh, right, you can read my thoughts."

"For now." He grinned. "But that will change soon too. Eve, let's take a walk so I can show you around."

* * *

The Archives, as Peter called it, was impressive; its sheer magnitude was incredible. Oval in shape, it had no discernable points of entry or exit. The walls were at least fifty feet high, interrupted only by a second-floor balcony that ran along the entire circumference of the room. It had a simple elegance that was almost contemporary in design, but it still held a certain old-world charm. The walls were covered in shelves upon shelves of books, complete with library ladders every fifteen or so yards. Wooden reading tables and chairs had been placed strategically throughout the inner perimeter of the large hall, while leather-tufted chairs and wooden end tables were grouped together on the outskirts of the room. Eight huge wrought-iron chandeliers hung from the ceiling.

But the ceiling itself was the most magnificent feature of the Archives. It was painted to look like the night sky. In fact, the expansive fresco looked so realistic that it seemed to radiate its own light from the illustrated moon and stars.

The floor was made up of wide walnut planks stained dark brown and laid in an oversized parquet pattern that stretched across the entire floor, everywhere except for the center of the room in which sat a huge sundial. It had to be twenty feet in diameter.

What an odd thing to see indoors, I noted. I wondered if the sundial actually worked. I looked up again at the ceiling, noting the night sky painted above it.

"It works," Peter responded.

"Hmm?" I muttered, lost in my own thoughts.

"The sundial—it works," he repeated once more. "The ceiling changes from dawn to dusk, and so forth, in accordance with how we keep time up here. During daylight, as the sun moves across the ceiling, it casts its light on the sundial so you can tell the time."

"Wow," I said in awe, "I'm sure I would've remembered seeing this before. You can't erase something like this from someone's memory." I was trying to drink it all in, but there was so much to see.

"It makes quite an impression. The sundial is the only one of its kind," Peter said.

Twenty feet from where we stood I saw a towering antique grandfather clock. Like everything else there, the clock made a statement.

"And that?" I inquired.

"Ah, that's the Time Keeper. It postdates the sundial and has become the primary way in which we measure how time passes up here," Peter explained.

I walked over to the Time Keeper to take a closer look. It looked like some sort of family heirloom you would find tucked away in a corner of an old European manor. The clock must have stood over ten feet tall. It was made of dark red mahogany. Its body was intricately carved from top to bottom. I wanted to run my fingers over the artfully-crafted designs, but didn't dare for fear I'd set off an alarm.

A pair of wood-carved angel wings sat perched on top of the clock, spread out like a bird about to take flight. The wings were flanked on either side by carved finials. The face of the clock was overlaid with brass that had been cut into a floral motif and gave it the impression of metal lace—strong and delicate at the same time. Large black Roman numerals were set on top of the brass layer. Decorative wood columns framed the long rectangular trunk of the behemoth clock, between which a large pendulum was visible through an amber-tinted glass door. At the base of the clock were two mischievous-looking cherubs carved out of the same wood, along with four wooden scrolls that served as the feet of the massive clock.

"It's beautiful," I remarked.

Across the room, at the other end of the Archives, I spotted an enormous globe. It appeared to be rotating slowly, but I couldn't be sure from my vantage point.

"What's that?" I asked Peter, pointing to the globe.

"Ah yes, that would be the Global Locator," Peter replied. "It lets us keep track of the whereabouts of all Shepherds on Earth—whether they are on assignment or not. You see, up here we can find each other easily by way of our thoughts. Down there, however, it's more difficult because we are unable to communicate telepathically with each other on Earth. But even on Earth, each Shepherd retains his or her unique signature. And when a Shepherd is on Earth, that signature is revealed as a distinct point of light on that globe, depending on the Shepherd's location," Peter explained. I started to walk across the Archives to get a closer look, but Peter politely took me by the arm and stopped me.

"Later," he said. "You'll have plenty of time *after* your training to study the Locator, as well as everything else here, including our extensive book collection. We have at least one copy of almost every book ever written, even some originals that have been long forgotten or abandoned. Not to mention, we have a prestigious collection of ancient scrolls, hides, and tablets—all original."

"Wow." I scanned the voluminous number of books that were shelved around the perimeter of the Archives. "Even books written in different languages?" I asked, still trying to grasp the full scope of my new *home*.

"Absolutely," Peter said proudly. "We all communicate in the same universal language, but one of the skills you inherited as a Shepherd is that you now can read, write, and speak every human language. Consider it another job requirement," he threw in for good measure.

"Oh," was all I could muster.

"Eve, I realize all of this must seem overwhelming, but in a few days time, you'll feel like an old pro. I promise." He squeezed my hand reassuringly and a twinge of *déjà vu* swept through me. I tensed up a little.

"What is it?"

"Nothing. It's just that I ... when you squeezed my hand ... it felt kind of ... strange." I wasn't sure why, but I didn't want him to know that his comforting gesture triggered a familiar feeling inside me. Maybe if I could keep remembering little things about my past, I could figure out who I was before I died. I quickly shoved the thought deep within the recesses of my mind.

"Don't fret," Peter remarked. "It's not uncommon at this stage to experience odd physical reactions or sensations, but that, too, shall pass as you get used to your new physical form. Your mind is still adjusting to your transformation; it's adapting to your *new*-old body, so to speak, and all the bells and whistles that come with it." He smiled at me.

"Oh, I should give you something before we get knee deep into your training." He reached into his pocket, pulled out a wristwatch, and handed it to me. It looked fairly ordinary with its brown leather strap and silver frame. On the circular face of the watch, however, were three separate timekeeping mechanisms.

"It's critical that you wear this watch *always*. Do not ever take it off. I can't stress this enough, Eve. *Never lose this watch.*

112

Certain elements, like time, for instance, take on a whole separate meaning for us. We experience time much differently up here than we do down on Earth." As Peter helped me fasten the watch on my left wrist, I couldn't help but notice that his watch looked remarkably similar to mine.

"What do you mean?"

"Each half-hour up here is equivalent to a half-day on Earth; each hour up here is the same as one day down there."

"Whoa, let me get this straight. Every *sixty minutes* up here in the Archives means that *twenty-four hours* have passed down there—on Earth?" I asked, baffled.

"Correct," Peter said calmly. I searched his face, his eyes, to see if he was joking, but I couldn't see a single hint of humor.

"I don't understand. How ... how is that possible?"

"Without going into too much detail, let's just say Shepherds defy many of the physical and natural laws that constrain mortals—time being one of them. You see, we need to concentrate our energy on the macro issues that affect the overall balance of good and evil. In order to stay focused on the big picture, we only need to catch glimpses of the human condition rather than track the daily grind of humanity minute-by-minute. Perched up here, our view of the human world could best be compared to flipping through a photo album that captures the highlights of a trip abroad instead of suffering through the unedited home movie of the same. To be required to do otherwise, to be forced to sift through every incident that occurred on Earth, would only distract us from our true purpose. We would be unable to flush out truly unnatural shifts in the patterns of good and evil from the less significant blips that mark everyday random acts. Believe me, it may seem strange at first, but it really is to our benefit.

"Okay, so without further ado," Peter continued, "let me explain the features of your watch. Every Shepherd has a

113

watch like yours—like mine. The Time Keeper tracks time up here, which we call *Aura* time. And the largest dial on all of our watches keeps *Aura* time in accordance with the Time Keeper. The Roman numerals on the big dial on your watch mimic those on the grandfather clock. See?"

I compared the face of my watch to the big clock and nodded affirmatively.

"What if the Time Keeper stops running?" I asked. Peter laughed out loud as if I had just asked the most ridiculous of all questions.

"Eve, the Time Keeper won't stop—it simply can't."

"Why not?" I was not too keen on the fact that Peter was laughing at me. The answer may have been apparent to him, but it sure wasn't obvious to me.

"Because if it did, it would mean that time as we know it would cease to exist. Disorder and chaos would soon ensue, throwing the natural order and balance of the existence of all creatures into a dark tailspin from which there could be no recovery." The words rolled off Peter's tongue so nonchalantly. Clearly, the impact of what he had just said was of monumental significance, but he seemed to treat it as casually as if he had just told me I would get wet if I stood uncovered outside in the rain.

"Okay, then," I said, staring at him wide-eyed.

"Not to worry, Eve. My point is that, in one form or another, the Time Keeper has been running since the beginning of time, and it will continue to run for as long as time exists."

"I'll just take your word for it." It was hard for me to treat what Peter was saying seriously when he seemed so relaxed about it.

"Now, let's get back to your watch. Within the *Aura* dial there are two other time-keeping mechanisms, one of which is a smaller face dial. Do you see it?"

"Yup," I replied. The second, smaller face dial was noticeably different from the *Aura* dial in that it used Arabic numbers rather than Roman numerals, and the Arabic numbers ran on a twenty-four hour cycle rather than on a twelve-hour one.

"This smaller dial keeps time on Earth, which we refer to as *Mora* time. Because time down there is accelerated when we are up here, it's easier for us to keep track of *Mora* time if it's measured on a twenty-four hour cycle. With me so far?"

"I think so. The larger dial on my watch keeps *Aura* time in accordance with the Time Keeper. Earth time, or *Mora* time, is measured by this smaller dial, which tracks time on a twenty-four hour cycle because time passes more quickly on Earth than up here in the Archives. Correct?" I asked.

"Correct," Peter confirmed.

"Wait, I just thought of something," I said, baffled again. "Which Earth time does my watch keep? I mean, does it keep time somewhere in the United States? Somewhere in Europe? In Australia? How will I know?"

"Your watch keeps *Mora* time in accordance with the time zone in which your charge is physically located. If your human is in Sydney, Australia, for example, your watch automatically will adjust itself and keep time consistent with the time zone there. If your assignment lives in North America, your watch will keep *Mora* time in accordance with the respective regional time zone there. Does that make sense?"

"I guess," I said. "So, seeing that I have no assignment yet, what *Mora* time is my watch keeping now?"

"Currently, your watch is set to keep Central Standard Time in the Midwest region of the United States—same as mine. Now let's move on to the third time mechanism on your watch, which is the digital window in the center—"

"Why Central Standard Time?" I interjected. "Is that where I'm from?" Somewhere deep inside I knew I was overstepping my bounds by pursuing this line of questioning, but I felt compelled to ask him anyway.

"Eve, it's no longer important for you to know where you *were* from, where you used to live, or where you died. Shepherds land themselves in a great deal of trouble for asking questions like these. Do you understand?" Peter warned.

I nodded affirmatively.

"Now, moving on—when you get an assignment, the third time-keeping mechanism on your watch will begin to run. We call this the Incident Timer." Peter pointed to the digital screen on his watch. I looked down and located the corresponding screen on mine.

"It's a digital countdown of when the human you've been assigned to protect will be in mortal danger next. We refer to the running of the Timer as the *Exitus* countdown. Naturally, the countdown is measured in *Mora* time because your charge is on Earth."

"Naturally," I repeated. I guess my tone was a little on the sarcastic side because Peter stopped and glared at me for a second before continuing.

"The digital window of the Incident Timer will stay blank until you get your first assignment. If we cannot correct the damage done to your charge's fate before the First Incident occurs, then the countdown immediately will refresh itself and begin anew for the next Incident—assuming, of course, that your human survived the First.

"But keep in mind," he added, "the Servants only have three opportunities, or Incidents, as we call them, to alter any one human's fate. If we fail to protect a charge during any one of the three Incidents, then the human's fate is sealed; his or her destiny will be carried out just as the Servants have rewritten it. But if we ensure that a charge survives all three Incidents, then the Servants must cease all future attacks on that human and let him or her live free from any further clan interference."

"Why must they stop all future attacks?" I asked.

"You're certainly not afraid to ask the more perplexing questions, are you?" He chuckled. "Our history tells us that, in the beginning, the Servants were ruthless in their killing exploits—often sacrificing many more humans than necessary when eliminating their specific targets. So an agreement of sorts eventually was reached between the Shepherds and the Servants, whereby the Servants would exercise some restraint and focus their attacks on only their intended targets. In return, the Servants would be given three opportunities to strike at each of their targets rather than just one. It's far from an ideal situation, but thousands of human lives, if not more, have been spared as a result."

"Why three chances?"

"Well, the number three has always had great symbolic, religious, and cultural significance," Peter explained. "For example, the number three represents the unity of the body, soul, and spirit. The number three also represents the ties between the past, present, and future.

"Most notable for our purposes, however, is that the number three has special significance with respect to a mortal's fate. Fate is controlled by the Three Sisters—immortal triplets: Aurelia, Perpetua, and Harmonia. Aurelia is a self-professed hopeless romantic, but that doesn't actually make her one. She weaves romance into humans' lives whenever possible, whether the romance is an affair of the heart or the body, fleeting or everlasting, it makes no difference to her—and, unfortunately, neither do the consequences of her actions. She has interfered in more mortals' lives for the sake of her own narcissistic curiosity and has caused more human heartache than words can say.

"Perpetua is another sister who seems to have perfected

117

the art of acting out her petty, egocentric side—only with respect to her wicked jealous streak. She has a habit of intervening in the lives of those mortals who either do or can possess the things she wants most, which tend to vary from century to century. Most often, however, she wants attention; she wants every immortal to respect, adore, and fear her. And, sometimes, she demonstrates what she's capable of doing at the expense of those humans who, unbeknownst to them, receive a bit too much attention from any one immortal or group of immortals.

"Harmonia, the most rational and logical of the Three Sisters, has the unenviable task of reining in her two sisters. She's the voice of reason, but they don't always listen. Her job is to keep sudden twists of fate to a minimum and make sure that the tapestry of life is free of as many botched stitches and tangled threads as possible.

"Together, the Three Sisters decide how and when to spin the threads of life. They choose the destined paths that any one human being can travel by weaving the thread of life into the fabric of a human's destiny; they create the advantages and obstacles a human will face given his or her predetermined path; and they snip the thread of life to determine its ultimate length, or when a human's life shall end.

"To change the course of a human's life for the purpose of prematurely terminating it, the Servants must successfully intervene at one of these three stages of fate. Any interference by a Servant will not go unnoticed by any one Sister for long. As I'm sure you can imagine, the Sisters do not take kindly to the Servants' meddling, and any one of the Three certainly will not allow their work, their *craft*, to be undermined if they can at all help it."

"Peter, do the Servants always try to *kill* a human? I mean, are our assignments always about saving humans from near-certain brushes with death?"

"Hmm," Peter mumbled as he thought for a moment. "Actually, I am unaware of any other kind of assignment, so I suppose the answer to your question is 'yes.'" He didn't let me linger on the point long as he quickly highlighted another feature of my watch.

"And, of course, your watch is also equipped with a date-keeping mechanism just underneath the Incident Timer that will help you keep track of the current month, day, and year on Earth."

"Of course. What watch doesn't have that feature these days?" I teased.

"Eve, I'm just trying to be thorough, but if you think you've got this all figured out, we can end your lessons here. I have plenty of other things I could be doing." Peter sounded annoyed.

"Sorry," I said, feeling foolish.

Apology accepted.

"Hey!" I looked at Peter wide-eyed with shock and excitement. "I *heard* that ... in my *mind!* How did I do that?"

"Oh, so I guess there are a few more things I can teach you," he said smugly.

"I get your point wise, old St. Pete." I raised my eyebrows in jest and exaggerated a grand gesture by tilting my head and shoulders downwards as if to curtsey before him. "By the way, when do I get to see the pearly gates?" I laughed.

"Go ahead—have your fun. But you just wait ... I'll be the one laughing soon enough. You have yet to meet the rest of my team." Peter flashed me a mischievous grin, which made me a little nervous. I wondered what he had up his sleeve.

11. You're a Shepherd—Not a Superhero

"Eve, clear your mind and close your eyes," Peter instructed.

I did as he requested.

"Okay, now open them," he said eagerly.

I opened my eyes to discover that Peter and I were standing in a quaint little garden; it was beautiful. Every single flower was in bloom. Bursts of purples, reds, yellows, whites, pinks, and blues were complemented with lush green bushes and herbs. A smorgasbord of floral and herbal aromas swirled around my head.

"Where are we?" I asked in awe.

"We're in the English garden outside of the Archives."

"How did we get here?" My eyes had been closed for only a second. I scanned the exterior wall of the Archives that butted up against the garden. The wall was draped with ivy; I didn't see anything that resembled a doorway.

"We traveled here by way of our thoughts. As we are no longer constrained by the physical restrictions of the human body, our minds can do many things we never could have done while alive," he explained.

I followed Peter to a little stone bench at one end of the garden near some bushes and a small fountain and sat down beside him. Immediately, I recognized the pleasant scent of a nearby lilac bush. I wondered how I knew it was lilac and whether I always had liked its smell. I looked around the garden and realized I recognized other flowers as well. There were roses, hydrangeas, gardenias, sweet peas, daisies, poppies, sunflowers, and a variety of herbs, including rosemary, dill, and mint.

"Peter, how is it that I can still remember the names of these plants? I thought my memory was erased. Wouldn't my memories include my knowledge about things I must have

120

come across or studied during my life? And another thing—if I'm dead, how is it that I can smell these flowers? I would have assumed that my sense of smell died with my body."

"You're one step ahead of me again." He chuckled. "Before I answer your questions, allow me to ask one of my own. Eve, do you happen to *hear* something deep within you?"

I sat still and listened. It was perfectly quiet—not even the chirp of a bird or the buzz of a bee around me. I focused on my "new-old body," my Shepherd body, and noticed something reverberating within. It was barely audible at first, but the sound quickly grew louder and louder to the point that I couldn't ignore it. In fact, I was surprised I hadn't heard it before. *Thump-thump. Thump-thump. Thump-thump.* I swore I was hearing my heart ... beating.

That's impossible, I said to myself. I listened again. There was something different about the sound; it actually wasn't a thumping noise at all—it was more like the ticking of a clock. I didn't understand. I was dead. I shouldn't have a heartbeat. Nevertheless, I definitely heard a rhythmic *pulse*, if that was what you could call it, deep within my chest.

"Is my heart beating?" I asked, half-bewildered and half-amazed.

"No, but I suspect you feel like it is," Peter remarked in amusement. "You no longer have a physiological heart, so you can't have a heartbeat *per se*. But your body, or, more accurately, *your mind*, has attuned itself to the Time Keeper. All Shepherds feel the ticking of the Time Keeper resonate within us—the Shepherd's pulse, so to speak."

"Why do we have a pulse if we don't need it?" I asked.

"Well, we may not need it *physically*, but having an inner rhythm does help us in several respects. For one thing, we are immortal. Like time, we can go on forever ... constant and without interruption. If we do not consciously keep track of time, we can lose decades, even centuries, only to look back and wonder where it all disappeared to. Having a pulse is a way for us to maintain some sense that time is continuously passing.

"Second, and most importantly, in my humble opinion, our pulse also reminds us of our own humanity. We were all human once. And in the afterlife, most Shepherds work closely alongside humans, spending the majority of their time on Earth, so it's important that we retain several human-like behaviors and characteristics to remind us of what it was like to be mortal. Plus, having a pulse helps us blend in better; it's simply another small detail of our mask, our cloak, which makes us *seem* more human to mortals when we're on Earth."

"Why would we need a cloak? Are we visible to humans?" I was intrigued. And I had to admit I liked the idea of spending my eternal days back on Earth.

"We are visible when we want or need to be. We even interact with humans from time-to-time," Peter noted. "Please understand, however, it is *crucial* that we hide our true identities from humans. All would be lost if they knew who we were and what we did. Our cloaks, namely, our bodies, help us appear anonymously human—just another soul that walks amidst the masses.

"I should note that our cloaks do serve another purpose while we're on Earth, albeit a fairly limited one." Peter paused for a minute to make sure he had my full attention. "Humans are not our biggest threat."

"Who is?"

"Some demons . . . and a few other types of immortals that are up to no good," Peter cautioned. "And while we can never be fully cloaked around them, if we must be visible, it's best to assume our human form in a crowd of people so as to make detection by these miscreants more difficult. Much like how a zebra's stripes make it difficult for a predator to tell one zebra apart from another when they stick together in their herd.

"That said, I will tell you that invisibility is almost always our best defense—particularly around our charges. Demons still may be able to *sense* us, but they won't be able to *find* us. And we will be less vulnerable to attack by them."

"But ... I thought we were immortal? How could anyone, or *anything*, threaten us?" Anxiety stirred within me.

"We may be immortal, but we are not indestructible," he clarified.

"So we can be ... killed?" I squeaked out.

"Killed? No." Peter smiled. "Eve, we're already dead; we cannot die again. But we can be destroyed."

"*How?* How then do I defend myself if I'm attacked by a demon? I mean," I rambled, "I hardly know anything about Shepherds ... much less demons! How am I even going to know what a demon looks like? Do *they* have cloaks? How will I know if one is close—"

"Relax, Eve. Relax," Peter interjected. "Chances are you'll never run into one; face-to-face encounters with demons are extremely rare. Nonetheless, you'll learn how to detect and avoid them and even to defend yourself against them if the need arises.

"Besides, we have no intention of ever letting you wander into harm's path. As your mentor, *I* won't let you." Peter took my right hand in both of his and smiled at me.

"Okay," I replied. There was something in Peter's eyes— he looked fiercely protective and affectionately tender at the same time. He made me feel safe.

"So," I took a deep breath, "back to my original question—if I'm dead, why do I still feel so alive? I mean, the mask, the cloak, whatever it is that we use to appear more human, seems to be working its magic on me. I *feel* human. I *look* human. I have a pulse ... of sorts. I can still breathe. I can still smell these flowers. I don't understand."

"Well, you feel human and alive because part of you still *is* human and alive. Remember, your soul and your spirit— *your mind*—still lives on in the afterlife, making you a member of a select group of beings that is neither wholly dead nor wholly living." Peter paused again to let the weight of his words sink into my mind. "To complicate matters further, you also were chosen to be a Shepherd, which makes you part of an elite order of ethereal beings.

"Nevertheless, with your living mind comes all of the knowledge, beliefs, values, and so on that you possessed in life. In a nutshell, you still possess the wisdom gained from your life lessons and experiences. We only erased the *circumstances,* the context, in which you gained such wisdom." Peter picked a small branch full of lilac blossoms and held it up for me to see. "You know this is a lilac bush, you just have no recollection of the first time you ever saw, smelled, or heard the name of this type of plant."

"So what about breathing?" I asked. Before he could respond, I took a deep breath and held it, counting in my head to see how long I could go before I felt the need to inhale again ... *forty-eight-Mississippi, forty-nine-Mississippi, fifty-Mississippi* ... My lungs started to burn. I fought off the urge to take another breath. *Sixty-two-Mississippi, sixty-three-Mississippi* ... The discomfort I felt could now only be described as sheer panic and desperation. I gave in and took a deep breath and then another as I sighed with relief.

Peter looked very amused by my little experiment. "You don't need to breathe, but you'll still do it. You breathe because it's what you've done your entire life. Breathing is a primal, involuntary, and necessary course of action for the survival of the human body. As such, you instinctively will continue to do it each time you assume your human form ...

at least for a while, anyway, until your immorality becomes second nature to you."

"Another thing," Peter continued. "As a Shepherd you can call on and take the shape of your past human form whenever you so desire—like you're doing right now. In fact, you will most likely prefer to be in your human form. In life, your mind was used to being anchored to a physical being—a human body. In death, your mind operates no differently. And along with the new version of your former human body comes many of your biological senses—your sense of smell being one of them, which is why you can smell this lilac." He waved the blossoms under my nose; I closed my eyes and inhaled, taking in its sweet floral fragrance.

"As an immortal," Peter added, "you also have several capabilities that go well beyond what is possible for a human being. Combined, your human and immortal traits make you quite a powerful force with which to be reckoned—a guardian of humans against evil."

"A Shepherd of the flock amidst the wolves," I threw in.

"Exactly," Peter said as a huge smile spread across his face.

"What did you mean when you said that along with the new version of my former self, my *new-old body*, came many of my biological senses?"

"You still possess certain of your human senses, such as smell, sound, sight, and touch, but each of these senses is now heightened. In fact, your senses are now much more acute than those of any human being—even the most perceptive of mortals."

"So I can see through buildings?" I threw out in jest.

"Eve, you're a Shepherd—not a superhero." He sounded slightly irritated. "Please do not make light of this; I need you to focus. This information will be of key importance when it comes time to carry out your assignment."

"Right—sorry." I cleared my throat and adjusted my posture to strike an exaggeratedly studious pose. Peter unsuccessfully fought off a grin and all of the disapproval in his eyes seemed to melt away.

"As I was saying," he continued, "your sense of smell, sound, sight, and touch are much more sensitive and finely tuned. For example, you will smell and hear things many miles away. And you will be able to see things from a great distance as well, that is, as long as your visual path remains unobstructed. Combined, these three senses alone will be invaluable to you when on assignment. You will be able to smell, hear, and see anything that would pose a threat to your human."

"If my sense of smell is so acute, how do things taste?" I tried to imagine what a bite of chocolate cake would taste like—or a ripe peach.

"You could say that your sense of taste died with your body. It actually makes perfect sense when you think about it. We cannot eat or drink anything because we have no means to digest food or beverages—in other words, what goes down must come back up. Thus, your mind will preemptively cure your hunger and thirst cravings, and you will soon lose your appetite completely. Anything you attempt to eat or drink will taste bland in flavor and texture and will be wholly unsatisfying. You won't even want to swallow it, which is the point. Don't get me wrong, you'll always have an appreciation for certain food and drink, but that's where your love affair with them will end."

Nothing to eat or drink ever again. I pondered that strange realization for a moment.

"Okay, so no food or drink. No sleep either?" I looked at Peter, who responded with an affirmative nod of his head.

"Then how do we stay strong?" I asked. "Where do we get our energy?"

126

"Eve," he laughed. "We *are* energy. We are the light of the stars, the sun, and the heavens above and the vitality of the spirit and the soul all wrapped up into one."

"What—so we don't need *anything* to rejuvenate ourselves? We have an endless reserve of energy?"

"Not quite. There are certain ways to deplete our energy, and when that occurs we need time to restore that energy." He lingered on this point like he wanted to add something else, but he didn't.

"So," Peter continued, "last but not least is your sense of touch, which is the most important sense you now possess. With respect to physical objects, your tactile abilities are much more acute now, so much so that you will be able to feel each imperfection on every tangible surface. The tiniest of physical disparities will be obvious to you, yet remain completely undetectable to a human's naked touch. You will be able to tell with utmost certainty the exact temperature of any object. Words like "hot," "cold," "smooth," and "rough" will be wholly inadequate to fully describe what you now experience through touch.

"Your extraordinary tactile sense will also affect your understanding of all living creatures," he explained. "Not only will you be able to see a living creature's aura, but you will feel its life radiating through your fingertips before you ever make contact with it. You will feel its life force, its heat signature, emanate from across the room. And you will learn how to interpret these signatures to determine how a creature is feeling, both physically and emotionally, at any given moment in time.

"And most significantly," Peter remarked, "you soon will learn that with your heightened sense of touch comes the power to heal."

"What?" I interrupted in disbelief. "Did you just say that I have the power to *heal* ... to actually *heal* living creatures? Like animals?"

"And humans too. But you also will discover that this power is to be used sparingly, if ever," he noted.

"Finally, your sense of touch also makes you a reliable moral barometer, capable of measuring the balance of good and evil in all living things. Like a magnet, you will be drawn toward those creatures that are good and repelled by those that possess a reckless disregard for humanity—or worse."

"The Servants?" I asked uneasily.

"Yes and no. Demons have no souls, so you will not be able to read them the way you would humans or any other living creatures. Nonetheless, demons have their own unique signatures, much like we do. But theirs are unmistakably dark and disturbing. Should you ever find yourself in the unlucky position of crossing paths with a demon, you will immediately discover that Hell itself rages deep within it." A haunted expression crossed Peter's face, which sent shivers down my spine.

This was all a little much for me. I needed time to absorb all of this.

"Take all the time you need," I heard Peter say with his thoughts.

"Thanks." Despite all of the crazy madness I had landed in, I still thought the idea of communicating telepathically was pretty amazing. It was like having a secret code or language, or it would be if my mind wasn't an open book for all Shepherds to read.

"Not all Shepherds," Peter remarked telepathically while he chuckled out loud. *"Just the ones up here in the Archives."*

"Great. That makes me feel much *better."* I hoped my thoughts still dripped with the intended sarcasm. *"So just how many Shepherds are up here?"* I asked.

"Right now? Maybe thirty or so—not including the Council, of course."

"The Council? What's that?" I was so curious, I forgot to *think* my question rather than verbalize it.

"Our governing body," Peter responded, also aloud. "The Shepherd's Council is made up of a group of twelve of our elders, who ensure our Rules and our purpose are being carried out consistently by all Shepherds. In fact, the Shepherds' Council developed our Rules. The Council is also called upon to determine if a Shepherd has broken a Rule, and if so, what consequences should be handed down."

"So members of the Council are the Rule makers, the Rule enforcers, the judges, and the jury? That seems like a lot of power to be given to one group, don't you think?" I asked skeptically.

"I wouldn't necessarily look at it that way. The Council is here to guide us and to remind us of our mission. Camouflaging ourselves as humans, working alongside them day in and day out, year-after-year, is more complicated and messier than you could possibly imagine. Trust me. We may not have the memories of our lives as humans, but we still have our personalities, our idiosyncrasies, our emotions, and our desires. The human side of us can wreak havoc on even the strongest and most self-disciplined Shepherd while on assignment."

"Well, when do I get to meet them?" I asked innocently.

"Who? The Council members?" Peter chuckled. "You don't. I mean, hopefully, you will never have to meet them. Typically, the Council only calls on a Shepherd when his or her actions or intentions are called into question and must be investigated further."

"So the Council only meets with Shepherds when they get in trouble?"

"Basically, yes," he replied.

* * *

Back in the Archives, Peter led me to a reading table to the left of the enormous sundial. I looked up at the ceiling; red, purple, and blue hues streaked across it as the evening stars were fading. It looked to be nearing dawn. I glanced at my watch and confirmed the same. Out of the corner of my eye, I noticed a small scroll rolled up at the far end of the table. I wanted to examine it more closely, but I knew better than to be so presumptuous as to walk over and pick it up. I would have to be patient and hope that Peter would let me see it eventually.

"Eve, in addition to your acute human senses, you also have several immortal skills, or *talents*, each of which will help you become an adept guardian. You've already experienced one of these immortal abilities—our communal mind. Any time you're up here, that is any time you're not on Earth, you will telepathically communicate all of your thoughts to every other Shepherd up here *unless* you shield a particular thought or the other Shepherds block your thoughts from entering their minds.

"For new Shepherds, thought-sharing can seem like a burden rather than a blessing. While human, you were used to keeping your private thoughts private, but that simply is not the case any longer. To be sure, it takes time for new Shepherds to adjust to the absence of privacy as the default state of mind. The benefit of our communal mind, however, is what you gain from other Shepherds' experiences through their thoughts while you learn how to successfully navigate the unfamiliar terrain of immortality."

I tried to focus and listen for the other voices in my head, but I could hear only my own thoughts mulling about. Maybe the communal mind needed to be activated somehow ... like I had to flip a mental switch or something.

"I can't hear any other Shepherds now."

"Hearing a constant stream of others' thoughts running through your mind can be quite distracting at first, especially during your training. I need you to focus solely on what I'm teaching you. Therefore, I temporarily blocked out other Shepherds' thoughts from your mind. I also took the liberty of shielding your thoughts from the others while you get used to the idea that we are all capable of hearing what you think, thereby giving you more time to adapt accordingly."

"You can do that?" I was intrigued and mortified at the same time. The thought of Peter—of anyone—manipulating my mind was downright creepy, and it made me uncomfortable.

"Yes. Because of our mentor-mentee relationship, we have a special connection—a unique bond that will last for eternity. And with that special connection, I have been given the power to shield and block thoughts for you so that I can better assist you through your training. It's very much like when I interfered with your thoughts before—"

"Before?" I interrupted, confused. I had no idea what he was talking about.

"Ah, yes, you probably don't remember."

"No, I don't." I looked at Peter, feeling even more uneasy now that I knew he already had controlled my mind once before and I had no memory of it.

"Well, then, I'll just have to show you again," he said, smiling. "Eve, think of an animal, any animal—picture it in your head."

I flashed him a lukewarm smile. I really didn't want to be part of this silly little exercise, but I knew there was no point in protesting. If Peter could influence my thoughts whenever he so desired, he would find some way to do whatever he had planned regardless of whether I was a willing participant.

I closed my eyes and focused on an animal. The first one that popped into my head was a cat. More specifically, a Siamese cat with bright blue eyes stretched out on a white windowsill basking in the sun. It seemed fitting enough—cats supposedly had nine lives. And in some strange way I had been given a second chance. I wondered how many "lives" I now had. My thoughts were interrupted when the image of the cat I just conjured began transforming into some large wild animal. My sweet little feline was now a white tiger with sapphire blue eyes moving stealthily through tall prairie grass.

"Whoa!"

Peter threw his head back and started to laugh out loud. He seemed very satisfied with himself.

"You … You did that?" I looked at him wide-eyed. Peter was barely able to contain himself, he was laughing so hard.

"I didn't realize you had *that* much control over my mind!" I exclaimed in awe. And, quite frankly, even though I didn't know Peter all that well, I didn't think he had it in him to turn my docile kitty into some ferocious predator.

"That was not very angelic of you," I said, feigning disappointment.

"Make no mistake, Eve," Peter declared after regaining his composure. "We are *not* angels. We are *Shepherds.* And we are hunters when we need to be."

I wanted to ask Peter what he meant by that, but there was something about the severity of his voice that made me hold back. Besides, my mind was buzzing with other questions.

"Can *I* do that? Can I interfere with others' thoughts?" I asked eagerly.

"Yes, but only under certain conditions, such as when a Shepherd isn't blocking out your thoughts or shielding his or her own from you. Humans are susceptible to such thought manipulation as well, but the Rules forbid us from interfering in their lives, which means that we can't use our mind tricks on them unless extreme circumstances warrant it.

"As I mentioned before, you also have the power to prevent a Shepherd from interfering with your thoughts," Peter continued. "You just haven't learned how to harness that ability yet. And, until you do, I'll watch over and guard your thoughts on your behalf.

"I should inform you, however," Peter threw in, "that even though I will always possess the power to shield your thoughts and block others' thoughts from entering your mind, I can and will only exercise my power to do so during your training. Mentors are limited to using this power of persuasion only while their mentees are adjusting to their new roles as Shepherds. For me to continue to shield and block thoughts for you after your training is complete would be highly inappropriate, not to mention a violation of our ethics. So once your training concludes, you'll experience our communal mind in full force.

"But, until then, I will make sure your thoughts remain private and others' thoughts are kept at bay." Peter smiled at me, and I couldn't help but return the gesture.

"Thanks." I liked Peter; and I hoped that my training would last for a while as I was in no rush to end our time together. I felt like I could trust him. Besides, he was the only one helping me make sense of all of this madness. I would be utterly lost without him.

"What is it?" Peter asked.

"Can't you read my mind?" I dared to ask.

"Eve, I'm trying to be respectful and let you maintain some semblance of privacy while you still can." Peter reached out towards my face and tucked some loose tresses of my hair behind my ear. His gaze grew more intense and his eyes darkened a bit. He abruptly turned away from me and cleared his throat. Despite Peter's assurances to the contrary, I suspected he had heard my thoughts. I felt my face getting warmer.

Please let me be fortunate enough to have lost the ability to blush, I desperately hoped. But when I saw Peter grinning, I knew I wasn't that lucky.

12. One Big Happy Family . . . and Cousin Eli

"Is this guy giving you any trouble there, missy?" asked the booming voice coming from behind me. Startled, I spun around, but I could see no one. Then I heard a roar of laughter to my left. I turned my head just in time to see someone materializing next to me.

"Hi, Eve. Nice to meet ya. I'm Theodore, but everyone calls me Teddy." He extended his hand out towards me.

"Hi ... Teddy. It's nice to meet you too." I shook his hand. Teddy looked like he was well into his sixties. His light, silver-blue eyes were framed by the deep lines of his weathered skin. He had a full head of thick white hair and a bushy white mustache that extended around the corners of his mouth and down both sides to his jawbone.

"Hey there, Petey. Long time, no see. Goodness, what's it been? Ten, maybe twenty *Mora* years?" Teddy extended his hand to offer Peter a handshake.

"Something like that. Whatever the period, it's been far too long." Peter accepted Teddy's hand only to be pulled forward into Teddy's arms and bear-hugged. Peter chuckled.

"Well, it's good to see you, my old friend." Teddy released Peter and slapped him on the back. "Still looking as good as ever, I see."

"And you're still a sight for sore eyes," Peter teased.

And he was. Teddy wore an obnoxiously loud, short-sleeved Hawaiian shirt that fit snugly over his bulging belly. A pair of thin legs peeked out from the end of his khaki cargo shorts. His outfit was complete with green Adidas sandals that he wore over white tube socks pulled up over his shins.

A perfect candidate for the fashion police, I mentally critiqued.

Peter shot me a glance that said "be nice." He obviously wasn't shielding my thoughts from himself at the moment.

"Well look at the guy? Who is he, anyway?" I asked Peter tele-

135

pathically. But, before he could answer me, Teddy offered his own two cents worth about me.

"Well, she's a pretty little thing, isn't she? … And so young." Teddy glanced over at Peter and, with raised eyebrows, shot him a curious look that I couldn't understand, followed by an impish little grin. Not surprisingly, Peter blocked Teddy's thoughts from my mind. Whatever the exchange, Peter must have not been too pleased because he was looking more and more uncomfortable—almost embarrassed.

"A penny for your thoughts," I chimed in. I didn't like being the odd man out of their private joke.

"And, apparently, a bit of a pistol too!" Teddy exclaimed with a crooked smile. He looked at me, thoroughly pleased.

"Eve," Peter cleared his throat, "I've known Teddy since the day I first became a Shepherd. I have asked him to teach you the arts of materialization and teleportation."

"Excuse me?" I asked, confused.

"Teleportation, sweetheart," Teddy repeated enthusiastically. "You know, how we travel from here to down there and vicey-versey."

Vicey-versey? I just glared at Peter. Did he really trust this guy to teach me anything about being a Shepherd?

"You're in good company, Eve. Teddy taught me almost everything I know, and I trust him implicitly," Peter said reassuringly. He glanced at Teddy and then added, "There is no one better when it comes to teaching new Shepherds how to phase in and out of sight and how to travel from one place to another by way of thought.

"So," Peter nodded at Teddy, "without further ado, I will leave Eve in your capable hands." Then Peter turned towards me and smiled.

"*You have nothing to worry about,*" Peter said to me telepathically. "*And, to put your mind at ease, I won't stray too far. If you need me, just call out my name and I'll be there."* With that Peter phased out of view.

"Huh," I remarked.

"What's wrong, kitten?" Teddy asked.

"Nothing, really. It's just that I had yet to see Peter do that."

"Phase in and out? Oh, that's easy. I'll have you doing that in your sleep by the end of the day," Teddy declared with the utmost of confidence.

"I thought we didn't sleep," I said distrustfully.

Teddy roared with laughter. "You are a feisty one, aren't you? Anyone ever tell you that? Oh, right, you haven't been around long enough to develop new relationships and memories," Teddy continued in between chuckles. "Don't you fret, little missy. In a couple of decades, you'll have more memories than you'll know what to do with."

"Wonderful." My sarcasm sent Teddy reeling with laughter again. I hadn't realized I was so funny.

"I can see why he's drawn to you," Teddy said.

"Why *who* is drawn to me?" I asked, bewildered.

"Oh come now, darlin.' Don't tell me you haven't noticed."

"I guess there's been so much to learn and process that I haven't really noticed much of anything," I replied naively, which made Teddy throw his head back and laugh again.

"Well then, honey, we better hop to it. We don't have much time, and it sounds like we may need every minute," Teddy joked as he looked at his watch.

I was a little shocked by Teddy's extensive knowledge of sexist names for females—and even more surprised that he felt comfortable enough to use his expansive vocabulary on me considering we had just met.

"Let's start with materializing in and out of our human forms. Phasing is the number one tool in our arsenal for protecting ourselves and our sheep."

"Our *sheep?*"

"Yes, our sheep—you know—our charges ... our *humans.* We're *Shepherds*—get it?" Teddy chuckled, clearly amused by his own little play on words.

"Okay, cupcake," he continued, "so the first thing you need to know is that most of our time on Earth is spent in our *ethereal* state. Humans *don't* know about us, and they *can't* know about us—plain and simple. In order to keep our identities a secret, we need to carry out our assignments in a clandestine fashion. So the more time you spend in your invisible state in the company of mortals, the more likely you will stay out of trouble. Got it?

"And remember," Teddy continued without giving me a chance to respond to his question, "in your physical form you still look the same as you did when you were alive. And while you might not have any memories of your past, others still do. All you need is to start walking around in the open and be recognized by someone who knew you *and* knew that you died. Holy moly, the Council surely would have a field day with that one!" Teddy chuckled to himself and slapped me on the back, jolting me forward a little.

"Oh, I forgot you haven't had your strength training yet. My sincerest apologies," Teddy said repentantly. Even though Teddy's personality was overwhelming, and arguably offensive at times, he was slowly growing on me. He was like a big, overeager puppy that meant no harm when it lovingly licked your hand while peeing on your leg.

"Apology accepted." I smiled at Teddy, at which point he bent backwards to stretch out his back while he rubbed his round belly with both hands.

"Okay, so where were we ... Oh yeah, don't be seen by *anyone* down there if you can help it. Of course, the Council members will do their best to take all the necessary precautions when giving you an assignment. They'll always try to pair you with a human who has no connection to you in a town you were never in while you were alive. That way you won't likely run into someone who knew you. But people move around a lot these days, and with the Internet and YouTube and the like, there's always a chance that someone from your past will cross paths with you in the future. And that would be *bad*."

"Bad. Right."

"Absolutely," Teddy confirmed. "If humans knew we existed, our entire operation would be jeopardized. I mean, just think about the repercussions. How would you feel if, while you were alive, you ran into someone you knew had died? Imagine the questions something like that would have triggered in your head?"

I tried to envision some of the questions that would have sprung to mind if I had found myself in such a situation. I'm sure I would have freaked.

"Besides," Teddy continued, "what good would it do if humans believed they had guardian angels?"

"I thought humans *did* have guardian angels," I corrected.

"Well of course they do—but they don't *know* it! And that's the way it has to be. For goodness sakes, if humans truly believed they had angels looking out for them, they would never watch their step! They would walk around assuming they could put themselves in all kinds of danger because their angels would swoop in and save the day. It'd be complete chaos down there." Teddy tried to hide a smirk, but I could tell he was clearly entertained at the thought of what the world he'd just described would look like.

"Anyway, I don't think we have to worry much about you running into anyone who knew you because you died so young. And according to your file, you weren't famous, you weren't involved in hardly any extracurricular activities, and you didn't travel a lot."

"Wow, when you say it like that, my former life seems so … dull. I must have been nothing short of ordinary." I hung my head down glumly, questioning how I could have allowed my brief life to be so uneventful.

"On the contrary, love," Teddy said warmly. "You had to be something real special to have found yourself up here—especially to get the likes of me teaching you the tricks of the trade." Teddy threw his arm around my shoulder and gave me a squeeze. I smiled.

For the next hour, I learned how to clear my head and focus solely on making myself feel solid as a rock and lighter than air as I slowly—very slowly at first—phased in and out of view. By the umpteenth time, I was able to materialize and dematerialize fairly competently and quickly.

"Good, good. You're a quick study. You'll do just fine," Teddy declared. "I'm proud of you, kid." He nudged me and smiled. "Let's take a quick break before we move on to teleportation. Here, take my hand and close your eyes or else you might get motion sick." I did as Teddy asked and the next thing I knew, we were standing on the floor of the Grand Canyon.

"Everybody always likes the view from the top of this place, but I think it's much more impressive down here at the bottom looking up at the canyon walls. What do you think?" Teddy asked.

"Yes, impressive," I agreed. It truly was incredible. The clear blue sky was a perfect backdrop for the red-orange rock walls that were visible for miles in every direction. I could hear the sounds of different animals from every direction, everything from soaring eagles above us to desert snakes slithering in the sand. But there wasn't a trace of a single human. The sun's rays were beaming down on us, and it felt good. I closed my eyes and inhaled deeply, trying to drink in the life that was bustling around me.

"So," Teddy said after a minute, "as you can see, teleportation can take us to amazing places. But it's not just for fun. It's another invaluable tool that can save your hide."

"What do you mean?" I said somewhat absentmindedly. I couldn't help but be distracted by the energy surrounding me. I was curious to see which of the two scorpions one hundred feet away would win the battle over the same half-dead beetle. I was entranced by the bees nearly one hundred yards away collecting pollen from the cactus flowers that were in bloom. I literally couldn't believe my eyes. Peter said I would have heightened senses, but I had no idea they would be this sharp.

"Eve," Teddy said authoritatively. I snapped out of my fog and gave him my full attention. In our brief time together, Teddy had called me by my name only once—the first time he introduced himself. I suspected he was about to tell me something important.

"A word of warning; we can't ever be wholly invisible to everyone—or everything," Teddy cautioned. "To the trained eye or psyche, a Shepherd's signature is always detectable. That's why the ability to transport yourself from place to place is what I deem to be the second most important skill we possess. Just remember, if you need to get out of Dodge in a hurry, teleportation is *the* way to do it."

"Teddy, are you saying some people can actually *see* us when we're invisible?" I asked, stunned.

"Not *see* us as much as *feel* us." He paused for a moment as if to collect his thoughts. "Some humans also have heightened senses. Take genuine psychics, for instance; they often know things that most other humans do not—or cannot—know because most humans are not in tune with their sixth sense.

141

"There are other ways humans can detect us as well," he continued. "For example, if a human had strong ties to a particular Shepherd when that Shepherd was a mortal. In that scenario, the human might possess the ability to sense the Shepherd's presence if nearby even when the Shepherd is invisible."

"So it's possible for a human to have ties to one of us?"

"Well, if a human developed a strong enough bond with a Shepherd when the Shepherd was alive, then, theoretically, that bond could be strong enough to survive death," Teddy explained. "Take twin siblings, for example, or a mother and a child. Even a husband and wife could have a deep enough connection. But to transcend death, the bond would have to run deeper than some familial or marital connection; it would have to be spiritual, divine . . . *soulful.*

"In any case," he went on to say, "that's why we've got to take the precautions we do when doling out assignments. We want to minimize the risk of a Shepherd being exposed at all costs."

"So," I tested, "the chances of me being assigned to someone from the same town are—"

"One in a trillion," he replied, cutting me off.

"And to anyone I know?"

"Not gonna happen, sweetheart," Teddy said, without as much as an ounce of doubt.

"What about demons? Should I assume that they can detect us?"

Teddy looked at me, surprised. He must not have realized I already knew about demons.

"Peter told me about them," I offered.

"Petey, huh?" Teddy unsuccessfully tried to stifle another knowing smile. "The truth is that most demons don't care if you're hanging out on Earth or not. And even if they did, they wouldn't dare do anything about it—well, except for maybe one group of troublesome wrongdoers ..." His voice trailed off.

"The Servants," I added.

"Petey?" Teddy looked at me with raised eyebrows. I nodded affirmatively. "That's a lot of information for a new Shepherd to process." He shook his head back and forth. "You shouldn't worry your pretty little head about the Servants. I suspect Hell itself would have to freeze over before you'd ever run into one.

"The Servants are a hunted group—and they know it. So they stay out of sight most of the time and rarely surface for air. They've got humans running around doing most of their dirty work. That said, if you ever feel like you're in danger, whether it be at the hands of a human, a demon, or whatever else that may come along, you teleport your sweet self right out of wherever it is you're located. Got it?"

"Um ... yeah." I might have understood what he was saying on some intellectual level, but I had absolutely no idea how to actually *do it*.

"Teleportation is really very simple—much easier than phasing," Teddy continued. "When we teleport, we travel at the speed of thought, which I'll have you know is *much* faster than the speed of light. Okay, so here goes—when you want to go somewhere, all you have to do is picture your destination in your mind and will yourself there."

"*Will* myself there?"

"Yup. Let's have you give it a go. See that big pile of rocks over there by the far canyon wall?" he asked, pointing to a pile of rocks that had to be a mile away.

"*That* pile? Way over there?" I asked meekly, pointing to the pile Teddy had singled out.

"Yup. Just picture yourself standing on top of those rocks and *will* yourself there—you know, make yourself *want* to be standing there on top of them."

"Just like that ... Picture myself on top of the rocks and *want* to go there." I looked at Teddy like he was nuts.

"Yup," he said confidently. "Go ahead, missy. You can do it." He nudged my shoulder.

"If you say so," I said uncertainly. "Here goes nothing."

"Oh ye of little faith," he said, chuckling.

I closed my eyes and mentally pictured myself standing on top of the pile of rocks he had chosen. *Okay, Eve—transport yourself to the rocks*, I told myself. *You want to be on the rocks. Go to the rocks. Go to the rocks.* I chanted to myself. *You can do this. You have to do this.* I waited for a second and felt nothing.

"See, Teddy, I told you I couldn't—" I opened my eyes and couldn't finish my sentence. Teddy wasn't there. I turned around to find him and almost lost my balance. I was standing on top of a small, jagged boulder. I looked down to see that I was at least fifty feet in the air.

"*What the—*" I exclaimed out loud. Immediately, I heard a roar of laughter and saw Teddy a mile away doubled over in hysterics.

"Would it be ill-mannered of me to say, *'I told you so'*?" he managed to spit out in between his fits of laughter.

I just stood there, wide-eyed in amazement. *I did it. I actually did it!* My mind was struggling to wrap itself around what had just happened. But once the initial shock wore off, I realized how incredibly cool it was to be able to teleport.

"That was mind-blowing!" I shouted to Teddy as I began laughing. I let out a scream of exhilaration and jumped up and down in excitement before losing my balance and almost falling off the boulder.

"Take it easy there, cowgirl! Okay, now come on back the same way you went!" Teddy yelled back to me. I pictured myself standing next to him and told myself to travel to that spot. I didn't even close my eyes—I didn't need to. Before I could even finish my thought, I was standing next to him, exactly where I had pictured myself standing. *Amazing.*

For the rest of the afternoon, Teddy had me teleporting myself all over the Grand Canyon—to the edges of the Canyon cliffs, to the banks of the Colorado River, and even on top of the smallest of river rocks that barely jutted out above the raging river rapids. He also taught me how to teleport in my dematerialized state, explaining that from now on I always needed to remain invisible when teleporting myself around Earth.

"You never know when you'll have an audience—unwanted or *not*. The biggest mistake you can make is to have some human see you materialize right before his or her eyes. Humans are not equipped to handle our kind of *magic*. Questions will be raised, possible investigations mounted—basically, a lot of hoo-hah will follow all because of some fancy little parlor trick. And the Council will not treat such a blunder kindly, that's for darn sure. So don't let me hear about how you went ahead and let the cat out of the bag. Capiche?"

"Capiche," I said with an affirmative nod of my head.

"All right then. Well, that's it for me. I've taught you the ropes and bestowed upon you my most clever words of wisdom," Teddy said with a cocky grin. "Any questions?"

What questions don't *I have?* I thought. *Where do I begin?*

"How did you teleport me here?" I began. "Can I do that with someone else?"

"Dual teleportation is pretty advanced stuff. It's only for seasoned Shepherds, and even some of them never master the art of dual transport. Before you can learn how to teleport with another being, or object for that matter, you need to master teleportation on a whole other level—like teleporting yourself to a destination you've never been before and can't even picture in your mind."

145

"Well, how do you do that? How do you travel to a place that you've never been before?" I asked.

"That is for another day, sugar."

"Oh c'mon. My mind is buzzing with possibilities. Give me a hint, please?" I smiled and batted my eyelashes slightly in hopes that he would succumb to my feminine wiles.

"Fine," Teddy sighed, "I'll throw you a bone. When you want to go to somewhere you've never been before, but you happen to be familiar with a landmark at that location, you can transport yourself there simply by conjuring up a mental image of that landmark and willing yourself to it. It doesn't have to be a perfect image—just close enough. Take Paris for instance. You don't remember if you ever went there during your life, but you still can picture what the Eiffel Tower looks like, right?"

"Yes," I was beginning to picture the structure in my mind.

"Okay then," he continued, "if you picture an accurate enough image of the landmark in your mind you can transport yourself there. But beware—if your image is sufficiently off target, like a wacky adaptation of the Eiffel Tower, you'll miss Paris and end up in some hotel in Las Vegas or at the seventh hole of some mini-golf course somewhere in the middle of nowhere with the Eiffel Tower as the hole-in-one." I looked at Teddy wide-eyed, and he just laughed at me.

"When in doubt, honey, look at a book. For goodness sake, we've got plenty of them up there in the Archives. Next question."

"Okay, so when I'm on Earth, but I'm not in my human form, what senses can I still use?"

"You will still have your sense of sight and sound while you're invisible. Your sense of touch and smell can only be triggered when you are in your physical form. And your sense of taste ... well, Petey should have told you by now that your sense of taste is pretty much shot."

"Makes sense, I guess," I mumbled. I was busily thinking of what to ask next when Teddy sighed, as if somehow disappointed with my questions, and then cleared his throat to get my attention.

"Are these *really* the things you want to ask me about, Eve?" He said my name again—I must have been overlooking something.

"What do you mean?" I was clueless as to where he was headed.

"*Petey* can answer these questions for you. And here we are on Earth, deep in a canyon where no other Shepherds can read our thoughts or hear our conversation ... even if *he* wanted to ... and you can't think of *any* other questions you wanna ask me?" Teddy looked at me, his eyes twinkling with mischief.

I couldn't believe it. Was he really going to give me the dish on Peter? *Fine*, I thought, *let's see how willing Teddy is to play ball.*

"Okay then. Tell me about him. Tell me about Peter," I dared. "He mentioned that he met you when he first became a Shepherd—when was that?"

"A while ago—just over a couple centuries ago now if memory serves me. I was his mentor."

"But ... that would make Peter over two hundred years old!"

"Well, not exactly. He died when he was twenty-eight. He's existed as a Shepherd for two-hundred-and-some-odd years, but he's never *aged* beyond his mortal years of twenty-eight."

"Oh, right," I said, feeling awkward and foolish. I still hadn't gotten used to the fact that I existed, but I was no longer alive ... I could no longer *age*. No Shepherd could.

Teddy looked impatiently at his watch, and I knew my time with him was almost at an end. Nevertheless, I still wanted to learn more about Peter.

"So tell me more about him," I pressed.

"What else do you want to know?"

"Why did you give him that *look* when you met me … right before I offered a penny for your thoughts? What was that look?"

"Now that's the million-dollar question, isn't it?" He chuckled. "The thing is, you remind me of someone, a young woman Petey and I knew a while back. It's not so much that you look like she did; I think you remind me of her because of the way Petey looks at you."

"How does he look at me?"

"Like he cares," Teddy responded, somewhat perplexed.

"I don't understand … He's my mentor. Isn't he *supposed* to care? Or is that not okay?"

"It's not a question of being okay or not okay inasmuch as it's a question of why Petey chose now—why he chose you—to start showing emotion towards someone again. It's just that the last time I saw Petey show emotion towards someone was with *her*—that is, until you showed up."

"What happened to her?"

"Madeleine was her name. She was a human, and she was Petey's last assignment. He fell in love with her, and she with him. He found himself going to extreme lengths to protect her; he was taking unnecessary risks, including revealing himself to her." Teddy paused for a moment. "You see, Petey not only let Madeleine *see* him, he also showed her *what* he truly was—a Shepherd. As you can probably guess, Madeleine had a hard time accepting the truth, and their relationship ended shortly thereafter. Petey was devastated when things didn't work out. But what could he expect? She was a human, and he wasn't. Not exactly what I'd call a match made in Heaven.

"Now if that would have been the end of it, if Petey could have just walked away from her and never seen her again, I suspect things would have been fine ... He would've gotten over her eventually. But it wasn't the end. Petey's assignment wasn't over yet. He had to continue protecting her; he had to see Madeleine every minute of every day while he remained invisible, broken, and alone."

"So what happened?" I asked.

"The Council felt it necessary to intercede," Teddy said. "Certain Council members were worried Petey would be incapable of successfully completing his assignment. As his mentor, I was instructed to act as his chaperone throughout the remainder of his assignment—something that rarely, if ever, has been done before or since.

"Thankfully, he admirably carried out his assignment without a glitch and that was that. He's never spoken of her since, but I could tell that the pain of losing her still lingered. Time heals all though, and Petey's no exception to the rule. Still, he's never quite been the same since then.

"And then you came along ... It would seem that there's something about you, little lady, that has given Petey a swift kick in the rear, catapulting him back from the land of the lost. I don't know what you did, but I guess I should be thanking you—we all should.

"Anyway," Teddy said, switching gears, "Petey never again took on another assignment. Oddly enough, the Council never pressured him to do so either. He was offered a few cases here and there, but he continued to decline. Now, he's one of our top mentors. In fact, he's the head of all of us mentors, which technically makes him my *boss*. So, with that said, we had better return you to the Archives before Petey puts my head on a platter. Just think about having to teleport your way out of that one!" He crinkled up his nose and then winked at me.

"Ready for your last lesson?" he asked.

"Uh, sure, I guess." My mind was reeling trying to make sense of what Teddy had just told me about Peter. I didn't know what to feel. Sad because Peter had lost someone he loved? Happy because I apparently helped him get over his enduring misery? Confused because I had no idea how Peter felt about me? I felt schizophrenic with emotion.

"Okay," Teddy began, "so when you want to teleport yourself back up to the Archives, just focus on the Time Keeper. Do you have a picture of it in your head?"

"Yes."

"Okay, then, go ahead. I'll be right behind you."

* * *

Teddy and I arrived in the Archives to find a very concerned-looking Peter and another male figure waiting for us.

"Miss me?" I asked drolly. He ignored my attempt at humor and glared at Teddy.

"You're late," Peter said.

"Sorry, boss. Little Bo Peep over here just had a few questions." Teddy looked at me out of the corner of his eye and winked. "But she's got a pretty good handle on phasing and teleportation. She's a quick study."

"Well, that's good to hear." Teddy's progress report seemed to relax Peter some. The features of his face softened and he flashed me a playful smile. "So, Bo Peep, are you ready for your next lesson?"

"Bo Peep, huh? Are you planning to make this nickname stick around for a while or are you just having some fun at my expense because we're late?"

"I don't know. I haven't quite decided yet." Peter chuckled and extended a hand out to Teddy. "Thank you, my old friend." Teddy and Peter exchanged their farewells and Teddy flashed a sly look at Peter who just nodded. Again, I couldn't figure out what they were saying to each other. It was like they were speaking in a code I didn't know how to decipher. I looked at the man standing next to Peter to see if I could read his face, but his expression gave away nothing. He either had a really great poker face or had no idea what the two of them were talking about either ... Or maybe he just didn't care.

"It was my pleasure, Petey. But I can already tell that this one's a handful." Teddy flashed me a big smile and winked at me again. "She's all yours, Eli," he then said to the figure standing next to Peter.

Faster than the speed of light, Teddy was gone.

* * *

It turned out that Eli was my defensive strategies teacher. He was petite in stature, being not much taller than me and not much bigger than me either. He wore a charcoal grey, velour jumpsuit and white socks—but no shoes. He looked to be in his early forties, but it was difficult to know for sure. Eli was a man of few words. In fact, compared to Teddy, it was like Eli had taken a vow of silence.

After a quick introduction by Peter, Eli took my hand and teleported me outside of the Archives to a small field adjacent to the English garden. I had no idea if I ever had any martial arts or self-defense training while I was alive, but I seemed to pick up Eli's teachings with relative ease. In addition to practicing several basic self-defense techniques used in various different martial arts, Eli also showed me how to disarm someone who was holding a gun, a knife, a tire iron, and a baseball bat.

For situations where I didn't have time to disarm an assailant, or was unsuccessful in my attempt to do so, Eli taught me how to do selective phasing, or phasing out only part of my body, so that the weapon used had no point of contact with me.

Eli made me practice selective phasing with my eyes shut, which I didn't like at all. But after one near hit with a bat aimed at my head, I paid much closer attention to the telltale sounds of an approaching weapon.

I also learned that I was much stronger than any human being. I easily bent tire irons and snapped two-by-fours in half.

"This is awesome!" I exclaimed when I crumbled a cement brick between the palms of my hands. I didn't care what Peter said—this was very much like being a superhero.

My least favorite part of the lesson was learning how to absorb and withstand blows. Despite being a man of few words, Eli did explain that there could come a time when I would have to step in front of my "sheep" and take a blow for him or her if I couldn't disarm the assailant in time.

"Here, take this knife and thrust it into my abdomen," Eli instructed while placing a dagger in my right hand. He took off his velour jacket and exposed his naked torso.

"*You want to me to do* what?" I exclaimed in alarm.

"Do it," Eli urged.

"No way!" I protested vehemently.

"Do it!" he demanded. He held his arms up towards the sky, closed his eyes, tilted his head back, and waited for me to stab him. But I couldn't. I just stood there, frozen.

A few seconds passed before Eli realized that I wasn't going to do his bidding. He opened his eyes and glared at me. Frustrated, he dropped his hands and took a step closer towards me. Before I could react, he grabbed my right hand and shoved the knife into his stomach. I heard it rip through his skin as I felt the knife enter his body. Instantly, I let go of the weapon, jumped backwards, and screamed. Horrified, I didn't dare to look down at the knife sticking out of his abdomen. I could only see his pain-stricken face. Sheer panic set in.

Borrowed Heart

Holy crap! Holy crap! Holy crap! my mind was shouting. I had no idea what I should do.

I was about to scream for Peter's help when I noticed Eli's abdomen begin to glow. I looked down out of the corner of my eye and saw one hand hover over the wound as the other hand slowly extracted the knife from his body. I just stood there with my mouth hanging open in awe.

In less than a minute's time, Eli was healed. I examined the wound—or where it should have been—but there was no trace of any injury, not even a scar.

"I ... don't understand. How did you ... What in the world just happened? I mean, I *stabbed* you. I'm sure of it. I felt the knife ... I saw it go into you. I saw your face," I rambled on, practically begging with my eyes for Eli to give me some answers.

"Getting injured does not have to be the end for us. As long as our minds remain conscious, and as long as we remain calm and focused, we can heal ourselves," he remarked calmly.

"We can heal *ourselves?*" Rage set in. "Well couldn't you have told me that *before* we conducted this little exercise?"

"Yes." Eli flashed me a smug little grin. He actually *enjoyed* scaring the daylights out of me. I thought about stabbing him again, but I mustered up enough self-control to refrain from doing so.

"Well, I sure hope it was better for you than it was for me," I said venomously. Eli was still smiling when Peter arrived.

I'll take that as a "yes," I said to myself.

* * *

"That was *not* funny, Peter." I was still seething when we returned to the Time Keeper in the Archives.

"Eve, I'm sorry. I should have warned you about Eli; he

153

has a rather sadomasochistic sense of humor." Peter was trying his best not to smile but failing miserably.

"Go ahead—get it out of your system," I said, annoyed.

"You should have seen your face." Peter busted out laughing. "It was truly priceless," he spit out.

"You mean you *watched* me suffer out there and you did nothing to help me?" Rage erupted within me again.

"Correct me if I'm wrong … but you weren't the one with a knife sticking out of your gut," Peter sputtered out in between laughs.

"Unbelievable. Has anyone told you that you're all a bunch of lunatics?"

"Oh come on, Eve. Cut us a little slack. It's not often that we get new faces up here. It's hard for us *not* to take advantage of such opportunities when they present themselves."

"Is that what I am to all of you?" I asked angrily. "An opportunity to be taken advantage of? So tell me—just how do *you* plan on taking advantage of me?"

"Eve, you have it all wrong." Peter had stopped laughing.

"Then explain it to me," I demanded.

"Eve, you are my mentee, my student. I'm here to help prepare you for your assignments the best way I know how. Look, I know that Eli can seem a little medieval, but his teaching methods are time-tested and proven to be effective. Eli has good shock value. He forces you to be in a frame of mind similar to what you'd experience during a real attack. Panic and stress are unavoidable in traumatic situations. You have to be able to think clearly and always be ready for surprises—"

"I'm not talking about Eli, or his *shock value*. I'm talking about *you*."

"Eve, I'm not sure what you mean." Peter shifted uncomfortably.

"Peter, do you only see me as your mentee?" I closed the distance between us, so he couldn't avoid making eye contact with me.

"Well, I do hope I'm not interrupting anything," said a sweet, melodic voice from behind me. I turned around to see an elegant, middle-aged woman in an impeccably tailored linen pantsuit.

"No, not at all, Agnes. As usual, you're right on time." I heard the relief in Peter's voice as he backed away from me a few steps. "Eve just returned from her lesson with Eli, and she's a little ... shaken up."

"Oh, Peter, when are you going to tell Eli to stop doing that awful 'stab me' thing. It's really nothing more than a platform for him to show off."

"Eve, I must apologize on the behalf of my colleagues." Agnes walked over to me and took both of my hands in hers. "You know what they say: men will be boys—and truer words could not be spoken about these fine gentlemen. Eli's lessons are real, but what these boys will neglect to tell you is that Eli never really gets hurt. It's all a trick—an illusion he creates in your mind. Then these boys get together and chuckle about you young ones and your reactions to Eli's supposed injury for decades to come. It's absolutely juvenile." She cast a maternal glance at Peter that seemed to say, *What am I going to do with you?*

"Now, first things first," she added, turning her gaze back towards me. "I don't know what Peter has told you about me, but I'm Agnes. I will be teaching you the art of healing. It certainly is a pleasure to meet you, my child."

"Likewise," I responded. I liked Agnes already. She had a very nurturing face—not to mention, she clearly had no reservations about busting the "boys."

"So let's leave these boys to their games and go somewhere a little more delightful, shall we?" Agnes took my hand

155

and smiled at me. I closed my eyes and wondered where she would be taking me. Suddenly, I could hear waves crashing over rocks.

"Go ahead and materialize, Eve," Agnes directed.

As soon as I did, the smell of the tropical ocean air overwhelmed my senses. I could almost feel the salt collecting on my skin. Warm water rushed up over my feet and then receded, causing the sand to tickle my toes as it was carried out by the current. I opened my eyes to discover that I was standing on a black sand beach tucked away in a little cove. The beach was small, surrounded by ocean caves; stone arches; and low sea cliffs covered in a lush, green blanket of tropical trees, plants, and flowers.

"Where are we?" I asked in awe.

"In Maui—on Wai'anapanapa Beach, to be exact," Agnes responded. "The beach is said to be a sacred place with sorrowfully romantic ties. I come here from time to time when I want to slow down a bit, think, or just relax."

"It's amazing. It's so peaceful, so ... perfect."

"Exactly," Agnes sighed, taking it all in.

"Well, Eve," she said, clapping her hands together, "I fear we don't have much time, so I think the best thing to do is begin with your lesson. Agree?"

I nodded affirmatively.

"Okay then, my child, why don't you close your eyes again and tell me what you hear."

I did as Agnes instructed. The sounds of the rainforest and the ocean filled my head. I could hear the ocean waves as the tide was rising. I could hear the saltwater-filled breeze rustling its way though the trees. I followed the sound of the wind deeper into the rainforest where I could hear cascading waterfalls ... and animals. I could definitely hear lots of animals—birds squawking; mongooses scurrying about; wild boar snorting; and a seemingly satisfied, well-fed, feral cat purring nearby.

Something caught my attention out in the ocean—the melancholy song of a humpback whale. I opened my eyes and scanned the surface of the ocean only to see water shooting out of a whale's blowhole about a half mile from the coastline. Every animal seemed so healthy, so free, so ... *alive*. A pang of jealously darted through me.

Eve, get a grip, my mind snapped at me. *You can't possibly be jealous of animals! You're lucky enough to have been given* any *kind of second chance, much less one like this.*

My self-admonishment was cut off by the sound of a very faint gurgling. Something was wrong; whatever was making that sound wasn't well.

"Agnes, do you hear that?" I asked apprehensively.

"From which direction is the noise coming?" Agnes asked calmly.

I closed my eyes and zeroed in on the origin of the sound.

"From over there!" I yelled as I ran towards a pile of rocks at the water's edge. Agnes was already there by the time I reached the shoreline.

"Oh, I guess I could have teleported myself here," I muttered, feeling a little silly.

"In due time, my child. This is all so new to you."

I looked down to see a young, injured sea turtle. I felt the turtle's instinctive need for self-preservation as it helplessly gasped for breath after breath. I was hit with what seemed like another moment of *déjà vu*—all I could see were blinding bright lights. My mind shuddered at the thought, but now was not the time to figure out what was going on in my head. The sea turtle's aura was so faint. I had an undeniable urge to help the baby turtle ... to heal it. But how? I looked at Agnes.

"Please teach me how to save this little guy," I begged.

"Eve, place one of your hands about an inch or so over the turtle," Agnes instructed. I quickly did as told.

"Good," she continued. "Now I want you to focus on the turtle's body. I want you to find the source of its injury."

"How do I do that?" I asked frantically.

"Just concentrate on the turtle's heat signature—where is it the weakest?"

I focused all of my attention on the tiny little body barely struggling before me. I scanned the turtle from its head to the tips of its flippers, over and over, trying to find the source of its pain, until I noticed that its signature was weakest on its underside. I gently rolled the turtle over and gasped when I saw that the turtle had been impaled by fishing hook. The turtle looked up at me, like it was silently pleading for me to help it.

"Now what?" I half-shouted at Agnes, anxiously bouncing on the heels of my feet.

"Take a deep breath and ever so gently remove the hook from the turtle's neck. Then place your hand an inch or so over the open wound and focus on healing it. You'll know when you are doing it correctly."

I took a deep breath and a big leap of faith. I carefully removed the hook from the near-lifeless body on the sand and then quickly concentrated all my efforts on healing the turtle. As my hand hovered over the helpless creature, its body began to glow. It took me a second to realize that the turtle wasn't actually glowing; rather, its wet body was merely reflecting the amber glow emanating from beneath *my hand*. Almost immediately, the turtle began desperately kicking its flippers back and forth as it tried to roll over onto its stomach. I pulled my hand away, afraid I was hurting it. Just then a big wave crashed over the rocks and flipped the little guy over. The turtle swam out to sea, carried away by the wave as it receded.

"Oh no!" I gasped.

"What could be wrong, my child? You just saved that sea turtle's life," Agnes announced proudly.

"I did? ... But it started kicking—I thought I was hurting it."

"Oh, poppycock! You accomplished quite the opposite effect. You healed the turtle and it was ready to heed the irresistible call of the ocean once again." Agnes smiled in approval.

"But ... it happened so fast. I saw my hand glowing and then ... then the turtle was gone."

"It was a small animal, so it did not require you to expend much of your healing energy."

"Huh," was all that I could muster. I allowed myself a moment to bask in the glory of saving the turtle before standing up to see if I could catch one last glimpse of it in the water. Once upright, however, I was hit with a dizzy spell.

"Ah, but it did require enough of your energy that you need to sit for a minute and let yourself rest." Agnes reached up for my hand and helped me back down to a nearby rock to sit. "The power required to heal a living being will take its toll on you; it will drain you of your strength," Agnes cautioned.

"So how much of my energy will be drained if I heal a larger animal or a—"

"Human?" She finished my question. "The healing process is the same for all creatures, including humans. However, the larger the animal, or the more critical the injury sustained, the more energy will be required to heal it." She paused for a moment before continuing.

"I must tell you, Shepherds rarely ever use this power—the goal being, of course, that we never find ourselves in a position of *needing* to use it. Healing a human will risk exposing your true identity. And, of course, there is always the danger of draining too much of your own strength in the process. Without your strength, even for a limited period of time, you will be rendered defenseless to protect yourself—or carry out your assignment. You will be incapable of guarding your human against the dangers that wait quietly and patiently in the wings, ready to strike when you make a mistake. Do you understand?"

"Yes. I mean, I'm pretty sure I do," I said thoughtfully. "If I'm on assignment, and I use my power to heal, my charge is essentially a sitting duck for the duration of time it takes for me to regain my strength."

"As are *you*," Agnes warned as she stood up and brushed off some of the black sand that clung to her linen pant leg before offering her hand to help me up. Once on my feet, she linked her arm with mine and began leading me back to the middle of the sandy beach.

"I think you've had enough for today, Eve. You did very well, very well indeed. It's not every day that you get to do some real good, hmm? And it's not every Shepherd who heals so competently on her first attempt." She smiled warmly and squeezed my arm as we walked slowly along. When we had gone far enough, Agnes stopped and turned to face me.

"I do wish we could stay and chat for a while, but we need to return to the Archives; I get the strange feeling that Peter is on pins and needles waiting for us to return."

"Agnes, thank you for bringing me here," I said sincerely.

"You're very welcome." She hesitated for a moment before continuing. "You should know, Eve, I do not invite just anyone here to this beach. But I can see that Peter is fond of you. He believes in you, and that means something to me. So please come and visit this little sanctuary anytime you wish. Maybe we'll be lucky enough to run into each other from time-to-time."

"I would like that," I replied.

"So would I." Agnes smiled warmly at me.

"Agnes?"

"Yes, my child?"

"Can I ever deplete *all* of my energy when using my power to heal?"

"Yes, you can." Agnes sighed deeply. "So you'd best be careful."

Before I could ask her another question, we were back in the Archives.

13. The Rules

Agnes and I returned to find Peter pacing the floor of the Archives.

"Oh dear," Agnes said. "I'm afraid I was right. You two do need to discuss something."

I had been so absorbed in my lesson with Agnes that I'd forgotten all about my conversation with Peter just prior to her arrival. I had the feeling Peter wanted to say what had been left unsaid. A knot formed in my stomach.

"Eve, it was such a pleasure to be able to spend time with you." Agnes hugged me. "You keep practicing doing good deeds when you get the chance." She smiled warmly at me. "And I'm sure we'll be seeing plenty of each other over the next several centuries. Ah," she sighed, "what a sweet, young child." Agnes gave me another quick hug.

"Peter," she said sternly, "treat her well—or you'll have to answer to me."

"Yes, Agnes," Peter replied in a respectful tone.

"Okay then, I should leave you two alone to talk." With that, Agnes was gone.

* * *

"You have something to tell me?" I asked nervously.

"Eve, your assignment has come through," Peter stated.

"What?" I felt like I'd been sucker punched. "But … I've barely had any time to adjust to all of this!" My mind started racing. "I thought I wouldn't get an assignment until I was fully prepared. Peter, I haven't even completed my training yet. There is still so much for me to learn—to practice …" Fear crept up my throat, strangling my voice.

"Eve, the Council wouldn't give you an assignment if they thought you weren't ready. Obviously, we've done a terrific job with your training thus far—maybe too good of a job." Peter forced out a chuckle, but his eyes told me a very different story; he looked worried.

"Besides, we still have a little time," he continued, trying to sound optimistic. "Your assignment isn't scheduled to begin for a few more weeks."

"Weeks? As in *Earth* weeks?"

"Yes."

"What's that? That's like ..." I did the math in my head. "Peter, that's less than a day up here!" I exclaimed.

"We have exactly twenty-two hours in *Aura* time." He took a deep breath. "Lucky for you, we'll just have to skip through some of the boring stuff and save it for a rainy day." He smiled at me, but the look in his eyes made me nervous, even more so than I already felt.

"It'll be okay," Peter said softly as he walked over to me. He cupped my face with his hands and stared into my eyes. "I will do everything I can to make sure of it."

* * *

"Even though we're forced to postpone a portion of your training, we still have quite a bit to cover before your assignment begins."

"Okay," I said numbly.

"Originally, I had planned on telling you about our origins—of how and why the Shepherds came to be—but, considering the circumstances, I'll save the history lesson for the end if we have time. It's more important that we cover the Shepherd's Rules that govern us; the Rules that we must follow *without exception*." Peter walked over to the table and picked up the scroll I had seen earlier; he untied the red, silk cord wrapped around it and unrolled it gently. The musty smell of the aged parchment filled my nose.

"The Shepherds' Rules have been transcribed on this scroll," Peter informed me.

"Should I be writing them down?"

"You won't have to," he said matter-of-factly.

"Well, then how am I going to remember them? How many Rules are there?" I inquired.

"Ten."

"You're kidding me, right?" I laughed. "Like the Ten Commandments? 'Thou shalt not kill.' 'Thou shalt not steal.' Those rules?"

"Are you quite finished?" Peter was not amused.

"Well, what if I don't remember them?"

"You will," Peter reassured me. "In fact, you know the Rules already; they're buried deep within the recesses of your mind. Once you review them, your memory will be refreshed, and the Rules will be as familiar to you as your name.

"By way of background," he continued. "The Rules have been set forth by the Shepherds' Council. They are not negotiable, and the consequences for breaking them can be quite severe—so review them carefully."

Peter handed me the scroll; the parchment felt so fragile between my fingertips, like the wings of a butterfly. The ink used to handprint the Rules had bled into the raw fibers of the aged paper, making the text slightly blurry.

The Shepherds' Rules

The following rules shall be known as the "Shepherds' Rules," as originally set forth and modified from time to time by members of the Shepherds' Council. The Rules shall be observed by all Shepherds without reservation or exception. Any apparent or alleged violation of a Rule, as stated herein, shall give just cause for a formal Inquiry, during which the Council Tribunal shall investigate the act(s) in question and, if necessary, shall discipline the offending Shepherd accordingly.

Henceforth, a Shepherd—

i. Shall not knowingly seek out any information relating to his or her own mortal life or former living identity;

ii. Shall have an ongoing duty to conceal our identities, existence, and mission;

iii. Shall conduct him- or herself in the utmost discreet manner at all times while in the presence of mortals;

iv. Shall not deliberately cause harm to come to any living creature;

v. Shall neither intervene in nor interfere with the life of his or her Assigned Charge;

vi. Shall disregard the preceding Rule only if such intervention or interference is necessary to protect the life or welfare of said Charge, and said Charge shall suffer serious injury or death without such intervention or interference;

vii. Shall be eligible for a new Assignment only upon successful completion of the previous Assignment;

viii. Shall not be transferred, removed, or reassigned from an ongoing Assignment unless the Council Tribunal deems it absolutely necessary;

ix. Shall not disobey any Rule set forth herein or any edict handed down from the Shepherds' Council or the Council Tribunal; and

x. Shall not attempt to shield or in any way conceal his or her thoughts from the Council should those thoughts pertain to either his or her own noncompliance, or the noncompliance of another Shepherd, with respect to any Rule set forth herein.

I handed the scroll back to Peter, reciting each Rule in my

head. He was right; as soon as I read them, they were committed to memory.

"So that's it, huh?" I asked. "These Rules are the nuts and bolts of how to be a Shepherd?"

"There's one more thing you need to be aware of. Although not a Rule, *per se*, it is important."

"What is it?"

"Shepherds cannot lie," Peter replied.

"It's against the Rules to lie— got it."

"No. The issue isn't whether or not we're allowed to lie— it's that we're incapable of doing so."

"Really?"

"Really."

"Okay," I said, somewhat dumbfounded. I couldn't grasp the concept of what it would feel like to not be *able* to lie, but I took Peter's word for it. "So the Rules-plus-one; it all seems straightforward enough."

"I wouldn't treat the Rules quite that casually if I were you. They may seem black-and-white on paper, but one can easily get lost in the shades of grey when it comes to their interpretation and implementation. Trust me." Peter's eyes darkened and he seemed to lose himself in his own thoughts.

I was just about to interrupt Peter's train of thought when an unfamiliar figure materialized and slipped a thin, brown file folder into Peter's hand. Peter read the piece of paper clipped to the front of the folder; he looked at the stranger standing next to him and a series of nods transpired between them. It was obvious they were communicating with each other telepathically, but since Peter was still blocking my mind, I wasn't privy to their conversation.

"Are you sure?" Peter finally said out loud.

"Yes," replied the stranger.

"Eve, wait here for a moment. I'll be right back." There

was a sense of urgency in Peter's voice that frightened me. Peter phased out, leaving me there with the stranger.

"Hi," I volunteered. "I'm Eve."

"I know," the stranger said flatly.

Okay then, I thought. I decided to give it another try.

"And ... you are?"

"Just leaving." In a flash, the strange, antisocial Shepherd was gone and Peter rematerialized.

"Who was that?" I asked, annoyed.

"That was Sergei."

"Well, *Sergei* isn't exactly the poster child for social graces. He could definitely use a refresher course or two in elementary etiquette."

"Yes, well, he's never really been the outgoing type. He's what you would call 'all business.' He works closely with the Council. Speaking of which ..." Peter grew quiet and looked down at the file folder he had been given.

"Eve, your training is officially over. We have to leave—now. Your assignment has begun and your charge, your human, is in danger. His *Exitus* countdown has been moved up from a matter of weeks to mere *hours*."

Peter grabbed my left wrist and held my watch up to my face. Sure enough the Incident Timer was flashing and the digital countdown had begun—T minus two hours in *Mora* time. I couldn't believe it. This was crazy! There was no way I was ready to save a human's life. My head began to swim.

Before I could protest, Peter grabbed my hand and teleported me to the edge of a remote cornfield in the middle of nowhere.

14. My First Assignment

"Where are we?" I asked, still trying to come to grips with what was happening.

"We're in a field about forty or so miles outside of Chicago," Peter responded. "I needed to get you down here as quickly as possible to slow down the *Exitus* countdown. Eve, we don't have much time, so I need you to listen to me very carefully. It is customary for Shepherds to carry out their assignments alone. That said, your training was cut short; you're not equipped with a full working knowledge of what's in your bag of tricks. Accordingly, the Council has agreed to let me to come down here with you this once. But I'm here to shadow you; I'm not supposed to assist you in any material way. Nevertheless, I think my being here will help you—not that you'll need it, of course." Peter smiled at me, but I was too nervous to return the gesture.

"What if I can't do this?" I squeaked.

"You'll do just fine," Peter said confidently. "Trust me, I've been doing this long enough to know what I'm talking about ... Besides, you've got me as your number one fan cheering you on the whole way."

"Is that your idea of a pep talk?" I asked, crinkling my forehead.

He just smiled.

"Well, thanks." I flashed Peter a little smirk as I nudged him with my shoulder.

Peter handed me the thin brown file folder. I glanced at the slip of paper attached to the front cover:

Assignment:	Thayer M. Harrison
Location:	Chicago, Illinois
Age:	20
Incident:	One
Shepherd:	Eve

168

"Thayer Harrison," I read aloud slowly. I looked up at Peter. "He's my assignment?"

Peter nodded affirmatively.

"How do I find him?"

"You and only you are intimately linked to your charge," Peter replied.

"What do you mean?"

"Our pulse serves an additional purpose—one other than what I described to you earlier. For the duration of your assignment, your pulse will no longer mimic the ticking of the Time Keeper. Your pulse will now echo the heartbeat of your charge."

"What? ... Why?" I asked, bewildered.

"Having your pulse linked directly to his will not only help you locate your human whenever necessary, but it will also help you connect with him ... understand him better. You'll always know how your charge is feeling by the pounding of his heart. When he's scared, his heartbeat will quicken ... and so will yours. When he's resting, his heartbeat will slow down ... as will yours. It's quite amazing, actually— almost intimate at times."

"Huh, a human heartbeat to call my very own."

"It's temporary, lasting only through the duration of your assignment. It's more akin to borrowing a piece of his heart."

"Well, what if his heartbeat ... stops?" I asked nervously. "Will mine stop too?"

"No. But make no mistake, Eve, protecting your charge's life at all costs is *expected*. After all, it's your job. His survival is essential, and the consequences for failing to do your job can be quite grave," Peter cautioned.

"Great. Just add a little more pressure why don't you," I scoffed. "Any other brilliant words of advice?" I asked.

"Yes, actually. The disparity between *Aura* and *Mora* time is too great. Therefore, it's best that you stay down here on Earth as much as possible while on assignment. If you don't, if you choose to watch your charge from our realm, you'll risk missing something that could mean the difference between life and death for your charge."

"Got it," I replied numbly. *Immortality, Shepherds, demons, charges, life-or-deaths situations, other realms—this was so beyond surreal.*

"Oh," Peter continued, "and remember to locate your human in your ethereal state—and do your best to remain invisible throughout your entire assignment. It makes things less … complicated. Charges are not supposed to see their Shepherds; it puts us at risk of attack and exposure unnecessarily. Making yourself visible is acceptable only in emergencies.

"Hopefully, you'll have a little more time to prepare for future attacks on your charge. In fact, in an ideal world, we would be able to prevent any Incident that threatens our charges well before the danger occurs. But life is far from predictable, and we rarely get much in the way of advance notice. So you must always be prepared to save the day in the knick of time.

"And in moments of uncertainty, call on your defensive strategies training. Remember, we are not allowed to deliberately hurt any living creature, meaning you can defend your charge with the blocking and disarming techniques Eli taught you, but you cannot purposefully harm another human or animal. If necessary, you can redirect the harm intended for your charge away from him and towards you. And if all else fails, you can place yourself in between your charge and the imminent harm and take the blow for him."

"But … wouldn't that mean I would have to become *visible* in front of my charge?" I didn't understand; it sounded like Peter was contradicting himself.

"Yes, it does. But as I mentioned, visibility is only acceptable if the circumstances are extreme enough to warrant it," Peter explained. He then took a deep breath and exhaled loudly. "What I'm saying, Eve, is just make sure this Thayer person stays alive at the end of the day—that's all you really need to do. The rest we'll figure out together later."

I nodded affirmatively. I took a deep breath and examined the farmland around us and wondered again why Peter had brought me here. Even though it was dark out, I could see the terrain around me clearly. I could hear the sound of leaves bristling in the night air and the crickets chirping for miles on end.

"Why don't you look at your watch and see how much time we have until the First Incident is scheduled to occur," Peter instructed.

I looked down at my watch; the *Exitus* countdown was running down … eleven minutes and thirty-two seconds … thirty-one seconds … thirty seconds.

"We have just over eleven minutes," I noted.

"One last piece of advice," Peter said, "always keep an eye on the time, but don't rely on it absolutely. Your watch will provide you with the best *approximation* of when a life-threatening Incident will occur; but as you've already learned, our system is not infallible. We do our best with the information we have, but things change. We simply cannot predict with any certainty the precise timeline of events for the humans we are charged with protecting.

"With that said," he sighed, "we better locate your human." Peter looked around as if he were trying to find my charge hiding in the field. "Even though we're considerably beyond city limits, we still should be close enough for you to find him with relative ease." Peter pointed his finger towards the north where I could see the distant glow of city lights hovering over the horizon.

"Okay, Eve, pay attention to the sound of your pulse and focus on your human's name. I'll follow your lead." Peter took my hand.

I did as Peter instructed. I closed my eyes, cleared my mind and focused only on my charge's name: *Thayer Harrison. Thayer Harrison. Thayer Harrison.* I tried my best to drown out the sounds around me and focus only on the pounding in my chest. I could no longer hear the ticking of the Time Keeper; it had been replaced by the rhythmic beat of my charge's heart … of my borrowed heart.

"Eve, I think we're here," I heard Peter whisper.

I looked around only to discover we were in the heart of the city. More precisely, we were standing at the corner of State and Maple, as I soon discovered from the nearby street signs.

People mulled busily around us, but no one paid us any attention. I then realized no one even saw us because Peter and I still were invisible.

"Over there. The alley," Peter whispered. A minute later, Peter materialized in a hidden doorway within the empty corridor.

"Eve, how much time is left?"

I materialized by his side and looked at my watch. "Just under seven minutes."

"C'mon, Bo Peep, let's go find your lost sheep and bring him home safely," Peter chuckled.

"Very funny," I snapped.

* * *

It was a quarter to ten on a Friday night, and my charge, my "sheep," was walking out of a restaurant with three other men and a woman, all of whom were at least ten years older than my human.

"Hey, you want to jump in our cab?" one of the men asked my charge.

"No thanks," he replied. "I think I'll walk off some of that meal." He patted his stomach.

"Suit yourself," the man responded and got into a cab along with one other guy.

"Have a good weekend!" the third man shouted as he and the only woman in the group were running across the street to catch a cab heading in the opposite direction.

"You too!" Thayer Harrison shouted back while waving his hand. He headed north, and Peter and I followed him in our ethereal states. We watched him stop at an ATM to get some money, which he shoved into his wallet without counting the amount before continuing to make his way north on State Street towards a nearby dimly-lit residential area.

He had only gone a block or so when I noticed the man following him. The stranger had not escaped my charge's attention either. My human glanced over his shoulder and picked up the pace slightly, turning down a small side street. The stranger turned down the side street as well. Suddenly, Thayer stopped dead in his tracks and turned around. I felt his heartbeat quicken.

"What is he *doing*?" I whispered in alarm.

"Who knows what goes on in their heads," Peter whispered in response.

"Can I help you?" my charge demanded. I was shocked. He was facing off with the stranger, who was now only a few yards away and closing in fast.

"Just give me your wallet, and I'll be on my way," the stranger ordered.

Crap! He wants to mug my human! I exclaimed in my mind.

The mugger was wearing ripped jeans that were at least two sizes too big and an oversized black hoodie that covered most of his face. He unzipped his hoodie halfway and flashed the gun concealed beneath it.

Well that certainly complicates matters. I could only hope my charge would do the smart thing and hand over his wallet.

"I don't have any money," Thayer responded. Although his voice sounded calm, I could feel his heart pounding in fear.

"Don't screw with me, man," the mugger shot back. "I *saw* you make a little visit to the ATM. Now, hand it over."

My charge slowly and reluctantly pulled out his wallet, but he didn't hand it to the mugger. In fact, my charge seemed to be hesitating.

Was he actually thinking this over? my mind shouted in disbelief. *What was wrong with him?* Still invisible, I darted over to my charge and stood just behind his left shoulder.

"Don't fight him. Just hand him the money," I whispered in my charge's ear, trying to reason with him.

He whipped his head over his left shoulder, looking for whoever had just offered him the unsolicited advice, but my charge couldn't see me. Thoroughly confused, he quickly turned his head around in the other direction, but I remained invisible. The mugger took full advantage of my charge in his distracted state, swiped the wallet clean out of my human's hand, and ran.

My charge abruptly snapped back into reality and began to chase the creep. The mugger was fast, but my human was faster; he was rapidly gaining on his attacker. I moved swiftly and invisibly alongside my human.

"Don't follow him. It's not worth it. He has a gun!" I whispered to him again, but he ignored my warning this time. He didn't even bother to pause and look around to see who might be behind the voice. He was determined not to let the mugger escape.

The stranger darted into a nearby alley, and my human followed. As he rounded the corner, however, he was struck in the head with a two-by-four the mugger had found in the alley. Thayer went down like a house of cards on the pavement.

"Stupid moron!" the mugger shouted, bending over him. Then the guy began pacing back and forth, getting visibly more agitated with each step. "You should have just given me the money. Now you pissed me off." The mugger kicked my human in the ribs and then proceeded to kick him a few more times. My charge just lay there, unconscious in a crumpled heap, his body heaving with each blow. His heartbeat began to slow down.

I didn't know what to do. I wanted to shove the mugger away from my charge, I wanted to kick him in the ribs and give him a taste of his own medicine, but I knew I couldn't. Rule Four prohibited me from deliberately causing harm to any living creatures—criminals included.

To makes matter's worse, kicking my human wasn't enough to fully vent the mugger's rage. Still pacing, the assailant pulled the gun out from under his hoodie, cocked it, and pointed it at my charge's head.

"This is what you get for being such a stupid jackass!" the mugger seethed.

Crap! I looked for Peter, but he was nowhere to be seen. I hadn't realized that Peter's idea of shadowing me would have such a literal interpretation. I had to do something—*fast*. I did the only thing I could think of doing. Making sure there were no witnesses, I materialized and turned the corner into the mouth of the alley.

"I wouldn't do that if I were you," I warned. Startled, the mugger looked up at me. He was standing not more than ten yards away. "I know what you look like. I can identify you, but I won't say anything if you leave him alone. You got what you wanted—just take the money and go. Leave him be."

Panicked, the mugger turned the gun away from my human and pointed it at me.

"That's good. Draw the attacker away from your charge and towards you." I couldn't tell if Peter was actually whispering to me or if I was simply repeating his advice in my head. Regardless, I felt like I should be nervous or scared. I mean, here I was staring down the wrong end of a gun. But I wasn't frightened. I was completely focused on doing my job—on finding a way to save the life of this human being lying on the ground.

Thayer stirred; he was coming around. The mugger turned the gun back on him.

So much for Plan A, I thought. *I guess it's time for Plan B.*

"I can't let you shoot him," I said, now standing a foot away from the mugger.

"What …? How the …? You … you were standing over there." The mugger stumbled backwards and did a double take to the entrance of the alley and then back to me.

"I won't touch you … as long as *you* don't touch *him*." I pointed at my charge, who stirred slightly again. "So my advice to you is to just take the money and get out of here."

The mugger eyed the wallet in his one hand and the gun in his other. I could see the waves of confusion, fear, and desperation flash across his face. I looked into his eyes; he looked totally strung out. He hadn't been thinking clearly to begin with; he only cared about getting enough money to score his next fix. I had the sinking feeling it would be utterly useless for me to try to reason with him. I was right. Without warning, the mugger pointed the gun at my stomach and pulled the trigger.

"Phase out! Quickly!" Even though I still couldn't see Peter, I heard his voice clearly this time. I dematerialized just in time for the bullet to pass through me and lodge itself in the brick wall behind me.

"Superhero stuff for sure," I remarked as I rematerialized.

Peter laughed out loud, which made the mugger spin around again, only to see no one behind him. The strung-out druggie was disoriented and confused; which, in turn, allowed me to grab the gun away from him with ease.

"That was not very nice," I said, flashing the mugger a menacing look. "Didn't your mother teach you to play well with others?" Now beyond spooked, the mugger dropped my charge's wallet and ran off and out the other end of the alley.

Out of the corner of my eye, I noticed my human stir again. The alley was dark, save for a few staggered streetlights, one of which was casting its light in our direction. I looked down at my human only to discover him staring up at me hazily.

I couldn't help but be drawn into his gaze. He had the darkest, deepest blue eyes; they were absolutely stunning. I had to force myself to look away.

My charge tried to sit up, but he was in no condition to do so. He clutched the side of his head where he had been hit with the two-by-four. There was a deep gash above his left temple, and he was bleeding.

"Don't try to get up. You're hurt." I heard the sirens off in the distance; they were heading in this direction. Someone nearby probably heard the gunshot and called the police. "Help is on its way."

"Evie? Is ... is that you?" my human mumbled weakly. He looked at me again, struggling to focus on my face. "I thought you ..." His voice was trailing in and out as he was teetering on the brink of unconsciousness.

Evie? I repeated to myself. *Did my charge know me?* I was beyond confused. I thought we were assigned only to humans who had no knowledge, personal or otherwise, of us when we were alive.

"I ... I'm sorry," I stuttered, "I think ... you have me confused with someone else." I began to doubt my words as soon as they stumbled out of my mouth. There was something about my charge, something vaguely familiar about him—about his eyes. It was like I had seen them before. But this was neither the time nor the place to figure it all out. The sirens were getting closer. I knew I had to get out of there.

"Help will be here soon," I reiterated. "You'll be fine ... Just don't move." I tried to remain calm, but it was difficult to do so under the circumstances. My adrenaline, if that's what you called it, was on overload. In a matter of minutes, I had revealed myself to a human, met my charge, saved his life by almost taking a bullet for him, disarmed a drug addict-mugger-murderer, and now had to come to terms with the possibility that my charge *recognized* me. I wondered if other Shepherds' first days on the job were anything like mine. *Probably not.*

I realized I was still holding the mugger's gun and laid it carefully into a shallow pool of water that had formed in a pothole about ten feet from my human. I made sure the handle of the gun was still visible so the police could locate and confiscate it with ease. Afraid to dematerialize in front of my charge, I just turned around and began to walk briskly out of the alley the same way I entered.

"Evie! Wait! Please!" my charge shouted weakly. His words haunted me, sending shivers down my spine, but I had no idea why.

I didn't dare look back. I rounded the corner and made sure there were no witnesses before resuming my ethereal form. I waited for the ambulance to arrive, not wanting to go anywhere on the off chance that the mugger would return to the scene of the crime while Thayer lay there injured and vulnerable. Two police cars and an ambulance arrived within a couple minutes of each other. As I'd hoped, the police found the mugger's gun and my human's wallet. They questioned my charge to see what happened, but he wasn't much help in his current state.

"A guy tried to … to swipe my wallet," my charge managed. "I chased him … but he hit me … Then a girl … she stopped him. I think he might have … shot her. Did you see her?" he asked more urgently as he unsuccessfully tried to sit up. "You … you have to find her."

Thankfully, the police did not take my human's version of the evening's events verbatim.

"Son, have you been drinking tonight?" one of the officers asked. He had pulled my human's driver's license from his wallet. "Says here you're only twenty."

"No … no drinking," my charge replied weakly. "Just dinner … with people from work."

The EMTs laid Thayer out on a stretcher and loaded him into the ambulance. I also rode inside the ambulance, careful to remain out of sight and out of the way. My human continued to slip in and out of consciousness. While in his semiconscious state, he uttered my name once or twice followed by bits and pieces of my whispered warnings. One of the EMTs administered a shot of something into my charge's arm, and in less than a minute he was out like a light.

I watched the EMTs treat his head wound and examine his body for additional injuries. In the ER, he was diagnosed with a concussion and bruised ribs. His head was stitched and bandaged, and he was admitted for the evening for further observation. I stayed by his side the entire night. My mind was racing, wondering if he really did know me.

15. A Case of Mistaken Identity?

Thayer was discharged from the hospital early the next morning with a handful of extra bandages and a bottle of codeine. He took a cab back to his place—a one-bedroom loft on the third floor of a mid-rise in the West Loop. He peeled off his clothes slowly, wincing in pain as he did, crept into bed, and slept most of the day away.

Knowing he would not soon wake from his drug-induced slumber, I materialized and stretched out my limbs. Peter was right; I did prefer to be in my human form. The ethereal, or "phantom," version of me felt too strange, too insubstantial—too *lifeless*.

Speaking of lifeless, it was a little unnerving watching my charge, my sheep, lying there so unbelievably still—his body battered and his face swollen, purple, and bandaged. The painkillers really affected him. He lay there motionless; I could barely see his chest rise and fall with each breath. And even though I could hear his heart beating steadily, I walked over to him and placed the back of my hand near his face to feel his breath as he exhaled. I stood there for a while, staring at him, studying his face, searching it for anything familiar, but I drew a blank.

I hung out in his apartment all morning, snooping around to learn more about him. I was sure that all the information I needed to know about Mr. Thayer Harrison was tucked neatly away in his file—the file that I hadn't had time to read while out in some cornfield in the middle of nowhere with only minutes to spare before needing to save his life. So now I had to resort to more covert tactics; I would turn over every stone and see what I could find out about him. I mean, I was assigned to protect this guy's life, right? Wasn't it in *his* best interest for me to learn everything I could about him?

I actually liked his apartment; it was open and airy and had a somewhat industrial feel about it. The living area was made up of a spacious common room with a combined kitchen. The room had high ceilings, complete with exposed pipes and ducts suspended above. A few oversized vintage posters of Chicago were hung on the walls.

In the northwest corner of the large common room was the kitchen. It had stainless steel and glass cabinets, black marble countertops, and stainless steel appliances. The only division between the kitchen and the rest of the room was a breakfast bar that jutted out from one of the two exposed brick walls. I opened the refrigerator to discover it contained only a half-empty gallon of whole milk, a six-pack of Coke, several bottles of water, and a few miscellaneous take-out containers.

Opposite the kitchen were wall-to-wall windows that extended from floor to ceiling, providing a partial view of the Loop skyline. I sat down in an upholstered wingback chair facing the kitchen and the hallway to his bedroom, propped my feet up on a dark wood coffee table, the length of which was positioned a few feet in front a sage green couch, and surveyed the rest of the space.

To my left were a big flat-screen television and a sleek stereo system. Two floating glass shelves were hung on either side of the TV, but the shelves were empty save for a few coffee table books, Chicago travel guides, and a short stack of CDs. On the other side of the couch, opposite the TV, was the dining room table, on which sat a stack of papers and a laptop. A charcoal-grey suit jacket was draped over one of the dining room chairs.

I stood up and wandered back down the hallway into my charge's bedroom. An alarm clock and an iPod docking station sat on one of the two bedside tables flanking the queen-sized bed, in which my charge was sleeping. The headboard was pushed up against the only exposed brick wall in the room, on which was hung an array of miscellaneous black-and-white photographs of Chicago tucked inside an eclectic collection of picture frames. The west wall of his bedroom also had floor-to-ceiling windows, which were hidden behind thick, dark curtains.

The apartment was in perfect order. Certainly no one could accuse Thayer of being a slob. Still, something was amiss. The apartment was devoid of any personal effects—no family photos, no mementos, and no knickknacks of any kind. And save for the scant summer wardrobe and business attire, the closets were virtually empty. No winter coats or boots, no sports equipment—nothing. There weren't any boxes of stuff yet to be unpacked either. In fact, there was very little evidence to suggest that my charge actually *lived* there. The one bedroom loft seemed more like a hotel suite than a home.

How odd. On a mission to find something more about my charge, I examined his medicine cabinet. He had the usual stuff: toothbrush, toothpaste, mouthwash, deodorant, hairbrush, some type of hair product in a jar, disposable razors, some aspirin, and a bottle of Motrin. In the shower, he had a bar of oatmeal soap and bottles of citrus-mint shampoo and conditioner.

My charge was either extremely low-maintenance or he hadn't lived here very long. Given the tourism books in the living area, I decided to go with the latter conclusion. I figured he was a recent transplant to Chicago, and I wondered if he was planning on staying here or if he was just passing through the city.

I walked over to the dining room table and rifled through some of his papers, but discovered no additional information about him other than that he was working on some type of third-party investment portfolio. I turned on his laptop, but it was password protected.

Crap, I muttered to myself. This part of my investigation into his background would have to wait until I watched him log on to his computer.

Someone buzzed my charge's loft from the lobby of the building. The noise startled me, and I jumped up so high my head almost hit one of the ducts suspended a few feet below the ceiling before I phased out of sight. I felt like I had been caught with my hand in the cookie jar, and my guilty conscience surfaced.

"Hey, Quinn!" I heard someone shout from the street curb as the front door buzzed again. The cell phone in his bedroom rang a few times, but Thayer didn't answer it.

"Quinny! Dude! I thought we were going to the game today!" I looked out the open window to see a couple of guys decked out in Cubs gear shouting up at me. Well not at *me* exactly; they were looking for my human—or, at least, I thought they were.

Quinn? I repeated the name in my head. A queasy feeling began to stir inside me. After another minute, the two guys gave up and left.

Wait a minute. I'm supposed to protect someone named Thayer— *not some guy named* Quinn. *Oh crap! Did I mistake this human for my charge? Did I save the wrong person?* Confusion, panic, and horror flooded me. If this human wasn't my assignment, then who was? More importantly, where was he? What had happened to him as a result of my careless blunder? I had to find Peter.

* * *

Peter was waiting for me in the Archives.

"I think I made a huge mistake." I was totally freaking out. "That guy ... that human that was getting mugged ... his name is *Quinn*—not Thayer. I think I saved the wrong person!"

"It all makes perfect sense now," I continued. "That Quinn-guy recognizing me and all. I mean, Teddy said I would never be paired with someone who knew me during my life. But if that guy I saved last night wasn't really my charge, then that explains it, right?" I stopped to catch my breath and collect my thoughts while I waited for Peter to give me an answer, a look—any sort of response. But he just stood there silently for an uncomfortably long period of time.

"Eve," he finally said after sighing heavily, "the human you saved is, indeed, your charge. His full name is Thayer *McQuinn* Harrison. Quinn is his nickname. You didn't have a chance to read his file, but I did. Trust me—you found your sheep last night." Peter flipped closed a thin brown folder, stood up, and handed it to me.

"But how is that possible?" I asked without even so much as glancing at the file in my hand. "Peter, I think my charge *knows* me. He called me *'Evie.'* Maybe that's what everybody called me when I was alive—I don't know; but it's too close to be a coincidence, you know?" I was pacing back and forth. "Ugh, I should *never* have let him see me. None of this would have happened if I had remained invisible." I could have kicked myself for being so foolish.

"Eve, you did the right thing. In fact, you really had no other choice given the circumstances and the time constraints. The truth is that sometimes we're put in situations where we are forced to do whatever we can to protect our charges—even if it's appearing in our human form. Believe me, it occurs more frequently than you might think. I probably would have done the same thing had I been in your shoes. At the end of the day, you saved your sheep, and that was the most important thing ... But I have to say ..." His voice trailed off as he looked down at the table and began leafing through another file.

"What? What do you have to say?" I demanded.

"Eve," he took a deep breath and looked up at me. "I am unaware of any situation in the past where a Shepherd was paired with a human with whom he or she had ever come into contact, or with whom he or she ever *could have* come into contact, during the Shepherd's life. Nevertheless, I have to agree with you—your charge does seem to think he knows you."

"Well *does* he? Did he know me when I was alive? I mean, I have no idea who this guy is or why he thinks he recognized me. I have no memories of my life, remember?" I said, flustered. "Besides, I thought you guys had the proper safeguards in place to prevent this sort of thing from happening."

"We do. And I can assure you that I am investigating this situation to find out what may have gone awry." Peter began sifting through another pile of papers on the table. "But as of right now, I can find nothing in either of your files that would suggest that your charge and you ever actually met." Peter seemed to be talking to himself. "Theoretically, I suppose it could be possible that a past meeting between the two of you was so inconsequential and brief that it would not have been recorded. But then you both should have forgotten each other, in which case, your charge shouldn't have recognized you.

"So the only thing I can think of—" Peter closed a file and shut his eyes as if deep in thought.

"Is what?" I couldn't handle the suspense. I wanted an explanation. Peter looked at me.

"Is that someone or something went to great lengths to erase any record of you from Mr. Harrison's life. That could explain why your association with him went unnoticed—and why you were paired with him."

"Why would someone do that?"

"I honestly have no idea," Peter conceded. "It's not anything I have encountered or heard of happening before. But whoever did it apparently didn't go as far as to erase you from Mr. Harrison's memory. Eve, if your charge did recognize you last night, that would complicate matters considerably. We have no protocol or guidelines for handling such a scenario. We would be venturing into uncharted territory. I must admit, I'm completely and utterly mystified."

"Great," I sighed. "Leave it to me to be the monkey wrench in the well-oiled machine." My mind suddenly flashed to my charge's deep blue eyes. *Quinn*—the name had a certain ring to it. Had I ever had heard it before? I quickly forced the thought from my head for fear that Peter was listening.

"Well, I'll just have to be reassigned to someone else then, right?" I suddenly felt anxious, almost like I was afraid of getting in trouble were it confirmed that there was a connection between my charge and me. Like it would be my fault somehow. But how could I be blamed for something I had no control over? I knew I was being irrational. Just the same, I wanted to rid myself of this assignment as soon as possible and leave this mess far behind me.

"It's not that easy, Eve," Peter began. "First of all, the Rules are steadfast and firm. A case transfer must be approved, and Council members do not like making exceptions—regardless of how *unusual* the situation. One exception would lead to another and then another and so forth. The Rules soon would become wholly unworkable and useless. They would be reduced to nothing more than mere guidelines or suggestions from which Shepherds could pick and choose. The Council won't stand for that.

"And second," he went on to say, "I'm not sure that transferring you to a new assignment actually would do any good. I'm beginning to suspect your pairing was handpicked by someone other than us. It seems too uncanny that your training was cut short only for you to be prematurely rushed into an assignment to protect someone who knew you in life. It would seem that fate might have something ... *different* in mind for you two, despite the fact that one of you is no longer living.

"So what do you suggest I do? Stay and protect him?" I snapped.

"Yes. For the time being, anyway. The Council has already been informed of your unique situation. I plan to consult with them later today," Peter added.

"In the meantime, you need to go back to Earth, back to your charge, and continue to carry out your assignment. Be mindful of your watch," Peter directed. "Don't let Incident Two catch you off guard. I'll contact you when I hear of any developments."

I nodded, making a mental note of Peter's instructions, but my chest sank as I heard Peter's words. I didn't want to go back to my human's apartment. I didn't want to take the chance of having another close encounter with him. But I had no choice. I was solely responsible for his safety. And minutes spent up in the Archives were equivalent to hours on Earth—hours during which my charge was alone, injured, and vulnerable to another attack.

Reluctantly, I closed my eyes and was just about to teleport myself back to my human's apartment when I felt Peter take my hand. I opened my eyes and looked at him.

"Eve, please be careful." His eyes were so full of concern and compassion. "And please, stay out of sight. Do not have any additional contact or communication with Mr. Harrison if you can help it. If he knew you when you were alive, then chances are he also knows you died. I'm sure this goes without saying, but another chance meeting with him could very well open Pandora's Box."

* * *

Dawn lit up the sky early Sunday morning. I was back in my human's apartment—Quinn's apartment. He was sleeping peacefully in his bed, and I had the feeling he would rest for at least another couple of hours. I resumed my human form and curled up in the wingback chair I had sat in earlier. I absentmindedly traced the length of the brushed chrome frame of floor lamp next to me with my fingers and was soon lost in thought over what Peter had told me.

Could Quinn and I really have known each other while I was alive? If so, if our paths had crossed once before, how could they have crossed again now that I was dead? Could my assignment really have been destined to happen? But why? Why would someone go through all that trouble to devise such a bizarre chain of events?

I didn't have the answers to these questions, and they only made me grow more restless. I stood up and began pacing, running my fingers over every surface of Quinn's apartment—the brick walls, marble countertops, glass shelves, plush fabrics, wool rugs, and even his silk tie. I was still getting accustomed to my acute sensory skills, my tactile sense being the most perceptive of all, and I had a compelling desire to touch every different texture I could find. Eventually, I found myself wandering back into Quinn's bedroom. I walked over to his bed to get a closer look at him. He was undeniably beautiful. I wanted to run my fingers through his thick, wavy black hair and caress his smooth golden skin. I wanted to feel how his soft lips were to the touch; but, of course, I didn't dare. I just stood there staring at him.

I still knew so little about Thayer McQuinn Harrison. What was he like? What was he doing in Chicago? Most of all, I wondered how he had been able to recognize me in the alley. I tried to remember something, some morsel of a fleeting memory of him … of the life I used to lead. But it was of no use.

I knew this was a dangerous game I was playing. There was a reason why I didn't remember my life. I had a job to do; I had to keep my charge alive. Investigating who I used to be would only distract me from my responsibilities. I knew I should heed Peter's advice; I should focus solely on my assignment, see it through, and move on.

"Besides," I whispered to myself, "you know what they say: 'curiosity killed the cat.'" I choked back a chuckle. *Yeah, but I'm already dead.* As soon the words entered my mind, I grimaced. Standing there, staring at this insanely attractive, *breathing* human before me, I didn't want to be reminded of how much I had lost the day I died.

Quinn shifted in his sleep, letting out a deep sigh. He looked as innocent and as perfect as an angel. The irony of my thought was not lost on me, and I smiled to myself.

16. Immaculate Recuperation

Several hours later, Quinn woke up still groggy from the codeine. He grimaced as he strained to sit, only to give up and lay clumsily back down. He reached over to feel his tender ribs and then felt the bandage on his forehead; I could tell he was in a considerable amount of pain. He stayed there for a good ten minutes before he managed to gradually get up out of bed and shuffle slowly to the bathroom. I heard him turn on the shower, and I decided to let him be. I was already invading his home by being there without him knowing. The least I could do was try to respect his privacy in its truest form. I even turned my back when he returned to his room, dropped his towel, and took an exceedingly long time struggling to put on a pair of boxers.

Only then did I dare to look at the extent of his injuries. I mentally winced at the sight of him. The entire left side of Quinn's torso was covered in dark purple bruises. The left side of his forehead didn't look much better; in fact, the stitches made his head wound look arguably worse. I watched Quinn survey the damage to his body in the full-length mirror in his bedroom and cringe. He went back into the bathroom and taped a new gauze bandage over his left temple.

Painstakingly slowly and carefully, Quinn slid his arms through the sleeves of a button-down shirt. After fastening only one of the buttons, he shuffled into the kitchen and poured himself a big bowl of cereal with milk and grabbed a can of Coke and both of the bananas left out on the counter. With breakfast in hand, Quinn maneuvered himself into the living area and eventually was able to lower himself onto the couch. He flipped through the cable channels until he settled on a movie and then ate his breakfast. Every time he laughed at a scene, however, he grimaced in pain, so much so that he took a couple more codeine and dozed off on the couch be-fore the movie was over.

I hated sitting there watching him suffer, especially since I felt like I was largely to blame for his injuries. Guilt surged through me. If only I had been quicker. If only I had stopped the mugger sooner, maybe Quinn wouldn't have gotten hurt at all. Hindsight was twenty-twenty, and it was a waste of my time to sit there playing the "would-have, could-have, should-have" game. Still, I wished there was something I could do to help him.

Then it hit me—there *was* something I could do; I could *heal* him. If my entire purpose for being here was to guard Quinn, to keep him safe from harm, then I shouldn't let him suffer physically because *I* had failed to act fast enough. I should heal Quinn—and I would heal him while he slept that night.

The rest of the day was pretty slow going. Quinn woke up from his "nap" at around four o'clock that afternoon, only to order some Thai food for delivery and watch another movie. Other than ordering food, he didn't make or accept any calls; although he did check his personal and work email accounts. Quinn also downloaded a few albums and a movie onto his laptop.

At around ten, he took a couple more painkillers and dozed off for the evening. He had set his alarm for six-thirty in the morning, so I assumed he was planning to go to work the next day. I knew that with the assistance of the drugs, Quinn would fall into a deep, sound slumber. An hour later, he started to snore softly.

Perfect, I said to myself. I materialized and tiptoed over to the side of his bed. Even though Agnes had told me that the healing process for animals and humans was basically the same, I was still nervous. My experience in this area was limited to healing one baby sea turtle, which was a far cry from healing a grown man.

Well, here goes nothing, I said to myself. I held my breath as I carefully unbuttoned Quinn's shirt and peeled it away from his chest, revealing the bruises that covered the entire left side of his rib cage and abdomen. I positioned both of my hands an inch above his battered body. I could feel the intense heat radiating from the injuries and assumed it was a result of his body working laboriously to repair itself. A twinge of remorse passed through me again.

Don't worry, Quinn. You'll feel better soon. I focused my energy and my mind on his injuries. I recognized the amber-colored glow emanating from the palms of my hands and knew I was healing him. Quinn's red-hot flesh was cooling down, and it wasn't long before the left side of his torso reached the same temperature as his right side. He abruptly shifted in his sleep and arched his back up slightly. Afraid we would make physical contact, I pulled my hands away, only to discover that all traces of his bruises had vanished—at least on the outside. I was surprised at the strength of my healing powers; I had no idea I could heal a human so quickly.

I smiled in satisfaction. My self-congratulatory pat on the back was cut short, however, when I suddenly realized how careless I had been. I shouldn't have healed Quinn's injuries completely. He undoubtedly would question what happened to him while he was sleeping.

Crap. Well, there's nothing I can do about it now. No use in crying over spilled milk.

My only hope was that Quinn would chalk up his immaculate recuperation to nothing more than a codeine-induced lapse in both memory and judgment that had initially led him to believe his injuries were more serious than they actually were. Following that line of reasoning, I figured there was really no point in leaving his head wound to fend for it-self. I would just have to be more careful this time around.

Quinn's head injury was logistically a little trickier. First, I removed the tape and gauze to uncover the wound, causing him to stir. I froze and waited until he began snoring again.

If his torso had been red hot, his forehead was blazing. Using the same technique, I allowed my hand to hover over his left temple and watched the glow emanate from under my fingertips almost immediately. I lifted my hand up periodically to examine the status of my work, stopping when the wound looked to be about a week or so old and the biode-gradable stitches had just started to dissolve.

I looked at the results of my handiwork with approval. Again, my moment of pride was interrupted. Only, this time, it was cut short by a whopping dizzy spell, one that was sig-nificantly stronger than the spell I'd experienced when I had healed the turtle. I felt drained and weak. Forget phasing out or teleporting myself anywhere; I couldn't do much of any-thing except sit down on the floor next to his bed for fear of fainting. I felt utterly defenseless.

Whoa, I thought. *So this is what Agnes was talking about.* Af-ter a few minutes, the spell had waned enough for me to be able to stand up, albeit shakily. I still felt depleted of energy, but I could feel my strength slowly returning with each pass-ing minute.

Quinn continued to sleep soundly, and I paused momen-tarily to look at his healed body. I reached down with the in-tent to re-button his shirt, but I gently caressed his chest and stomach muscles with my fingers instead. I traced the faint line of hair that led from his chest down to just below his na-vel. I couldn't help myself. Watching him the past couple of days, letting my hands hover just above his body, healing him—it had been too much. I couldn't resist this stolen mo-ment to indulge myself. I closed my eyes and inhaled. His scent was intoxicating—and oddly comforting and familiar at the same time.

Maybe Quinn's memory of me wasn't the only link to my past. Maybe somewhere in the deep recesses of my mind, I remembered him too. I wondered how we knew each other. Were we friends? Were we something else ... something more? I pictured us kissing. I imagined what it would feel like to have his hands on my body. A ripple of electricity slowly made its way from my head to my toes, leaving a warm tingling sensation in its wake.

I snapped out of my fantasy. I couldn't go there. I couldn't afford to be distracted by some silly fantasy. Quinn was in real danger, and it was my job to make sure that he survived unscathed. Where my Shepherd had failed, I would succeed. No Servant was going to end Thayer McQuinn Harrison's life while I was still able to walk the Earth.

I quickly re-buttoned his shirt and re-bandaged his head wound in an attempt to mask all signs of my meddling—well, almost all signs; there was no way to hide his quick recovery. I looked at my watch to discover it was just after one in the morning in Chicago. I had a few minutes to check back in with Peter to see if he had learned anything from the Council. I turned around and began to walk out of Quinn's bedroom.

"Evie," Quinn mumbled.

I froze in the middle of the room. I didn't dare breathe or make a sound. I was terrified to look over my shoulder for fear that he would be awake and staring at me. My only saving grace was that the room was nearly pitch black. Maybe, just maybe, he couldn't see me. I crossed my fingers and slowly turned my head around just enough to glance at Quinn in his bed. He was still sleeping. I threw my head back and sighed silently in relief as I felt the tension slowly drain from my body.

I had been given a fortuitous break, one that would not likely be repeated. I phased out of sight. I knew I should leave, but I stood there watching Quinn. *Evie*—his voice was echoing in my head; my name never sounded better—or more fitting. My mind was overflowing with intrigue and excitement as one thought ran laps through my head at record speed: *Quinn was dreaming about me.*

* * *

"Having a little fun with your sheep, Bo Peep?" Peter asked as soon as I materialized in the Archives.

"I don't quite know what you're talking about," I said, caught off guard. Was Peter referring to the fact that I had healed Quinn? Or was he referring to my stolen caresses over Quinn's body and the thoughts that followed? I suddenly dreaded the idea of coming here. I sped up the pace of my thoughts, hoping they would sound jumbled to the other Shepherds now privy to the secrets in my mind. Still, I feared my thoughts weren't running through my mind fast enough. I swallowed hard and looked at Peter anxiously.

Peter didn't bother to return my eye contact. He was preoccupied with the various files and books scattered about on one of the reading tables. Maybe he wasn't listening to my thoughts. Maybe he had no idea what I had just done.

"Be careful when you heal," Peter said telepathically. He stopped shuffling though the papers in front of him long enough to glance up at me briefly. *"It's considered a grey area, although some Shepherds still believe it's a clear violation of the Rules."*

"Oh, so you were paying attention," I mumbled out loud, dropping my head slightly and clasping my hands behind my back like a child being scolded. *"Well,"* I continued telepathically, *"I just thought that ... I mean, since it was my fault that he got injured, I thought the least I could do was ease some of his suffering."*

"I know. Just be aware that some of our kind would not view your

195

actions as acts of kindness." He took a deep breath. *"And you should also know that I wouldn't be the only one listening in on our conversation right now if I had stopped blocking and shielding thoughts for you."*

"But … I thought … you said …," I stammered. "You told me that you'd stop blocking and shielding thoughts for me once my training was over … that you *had* to stop because it was some sort of … ethical violation or something." It suddenly dawned on me that the only thoughts I was hearing were my own. That was, until Peter replied.

"Yes, that's true. However, since your training was cut short so abruptly, you never completed your education. You have yet to learn how to telepathically block and shield thoughts. Technically, one could argue that your training isn't over. So I suppose I am still permitted to help you with this part of being a Shepherd—that is, until you learn how to do it on your own."

"And when will that be?"

"I'm not sure," he replied, this time out loud. "But I suspect it won't be for quite some time. First, we have to get a handle on your assignment." Peter shook his head from side to side slowly and sighed. "I'm still baffled by the chain of events that led you here—led you to *him*." He wrinkled his forehead and began flipping through the pages of a book. I couldn't hear what he was thinking, and I just assumed he was deliberately preventing me from eavesdropping.

"Eve, I spoke with the Council," he announced.

"And?" I asked anxiously.

"The Council members have questions of their own about your assignment. It would appear that whatever is happening is not their sole doing. I can't even be sure this is the work of the Servants alone. It seems more likely that this is the result of some stronger force."

"The Order of the Realms?"

"Perhaps."

"But why?"

"I wish I knew. The Sisters are working arduously to identify exactly which part of Mr. Harrison's fate has been manipulated, but it is a very difficult task. Your charge's destiny continues to shift even now. To be quite honest, I'm not sure what will happen next. It's almost as though whoever is doing this is staying one step ahead of us, preempting our moves. Once you were assigned to protect Thayer Harrison, the First Incident reared its head so quickly we almost couldn't catch it in time.

"Eve," Peter said urgently. "What does your watch say? How long until the Second Incident?"

"Nothing—it's blank," I responded as I looked down at my watch.

"What do you mean *'it's blank'*? That's not possible!" Peter exclaimed as he walked over to me, grabbed my left wrist, and pulled it towards him. He looked at the Incident Timer on my watch and then at me. A dumbfounded expression crossed his face. Peter dropped my wrist, ran over to one of the books laid out on the table, and frantically started flipping through pages again.

"That doesn't make any sense. The dates of next Incidents are *always* indicated—even if they aren't scheduled to occur for several months—or years even. This is very unsettling, indeed." Peter tossed one book aside and grabbed another.

"Eve, it's time you go back and watch your charge carefully," he directed, his head still buried in the pages of a book. "Do not leave his side unless absolutely necessary. I'll come to you once I have some answers."

"How will you find me?" I asked. Peter must have heard the apprehension in my voice because he tore himself away from the book and looked up at me.

"Eve, don't worry," he said in a calmer tone of voice. "As your mentor, I can find you almost as easily as you can find Mr. Harrison. And as your mentor, it is my job to keep you out of out of harm's way. Okay?" He smiled at me reassuringly.

"Okay," I replied.

"Peter?" I asked.

"Yes?"

"Thanks."

"For what?"

"For being my mentor, for being there for me—*and*," I threw in telepathically, "*for finding that loophole ... you know, to continue to shield and block thoughts on my behalf. If I haven't said it before, I really do appreciate it.*" I walked over and hugged him.

"Don't mention it," Peter responded as he accepted my embrace. I swore I could feel a rapid pounding like a drum in his chest. Oddly enough, it was as if his inner rhythm didn't mirror the ticking of the Time Keeper. It was as if his pulse had a beat all its own.

* * *

Quinn was still sleeping when I returned to the loft.

Good, I haven't missed it. I was more than a little curious to see his reaction when he woke up and realized he felt better.

When Quinn's alarm went off fifteen minutes later, he instinctively swung his left arm around and shut it off without hesitation. Yet, rather than let his arm drop back down onto the mattress, he stopped short, holding his arm up in midair.

No way! I thought. *He couldn't still be in pain, could he? Maybe I didn't heal him as well as I thought I had.*

Quinn rotated his arm around in the air, testing it. He reached across with his right hand and poked around the left side of his rib cage. Then he cautiously sat up in his bed, reached up towards his left temple, and removed the gauze pad that I'd so carefully replaced last night. He gently touched his forehead and realized that it, too, had healed considerably.

The look on his face was priceless. He looked both confused and relieved, sitting there wondering how he had healed so quickly. I giggled to myself. This was definitely the amusing part of my job, of my new existence, even if I had taken an unnecessary risk for the reward. I figured that as long as Quinn didn't see or hear me again, everything would work out just fine. My identity would remain a secret.

For one thing, I was confident he wouldn't mention either his miraculous recovery or his "vision" of me to anyone. I mean, how could he? No one would believe him. Moreover, there would be no way for Quinn to make sense of the events over the past couple days, and there had been no other witnesses to help him rationalize what had happened. Aside from the food delivery guy, Quinn hadn't talked to or seen anyone. No one else could verify the state of his injuries as the weekend had progressed. Not to mention, he spent most of the last two days semi-conscious, thanks to a healthy dose of codeine.

Knowing what I now knew about the human mind and what it was capable of doing to shelter itself from the strangely inexplicable, I was led back to my original theory: Quinn would chalk up recent events to a side effect of the painkillers he was taking and let the whole thing go. Eventually, this would all be repressed somewhere deep within his mind, not to be pondered, questioned, or revisited again.

Besides, it felt good to do good—to be able to heal injuries inflicted at the hands of someone else. Without warning, my mind ached with a twinge of sadness. I wasn't sure why, but I suspected it had something to do with how I'd ended up a Shepherd. I still didn't know the details of what happened to me and why my Shepherd was unable to save me. Peter had said it had all happened so fast. Maybe my Shepherd couldn't prevent the car accident. Maybe my injuries were so extensive, I couldn't be healed in time.

Quinn got out of bed and walked over to the full-length mirror in his bedroom. He removed his shirt and examined his torso in the mirror. He poked around some more with his hands and then twisted and turned his body this way and that. When he was convinced his ribs had healed, he examined the extent to which the wound on his forehead had healed. It was easy to see Quinn was more than just a little baffled. Nonetheless, he went on with his morning and got ready for work.

I remembered Peter's orders not to leave Quinn's side *unless absolutely necessary*. And, although Peter's words would seem to justify my desire to peek at Quinn while he was in the shower, I resisted temptation and gave him his privacy until after he was dressed. When he emerged from his bedroom, he was wearing a sky-blue Oxford with white pin stripes, black suit pants, and dress socks. The light blue color of his shirt only made his gem-colored eyes look more brilliant. He put on his suit jacket, which was hanging in his coat closet, and black leather loafers. I was taken aback by how professional he looked. Somehow, he seemed different— older and more serious than I had expected. That I had *any* expectations of how Quinn *should* look was odd in and of itself considering I didn't know him. But something was definitely off—like he wasn't supposed to look quite this ... grown up.

Within a matter of minutes, Quinn scooped up his laptop and a stack of documents, stuffed them in his computer bag, and shoved his wallet, phone, and keys into his pockets. One last glance in the hallway mirror to tuck his wet hair behind his ears, one last minute to examine the new bandage on his forehead, and he was out the door.

I followed Quinn down the stairs and out onto the street where he walked into a nearby Dunkin' Donuts and ordered a coffee and two chocolate-frosted doughnuts before hopping into a cab and heading downtown to work.

Having spent the majority of my assignment in the solitude of a quiet hospital room and his apartment, I was immediately taken aback by the sounds and sights of the city as everyone scrambled to get where they were supposed to go. Honking horns, screeching brakes, the El overhead, conversations, music, and footsteps—*tons* of footsteps—it was deafening.

Not to mention the overwhelming amount of visual stimuli that bombarded me at every turn. A sea of people, cars, taxis, and buses, each one vying to carve out their own little space in the morning madness. Most everyone was wearing unremarkably drab or benign colors, but every so often the beiges, greys and blacks were punctuated with splashes of color worn by a few pedestrians.

And the auras that emanated off of people—it was a sight to behold. It was hard to explain, but like humans' clothes, most of the auras were indistinctively similar. Once in awhile, however, a more unique signature would stand out from the crowd. I didn't see anything that matched Peter's description of a demon. I also didn't see anything that would resemble a guardian angel, although I really had no idea what one was supposed to "look" like.

17. The Daily Grind

Quinn was a summer intern at Hamil and Mueller, a high-end boutique firm that specialized in financial planning and wealth management—at least that's what the firm's promotional materials boasted. Quinn shared an office with another summer intern, a goofy-looking blond guy, who seemed to be about the same age as Quinn. From the nameplates outside the office door, I discovered that his office mate's name was Kyle Williams. And from the few personal items they had on their desks, I surmised that Kyle was recruited from the University of Michigan because the school logo was emblazoned on his mouse pad. Quinn's mouse pad had Indiana University's logo printed on it.

Huh, I thought, *so my human was recruited from IU—good to know.*

Their office was nice, but fairly plain. Two desks sat side-by-side, each complete with a large flat-screen computer monitor and an ergonomically correct keyboard. Quinn and Kyle connected their laptops to their respective desktop components. In front of each desk were leather-bound chairs for visitors. A worn, navy-blue, polyester-tweed loveseat sat on the opposite end of the office. The only picture was a framed copy of Vincent van Gogh's "The Starry Night." Quinn was fortunate in that his desk was closer to the two large office windows that faced east towards Lake Michigan.

Kyle bombarded Quinn with a never-ending stream of questions about the particulars of his head injury. It was obvious that Quinn was uncomfortable talking about the incident, but Kyle was relentless; he was not going to let this go until he pumped Quinn for every last detail.

Someone was unwittingly kind enough to dial Kyle's extension, saving Quinn from recounting the mugging blow-by-blow. Clearly, whoever was on the other end of the line was someone of apparent significance to Kyle because he looked at the caller ID, cleared his throat and straightened his posture before picking up the receiver. Quinn snickered a bit under his breath when he saw Kyle's little performance. Kyle's conversation consisted of several *"Yes, sir's"* and *"Of course's"* before he said he'd be right there.

"Well, got to go," Kyle said as he grabbed a legal pad and pen and stood up to leave. *"Mueller* just called; he has a *big* project for me," he noted smugly. Quinn just rolled his eyes in response, but Kyle didn't see.

"Hey, want to grab lunch later?" Kyle asked as he was almost out the door.

"Um, I'll see. I know Jones wants a status update at the end of the day on a research project I'm doing for him, so I was planning to work through lunch today."

"Oh, okay." Kyle sounded disappointed. "Well, I'll check back in with you later to see if you've changed your mind."

"Sounds good." Quinn's voice was sincere, but he shook his head, seemingly annoyed, as soon as Kyle walked out of the office.

So Quinn was not a fan of Kyle. That made two of us. I got a bad vibe off of him. His heat signature told me all I needed to know—I wouldn't trust Kyle as far as I could throw him—which was saying a lot considering how far I actually could throw him.

And despite his assurances that he wouldn't tell anyone about Quinn's mishap, I knew there was no way he would keep his mouth shut. Sure enough, not fifteen minutes had passed before all sorts of people were stopping by Quinn's desk to see how he was feeling—and more importantly, to hear him rehash the details of his attack. I couldn't believe how morbidly curious humans were about traumatic events; it was truly appalling. I couldn't have been like that when I was alive, could I? Considering I couldn't remember my life, however, all I could do was hope for the best. By lunch, Quinn must have told the story to twenty different people.

"I should have just sent out a freaking memo—it would have been quicker," Quinn muttered under his breath when the last tag-team left his office.

Just after lunch, Mr. Mueller stopped by Quinn's office to check in on him. He apologized to Quinn for not offering driving him home from dinner on Friday night. Quinn told him that it was no big deal. Nevertheless, Mr. Mueller must have felt pretty guilty because he insisted Quinn take the rest of day off. Quinn tried to explain that he felt fine, but to no avail. So he packed up his laptop and left work at one thirty in the afternoon.

It was a beautiful day, and Quinn walked the mile back to his place. When he arrived at his building, he bypassed his mailbox and walked straight upstairs to his loft. Once inside, Quinn tossed his stuff onto the kitchen counter and took off his suit jacket, draping it over one of the wingback chairs in the living room area. He walked into his bedroom and a few minutes later emerged wearing only an IU T-shirt and black boxers.

Quinn got a Coke from the refrigerator and then rifled through his wallet and pulled out a business card. He dialed the number on the card and asked for Dr. Jenson. When Dr. Jenson wasn't available to take his call, Quinn asked the nurse if she knew when he could expect his injuries to heal. Even standing across the room, I could hear the nurse's reply over the phone.

"Your head should heal in about seven to ten days, but your ribs will take a little while longer. All in all, you should feel as good as new in two to three weeks," the nurse stated. "The doctor wrote in your chart that you should take it easy for at least another week or so," she reported. "I see here Dr.

Jenson gave you a script for the pain—do you need a refill, honey?"

"Uh, no thanks. I haven't used up the first prescription yet." Quinn ended the call, opened the refrigerator again, and stared blankly at the scarce number of contents within until he settled on a day-old container of Thai food. He grabbed the pair of disposable chopsticks on the counter next to him, but just used them to poke at the food, looking at it as if it was the least appetizing thing in the world. Finally, he gave up and set the container down on the counter.

I followed Quinn into his bedroom, where he took off his T-shirt and examined the left side of his torso in the full-length mirror. As if still unconvinced that his injuries were gone, he pressed his fingers into where the bruises used to be, but he clearly felt no pain. He peeled off the gauze pad over his forehead and inspected the status of his head wound again. Then he walked into the bathroom and turned on the light to get a better look. He grabbed either side of the sink, leaned into the mirror, and stared at himself for a few minutes. I knew he was struggling to figure out how his injuries had healed so fast. Thankfully, he had no idea how to answer this riddle.

I began to regret my hasty decision to heal Quinn. Maybe I should have let nature take its course. At the very least, I should have healed him more slowly, a little bit day-by-day, so the changes would have gone unnoticed. Regardless, I was still confident that Quinn's mind eventually would help him trivialize, rationalize, or in some other manner explain away his miraculous recovery. As I'd recently learned, it was the most common way humans dealt with issues that could only be described as mystical, spiritual, or supernatural.

Quinn walked over to the stereo in his living room and turned it on. He grabbed a bottle of water out of his fridge and a bag of chips from the pantry before sprawling out onto the living room couch. He closed his eyes and listened to the music. I didn't recognize the song, but that didn't surprise me considering my state of amnesia. Hours passed, and he just listened to music with his eyes closed and his hands behind his head. Every time I suspected he had fallen asleep, he would take a swig of water from the bottle he was holding between his knees. He had been laying there the whole time thinking, and it wasn't too hard to guess what he was thinking about.

Out of nowhere, Quinn opened his eyes, stood up and began pacing back and forth slowly, gesturing with his hands as if he was talking to himself. Then he walked down the hall and into his bedroom. He lifted the shades just as the sun was about to set. He paused momentarily to appreciate the faint orange hues that were spreading across the sky before he fell backwards onto his bed and looked up at the ceiling, still lost in thought.

As the sun dipped below the horizon, shades of pink, red, and orange flooded the sky. Still invisible, I positioned myself in front of the window to soak up the warmth of the sun before it said good night. At the peak of the sunset, Quinn also seemed to take notice of nature's amazing display. He looked right at me—well, right through me—at the fiery sky.

Even though Quinn and I were as far apart as two souls could be, it felt like we were in his room *together*. It was as if we were both in sync with each other as we silently watched the sun disappear behind the buildings. I knew I couldn't let him see me. Yet, for one minute—for one brief moment—I let my guard down just enough to allow myself to feel closer to him.

"Evie?" he asked nervously, looking at the window.

Could Quinn see me? I asked myself. *How could he? I was invisible.* I was stunned. Every defense mechanism I had learned during my Shepherd training kicked in reflexively. I immediately teleported myself from his bedroom into his living area. I didn't dare breathe as I waited to see if Quinn would follow me.

"Evie? Is ... is that you?" I heard him call out hesitantly from his bedroom.

Crap! Crap! Crap! my mind was shouting. This was not good. Of course, I didn't dare answer him. But, I didn't know what to do other than to remain invisible and be ready at a moment's notice to "get out of Dodge in a hurry," as Teddy had so eloquently put it.

"This is crazy," Quinn said to himself from his bedroom. "I must really be losing it fast." I heard him get up from his bed. He walked down the hallway and into the living area, stopping near the breakfast bar. I moved across the room towards the windows to put as much distance between us as I could. "I'm sure I look like a total whack-job." He chuckled. "Quinn, dude, you're lucky you don't have a roommate listening to you right now."

Little did he know, he *did* have a roommate—an uninvited one ... *me.*

Quinn still looked troubled. He started to trace the stone veins that ran through the marble countertop with his fingers before sighing heavily and looking up at the ceiling.

"Evie ... if it's even possible that you're here somehow ... that you were there the other night ... I just wanted to say thanks for helping out. I probably should have listened to you. And I'll admit it wasn't one of my most brilliant ideas to chase after that guy." He smirked. "And, well, if you had something to do with this—" Quinn felt his side, "then thanks for that, too, I guess."

He looked almost relieved to have given a voice to this outrageous notion that he had been entertaining in his head. As though verbally acknowledging my existence and my aid was cathartic in some way. As though saying it out loud would exorcise this nonsense from his mind. Maybe this was exactly what Quinn needed to do to let go of what happened … to let go of me. I could only hope.

Even so, Quinn was smarter than I had given him credit for. Instead of repressing the trauma he had experienced, instead of coming up with some superficial, Band-Aid excuse to write off what had happened, his mind was making leaps— correct ones—to fill in the inexplicable voids for which no logical explanation made sense. He was connecting his vision of me not only with the botched mugging but his accelerated healing as well. And he was struggling to find some resolution to the questions that kept running through his head.

I was beginning to worry that his mind wouldn't let go of this phenomenon, or whatever he believed it to be, without getting some answers … some certainty. Unfortunately, I couldn't think of a way to give Quinn the answers he sought without revealing too much about myself—without breaking the Rules.

"Evie … Wow. I haven't thought about you for a while," Quinn said wistfully. "It would be awesome to be able to see you again." He walked towards the windows in the living area, right beside me. It was like he was looking right at me. I was so taken aback by his words and so mesmerized by his eyes that I couldn't move.

"I remember the first time I saw you in class," Quinn continued, "the first time I got up the nerve to talk to you. Your long hair was bunched up under that funny little hat. I can still see your green eyes from behind your glasses … And then there was that night at the party, when we …" his voice trailed off and a tiny smile hit the corners of his mouth.

When we what? I wanted to scream. *What happened that night at the party? What did we do?* I desperately wanted to know—I desperately wanted to remember. I could barely contain the curiosity and anticipation welling up inside of me. I felt like I was about to spontaneously combust. For a split second, I stopped to ponder whether I actually could combust into a million little pieces, before concluding the odds of that happening were infinitely small.

"Then ... you got into that car accident and just like that ... you were gone," Quinn continued, shaking his head. "I had a bad feeling about that road trip. I should've found a way to stop you from going. I should've found a way to make you stay in Bloomington." He glanced down at the floor and then he looked straight into my eyes—eyes that he couldn't possibly see. But I could see into his. I could see he was upset. I could tell he was hurting.

"One minute you were standing in front of me and the next minute ... I couldn't believe it. Part of me still can't believe you're gone."

I'm not gone! I wanted to shout. *I'm standing right in front of you!*

"I've really missed you these past months ... I still do." He turned around, walked over to the couch, and collapsed down on it. "Hearing the words come out of my mouth right now, it doesn't make sense. I mean, I didn't know you that well or even for that long, but there was something about you that was different. You made me feel different.

"And then out of nowhere, it was like you were there ... standing over me the other night. I *swear* it was you. It *had* to be," Quinn muttered. "And ... I wake up and discover my ribs are healed ... and my head. I just don't get it." The tortured look on his face was almost more than I could bear. My actions over the past few days had caused him to dredge up memories that were better off buried in his past.

An overwhelming urge to reveal myself to Quinn came over me. I had to leave. I had to get out of there before my guilt caused me to do something I would no doubt regret later. I teleported myself to the rooftop deck of his building.

When I saw that no one was around, I materialized into my human form, stretched my limbs, and walked over to the railing. My chest began to ache, and I realized it was Quinn's heart I was feeling.

I stayed up on the rooftop deck for a while staring at the expansive Chicago skyline just as the moon was beginning to settle into the evening sky. I needed time to sort through what Quinn had unknowingly revealed to me. This added a whole new layer of "complicated" to my assignment. Anger stirred inside of me. To assign me to Quinn's case was grossly unfair—no, it was downright cruel—to *both* of us. Quinn not only *knew* me when I was alive, he'd actually had feelings for me. More to the point, it appeared as though he *still* had feelings for me.

And to top it off, he had information about my life. In the span of a few minutes, I'd discovered Quinn and I were in a class together, presumably at Indiana University. I knew we had at least one memorable evening together. I knew I took a road trip somewhere, which resulted in the car accident that claimed my life. I'd also learned Quinn didn't want me to go on that trip. And I'd found out that *Quinn missed me.*

The Rules forbade me from seeking out information about my past, but what if the information was volunteered freely? What if I learned about my past accidentally? Quinn had let the cat out of the bag. Now I wanted to know more—about who I was, where I was from, and what I was like.

It was a risky enough proposition to even dare to consider fulfilling this desire of mine, much less pursue it. I couldn't make this decision lightly. Once I opened this door, there was no going back. I'd have to play my cards *exactly* right; I couldn't afford one misstep. Moreover, I couldn't let a soul know what I was doing—not even Peter.

Was I really considering this? Could I really *use* Quinn to find out about my former life? How would I even go about doing it? How could I get him to volunteer more information about me? I still couldn't let him see me. What was I going to do? Drop constant reminders of myself around him? No way. I wouldn't feel right toying with Quinn's emotions like that just to get him to talk about me.

Besides, I had to look at the other side of things. Just how important was it for me to know about my life? And what was the cost of finding out about my past? Peter told me focusing on such distractions could be dangerous, even fatal, for my charge. What's more, Quinn had said he didn't even know me all that well or for that long. Was I really that callous that I could risk his life for a few details about my own—about a life that was no longer mine?

I may not have had the answers to all of my questions, but I certainly had the answer to the last one: *No.* I wasn't so cold and insensitive that I would risk the well-being of another for my own selfish gains. My entire reason for being was to keep Quinn safe from harm. I was given a second chance so I could protect him. And that was exactly what I was going to do.

18. I've Been Made

When I returned to Quinn's loft, he was eating pizza and checking his email. The rest of the evening was uneventful. He didn't speak another word either to or about me. But he still looked uneasy, like he was mentally wrestling with something. I knew that "something" had to do with me.

He went to bed and tossed and turned until he fell asleep. I wasn't sure what came over me, but I felt compelled to heal his head wound again—not enough for him to notice, but a sufficient amount to help it heal faster. I supposed it was because every time I looked at his face, I was reminded of my own shortcomings as his Shepherd. Plus, I also felt guilty about messing with his mind—with his life. Quinn shouldn't have seen me the other night; I realized what a big mistake it had been on my part. Now I just wanted to help him through this rough time, and healing him was the only way I knew how. The sooner he healed, the sooner he could put the entire chain of events behind him, and the quicker he could move on with his life.

Whatever my reasons for wanting to heal Quinn again, I promised myself this would be the last time I worked my magic on his injury. I would let nature do the rest.

Quinn was restless, even in his sleep. Knowing I had to be particularly careful tonight, I slowly removed the gauze bandage from his head and began the healing process. I stopped when the left side of his forehead cooled down to a few degrees above his normal body temperature. I stepped back to survey my work.

That's it, I proudly said to myself. He would never suspect I'd helped out again. I gently replaced the bandage and immediately backed away from him. I didn't trust myself to be within arm's reach of his body for very long and resist the temptation of running my fingers over his bare skin.

I turned around and walked out of his bedroom, pausing in his doorway as I imagined what memories he had of me … of us. I shook my head in an effort to empty it of images of him and I together. This assignment was really turning out to be a huge mess—one that I feared would only get worse. How could the Council have made such a colossal blunder by assigning me to him? Where were the warning signs? The red flags?

I wondered if Peter had any new information that could help unravel the mysteries plaguing my assignment.

Ugh … Peter. I knew I should fess up and tell him everything that had happened today, but he was the last soul I wanted to run into right now. I could just hear him run through his "I-told-you-so's:" *"Eve, I told you the only way you'll be able to do your job is if you maintain a safe distance from Quinn,"* or *"Eve, need I remind you that your only job is to save Quinn's life—not to get wrapped up in his personal issues?"* or—

"Evie?"

No, that wasn't right, Peter didn't call me Evie. The only person I knew who called me that was—

I immediately looked down at myself. *Crap!* I was still visible. Dread filled me instantly. I was so preoccupied with my thoughts, I had forgotten to phase out of sight and was still standing in Quinn's bedroom doorway. It was a rookie mistake—actually, it was more like a Freudian slip, and a big one at that. I felt like I was going to be sick.

"Evie? … Is that you?" Quinn asked in a groggy voice.

"Damn it," I muttered under my breath.

I didn't have to turn around to confirm what I already knew to be true—Quinn was awake, and he saw me plain as day. My cover was blown. *I've been made.*

I couldn't help but turn around anyway. Just as I suspected, Quinn was sitting up in his bed, struggling to see me clearly, his eyes still out of focus from just waking up.

"Are … are you really here?" he asked in disbelief.

I just stood there speechless. If I phased out now, would he think it was all just a dream in the morning? How could I get myself out of this mess? Did I really even want to get out of it? Maybe this was for the best. My mind was running through possible scenarios—both good and bad. I couldn't figure it all out right now. But I knew the longer I stood there, the more convinced Quinn would be that his "vision" was real.

At a loss for what to do, I quickly spun around and walked down the hall towards the kitchen. I would dematerialize once I was out Quinn's line of sight. Unfortunately, I never had the chance to execute my escape plan. He leaped out of bed and ran after me as soon as I rounded the corner.

"Wait! Evie! Please don't go!"

I froze in place, my back still towards him.

"Please," he begged, "just stay for a few minutes."

"I … I can't," I replied, unable to move.

"Why?"

I didn't answer him.

"Fine. Go ahead. Leave … I guess some things never change." His words stung. He sounded so bitter and upset.

But how could I blame him for feeling that way? In the short time I had been his Shepherd, this would be the second time I'd walked away from Quinn after he'd pleaded for me to stay. Who only knows how many times I'd done this to him when I was alive. But I couldn't deal with that now. I had to leave. The ramifications—the consequences of Quinn having recognized me a second time—were much more serious than me hurting his feelings or his pride.

"I'm sorry. It just has to be this way." I stole a glance at Quinn and gasped quietly. He was wearing only his boxers. And even though it was dark outside, the streetlamps were casting their light through the living room windows and down the hall, outlining every curve and ripple of his toned body. If I didn't know any better, I would have sworn the pounding in my chest came straight from my heart. I had trouble catching my breath. I didn't dare look at his face for fear that I would lose myself completely in his eyes.

I didn't want to leave, but I had no other choice. I opened Quinn's front door and walked out. The door shut behind me with a hollow thud that rang in my ears. I just stood there pressing my face against the door, feeling the chill of the metal against my cheek.

I knew I should be watching over Quinn, but I couldn't return to his apartment just yet. I no longer trusted myself to make the right judgment calls or to do what I needed to do—what I should have done all along, which was to stay hidden and to keep my distance.

But I couldn't go to the Archives either. It wouldn't take long for Peter to read my thoughts and figure out Quinn had made contact with me again. I wouldn't even know where to begin explaining my mistakes to Peter, and I sincerely doubted he would understand my actions after the warnings he had given me. I shuddered to think about his reaction to how much trouble I had landed myself in—and in such a short period of time. Something deep in the pit of my stomach began to stir as anxiety crept up the back of my throat. *I really screwed up this time.*

That's when I remembered her—the faceless statue at the top of the Chicago Board of Trade. I had read about her in one of the few books in Quinn's loft and then saw her from Quinn's office window. Her name was Ceres; she was the Roman goddess of agriculture—grains mostly, I think—and was thought to be responsible for nurturing mankind in matters relating to the cultivation of the land. The statue of Ceres stood on top of the Board of Trade to serve as a symbol of the commodities traded within the building. And even though she had a name, she was a mystery, having been given no face; the architect had never bothered to give her one because he wrongly assumed the Board of Trade would remain the tallest building in Chicago. For some inexplicable reason, I wanted to be near this Chicago icon. Maybe I could find some answers there.

I teleported myself to the top of the Board of Trade and heard nothing but the sound of the wind whipping around the statue. Perched up there with her, I was finally able to escape most of the noisy chatter down below. And, oddly enough, the quietude revealed everything I needed to know. It was as if by majestically standing there in complete silence for all those years, Ceres was showing me what I needed to do. She had stood alone at the top of this building for decades, silently watching over the city, guarding it from a distance. Most people probably never knew she existed; they probably never bothered to take a break from their daily routines to notice her at all. Yet, there she remained, year after year, an invisible symbol of growth—a symbol of life.

I, too, was a symbol of life—a protector of it. I was charged with guiding Quinn safely through the unknown dangers that awaited him. I, too, had to do it alone, unnoticed and in quiet solitude. If he was supposed to know about his destiny, if he was supposed to fend for himself against the demons that manipulated his fate, then there would be no need for the secrets, there would be no need for the Rules, and there would be no need for me.

But here I stood. It would take a leap of faith larger than most humans were capable of making to be able to contemplate, much less understand and accept, the details of how I came to stand here. I could not expect Quinn to take such a leap—in fact, I couldn't let him. It would only distract him and me from the real issue at hand ... the only issue that mattered—his life.

And so it was decided. I knew I had to keep my distance from Quinn. I could not under any circumstance let him see me again. I could not communicate with him again. And I would ignore any future attempts by him to contact me. As hard as it might be for me to do, in the long run, I knew it was far better for him to think he'd suffered a spell of temporary insanity than to figure out what was really going on and why I was sent to him.

I returned to Quinn's apartment before his alarm went off Tuesday morning. With my new plan in full effect, I sat invisibly in what was quickly becoming my favorite seat, the wingback chair next to his couch. I dared not move while Quinn got ready for work. Understandably, he was on edge all morning. He was cautious, almost self-conscious about his actions, like he knew someone—like he knew *I*—was watching and listening to his every move. You could hear a pin drop, it was so quiet—no morning news, no music, nothing. Even he was silent the entire morning. It went without saying that I remained silent as well.

Quinn grabbed his stuff and was just about to open the door when he turned around and looked into his living area.

"Evie, I just want you to know that I'm okay with you being here. I … I want you to stay," Quinn announced. Then he opened the door and left to go to work.

I just sat there in utter shock as I watched him leave.

* * *

Sticking to my guns, I kept my distance from Quinn for the next couple of weeks. And each day it seemed to get a little easier. It was pretty easy to follow his schedule, which he maintained diligently. From what I could tell, Quinn was a creature of habit. During the workweek, he'd get up, get ready for the day, stop at one of two places to pick up breakfast, and hop in a cab to go to work.

Quinn's office life was fairly monotonous. Kyle remained a pesky thorn in his side, but things were going well for Quinn overall. It seemed he was well regarded by everyone at the firm.

In the evening, Quinn typically would come back to his apartment and then go for a run or a bike ride if the weather permitted. Frequently, he would swim laps at a nearby health club. Later, he would review some files he'd occasionally bring back from work or surf the Internet while eating whatever take-out or delivery he had gotten for dinner. He would end his evenings by checking his email and watching TV or listening to music before heading off to bed. The weekends were filled with more bike rides, runs, and laps at the pool; more TV and music; and more takeout.

Sometimes Quinn would meet up with friends, but he generally seemed to prefer being alone in his loft. I couldn't figure out if he was really that solitary by nature or if he deliberately hung around his apartment in the off chance that I would show up again.

Most of the time, Quinn wouldn't mention me while he was awake. He did, however, mention my name in his sleep from time-to-time. On a few occasions, he was so bold as to talk to me in his apartment. It was like a game to him. He would say things like, "Evie, I sure hope your day was more interesting than mine," or "Evie, it's too bad that you don't have the pleasure of hanging around my office mate all day." Once in a while, he would even wish me good night.

I didn't risk materializing in Quinn's apartment again *ever*—even while he slept. But after an entire day of shadowing, or "ghosting," him, I was itching to be in my human form. So the only solution was for me to leave his apartment while he slept. I used this time to travel to other destinations around Earth.

In fact, I had gotten quite proficient at teleporting myself to different cities and landmarks. I even practiced teleporting myself holding different objects—a dead pinecone I found in Yellowstone or a handful of pebbles I picked up from the California coastline. I also discovered that I preferred to visit time zones when it was still daylight so I could feel the warmth of the sun on my skin.

The majority of my evenings, however, were spent walking around Chicago. I was too nervous to stray far from Quinn for any considerable amount of time even though he was only ever a thought away. Each time I strolled the city streets I was reminded of little things that I had witnessed Quinn do or say; things that showed me what I already knew to be true: he was a kind and thoughtful person. There was the bus stop in the West Loop where Quinn was the only person who bothered to help an elderly woman gather her groceries scattered about the sidewalk after her collapsible shopping cart had tipped over. There was the Lincoln Park Zoo where he stopped mid-stride during one of his afternoon runs to scoop up and return a stuffed animal that, unbeknownst to a mother, her baby had dropped.

And then there was Ronald—a homeless man—who perched himself on a couple of milk crates, peddling *Streetwise*, a local paper, at all hours of the day and night outside the twenty-four hour convenience store a few blocks from Quinn's apartment. Most people ignored Ronald, but not Quinn. Like clockwork, every Friday when he walked home from work, he would buy the latest edition of *Streetwise* from Ronald and talk to him for a few minutes. Other afternoons, Quinn would randomly slip Ronald a couple of bucks and ask how he was doing.

Ronald always smiled when he saw Quinn walking down the street. I could tell he appreciated how Quinn treated him like a person instead of a contagious disease.

Ronald also seemed to have taken a liking to me, despite

the fact that I'd never once stopped to talk to him during my solo nightly strolls.

"There's my favorite angel!" Ronald would call out to me in a deep, bluesy sing-song voice while flashing me a goofy, cheerful grin as I passed by the convenience store. I doubted he actually knew how close to the truth he was about me, but he always made me smile.

19. Time to Meet the Parents

One evening the phone rang. Quinn looked at the caller ID and then sighed, debating whether to answer it or not. Finally, he picked up. To respect his privacy, I had gotten into the habit of mentally tuning out whoever was on the other end of the line.

"Oh, hi, Mom … No, I'm fine, really. I was … in the shower … Yeah, sorry about that … I haven't been feeling well. I think I caught a summer bug or something … No, no, I'm fine … Really, there's no need for you … Oh, you are? Uh, Mom, I don't think that's such a … But, Mom, I'm really busy … No, of course I'm not too busy to see you and Dad … Okay, then, tomorrow night … six thirty … Pegasus … Yup, I know where it is … Okay, Mom. See you then … I love you too."

Quinn tossed the phone on the couch and sighed again. He walked over to the hallway mirror and looked at the scar on his forehead.

"They are going to love this," he said.

Quinn's parents, I said to myself. *This should be interesting.*

* * *

The next evening, Quinn left work and headed directly to Greektown to have dinner with his parents. I ghosted him into Pegasus. The backdrop of the restaurant was a painted scene straight from Greece—a fresco of white stucco buildings was painted across the entire back wall. It made me curious to see what the Greek Islands really looked like, and I decided to visit them the next time I "traveled."

Quinn saw his parents sitting at one of the tables pushed up against the painted backdrop. He took a deep breath, forced a smile, and walked over to them.

"Hi, Mom," Quinn said enthusiastically as he leaned over

to kiss her on the cheek. Mrs. Harrison was a petite woman with long black hair that was pulled up into a ponytail. She had bright blue-green eyes and beautiful alabaster skin. She was wearing a white Oxford that was unbuttoned just low enough to show off a large turquoise pendant hanging from a silver chain around her neck. She was quite attractive and youthful in appearance. In fact, I would have never guessed she had a son as old as Quinn.

"Hi, Dad," Quinn said, extending his hand towards his father, who was now standing. Smiling, his father grabbed Quinn's hand and then pulled him into his arms for a big hug. His father was built like a former college defensive line backer. He was a little taller than Quinn and about twice his size, taking into consideration his robust belly. He had salt-and-pepper hair and bright blue eyes. The crow's feet around his eyes and laugh lines around his mouth gave his age away. Quinn's father kind of reminded me of Teddy, except Mr. Harrison was a more low-key dresser, wearing a navy-blue polo tucked into jeans and brown leather loafers.

"So, my dear. *What* is going on with you?" Quinn's mother cut right to the chase. "We haven't seen or heard from you in weeks!"

"Nothing, Mom," Quinn responded as he sat down. "I told you I've been busy, that's all." He lowered his eyes as he spoke.

Hmm, I thought, *not a very convincing liar.*

"Quinny, I'm not buying it," his mom declared. "You don't think a mother knows her own children? You don't think I can tell when you are full of it? You haven't returned any of our calls or any calls from your brothers." Quinn's mother softened her tone. "Sweetheart, it's just so unlike you to pull away from us. We're worried about you. Is there something going on?" She lifted Quinn's head up towards her and then gasped.

"Oh, good Lord! Quinny—what happened to your fore-head?" His mother had just noticed the fresh, red raised scar on his forehead.

"Oh." Quinn touched the scar with his fingers. "It's noth-ing. Really. Someone tried to take my wallet."

"Tom, did you hear that? Quinn was mugged!" Quinn's mother looked towards her husband in alarm.

"Did you stop him?" Quinn's father joked, but he couldn't hide the concerned look on his face.

"Well, let's just say that I still have my wallet. And … I seem to have made a miraculous recovery." Quinn's eyes darkened for a moment and he grew quiet. I knew Quinn was thinking about me, but I also knew he wasn't about to tell his parents about our encounters. He forced a smile and then added, "I'm fine, really. No harm done."

"That's my boy," his dad said with pride. "See, Maggie—he's fine. He knows how to take care of himself." Looking back at Quinn, his dad asked. "Hey, did they catch the son of a bitch?"

"Tom, language please," Quinn's mother chastised.

"Mags, take it easy."

"Take it easy," she huffed. "Tom, our son almost got killed by some … hoodlum, and you want me to take it easy? I knew I should have insisted that Quinny live with us this summer instead of subletting that apartment downtown. I would feel so much better knowing he was home safe with us."

So would I, I seconded silently.

"Come on, Maggie, the boy is twenty years old. He's an adult. When we were his age, we were already married and waiting for the arrival of Tom, Jr."

"Times were different then, Tom."

"Not *that* different," his dad said. "Look, Quinny," he continued, turning towards his son, "obviously you've discovered firsthand that city living carries with it certain risks. This isn't like living at home—or in Bloomington for that matter. You have to have your wits about you all the time around here, okay?"

"Okay, Dad," Quinn replied. He seemed to genuinely appreciate his father's advice. Quinn took his mother's hand. "Mom, I like living in the city. I'll be more careful. I promise. Besides, I'll be back at IU before you know it." He squeezed his mom's hand lovingly, looked at her, and flashed a big smile. Her face softened immediately. She returned his smile and caressed his forehead.

"Ugh, you know I can't resist that smile of yours. You ought to have a warning label attached to that thing!" She took a deep breath and sighed.

"Good. So can we talk about something else now, please? I'm sick of focusing on my dull, uneventful life," Quinn said, chuckling in jest. "How's the rest of the family?"

His parents shot a knowing glance at each other. They had shared a similar look when Quinn arrived. I'd thought their exchange was nothing more than the concern of two parents who hadn't seen or heard from their son in a while. But now I could see there was something else—something about their family that they needed to discuss with Quinn. He also noticed the sobering glance his parents had shared and shifted uncomfortably in his seat.

"Mom? Dad? What is it?"

His mother went on to brief him about his oldest brother, Tom, Jr., and his wife, Samantha, who had just purchased their first house and would be moved in well before the arrival of their first child. Quinn smiled hopefully and asked whether they had found out if they were having a boy or a girl.

"Not yet. They should find out in a few weeks," his mother replied. She continued to explain that Tom, Jr. still worked for a small public accounting firm, but he was looking to move to a bigger firm downtown.

"Of course that would mean longer hours for Tommy, but it would also mean more money, which would allow Sam to quit her job and stay home full time with the baby," his mother added.

Then his mother updated Quinn on his second oldest brother, Doug, who was preparing to enter into his third year of law school at the University of Illinois. His mom added that both Tommy and Doug were upset with Quinn for blowing them off the other weekend when the three of them had plans to go to the Cubs game together.

"It's not like you to be that inconsiderate, Quinny," she said in a disappointed tone. "They are your *brothers*. You really should call them and apologize."

"Fine. You're right. I will." Quinn poked the food on his plate with his fork.

"And Brady?" he asked warily, changing the subject. "Have you heard from him?"

His parents stole another glance at each other. *Ah—there was something going on with his brother, Brady.*

"No, not recently," his father said, clearing his throat. Quinn's mother looked at her husband; I could see the distress in her eyes. "It's been about a month now."

"Last we heard, Brady was still in Vegas," his mom continued. "Quinny ... we cut off all contact with him."

"What? Why would you—" Quinn stopped short. He actually didn't seem all that surprised. Still, he shot his parents a look that told them he wanted an explanation nonetheless.

"Oh, Quinny," his mother cried, "you know why. Brady's gambling is out of control, and we can't handle the roller coaster ride anymore. Every time he calls it's to ask for more money. It's always another story about how he's on to the next big thing ... or how his bookies are looking for him, and if he doesn't give them the money he owes, they'll ..." Quinn's mother couldn't finish her sentence. She closed her eyes, rubbed her temples with her fingers, and took a deep breath.

"Sweetheart," his mother continued as she looked back at Quinn, "we just can't take it anymore. Brady has to hit rock bottom on his own before he will ever be serious about getting help. So we told him there would be no more assistance on our part—no more money, no more attempted interventions—and, in return, he wouldn't have to go through the motions of making promises he knows he can't keep."

"Quinn, we told Brady he can't come home until he's ready to give up gambling for good," his father added.

Quinn was silent.

"Quinny, say something, please," his mother begged.

"I hope he survives long enough to hit bottom." Quinn sounded bitter and sympathetic at the same time. "Look, I know that Brady is difficult, but don't give up on him yet, okay? Just don't write him off completely. He's still a part of this family."

"We're doing the best we can with him, Quinn," his father said.

"I know, Dad, I know. I just wish there was more *I* could do."

"There is," his father offered. "If he calls and asks you for money, do *not* give it to him—no matter how much he begs. You know handouts and loans don't do him any good—he just gambles the money away as soon as he gets it."

Quinn remained silent.

"Quinny," his mother wrapped her petite hands around Quinn's, "Brady knows that you're working this summer. He knows you have some extra cash. If he calls, promise us you won't let him manipulate you into giving him any money.

Please, sweetheart. Your father's right—Brady will just throw it all away. Promise us," she begged again.

Quinn still didn't say anything.

"Quinn?" his father chimed in.

"I promise," he agreed reluctantly.

The evening wrapped up, and Quinn's parents dropped him off at his apartment building before they headed back home. Quinn climbed the stairs slowly, opened his front door, and just stood in the open doorway for a minute. He dragged himself inside, set his computer bag on the floor by his closet, hung up his jacket, and emptied the contents of his pockets onto the breakfast bar. Then he walked over to his stereo and popped in a CD. The song Quinn played was intense, almost angry, and he played it loudly—very loudly. He collapsed onto the couch and just stared up at the ceiling, allowing the music to engulf him. Quinn let the music blare for a good fifteen minutes or so until his neighbor below started banging his ceiling up through to Quinn's floor.

"Hey! Turn the music down!" his neighbor screamed.

An annoyed expression crossed Quinn's face, but he got up and turned off the music. He just stood there for a minute with his hands on his hips before bowing his head slightly and shaking it with disapproval.

"Damn you, Brady," he muttered under his breath. He turned off all the lights and went to bed.

That night, my heart went out to Quinn and his family. Quinn was my priority; but I wondered if there was something I could do for the Harrisons as well. I wondered if there would ever be some way in which I could help his family.

20. Shell-Shocked

The next morning, Quinn was like a different person. He seemed more focused and determined. It was as if somehow the news about Brady had been some huge reality check for him.

There was no mention of me. In fact, there had been no mention of me at all in his sleep. And Quinn wasn't at all self-conscious about getting ready for work. I even found myself shielding my eyes for a good part of the morning to give him some privacy.

I wasn't the only one to observe Quinn's renewed sense of purpose; the partners at the firm noticed as well. That day, Quinn actively volunteered to shadow partners in meetings, he sought out research assignments, and spent the better part of the afternoon diligently sifting through boxes of documents stashed in a small, interior conference room commonly referred to as the "fishbowl," as three of the four walls were made entirely of glass. Every so often, Quinn would take a break and glance around. He seemed to be looking for someone.

Only when I saw her enter the fishbowl did I comprehend just who Quinn had been hoping to see. She looked like she had walked right off the pages of a fashion magazine. She was probably in her mid-twenties. She was tall and had long, light-brown hair that fell past her shoulders in thick waves of perfectly tamed curls. Her dark, hazel eyes complemented her golden skin. And her body was perfect—thin but curvy in all the right places. To top it off, her clothes and makeup were flawless; I wouldn't have been surprised if she had her own personal wardrobe and makeup assistants stashed away somewhere close by. I glanced back at Quinn and saw the look in his eyes. Clearly, I wasn't the only one taken by her beauty.

"Ashley, you're back," Quinn remarked.

"I am," she smiled at him. "That project in Philly took a lot longer than anticipated, but I got home last night. Hey, is it true that you were mugged while I was gone?" She sounded overly concerned.

"Well, technically, no—he never got anything from me."

"Well, are you okay? I hope you weren't badly hurt." She walked up behind him and innocently tousled his hair before walking across the room and sitting on the corner of the desk pushed up against the only opaque wall. "Ugh, I must be the worst mentor ever—leaving you high and dry for weeks at a time only to come back and learn that you got assaulted while I was away."

"Don't worry about it, Ash, it would have happened had you been here or not," Quinn commented. "It was destined to happen," he joked, without realizing that he'd just nailed the bull's-eye.

"Wow, you really *did* get hurt, didn't you?" she asked, sounding more genuinely concerned. She must have noticed his scar.

"Oh, yeah—that. It's no big deal, really." Quinn tried to sound as nonchalant as possible as he rubbed his left temple.

"Well, it *looks* like a big deal. I want to hear all about it tomorrow night. We're still on for dinner, right?" Ashley asked. "Of course, if you're still not feeling that well, we could always just stay in," she said seductively. Her eyes twinkled as she smiled at Quinn playfully.

Holy smokes! my mind screamed as I attempted to recover from the newsflash that had just slapped me across the face. *They're involved!* I was flabbergasted. Nowhere in my mind had I expected this turn of events. I felt like such an idiot. Of course they were involved! They were a perfect pair; her beauty rivaled his own. They were *that* couple, the couple everyone envied but secretly longed to be a part of.

"No, I could definitely use a night out. I've been cooped up in my place for so long I've started seeing things—not a healthy sign." Quinn chuckled and flashed his charming smile at her.

"No, definitely not. Let's go out. Do you want to leave straight from here—say around six?"

"Yeah, six should work."

"Okay, see you then." She winked at him and walked away.

I couldn't keep pace with the thoughts streaming through my mind. I suddenly felt wholly inadequate. Even with my immortal abilities, I was no match for her. Ashley was stunning. She was his mentor at work. More importantly, she was *alive*.

I was jealous, even though I knew I had no right to be. Quinn and I were not together nor were we meant to be together. He was supposed to forget about me. I had *wanted* him to forget about me ... to move on with his life. I just hadn't given a lot of thought as to what "moving on" really meant. I certainly didn't think it would mean having that siren make a move on him.

* * *

The next evening dragged on at an excruciatingly slow pace. Quinn and Ashley went to the Italian Village for dinner where they got seated in an intimate booth tucked away in a corner of the restaurant. Ashley smiled with satisfaction when the host seated them. I could see her scheming, planning out every last detail of their romantic night together.

If I'd known what was good for me, I would have left. I knew I could travel to the ends of the Earth twice and be back before they finished their appetizers. But I didn't leave. I couldn't tear my attention away from them for even one second. I studied her every move. I mentally cringed at Quinn's every reaction towards her. It was like watching some awful horror flick unfold. I could see the monster hiding around the dark corner. I could hear the bone-chilling music in the background. I just couldn't do anything to stop the impending massacre.

Ashley strategically sat next to Quinn rather than across the table from him. *Very smooth*, I thought as I mentally tallied a point in her favor. I gave Ashley another point every time she managed to slyly inch her way closer to him. She fed him some of her pasta, leaning into him so that her breasts brushed against his arm. Using her finger, she gently wiped the Alfredo sauce from the corner of his mouth and fed it to him—another point.

Ashley definitely wanted Quinn, and she was not at all shy about letting him know just how physically attracted she was to him. And Quinn seemed to be welcoming Ashley's advances. Yet, I couldn't help but notice some part of him seemed closed off—some small part of him was keeping her at bay. Ashley didn't notice, or if she did, she didn't look like she cared. She continued to confidently and expertly execute her seduction. She clearly had no doubts she would be spending the *entire* evening in Quinn's company—that was, until they left the restaurant.

Ashley was tracing the buttons of Quinn's shirt with her fingers as they waited outside for a cab. As one pulled up, Quinn opened the door for her.

"Please take us to the corner of Morgan and Adams," Ashley directed the cab driver as she stepped inside. She knew where Quinn lived, which could only mean that she had been to his apartment before. *Ugh.* An aching pain streaked through my mind.

"Um … Ashley," Quinn muttered somewhat uncomfortably, "I think maybe it would be best if you went back to your place tonight."

Ashley looked up at him, bewildered. *I* was bewildered. He wanted to go home *alone*. Relief mixed with a hint of joy swept through my mind.

"Why? Is something wrong?" Ashley asked, disappointed.

"No. It's just that I'm still supposed to take it easy for a little while longer," Quinn said, pointing to his forehead, "and I know I won't do that if you come over. In fact, my head is already starting to spin." He flashed her his seductive, charming smile, which seemed to placate her some.

"So … I make your head spin, do I?" Ashley smiled impishly at him and winked.

"Like you don't know." He returned her grin and leaned down and gave her a quick peck good night. Not letting him off that easy, Ashley pulled him towards her and kissed him passionately. My mind flooded with envy.

"Are you sure I can't change your mind?" she tempted.

"Oh, I'm pretty sure you could," Quinn replied, "but I'm still under doctor's orders … How about a rain check? Dinner will be on me next time—I insist."

"All right, but I'm going to hold you to it." Ashley sighed melodramatically as she smiled in partial victory. "Good night, Quinn."

"Good night, Ash," Quinn replied as he stepped back, closed the cab door, and knocked on the top of the car's roof to signal it was okay to drive off. He took a deep breath and sighed as he watched the cab get smaller and smaller in the distance. I knew that part of him wanted to be in that cab with her, and I mentally winced.

When Quinn walked into his loft, he hung his suit jacket up in the coat closet. He unbuttoned his Oxford and took it off, but before draping it over one of the dining room chairs, he brought the shirt up to his face and inhaled deeply. Ashley's perfume must have been lingering on it; he was taking it in, letting her scent invade his senses.

This was just too much to handle. I didn't know which was worse—knowing that Quinn wanted to be with her or that there was no chance he could ever be with me. I knew he and I would never be together. I knew that I could never offer him what a living, breathing woman could offer him. But I hadn't thought about him actually *wanting* someone else … wanting *her*. I hadn't thought about how it would make me feel. I certainly wasn't prepared to be emotionally twisted and ripped apart while I was forced to silently watch Quinn with another woman from the sidelines.

I teleported myself to Quinn's rooftop where I materialized into my human form and stretched; the hot summer breeze felt good. I even welcomed the smell of hot asphalt combined with the hodgepodge of aromas emanating from the exhaust vents of nearby restaurants and coffee shops. I anxiously paced the length of the deck until he fell asleep.

Did protecting Quinn honestly mean I had to stand by and suffer while I watched him with *her*? I already knew the answer was "yes." This was the job, whether I liked it not. That being the case, only two questions now remained. First, how much longer was this assignment going to last? And, second, just how much of Ashley was I going to have to endure?

I looked at my watch. The Incident Timer itself was still blank. It could be months—years, even—before the Second Incident occurred. I dropped my face in my hands. I felt like my body was being crushed from the weight of the misfortune bearing down on me.

I can't do this. I just can't, my mind rambled in a panic. *I'm getting in too deep. I'm sinking too fast.* I felt like I was suffocating. I had to find a way to breathe. I had to get away. I had to escape. I needed to go somewhere calm and peaceful to think things through clearly. Black sand beaches and ocean surf flashed through my mind. That was it—that's where I needed to be; that's where I *wanted* to be.

Instantly, I found myself on Wai'anapanapa Beach. The sun had set, and the stars were beginning to sprinkle their brilliant, twinkling lights across the young night sky. The moon was rising, casting its mystical glow across the water. I materialized into my human form and walked knee-deep into the water as I breathed in the salty ocean air. I closed my eyes and drank in the sounds of nature all around me, letting them drown out the noise of my own thoughts. I immediately felt more relaxed.

"This is quite a magical place … especially if you need to figure a few things out. Don't you agree, my child?"

Startled, I opened my eyes and turned my head around to see Agnes standing about fifteen feet from me at the edge of the shore. I noticed she was wearing a different linen pantsuit than the one she'd been wearing when I first met her.

"Yes, I do," I mumbled awkwardly, unsure if Agnes's previous invitation for me to return to this spot had been genuine or said out of sheer politeness. I hoped she wasn't upset that I had come back so soon.

"I'm sorry to bother you. I can leave if you would like to be here alone," I offered.

"Nonsense," Agnes responded, smiling. "It's wonderful to see you again, Eve. Besides, you look like you need this place more than I do at the moment. I can see something is bothering you. Would you prefer to be alone with your thoughts or would you like a friendly ear to listen to you?"

"Actually, I'd appreciate it if you could stay for a few minutes—that is, if you have the time." I didn't know how else to answer Agnes. I was glad to see her, but I wasn't sure I wanted to tell her anything.

"For you, my child, I'll make the time." She gave me another warm smile and extended her hand to help me out of the water.

Borrowed Heart

We walked the length of the beach arm-in-arm and sat down on some rocks near the shoreline. The moonlight bounced off Agnes's skin, making it glow like iridescent silk. She was a very elegant-looking woman. I took a second look at her new outfit. I surveyed my clothes only to realize I had been wearing the same white T-shirt and jeans for as far back as I could remember. As far as I knew, they were the only clothes I owned.

"How did you do that?" I asked Agnes curiously. "How did you change your outfit?" I knew my small talk was just a way to beat around the bush, but I wasn't ready to talk about Quinn just yet. Besides, I was intrigued by the idea of being able to expand my wardrobe.

"I just willed it," she replied. "It's much like teleporting; you picture what you would like to be wearing and then you simply *want* to wear it. The trick is remembering that it's all an illusion. The clothes you're wearing, the ones we're all wearing, are merely mental projections of ourselves—the way we want others to see us. Once removed, however, they disappear into thin air like magic ... like the illusion they really are." Agnes took off her blazer and let go of it. I watched it disintegrate before it ever touched the ground.

"See? ... And you can appear to be wearing anything you like whenever you wish." She closed her eyes for a brief moment and instantly her clothes shimmered, and she was wearing an exact replica of the T-shirt and jeans I was wearing.

"Wow." I laughed. "Something tells me you pull these rags off a lot better than I do."

Agnes shimmered back into her pantsuit, took my hand, and smiled at me. "Eve, did you really want me to stay with you so you could ask me about altering your wardrobe?" She cast me a knowing glance.

"No." I dropped my head down and sat there silently for a moment. I looked up at her. "It's just that ... Oh, Agnes, I don't even know where to begin," I said helplessly.

"Sometimes it helps to just start talking," she advised.

"Okay." I took a deep breath and exhaled, mustering up enough courage to tell her what had been happening. "I feel like I'm totally messing things up ... And I feel like I'm totally messed up." My eyes stung, longing for the tears I knew wouldn't come.

I opened up the floodgates and pretty much told Agnes everything, letting my emotions do most of the talking. I told her that Quinn had recognized me when I rescued him the first night of my assignment and how Peter had yet to find an explanation for this unexpected connection between Quinn and me. I told her that he'd been talking to me when he suspected he was not alone in his apartment ... how he had revealed things about who I was when I was alive. I told Agnes about the second time Quinn had seen me, how I had let my guard down after healing him a second time, how maybe I had *wanted* him to see me. And, I told her about how I had avoided any contact or communication with him ever since.

Then I told Agnes about Ashley and how awful it was to see her with Quinn ... to watch her seducing him. My skin crawled as I relived the evening in my head.

I confessed that deep down, *I* wanted to be the one to caress Quinn's face and trace its contours with my fingers. *I* wanted to be the one to tousle his hair ... to brush my body up against his and kiss his lips. I told her it wasn't just my physical attraction towards him that had gotten the best of me, but it was him—his random acts of kindness and his reactions to and feelings towards his family. And I told Agnes I couldn't help but feel as though there was something so hauntingly familiar about Quinn.

I admitted that I knew my feelings were irrational and ridiculous. I knew that allowing myself to entertain these notions was nothing but self-destructive. I knew that Quinn and

I could never be together.

"Still," I conceded, "knowing all of this—knowing that I can't be with Quinn, knowing that he wants to be with someone else, knowing that I'm now forced to sit back and watch him be with her—it doesn't change anything. I *still* want to be Quinn's Shepherd. I want to protect him—and not just because it's my job to keep him safe, but because I want to be near him ... close to him. I'm like a moth to a flame. Pathetic, isn't it?" I sighed.

"Agnes," I continued, before she could answer my question, "what if I'm already too close? What if I've crossed the line? What if ... what if I'm falling for him?"

"Did you ever think that maybe this isn't the first time?" Agnes asked.

"First time for what?" I asked, thoroughly confused.

"The first time you've had feelings for this young man," Agnes clarified.

"What are you saying?" I stammered, my eyes wide in astonishment.

"Did you ever stop to consider that maybe you already fell in love with Quinn once before while you were alive?" Agnes asked. "Have you ever considered that you aren't falling for him so much as you are reawakening the feelings you once harbored for him?"

I shifted my gaze towards the ocean while I tried to make sense of what Agnes was saying. Waves of excitement, hope, self-doubt, and anxiety were pounding my mind like the waves of the ocean crashing into the black, sandy shore.

"Eve, this is a delicate matter," Agnes explained. "Shepherds have been known to fall in love with their charges in the past—even without having a past mortal connection. You, on the other hand, apparently do have a history with Quinn. Even though you have no memory of him, your soul and your spirit obviously still do.

"It seems to me, Eve," she continued, "that your situation is further complicated by the fact that you were paired with a human who also possessed strong feelings for you before you died. And despite the fact that your life ended, fate somehow saw fit to draw you two together again—a consequence of which led you to rekindle your feelings for each other. There are rare cases where soul mates actually find each other in the afterlife; their souls survive death to be together for eternity.

"If Quinn and you are soul mates," Agnes went on, "well then, quite frankly, I'm not sure you could have avoided revealing yourself to him no matter how hard you tried. Indeed, knowing the Three Sisters—knowing *Aurelia*—I'm surprised you've been able to avoid him for this long." Agnes paused to chuckle softly. "If you two aren't destined to be together, if this is not a case of true love, then I don't know what is. And, let me tell you, I've seen a lot in my five-hundred-and-some-odd years."

"Why are you telling me this?" I asked, completely distraught. My mind was spinning a million miles an hour. Did she think this information made things easier for me? Did she want me to get in trouble? "Do ... do you want me to break the Rules?"

"No, of course not, my child," Agnes said in a reassuring voice. "I'm just saying that in life *and in death* things are often unpredictable. With that uncertainty comes untraveled roads, unforeseen choices ... and *inevitable exceptions*." She looked me in the eyes with raised eyebrows.

"Eve, I'm telling you that we *all* make mistakes—even Shepherds. But if the *reasons* underlying such mistakes are *pure* and *true*, then such mistakes *can* be forgiven." She paused for a moment before continuing.

"Take love for instance—there is nothing more pure and true than love." Agnes was staring intently into my eyes, trying to convey something through them that she couldn't—or wouldn't—admit verbally.

"Are you saying that it's okay for me to *break* the Rules if I truly love Quinn? That I will be forgiven?" I asked incredulously.

"No, my child, I am not saying that," Agnes clarified. "Truthfully, I don't know what will happen if you ignore or deliberately defy the Rules. And I cannot condone what you have done. In fact, if I were your mentor, I would counsel you to be very careful and to watch yourself. If I were your mentor, I would advise you to focus on your job and to refrain from having any additional contact with Quinn.

"But I am *not* your mentor." Agnes grinned. "So I can offer you a slightly different perspective. Hypothetically speaking, of course, *should* a Shepherd fall in love with a human and *bend* the Rules a bit for the sole purpose of furthering such a *true* love, that Shepherd may be forgiven his or her transgressions … *Peter was.*" She paused again, waiting for me to process her words.

That's right. Peter had fallen in love with a human and the Council had forgiven him. *Did Agnes really know a way for Quinn and me to be together?*

I looked at Agnes inquisitively. Why was she was telling me this? Why would she encourage me to bend, or possibly even break, the Rules? Particularly when the first time we met, she had hinted that Peter liked me. I searched her eyes for something disingenuous, but I could neither see nor feel anything but the sincerest of intentions.

"But I don't really need to be telling you any of this, do I?" she asked. "I suspect your mind was made up before you came here this evening. You're going to fight for him. You've already decided to test the Rules."

"If you really believe that, then why are you telling me all of this?" I asked. And, honestly, I had yet to decide what I was going to do.

"I'm a sucker for a good love story—always have been." Agnes flashed a big smile.

"But what about Peter?" I asked suspiciously.

"What about him?" She turned the question right back at me.

"Well, I thought … I mean … I've been told that Peter … that I'm …" I couldn't find the right words. Thankfully, Agnes quickly put me out of my misery.

"Peter is a big boy. He's fully capable of picking and choosing the battles he wants to fight. And when he does, he surely doesn't need any assistance from the likes of me." She chuckled.

"Eve, before you return to your knight in shining armor with high hopes, I do feel the need to warn you of something. Should you choose to pursue Quinn, the path you will no doubt find yourself on will be a long and difficult one. You will constantly be forced to walk a thin line between love and passion. You need to realize that acts of love and acts of passion, while often related, are *not* the same thing. To have any fighting chance of success, you will have to find a way to separate the two and act only out of love.

"I … I'm not sure I understand you. What do you mean by acting only out of love?" I asked, confused.

"Oh my!" Agnes laughed out loud. "You really are quite young, aren't you? Such a sweet child." She took both my hands in hers.

"Love is the truest and purest form of emotion that anyone can experience. Passion is also pure, but not purely emotional. Passion is the result of the human response to raw desire and sensuality. Love comes from the heart, but the root of passion comes from here." She made a circular motion with her hand over the lower part of her torso, from her belly to her loins.

"Love and passion can evoke the most intense feelings a *human* can experience," Agnes continued. "For *us*, these feelings can be overwhelming and extreme. As with our senses, our feelings are much more heightened and acute than any human's, making us particularly vulnerable to them. We have to be careful not to overindulge in our feelings for they can consume and, ultimately, betray us if we let them.

"Eve, as a Shepherd, it is crucial that you learn to identify and rein in whatever feelings you are experiencing at any given moment, especially feelings stemming from love or passion. Confusing the two, or losing control of yourself when experiencing such strong emotions or feelings, will signal the beginning of the end for you and Quinn."

"How do I control my feelings?" I asked, concerned. "How do I know which feeling is which?"

"It's not an easy task," Agnes responded. "And it's different for each individual involved. All I can tell you is that love and passion are often linked, but they are not inevitably intertwined. It is possible to feel one without the other—even romantically. And you must find a way to do that, Eve. You must find a way to recognize and isolate when you are feeling a moment of love and when you are feeling a moment of passion.

"Acting out of the love you feel towards another can mark the truest of all selfless and altruistic intentions," she explained. "On the other hand, acting out of passion often marks one's desire to satisfy one's own selfish and hedonistic pleasures … In other words, Eve, acting out of love is arguably justifiable; acting out of passion is not."

"Acting out of love is arguably justifiable, while acting out of passion is not," I repeated out loud, memorizing Agnes's words, etching them into my mind.

"Eve, I also feel it would be unfair of me to let you embark on this journey without letting you also know that there will be consequences if the Council determines that your actions, even if done out of true love for Quinn, are inexcusable. And believe me when I tell you, there *are* some things worse than death." A haunted expression crossed her face.

"Like what?" I asked uneasily.

"Just be careful, my child. Always keep in mind that the sum of your morals, your values, and your choices in life tipped the scale in favor of your soul being brought up to us to become a Shepherd. But your soul is still alive, and your future actions can tip the scales again. Angels have been known to fall ... and so have we."

Angels have been known to fall... and so have we, I repeated silently. Her words sent chills running down my spine.

21. The Big Reveal

It was about a half-hour before sunrise by the time I returned to Quinn's loft, and I knew his alarm would be going off soon. I walked into his bedroom and ever so carefully sat on the edge of his bed for a moment. My mind was buzzing. Was I falling for Quinn? Or was Agnes right? Had I already fallen in love with him once while I was alive? Did I dare entertain the idea that maybe we could be together? Did I dare fantasize about telling him who, or better yet, *what*, I was?

The questions themselves were enough to make me feel hopeful. Any optimism I felt, however, was tempered as it neared time for Quinn to go to work. I was sure Ashley was waiting for him. I pictured the two of them at dinner the night before; I remembered Quinn offering her a rain check. My stomach turned over.

If I did go through with this, if I did pursue Quinn, I suspected Ashley was not the type of girl who would quietly step aside for another to take her place. I would have to figure out some way to overcome this obstacle—but, thankfully, not today.

Ashley had to go to Los Angeles to consult with a client on a last-minute project and would be gone for at least a week. Relief washed over me. Maybe Aurelia did have her hand in this after all. With Ashley temporarily out of the picture, I was able to relax a little. There was no reason to jump the gun; there was no pressure for me to do anything rash. I could take my time and consider what Agnes had said. I could carefully weigh all the pros and cons before making my decision.

For the next couple of days, I maintained the status quo. I still kept my distance from Quinn. I didn't attempt to reach out to him in any way. Unfortunately, he didn't try to reach out to me either.

* * *

An electrical storm blew through Chicago just after eleven that Sunday evening. I could feel the static energy in the air; lightning, thunder, and rain were unleashed on the city with such a vengeance that it amazed even me. It was like the heavens themselves had opened their floodgates over this tiny little piece of Earth. Still invisible, I walked over to Quinn's bedroom windows to get a better view of the storm passing over the city.

Although asleep, Quinn was tossing and turning in his bed, and I assumed it was because of the storm. A streak of lightning blazed across the sky just above Quinn's building, followed closely by a loud crash of thunder. The booming noise woke him up. He flung his covers to one side, threw his legs over the edge of his bed, and sat there for a minute rubbing his eyes. Caught off guard, I froze, too afraid to move.

Quinn stood up, but rather than walk out into the hallway to the bathroom as I had expected, he walked right over to his bedroom windows. I tried to jump out of his way, but it was too late; Quinn passed right through me, leaving me tingling from head to toe. It was an indescribable feeling. It was as if he had reached out and touched my soul.

He stopped dead in his tracks. He sucked in his breath and closed his eyes.

Could he feel me too? I couldn't imagine any way he possibly could. I was in my ethereal state, I reminded myself. There was nothing tangible about me. But then Teddy's words repeated themselves in my head: *"We can't ever be wholly invisible to everyone."*

"Evie?" he asked cautiously.

Not again. I remained motionless.

"Evie?" He took a step backwards, reaching out with his hands, waving them slowly in the air. This time I managed to

244

slide out of the way and avoid him just in the knick of time. I still didn't answer him. I wasn't sure I was ready to at this point.

Quinn walked out of his bedroom into the hallway, and I followed him. He turned on the lights and looked around. When he didn't see me, he leaned his forehead against the wall opposite him in the hallway, hitting the plaster with his fist. Then he turned around and leaned back against the same wall before sliding down the length of it into a crouching position with his head in his hands.

"Evie, if you're here ... please let me see you," Quinn begged. "I want to see you. I *need* to see you." He waited a moment to see if I would appear, but I didn't.

"Evie, please don't do this to me. I feel like I'm losing my mind. I can't focus. I can't relax. Just help me out here. Give me *something* ... some sign to let me know that I'm not losing it ... that this whole thing ... that *you* ... weren't just some crazy hallucination." He paused again, waiting to see if I would answer his plea, but I couldn't—not yet.

"I keep going over it in my mind again and again," Quinn continued. "That night I was mugged ... and that night I healed so quickly ... And I keep seeing you standing in my room ... in this hallway. I keep thinking about you ... hearing your voice in my head. And now ... now it's like I literally just ... *felt* you." He looked up at the ceiling. I could see he was growing more and more frustrated.

"Look, I just want to know what's happening. I just want to know if you're real. I just *need* to know." He paused again, waiting for some response. When I still didn't answer, he shook his head.

"How can you be real?" he asked bitterly. "You're *gone*." He stood up hastily and ran his fingers through his hair. "Face it, Quinny, it's finally happened—you're losing your mind. You're officially going nuts."

Since becoming Quinn's Shepherd, I had committed to memory every detail of his beautiful face. I had memorized every expression, but I'd never seen him look like this. I had never seen him so distraught and upset. I wanted to go over to him and let him know that he didn't have to torture himself like this anymore ... that I was real. I wanted to *show* Quinn that I was real. There was a stirring in the pit of my stomach—the warm embers deep inside of me began to smolder.

I didn't know what came over me, but I began toying with the idea of doing something extremely stupid. This was the Pandora's Box Peter had warned me about, and I knew I was on the verge of blowing the lid right off of it.

Could I really trust Quinn with my secret? What if he couldn't handle the truth about me? I thought about Peter and Madeleine and how the truth had ripped them apart. What if Quinn didn't even want me in the same way I wanted him? I thought about Ashley ... and how Quinn looked at her.

I refused to allow myself to dwell on these questions for fear that I would lose my nerve. I sat down in the wingback chair I had come to call my own and materialized. I took a deep breath as every hair on my body stood on end, as every part of me tingled with both fear and excitement.

"I'm over here," I said out loud.

Quinn snapped his head up and looked at me.

"Evie," he whispered breathlessly. He practically leaped across the room to where I was sitting, like he was afraid I would disappear before he could get a closer look at me. He kneeled down in front of the chair, inches away from me, and stared at me. How easily I could get lost in his eyes; they were like the night sky just after dusk. Quinn didn't try to touch me, and I was thankful for that.

"Oh my God, it's you," he whispered. "It's really you. You're here. You came back. When you left Bloomington that day ... you know, the day of the car accident ... I had this feeling I'd never see you again. And then—"

"I'm sorry," I interrupted, "but I don't remember you." I said the words so curtly I was afraid Quinn would think I was being rude, but I had to take that chance. I was foolish enough to reveal myself to him, but I wasn't about to go breaking another Rule by finding out more details of my life—even inadvertently so. My nerves were already shot. I was kicking myself for having been so weak as to give in and let Quinn see me again. I had a sinking feeling that I had just made a mistake—a colossal mistake.

Quinn studied my face, my eyes for a minute. His smile disappeared and his brow furrowed.

"You're not kidding, are you?" he asked. "You really have no idea who I am. Huh, some impression I must have made on you," he said sarcastically, trying to mask his disappointment. I tried to put myself in Quinn's shoes and imagine my reveal from his perspective, and I felt more sympathetic.

"It's not your fault," I reassured him in softer tone of voice. "*All* memories of my life have been erased."

"Erased? Why?"

"My memories would only serve as a distraction, and it's crucial that I be able to stay clearheaded and focused."

"Focused on what?" he inquired.

"On my assignment," I responded.

"Your *assignment*? What assignment?" Quinn looked thoroughly confused.

"The details are not important," I said, avoiding his question.

"Not important, huh? Is that code for 'I'm not going to tell you'?" There was more than a hint of irritation in his voice.

"Quinn, it's not that I don't want to tell you. It's just that … I can't."

"You can't," he repeated.

"Honestly, you're not supposed to know *anything* about me. I'm taking a huge risk just by being here."

"What do you mean?" he asked.

"Let's just say that not too many people are very … accepting of me."

"Why?" he pressed. I realized he still didn't get it.

"Quinn," I frowned slightly, "need you really ask?" He sat there for second before it registered.

"Oh, you mean because you should be dead," he remarked.

"Not *should* be, Quinn. The *Evie* you knew *is* dead."

* * *

"Okay, so let me get this straight. You died in that car accident last winter, right?" Quinn asked, puzzled.

"Yes, I was told that I died in a car accident," I replied.

"And now you're like some sort of ghost—hey, are you an angel?"

The curiosity and excitement in his voice surprised me.

"It's complicated."

He looked utterly dissatisfied by my response.

Well, I thought to myself, *I've already gone this far; I might as well take another step closer to the edge of the plank*. I took a deep breath and exhaled slowly.

"Quinn, I don't really know how to explain all of this—in fact, it's still new to me," I began. "Even though I'm no longer a living, breathing mortal, I still *feel* more like a human than an angel or a ghost. Obviously, I can still look human, but I also can be, and often need to be, invisible … in an ethereal state. Nonetheless, I actually prefer to be in my human form. And memory loss aside, I still consider myself to

248

be human most of the time. In fact, I still experience many things the same way you do … well, almost the same way anyway … I mean … except for the *living* part," I said awkwardly. I flashed Quinn a crooked grin.

"So I can … touch you?" Quinn asked, intrigued.

"It's possible."

Quinn reached out for my hand, but I jerked it away just before he made contact.

"Why'd you do that?" Quinn looked up at me, confused and a bit offended.

"I said it was *possible*—not that you should," I stated. Actually, I was afraid of how Quinn would react if I let him touch me. What if I felt different than I used to? And I was afraid of my own reaction to his touch. I still needed to learn how to control my emotions—my impulses. I remembered what Agnes had told me—acting out of love was one thing, acting out of passion was something completely different … something wholly unacceptable. I had to proceed slowly; I needed time to absorb the aftershocks that no doubt would follow what I had just done.

"Look, we need to take this one step at a time … Our situation is a little … unique. Apparently, you seemed to have known me when I was alive, but I don't remember you. I don't even remember *me*. That said, I can assure you that I'm not the Evie that you once knew. And I don't want to mislead you into thinking that I am. For one thing, my name is *Eve*.

"And," I continued, "despite the temptation of wanting to learn about my past, I just can't. So please don't tell me anything about myself when I was alive. It's just too risky. I won't be able to do what I need to do if I'm bogged down with those kinds of distractions." I paused for a moment. "Quinn, I'm asking you to please promise me that you won't tell me anything about my past."

"Wait a minute," he said in disbelief. "You have no idea who you are because your memory was somehow erased. And, even though I can fill in a few gaps and answer some of the questions you may have about your life, you're honestly telling me that you don't want me to tell you *anything* about yourself?"

"In a nutshell, yes. It's for your own good."

"For *my own* good?" Quinn asked, confused, before he started firing off questions. "Okay, what's going on? Why are you really here? Why did you show up that night when I was getting mugged? What were you doing out there? Trying to save me or something?"

"Excuse me? *Trying* to save you?" Now I was the one who was mildly offended. "Um, I think you can give me a little more credit than that—the guy would have killed you if it wasn't for me!"

"Maybe he wouldn't have snatched my wallet away from me so easily if you hadn't distracted me. Did you ever think of that?"

"Quinn, if you believe that, then you really *are* losing your mind," I snapped.

"Whoa there, Miss Feisty!" Quinn spit out as he laughed. "I must say, you sure *sound* like the old *Evie* to me."

Feisty. I backed down, caught off guard by what Quinn had said. Teddy had used that exact word to describe me, and although Teddy hadn't known me for all that long, he had to be able to read people fairly well given that he had been around them for centuries. Quinn, on the other hand, was a twenty-year old college student. What in the world did he know about people? Quinn's choice of words made me wonder just how well he had known me.

Our eyes met and we held each other's gaze. His deep blue eyes darkened to the color of midnight, and I noticed the expression on his face change. It made my stomach stir with excitement. I quickly cleared my throat, interrupting the moment.

"Quinn, this is serious. I have to stay focused on my assignment."

"*Your assignment*," he teased. "*Right.*"

I was surprised by how quickly Quinn was able to fluster me, but he did. In fact, his mocking infuriated me.

Fine, I said to myself, *if he thinks this is all a joke, let's see how much humor he finds in this bit of information.*

"I'll have you know," I stated arrogantly, "that my assignment … is *you.*"

"What?" That was enough to grab Quinn's attention.

I knew I should have fought the urge to tell him, but I suspected he would find out the truth sooner or later. Besides, judging by how he seemed to be taking all of this in such stride, maybe a little reality check was in order.

"I'm here to protect you from getting hurt, to protect you from other dangerous encounters like the attack."

"So you're supposed to be like, what, my guardian angel?" Quinn half-stated and half-inquired.

"If that's the way you want to look at it—then, sure."

"Am I still in danger?"

"Someone seems to think so."

"My own personal angel," Quinn teased as he flashed me that smile—that amazing, heart-melting smile.

"Hey, don't go letting this feed your already over-inflated sense of self. I'm far from the only one of my kind."

"Then why are *you* here to protect me?"

"What—you don't think I can protect you?" I asked defensively. "Haven't I proven myself to you once already?"

"No, it isn't that," Quinn said quickly. "I just think it's a little weird that your memory was erased so you wouldn't remember your life, but then you were assigned to protect me—not that I mind that it's you, of course, because I don't—trust me." His eyes sparkled and he flashed me that amazing smile of his. "I mean, when I first met you, I thought you were—"

"Please, no personal information about me, okay?" I reminded him.

"Okay," he agreed reluctantly, frowning.

"And, in response to your original question, it wasn't supposed to happen like this. Yet, here I am, standing before you, charged with protecting you."

"Are you saying that your being assigned to me was a *mistake*?" Quinn asked.

"It's not clear." I was divulging too much information. What was I talking about? I had already said way too much. I could probably get my immortal abilities stripped for the next five centuries based on my actions in the last twenty minutes alone! "Look, Quinn, I think it's safe to say I have now told you considerably more than you're supposed to know. I have to ask that you please not tell anyone about me ... or about your—*our*—situation."

"Back in my life for five minutes and you're already asking me to make *two* promises. I don't know about this," Quinn joked.

"This is not a joking matter." I shot Quinn a glance that said I meant business.

"Okay, so let me just run through the highlights: I now *know* that there is indeed life after death—case in point: *you* sitting here in my apartment. And, even though we knew each other while you were alive, you have no recollection of your past and you *don't want* to know about it. You're here to protect me because I am apparently in some kind of danger, although I have no idea what kind. And I'm not supposed to tell anyone about *any* of this. Does that about cover it?"

I nodded affirmatively.

"Don't worry. I'm not about to breathe a word of this to

anyone. I mean, what would I say? Who would even believe me? I've been acting weird enough lately; I don't want to end up locked in some padded room somewhere. I mean, I'm not sure I even believe all of this; you could simply be a dream." He suddenly looked lost and unsure of himself.

"Quinn, I know my being here has to be blowing your mind. I would have trouble believing it if I were in your shoes. I want to try to help you understand what is going on, but I'm just not sure of the best way to do that. I can promise you, however, that this is *not* a dream and that you *are* in need of protection."

"And you?" he asked. "Are you a dream?"

Against my better judgment, I reached out and touched Quinn's hand. Electricity surged through my fingertips the instant we made contact, but he didn't flinch or try to move. He just looked down at my hand resting on top of his own. The electric current raced up my arm. I held my breath not knowing how much longer I could fight the urge to move closer towards him. I lifted my hand off of his, leaving only the wake of the tingling sensation rippling through me. Quinn kept gazing at his hand.

Proof enough, I thought.

"So you won't tell anyone about this evening, about anything that has to do with me or why I'm here?"

"I promise—scouts honor." He flashed his huge, beautiful smile and held up his hand like he was a boy scout. "But don't expect me to call you Eve. You were, and you always will be, *Evie* to me."

"Fair enough," I conceded. It was a small price to pay for him to keep my secret, my anonymity. Besides, I believed Quinn wouldn't tell anyone about me regardless of my concession. Though I had no real reason to trust him with protecting my identity, I did. That said, I wasn't so sure about my other request. I wasn't sure he would respect my desire to remain in my current state of amnesia.

"And what about my first request—that you promise not to tell me anything about me or my life?"

"Are you sure you don't want me to tell you *anything*?"

I shot Quinn a stern look.

"Yeah, fine, that one too," he agreed unwillingly.

"Thanks," I said sincerely. The truth, however, was that I did want to find out something.

"Um, Quinn, before you make good on your promises, I do feel like it's important for me to know one thing."

"I knew it!" he declared triumphantly.

"Just this one thing and that's it. Then the promises kick in."

"Shoot."

"Well, uh," I stumbled, "I have no idea about us ... or ... if there ever was an *us*. Could you just tell me in what way ... I mean if ..." I cleared my throat, rephrasing the question in my mind before spitting the rest of it out. "Were we ever ... *involved*?" I felt like an idiot for asking, and the pleased look that crossed his face did not do much to reassure me.

"Are you asking whether our relationship was ever more than platonic?" Quinn's patronizing smile was almost more than I could bear—I was humiliated enough as it was. But his playful expression was soon replaced by a dark, stormy look in his eyes.

"I wanted it to be. And I honestly believed you did too. But there was an ... obstacle of sorts. And then you were gone."

22. Reunited

Quinn would only go back to sleep that evening after I promised him I would be there when he woke up. True to my word, I was sitting in "my" chair before his alarm went off, and watched as he groggily stumbled across the hall from his bedroom to the bathroom. As if the events of the prior evening had just resurfaced in his mind, he stopped mid-step to the bathroom and glanced in my direction. When he saw me, he flashed me a funny little grin, which made him look goofy and sweet when combined with his out-of-control bed head.

* * *

"So how does this work?" Quinn asked. He was dressed in a charcoal grey, pinstriped suit, stuffing documents into his computer bag.

"How does what work?" I asked.

"You know—*you* ... *this*. What do you do when I'm at work? Can you leave this apartment?" he asked curiously.

"Yes, I can leave this apartment," I scoffed. Not wanting Quinn to think of me as a stalker, however, I answered his first question more vaguely. "I like to travel. In fact, I can go anywhere in the world I want to in a flash. But I'm always just a thought away. So if you ever want me—"

Almost immediately, I saw a playful twinkle appear in his eye.

"Let me rephrase that," I said, smirking, "if there's ever a time when you *need* me, if you're ever in trouble, I'll be there."

"So you'll be here when I get back?" Quinn asked somewhat tentatively.

"I guess that all depends ... do you still want me to be here?" I asked just as hesitantly. A part of me was afraid he had changed his mind overnight.

"I can't believe you even have to ask." He sounded so insulted.

"Quinn, you have to admit that my being here—my existence—is pretty strange at best. I would understand completely if this was too much for you to handle. I mean, this isn't a test; I'll do my job whether you want me here or not. You don't have to make this some personal quest to see how far you can push the boundaries of what your mind is willing to accept."

"Evie, you obviously have *forgotten*, but I'm not one to walk away from a challenge—especially if that challenge involves you." He smiled at me and my insides melted. I was thankful to be sitting, afraid my knees would have given way had I been standing.

"Okay then," I said weakly, "I'll be here when you get back."

Quinn smiled at me once more before he walked out of the apartment.

He wanted me to stay. I couldn't stop smiling. It took me a moment to collect myself before I phased out and ghosted him to work.

* * *

The next few days were much the same. I would say good night just before Quinn went to bed, leave his apartment, and hang out on his rooftop until I knew he was asleep. At night, I mostly strolled the city streets, Lincoln Park Zoo, Grant Park, and the bike path along Lake Michigan. Having now visited several other cities around the world, I had come to appreciate Chicago; it was beautiful, charming, and friendly—qualities I had thought were absent in most cities this size. I wished I could have walked around the city during the daylight hours so I could feel the sun on my face and the energy of the city buzzing all around me.

I would return to Quinn's apartment just before his alarm went off in the morning, sit in my chair, and wait for him to walk out of his bedroom, only to resume my phantom-like state during the day, invisibly observing him while he was at work.

Quinn kept to his daily routine at the office but seemed to grow increasingly more anxious towards the end of the day. Instead of volunteering to stay late to rummage through boxes of documents, he would duck out of the office or take a short online research project that he could complete at his apartment. Instead of stopping off to pick up dinner on the way back, he would order it for delivery. And, instead of spending the extra few minutes talking to Ronald outside the nearby convenience store, he would give him a few dollars, apologize, and tell him that he had to run home. Then he would race up the stairs to his apartment, and a look of relief would cross his face as soon as he saw me waiting for him in the wingback chair that faced the front door. I had to admit, it was very cute.

Careful not to touch on any off-limit topics of conversation, we kept the subject matter of our conversations pretty light and superficial, sticking mainly to "how was your day" stuff and current events. Occasionally, he would offer me some of his dinner but wouldn't pry when I politely declined. We would watch TV together, and he would usually defer to me when it came to picking the evening's tube entertainment, which ultimately meant a lot of the Discovery Channel.

During Quinn's lunch hour that Friday, he picked up a handful of major newspapers and a bunch of magazines, everything from *Newsweek* to *Us! Weekly*, and "surprised" me with them later that night before he went to bed.

"I thought you might get bored while I'm at work or at night when I'm sleeping, so I got these for you to read. If there's anything you like, or if you want something else, just let me know and I'll get it for you."

"Thanks, that was really considerate of you." I smiled at Quinn's kind gesture. I didn't have the heart to tell him that I had watched him buy the magazines earlier in the day. I also didn't want him to worry about me; I wasn't his concern.

"You know," I added, "I can find plenty of ways to entertain myself. Take last night for instance—I went to Rome. I wanted to see the Pantheon." Strange as it might seem, looking at Ceres standing not far from Quinn's office window day after day had made me want to feel closer to the gods while here on Earth.

"You went to *Rome?*" he asked, shocked.

"Yes." I was amused by his reaction. It reminded me of my own disbelief when Teddy was teaching me the art of teleportation. "It was really quite easy," I teased in a nonchalant tone.

"Oh, sure—for an *angel*," Quinn teased back.

"Hey, there have to be a few perks to my job. Otherwise, what fun is it to be the walking dead?" I winced a little as soon as the words "walking dead" escaped my lips. Quinn looked as uncomfortable as I felt.

"Sorry," I apologized. "I shouldn't joke like that."

"No, it's not that, Evie. It's just that ... even though you don't remember who were you, you still *say* a lot of the same things you used to say ... Even your mannerisms are the same." Quinn looked down at his hands and then at me. "But our relationship, if that's what you call this, is *so* different. I'm walking around on eggshells—and so are you. I *know* you are, so don't even try to deny it. And that's *not* like you or me— and it definitely wasn't like *us* ... even for the short period of time we were together."

"Quinn," I broke in.

"Wait," he said firmly. "Please just let me get what I have to say off my chest."

I closed my mouth, leaned back in the chair, and let him continue.

"Evie, I don't know what to do here." Quinn crouched down in front of me. Instinctively, I pulled back a little, afraid that he would try to touch me. He noticed my reaction and sighed in frustration.

"Evie, you *still* can't remember anything? About yourself? About me? Not even in the slightest?" he asked. I could feel his heart begin to pound a little faster, and it made me nervous. Quinn's eyes grew dark, but the expression on his face was not one of desire; it was more reminiscent of someone who was suffering.

"No," I replied matter-of-factly.

Quinn bolted up, walked into the kitchen, and grabbed a bottle of water from the fridge.

"God, I can remember it all like it was yesterday," Quinn said, exasperated. "It practically was yesterday! And right now, all I want to do is pick up where we left off. But I can't. I'm not exactly sure *why* I can't, but I know that I can't. So, instead, I'm resigned to sit on a couch and act like some freaking choirboy. Hell, at this point, just holding your hand would be a major step forward for us … This really sucks."

"Quinn, I'm sorry. I can't begin to imagine how frustrating this is for you. It was selfish of me to reveal myself to you." All of a sudden I remembered Agnes's warning that acts of passion are often the mark of selfishness, and I cringed inside, wondering if my letting Quinn see me was really about satisfying my needs rather than his. "Maybe … maybe this was a bad idea. Maybe I should go." I stood up to leave.

"No! Don't!" He leaped over the couch to block my way, spilling water all over himself in the process. "Damn it!" he exclaimed when he looked down and discovered he was wearing most of his drink.

"Wait there! *Don't—go—anywhere!*" he commanded. I just stood there, amazed at how quickly he'd cleared the couch to get to me. Quinn put the bottle down, pulled off his shirt, and used it to wipe off his chest and stomach before tossing it onto the floor. I stared in awe at the muscles that rippled beneath his chest, his shoulders, his stomach, and his arms. I thought back to the first time I'd seen his body, battered and bruised from the attack, and how I had healed it. I remembered how I had indulged myself by caressing him while he slept. My insides began to ache. It took all my strength to stop myself right then from reaching out and touching him. I swallowed—hard.

"You can't just mysteriously reappear in my life one day and then unilaterally decide to take off at the slightest whim." His voice cracked. "It's not fair for you to screw with me like that." He took a deep breath to calm down. "This … thing we have—it can't be solely on your terms. We're in this together, okay? We have to play this out as a team." He looked for some kind of sign that I accepted his terms.

"Quinn, I can't promise anything."

"Just do me a favor and at least try, okay?"

"Okay. I'll try."

"I guess that's the most I can ask for," Quinn muttered in dissatisfaction. I knew he wanted more from me—a pledge that I wouldn't disappear out of the blue and abandon him, and he deserved as much. But his wish was impossible for me to grant. One day my assignment would be over. One day I would have to leave.

"I know the Rules suck, but they're the Rules I have to follow. I can't change them."

"Yeah, well some Rules are meant to be broken," Quinn said, sulking.

"Please try to understand, I've already risked too much by revealing myself to you and telling you why I'm here."

He just stood there without saying a word. Of course Quinn didn't understand. How could he when even I had trouble adjusting to the Rules and to my "life" as a Shepherd. But I did understand there were consequences, potentially dire ones, for those of us who got caught breaking the Rules.

Just then my watch beeped three times. I looked down and saw that the Incident Timer was flashing as numbers raced across the screen like a slot machine in motion.

Crap! I thought. *The Second Incident.*

"What was that?" Quinn asked apprehensively.

"Um, it's nothing you need to worry about." I saw the look on his face and knew he didn't believe me. "Quinn, there's no need to look so worried—really. I just have to go find someone and talk to him for a minute."

"Now? Evie, it's late." Quinn sounded so overprotective I had to smile.

"And here I thought *I* was the one who was supposed to be concerned about *your* welfare—not the other way around," I said, still smiling.

"I did mention we were a team, right?" His face brightened up a bit.

"Quinn, I'll be back," I said reassuringly.

"Promise?"

"Scouts honor." I flashed him the most enthusiastic smile I could muster and held up my hand just like he had days before, which made him laugh.

"Well, you'd better hurry because I'm going to wait up for you—just to be sure you keep your promise."

"Quinn ... you really don't have to do that. I might be gone most of the night."

"Hey, I have nothing but time—tomorrow's Saturday. I'm sure there's some kind of movie marathon on tonight."

"Okay, then. Have fun with that." I just shook my head at him, knowing there was no way to talk him out of his plan.

Even though I could have just teleported myself out of his apartment, I didn't. I tried to appear as human as possible in front of Quinn. The last thing I wanted to do was highlight my immortal side any more than I already had. I didn't want him to think of me or treat me differently than he would any other human—well, any other *girl*. So I walked over to his front door and opened it. I glanced back at him and noticed how uneasy he suddenly looked.

"Evie ... promise me you'll be careful." Instantly, a moment of *déjà vu* hit me. Puzzled, I studied Quinn's face for a moment.

"What is it?" he asked.

"It's just that ... I feel like you've—" I stopped and smiled to myself, feeling pretty silly. "I'm sure it's nothing. I'll see you in a little bit ... And try to get some sleep!"

I heard Quinn chuckle as the door closed behind me.

* * *

"Peter!" I whispered as loudly as I could from Quinn's rooftop. I had teleported myself up there and resumed my human form so Peter would be able to see me—that is, if he could hear me. Now that Quinn's Incident Timer had begun to run, I didn't want to take the chance of leaving Quinn's side to go to the Archives. Plus, Shepherds couldn't read each other's minds on Earth. Here, my thoughts were truly my own, and I didn't want to take the chance that Peter, or anyone else for that matter, would discover what I had been up to.

"Peter! I really need you," I said a little louder. "Quinn's Incident Timer is going haywire, and I don't know what to do. Please, I need to talk to you!"

"It's been a while, Bo Peep." I heard Peter's voice from behind me, and I turned around to see him standing there smiling at me. "Still having trouble with your sheep?"

"Peter!" I exclaimed. I was so happy and relieved to see him that I ran over and jumped into his arms.

"If I knew you would be this happy to see me, I would've come and visited you sooner," Peter responded as he was forced to catch me before I slammed right into him.

"Well, you *should* visit more often." I pouted. "It can get lonely down here, especially at night, and I could use a little company from time to time."

"You know you're always welcome to drop by the Archives."

"Hey, you're the one who told me I couldn't leave Quinn's side unless it was *absolutely necessary*," I reminded him.

"Yes, but I didn't realize you would take my words so literally."

"Well, you really freaked me out during my last visit up there." It was true, Peter was usually the epitome of self-control, or at least he always looked the part. But the last time I'd seen him, he was so preoccupied and distraught.

"Well, I apologize for my demeanor during our last encounter." Peter bowed his head a little. I would have sworn he was a little embarrassed.

"So," he said more lightheartedly, "what has you howling my name from the rooftops in the middle of the night?"

"Very funny!" I snapped. "Look at my watch. It looks like the Second Incident is being planned as we speak. See?" I shoved my watch within an inch of his face. "The month and year are set, but the day is still unclear."

"Interesting. The exact date of the Incident must still be in flux. It happens occasionally. For example, your charge could be planning a trip and is yet unsure of the exact date of departure or arrival." He continued to examine my watch.

263

"But, whatever the day, the Incident isn't scheduled to occur until November of this year—that's months away. So I wouldn't worry too much right now. We have plenty of time to figure out what's going on."

"*We* have plenty of time to figure out what's going on?" I repeated hopefully.

"Eve, you know I'm always here for you. I'll help you out in any way I can."

"I know. It's just good to hear you say it," I said, feeling much more self-assured knowing that I had Peter's support.

"So," Peter asked slowly, "does he know?"

"Does who know what?" I tried to sound innocent, but so much had happened over the last several days, I didn't dare try to guess the particular thing to which Peter was referring.

"Does *who* know *what*," Peter repeated in exasperation. "Your sheep—that's who! Does he know about you? Has he seen you again?"

"Do you really want to know the answer to that?"

"I'll take that as a 'yes.'" Peter said, disappointed. "What am I going to do with you?" He sighed. "Eve, *please* think long and hard about the decisions you are making—or are about to make. And please take care of yourself. The expression 'playing with fire' takes on a whole new meaning for us." He walked up to me, embraced me, and gave me a kiss on top of my head. "Keep an eye on your watch and let me know if anything changes. And call me if you need me." He took a step back and winked at me before he dematerialized right in front of my eyes.

I wanted to heed Peter's warnings. There was still time to reverse some of the damage I had done. I could go back and somehow make Quinn believe that I was ordered to stop seeing him, or that I was reassigned even. But all I could think of was that my days with him were numbered—literally. We had a handful of months until his Second Incident. Assuming I saved him, who knew how quickly after that the Third Incident would occur.

I returned to the apartment only to discover Quinn already fast asleep on the couch. All the lights were on, as was the TV. I smiled to myself as I took a mental snapshot of this moment.

23. A Walk in the Park

The next day was beautiful; the sun was shining and there wasn't a cloud in the sky. Quinn had opened the windows in his apartment earlier that morning, and I could feel the cool breeze that had come off the lake and wound itself through the corridors between the buildings downtown before making its way to the West Loop.

I stared longingly out one of the windows of Quinn's loft. I was antsy; I felt like a caged tiger at the zoo pacing back and forth in its "cell." I wanted to walk outside. I wanted to feel the sun's warmth radiating above me.

"It's a beautiful day out," Quinn said.

"Mmm," I mumbled in agreement.

"It's not right to be cooped up inside on a day like this."

"I agree," I said and turned towards him. "Why don't you go out and enjoy the day. I'll be back here when you return." Of course, I would ghost Quinn the entire time, but it wasn't the same thing as being outside in my human form. I wouldn't be able to feel the warmth of the sun or smell the summer air.

"That's not what I meant." He moved towards me. "Evie, I want to take a walk outside *with you*." He drew out the last two words for emphasis.

"Excuse me?" I asked in disbelief.

"You heard me. I want us to take a walk *together*. We're always stuck inside here. I think a change of scenery will do us some good."

He was right; I would love a change of scenery. Still, as tantalizing as his idea sounded, the thought of actually walking around with him in plain sight made me nervous.

"Quinn, I'm not so sure that's a good idea," I said cautiously.

"Why not? Am I in imminent danger?" he asked calmly,

266

like he already knew he wasn't.

"No, not that I'm aware of," I replied. The Incident Timer on my watch had finally settled on the end of November, a couple of days after Thanksgiving.

"Okay, then, let's go. C'mon, just a short walk—that's all I'm asking," Quinn pushed.

I just stood there, visibly hesitating.

"What—is it against the Rules for you to take a walk outside?" Quinn asked.

"What if someone recognizes me?"

"Hold on." Quinn grabbed a Cubs baseball hat from his coat closet and his sunglasses from the kitchen counter and placed them both on me. He stood back to survey his work. "Perfect! No one will recognize you with these on." He seemed very pleased with himself, clearly believing that he had single-handedly deflated my argument in one swift blow. I took off the hat and glasses, looked at them, and then glanced back at him, my face still riddled with concern.

"Come on. Just try it," Quinn said, sensing my continued reluctance. "If you're still uncomfortable after a few minutes, we'll turn around and head back here. I promise." He flashed me that irresistible smile of his, and I found myself giving in.

"You know, you should be required to carry a license for that smile of yours," I said.

"That's funny," he chuckled. "My mom says almost the same exact thing."

I know, I thought to myself. *And she's right.*

"So are we going to do this or what?" he pressed, still smiling at me.

"Okay, okay," I conceded. "I'll take a *short* walk with you. Just give me a minute." I stood up and walked into Quinn's bedroom, closing the door behind me. I put on the hat and glasses and stood in front of his full-length mirror. I gave myself a once-over and realized that I *still* had been wearing the same T-shirt and jeans that I had worn from day one. I remembered what Agnes had told me, and I morphed myself into a pair of light-khaki cargo pants and a black tank top. I looked at myself again in the mirror. *Hmm ... black—the color of death. Nope, that won't do.* Instantly, I changed the color of my top from black to a shade of blue barely lighter than the color of Quinn's eyes.

"Much better," I announced out loud when I looked in the mirror again. Then I morphed my hair into two pigtails at the base of my neck and put the Cubs hat back on my head, adjusting the strap for a better fit. Last but not least, I put on Quinn's sunglasses. I glanced at myself once more in the mirror and shrugged my shoulders. It would have to do. I walked out into the hallway towards him.

"How ... how did you do that?" he asked in amazement.

"Do what?" I asked, feigning ignorance. I knew he was baffled by my wardrobe change.

"Change your clothes? Do you have some stuff stashed away in here?" Quinn quickly scanned his apartment trying to find anything that stood out or didn't belong to him.

"Nope. Just another one of my many talents." I stifled a giggle.

"Oh, come on. You've got to tell me how you did that. Better yet, why don't you *show* me," he teased as his eyes sparkled with mischief.

"You would like that, wouldn't you! Well, sorry to disappoint, but it's not going to happen. Magicians never reveal the secrets behind their tricks," I replied, just as playfully.

"Something tells me that you will never reveal all your secrets to me." I could hear the edge in his voice.

"Look, Quinn, it's not that I don't want to ..." My voice trailed off momentarily. I looked down at the floor of his loft, avoiding his face.

"I know … don't worry. I'm getting pretty used to hearing that response."

Inside, I cringed. I was doing exactly what I didn't want to do—upset him. But this was the way it had to be—the only way it could be, whether he liked it or not.

"Come on, let's go outside. The day is slipping away," I said, changing the subject. Quinn's face brightened as he remembered his initial goal of taking a walk with me. He looked me over once more and then flashed me a little grin.

"Um, Evie, you might want to put on a pair of shoes," he remarked.

"Oh! Right." I ran back into his bedroom and re-emerged wearing a pair of sandals. Quinn just shook his head back and forth and smiled at me in wonderment.

* * *

We headed east from his apartment into the Loop; it was like a ghost town. The only signs of life were the occasional car or pedestrian.

"Wow," I remarked. "It's hard to believe that this place was teeming with life just yesterday."

"I know. Pretty amazing, right? I guess people avoid the place they work like the plague on the weekends if they can help it," Quinn commented.

When we reached Grant Park, I quickly realized why nobody was downtown. There were softball games to the south; people meandering about Buckingham Fountain ahead of us; music being played to the north; and boats, hundreds of them, out on the water. The scene was so picturesque. I turned around, admiring the skyline behind us. By all standards, no one could deny that Chicago was impressive.

There were no buildings to shade me from the sun. I looked up and felt its rays beaming across my face and my arms. It felt amazing. I took a deep breath, inhaling the hot summer air and the smells around me. I looked at Quinn and noticed that he was observing my reaction. He smiled.

"I told you this was a good idea," he said smugly.

"What can I say—when you're right, you're right," I admitted.

We walked through Grant Park and up north along the lakefront. I watched people playing Frisbee, running, biking, and rollerblading. Men and women were playing in beach volleyball tournaments. Children were digging holes in the sand, building sandcastles, and frolicking in the water. And couples were walking hand-in-hand.

I saw one especially cozy young couple walking with their arms around each other's waists. The couple stopped momentarily in the middle of the bike path to give each other a sweet little kiss and stare affectionately into each other's eyes. I looked up at Quinn; he had noticed the same couple. He looked at me longingly for a second. I knew seeing the couple was like a slap in the face for him, reminding him of what he couldn't have with me.

"Quinn," I began somberly, but he didn't let me finish.

"I know. *You can't,*" he said bitterly.

I hated when he threw my own words back at me. He sounded angrier than ever. I couldn't let him stay this upset; it wasn't fair. He deserved a better explanation.

"Don't you think I wish we could be like that couple? Don't you think I would love to have the freedom to hold your hand? To hug you? To kiss you?" My body tingled a little at the very thought.

"How in the world would I know that, Evie?" He maintained control of his voice, but I could tell he was angry. He kept on walking, looking straight ahead. "You flinch every time I get close to you—like I'm some kind of creep," Quinn continued. "And, other than putting your hand on mine *once,* you haven't said or done *anything* to indicate that you're even the slightest bit interested in me. So, tell me, Evie ... please explain just how I'm supposed to know what you think about me or how you feel about me." He stopped and turned towards me. "Just how long do you expect me to sit back and wait ... hoping that you'll remember me?" he demanded.

I didn't know what to say. What *could* I say? That I felt a rush every time I said his name? That the very thought of him touching me sent shock waves surging through me? That I couldn't wait until we were alone in his apartment so I could spend time with him? That I didn't have to remember him to know I was in love with him?

I wanted Quinn to know all of it—everything—but I would be crossing too many lines already drawn in the sand. Not to mention how unfair it would be to him. How could I justify being so selfish as to tell him that I loved him? I couldn't expect him to give up what life had to offer him—a wife, children ... a real future—for me, even if only temporarily.

I looked at him, struggling to think of something to say. I opened my mouth, but no words came out, so I promptly shut it and looked straight ahead. Quinn followed suit. We continued to walk next to each other without so much as saying a thing. But his silence was eating me up inside, and I couldn't stand it any longer.

Against my better judgment, I took a step closer towards Quinn. I let my hand wander even closer towards him until the back of my hand purposefully brushed against the back of his. He continued to walk, his head still facing forward. But I could see that his expression had softened a little. My fingers found their way around his; they intertwined together so naturally, as if we had held hands a thousand times before. Maybe we had. I looked up at Quinn, who was now glancing down at our hands. Maybe he'd just realized how perfectly our hands fit together too. Or maybe he was just reminded of the same.

"Quinn," I said, barely louder than a whisper as knots formed one on top of another in my stomach. "I *am* interested in you—and it terrifies me."

He said nothing in response to my admission. He simply squeezed my hand and flashed a quick smile. He knew he had won this battle. More importantly, though, he knew he had won me over. In my own way, I had just let him know how much he meant to me.

We continued to hold hands as we walked past Oak Street Beach all the way to Diversey Harbor. I walked on the beach whenever possible; I loved the feel of my toes sinking into the sand. Most of the time we didn't speak—we didn't need to. What we were doing was much more intimate. It was as if in that one gesture of taking his hand, I had touched his soul, and by him accepting my hand, he had touched mine.

As we headed back south, Quinn told me about his upbringing, his parents, and his brothers. He left out the more sordid details about Brady, and I understood why. I never did tell Quinn that I had eavesdropped during the dinner with his parents in Greektown.

Quinn also spoke of his experience attending IU, carefully omitting any mention of me—or any other girls—and working at his summer internship here in Chicago. He was subletting his place until the middle of August, at which time he would go back to IU to complete his junior year. Quinn was planning on quitting the swim team at the end of the coming season, although he had yet to tell anyone, including his parents. He wanted to travel abroad his senior year, and staying on the swim team would prohibit him from doing so. Moreover, swimming wasn't a part of his future, not swimming competitively anyway. The only issue that remained would be his scholarship—Quinn would lose it if he quit the team. But, he figured, he would make enough this summer and the next to cover his tuition abroad and living expenses during his senior year.

"I feel like I've been boring you with my life story," Quinn said apologetically. "What about you? I mean, if you can't remember your past, and you won't tell me about your *existence* now, then what can you tell me about yourself?"

"I'm … I'm not sure, exactly." It seemed like a simple question, but it was nearly impossible for me to answer.

"Well, what kinds of food do you like? What kind of music, or movies, or books do you like? What do you like to do in your spare time?"

"Oh, you mean the few minutes I get here and there when I'm not busy watching over you?" I teased.

"Yes, aside from *that* tedious imposition," he joked.

"Well, to tell you the truth, I don't really know." I looked at him. "I know that sounds like a cop-out response, but I really don't." I was scanning my mind for something, anything, but it was a blank slate. Further, since becoming a Shepherd, my sole interest was—well, *had to be*—Quinn, and I was *not* about to profess that to him.

"I haven't been … who I am … for all that long. In fact, you're my first assignment. So, aside from my training," I said rather pathetically, "I've spent most of my time with you—and traveling. I like seeing the world."

We kept walking for a few minutes before Quinn stopped and turned towards me. A mischievous grin spread across his lips.

"Hey, are you busy tonight?" he asked.

"Very funny," I replied. He knew full well that I would be watching over him in some capacity.

"Well, it just so happens that I have come up with an ingenious idea." Quinn's smile got wider and there was a definite sparkle in his eyes. No doubt he was up to something.

"What is it?" I asked suspiciously.

"Well, it's a surprise of sorts—for you. I mean, I don't know how much of a surprise it can be considering you can hang around without me knowing and all. But I really want to do this—or at least try to anyway." He was buzzing with excitement. "I don't mean to sound like a prick, but can you leave me alone for a couple of hours when we get back to my place? I need time to prepare. Oh ... and can you give me some forewarning before you come back?" He stood there smiling like a little schoolboy.

"Time away from you ... so you can surprise me, huh?" I pretended to give it serious consideration. Quinn was practically bouncing up and down in anticipation, hoping I would agree.

"I think it can be arranged," I said, smiling playfully.

Quinn was so surprised by how quickly and easily I'd agreed to his plan that he swept me up in his arms and swung me around. He suddenly stopped, tensed up, and put me back down.

"Sorry about that," he said apologetically.

"It's okay. But I'm glad breathing is no longer a requirement for me," I said, holding my ribs as I began to laugh.

Quinn relaxed his expression and laughed too.

* * *

We didn't get back to Quinn's building until half past four in the afternoon. Rather than going up with him, I said goodbye in the lobby. We agreed I would return in two hours. I watched him bolt up the stairs two at a time. Once I made sure he was safely in his apartment and checked my watch to confirm nothing had changed on that end, I left. I really did want to be surprised. He looked so eager and hopeful that his idea would work that I didn't want to disappoint him, and I knew I wouldn't be able to fake it if I had discovered his plan prematurely.

24. Our First Date

Two hours later, I stood outside the front door of the apartment and knocked, giving Quinn the forewarning he'd requested.

"Hold on!" Quinn said loudly. I could hear him running around his apartment, scrambling to finish last minute preparations for my surprise. A minute later he unlocked the door and opened it. I had to catch my breath when I saw him; he looked absolutely stunning. He was showered, clean-shaven, and his hair was tucked loosely behind his ears. He was wearing a white linen shirt with the sleeves rolled midway up his forearms and khaki pants. He was barefoot, which only perfected the look. I glanced down and surveyed myself; I was wearing the same clothes from that afternoon. I suddenly felt underdressed for the occasion.

"Maybe I should go change," I said self-consciously.

"No need. You look great!" Quinn exclaimed as he opened the door and invited me inside. I peeked over his shoulder through the door only to confirm that my appearance was definitely sub par for the evening he had in mind. The blinds were pulled, the lights were dimmed and there must have been two dozen candles lit and strategically placed throughout the living and dining room areas.

"Now I *know* I'm underdressed," I remarked as I wondered what was going on. That's when I paid attention to the smell—or should I say smells—wafting through the door and into the hallway. I had been so curious about the evening and so taken by Quinn's appearance that I hadn't even noticed the variety of scents permeating the air around me.

I walked inside his apartment and was blown away. I had to laugh. The breakfast bar, the dining room table, and the coffee table were lined with every type of takeout you could possibly imagine. There must have been three dozen different containers of food. I was truly astonished … and more than a little impressed.

"Wow! You did all this in a couple of hours?" I asked, still trying to get over the shock of what I was seeing.

"Internet," he replied nonchalantly, but he couldn't hide his smile. He knew he had succeeded in surprising me.

I suddenly felt horrible. How was I going to break it to him that I couldn't *eat* any of this? I took off his baseball cap and set it on the glass shelf to the right of the front door along with his sunglasses.

"Um, Quinn," I said reluctantly, avoiding eye contact.

"I know," he interjected immediately. "You can't eat any of it, right?"

"How did you know that?" I turned to look at him, even more surprised.

"Evie, I have yet to see you eat or drink anything, even when I am, so I just assumed you probably couldn't, being … you know …"

"No longer capable of digesting food?"

"Yeah … that." He shifted uneasily. I wondered what made Quinn more uncomfortable—hearing me say the words or trying to come to terms with why I couldn't eat; I presumed it was the latter.

"But," his eyes twinkled slightly, "I also remembered one night last week when you commented on how good my pizza *smelled*, and I figured you still must have some appreciation for food. I mean, you obviously can still tell which foods you like and which ones you don't through your sense of smell, right? So I thought we'd try it out. We'll have our own private culinary aromatic adventure to help you discover more about yourself—even if only in a small way."

"Quinn … I don't know what to say," I stammered. I didn't even remember making the comment about his pizza. I was truly taken aback, overcome with emotion. I was so grateful for what Quinn had done—what he had even *thought* to do. I wanted to hug him, but I didn't dare. I found myself really looking forward to this "aromatic adventure," and I didn't want to complicate the evening.

"I can't believe you did all of this … I'm just so surprised." I looked up at Quinn. "Thank you."

"So what would you like to try first?" He flashed me a big smile, satisfied with my reaction.

"*First*, I'm going to freshen up," I insisted. "If you went through all of this trouble, the least I can do is dress up a little for the occasion." I ran into his bedroom before he could protest. After a few minutes, and several outfit changes, I settled on a summer dress that I remembered seeing in one of the fashion magazines Quinn had bought me. It was a simple, long, white spaghetti-strapped dress that reminded me of ancient Rome. It was very feminine and not too sexy—although it did cling to the curves of my body. I wore my hair down in loose curls and added a hint of makeup.

"Being immortal does have its advantages," I noted as I looked myself over with approval in Quinn's bedroom mirror.

I walked back into the candlelit room. He was sitting in my chair waiting for me.

"Whoa," he gasped when he saw me, his mouth hanging open slightly. He stood up and walked over to me.

"Too much?" I asked nervously.

"No … not at all. I just … I mean, you look absolutely … angelic." Quinn paused for a moment and chuckled slightly, having realized the unintended humor in his choice of words. "No pun intended."

"I guess this outfit would suggest that, wouldn't it," I added, feeling a little silly.

"Well, you look stunning." He just stood there and stared at me. Now I really felt self-conscious.

"Funny, I was going to say the same thing about you when you opened the door," I said a little awkwardly. I cleared my throat and looked at the tables of food.

"So what's on the menu?" I asked, purposefully breaking up the moment. I walked past Quinn and into the living area to survey the variety of food out on display.

"Well, Mademoiselle," he said with a fake French accent as he rubbed his hands together and walked over beside me.

I looked at him like he was nuts.

"Lose the accent?" he asked.

I crinkled my nose and nodded in confirmation.

"Okay." He cleared his throat, dropping the accent. He quickly got back into the swing of the evening as the anticipation of our endeavor took over.

"So over here," he explained, walking over to the kitchen counter, "are your classic American favorites." He pointed to each item as he ran through the list of my choices. "Here's a hot dog with relish, onion, and mustard. To its right is a half slab of barbeque ribs, followed by a cheddar bacon cheeseburger and ultra spicy buffalo wings with blue cheese dressing on the side.

"Next stop is Italy," Quinn continued. "I don't know if this food looks as appetizing as what you saw in *Rome*, but it's the best I could come up with on such short notice. We have a personal-size, deep-dish, Chicago-style pepperoni pizza; spaghetti Bolognese; gnocchi in tomato vodka sauce; and chicken marsala.

"And, of course, we can't forget Mexican food ... one of my personal favorites."

"Of course," I repeated in jest. I was already overwhelmed by the selections thus far.

"I ordered some beef burritos, chicken enchiladas, and chicken and pulled pork tamales," Quinn announced. He took my hand and walked me over to the dining room table.

"Over here we have a small sampling from France, namely, French onion soup, duck pâté, and escargots, as well as some Indian dishes including lamb kebabs, chicken tikka masala, vegetable curry, and something called palak paneer."

"What's palak paneer?" I asked.

"I have no idea, but I'm willing to sacrifice my taste buds for you," he replied.

I had to laugh.

"It's good to hear you laughing, Evie," he said sweetly.

"It *feels* good to be laughing," I noted, smiling. The candlelight hit Quinn's face in such a way it made his skin look as though it was glowing softly. It actually reminded me of the glow that emanated from my hands when I had healed him, which was strangely appropriate considering that Quinn was healing my spirit ... my soul. What had been a dark and empty void within me not long ago now seemed so full of energy and ... *life*. I no longer felt alone. I felt happy.

"All right, we're not done yet. Next to the Indian food are some traditional Greek dishes. Over here we have mousaka, a gyros plate, spanokopita, and tzatziki." Again, he pointed to each item so that I could get them straight in my head.

"At the end of the table over here, we have another favorite of mine—Chinese food. I got some hot and sour soup, kung pao chicken, Mongolian beef, and moo shu pork.

"And for the grand finale," he said as he led me to the coffee table, "I got a variety of desserts. Over here is baklava, and to the right of that is crème brûlée. That over there is chocolate lava cake. Of course, I had to include a few childhood favorites—Reese's chocolate peanut butter cups and Nestle's chocolate-chip cookie dough. And, last but not least, I have some mango sorbet in the freezer." Quinn stood back and surveyed the room. When he was satisfied that he'd explained everything, he sighed.

"I guess that's about it."

"*That's it?*" I asked, astonished. "Quinn, there is enough food here to feed an army! How are you going to eat all of this?"

"Hey, I'm still a growing boy with a big appetite." He smiled as he rubbed his stomach. "And, in case you haven't already noticed, I'm a big fan of leftovers."

"I've noticed," I replied. Since I had been assigned to Quinn, I had yet to see him open a can of soup or turn on the oven, much less make an actual meal. He was the king of takeout.

"So where do we begin?" I scanned the room again, feeling more overwhelmed. It was obvious he had put a lot of effort into this evening, and I was going to make sure I didn't miss anything.

"Anywhere you want," he responded excitedly.

"Hmm." I decided the best thing to do was start from the beginning. I walked over to the breakfast bar and pointed to the hot dog. "Let's start with the American classics."

"Wise choice, Mademoiselle." Quinn tried out his French accent once more and it made me laugh.

I picked up the hot dog and examined it carefully, rotating it horizontally three-hundred-and-sixty degrees to get the full picture.

"Well?" he asked anxiously.

"It *looks* okay," I said. But as I brought the hot dog to my nose and inhaled, the smell of raw onions assaulted my nose.

"Um, Quinn, I'm pretty sure I'm *not* a fan of raw onions." I pushed the hot dog into Quinn's hand like it was a dirty sock. He graciously accepted my offering and took a huge bite.

"Oh, totally," he said in between chews, "I could see how this would completely offend the senses. I'll never eat one again for as long as I live!" he proclaimed as he proceeded to take another couple of bites, clearly enjoying every morsel of it.

"Just disgusting!" he exclaimed. I laughed as he pulled out a huge garbage can from behind the kitchen counter and took one more bite before tossing the hot dog in the trash. "Check this one off in the 'no' column." He looked up at me and smiled, which only made me laugh even harder.

"What's so funny?"

"You have ... mustard ... on your nose!" I could barely get the words out, I was giggling so hard. Quinn wiped it off with the back of his hand.

"I think we're going to need some reinforcements here," he said as he grabbed a roll of paper towels from under his kitchen sink.

There was no easy way to pick up the ribs, so I pulled my hair back and bent down to smell them. "Now *these* smell good." I leaned over again to inhale the sweet smell of molasses and brown sugar and the savory scent of vinegar and whole grain mustard. "Mmm. If I could eat, these would definitely be up my alley."

Quinn quickly devoured a few ribs. "I agree with your assessment. Strike this one up as a 'yes.' These have earned themselves a spot as an official leftover."

We tried the rest of the items in a similar manner. I discovered that I was so-so on the cheddar bacon cheeseburger; it smelled good, but it looked too greasy. I also didn't like the ultra spicy buffalo wings, which all but set my nasal passages ablaze when I took a huge whiff. As if on instinct, I felt the undeniable urge to cough and had a hard time stopping my coughing fit once it started.

Quinn roared in laughter—that is, until it was his turn to actually *taste* them. Then it was me who was fighting the fits of laughter on the brink of escape. Beads of sweat formed on his forehead almost immediately, and his face turned bright red from the heat.

"What?" he gasped. "These are good … really," he insisted in a hoarse whisper, trying to convince me that he was okay as he took another bite. It was when I saw him affectionately eyeing the can of Coke on the table next to him that I just lost it and began laughing uncontrollably. Quinn finally gave in and took a huge swig of Coke, quickly followed by a few more gulps until his cheeks began to resemble a rosy shade of pink rather than bright scarlet.

"Yeah, so I don't think I'll be saving the rest of these for later," he said as he scooped up the cardboard container of wings and threw it in the trash, which sent me into a fit of giggles again.

The pizza, spaghetti Bolognese, gnocchi in tomato vodka sauce, and chicken marsala were all hits for both of us, making them eligible as finalists in the leftover category. I liked the chicken enchiladas, and the tamales smelled delicious. Quinn promptly demolished them both. But the beef burritos were a no-go because I didn't like the smell of refried beans. He frowned as he slowly walked the burrito over to the trash, taking one last memorial bite.

"Adiós, mi amigo. Down the hatch you go." He pretended to be sad as he dumped the burrito.

I also was not a big fan of French food—or I should say, the French items Quinn had selected. I realized that it wasn't just raw onions that offended me; *all* onions bothered me—even in soup. The pâté and escargots freaked me out in both appearance and smell. Quinn, who apparently loved pâté and cooked snails, urged me to give them each a second chance, but I refused. So he begrudgingly walked over to the garbage can and turned his back towards me for a second as he gulped down a few more escargots and another spoonful of pâté before pitching them.

Saving the Indian food for last, we tried the Greek food next, followed by the Chinese dishes. I passed on the mousaka and gyros plate, but I liked the smell of the spanokopita and tzatziki. Quinn ate the spanokopita and half of the gyros, throwing the rest of it out. The tzatziki and mousaka made it to the leftover list. Same with the kung pao chicken, Mongolian beef, and moo shu pork, each of which I loved—as did Quinn. The hot and sour soup was not a huge hit for either of us, so it was tossed.

Finally, we got to the Indian food. I really enjoyed the smell of the vegetable curry, but Quinn wasn't a huge fan of vegetables—or curry, it would seem. I tried to convince him to take another bite, but he wouldn't budge. And when I wanted to put it on the official leftover roster, he looked at me like I was nuts.

"What are you going to do? Open the fridge in the middle of the night, and *smell* it for a while?" he teased.

"I don't know … maybe." Admittedly, it wasn't the strongest of arguments. Quinn took the container and threw it away. We both liked the lamb kebabs, and the chicken tikka masala was okay, but not good enough to make it a keeper. Then it was time for the palak paneer. It looked like some type of pasty spinach dish with cubes of tofu or some type of cheese swimming in it.

"You first," Quinn offered.

"Are you sure? I mean, I don't mind at all if you want to go ahead," I said, trying to graciously pass.

"Nope. You know what they say … 'ladies first.'"

Great, I said to myself as I bent over and inhaled the scent of the dish. To my surprise, it actually smelled pretty good— earthy with a little garlic and other kinds of spices I couldn't quite place—maybe coriander and cumin. It wouldn't have been one of my first choices, but I liked it overall. Instantly, however, I knew Quinn would *not* be a fan. Nonetheless, I desperately wanted to see the look on his face once he tried it.

"Mmm, it smells good," I said in an exaggerated tone and bent down to smell it again.

"Really?" he asked me incredulously.

"Absolutely; you should try it," I remarked enthusiastically.

As Quinn scooped up a heaping spoonful of spinach, I could barely contain the laughter that was welling up inside of me. He put the entire bite in his mouth, and the expression on his face immediately changed; it looked contorted, twisted, and miserable. He just sat there for a minute not knowing what to do with whatever it was in his mouth that he clearly disliked. Like a little kid who had just been tricked into eating a mouthful of Brussels sprouts, Quinn shot me a look of contempt before running to the kitchen sink and spitting it out. I couldn't contain myself any longer; I began laughing.

"You think you are *so* funny, don't you?" Quinn asked in between his gulps of water directly from the kitchen faucet. "I thought you were here to protect me—not kill me!" I was still reeling in laughter as he picked me up, carried me over to the couch and fell back into it with me in his clutches.

We sat there for a good hour before we—well, before Quinn—could even think about eating anything else. We talked about our walk that day, the people we observed, and the sites we passed.

When we finally did move to the desserts, I discovered that I liked the crème brûlée and mango sorbet the best, while Quinn stuck with his old favorites—chocolate peanut butter cups and raw cookie dough.

At some point, he looked at what would be his umpteenth spoonful of cookie dough, debating with himself as to whether he should eat it. He ultimately decided against it and tossed the spoon onto a nearby plate and moaned.

"Boy, am I stuffed." Quinn sighed as he dragged himself up off the floor and crawled onto the nearby couch. He looked at me still sitting on the floor in front of the coffee table. "But it was worth every bite." He smiled at me, and my insides swelled with joy. I climbed up onto the couch next to him.

"Quinn, I can honestly say I don't believe anyone ever has done anything like this for me before."

"Well, someone should have." His voice was husky, his face grew serious, and his eyes sparkled. I felt his heart beating faster in my chest.

"Well, thanks for being that someone."

He looked like he was going to lean in any minute and kiss me. But he picked up a lock of my hair that had wandered out of place and wound it gently around his fingers before tucking it behind my ear instead. His fingers brushed the nape of my neck as he did and my skin tingled at the site of contact. Afraid of getting lost in the vast oceans of blue staring intently at me, I glanced down at the floor.

I was acutely aware that I was treading on very thin ice. The desire I felt for Quinn was growing stronger with each passing moment. I was on the verge of losing all sense of self-restraint, and I knew it wouldn't take much for me to give in to my intense urge to kiss him.

The smart thing for me to do would be to say good night. Orchestrating my escape, I checked my watch. It was after midnight.

"It's pretty late." I stood up and grabbed some of the dessert containers on the coffee table in front of us. "Here, let me help you clean up."

"Wait!" Quinn exclaimed urgently, startling me. Then he jumped to his feet. "I almost forgot—there's more!"

"Oh, please tell me there's no more food," I begged. "I don't think I can suffer *watching* you eat another bite."

"Don't worry. No more food." He smiled. "I have something else in mind, so you can't leave yet."

I frowned. I didn't need sleep, but he did. The expression on my face must have given away my thoughts.

"Look, *Mom,* I think I'm old enough to decide when I should go to bed. Besides, tomorrow's Sunday—the day of rest. So I can catch up on my sleep if I'm tired." He took the containers from my hands and put them back on the table and then gently sat me back down on the couch.

"Evie, don't go just yet." His eyes pleaded with me to stay.

"Okay." I couldn't resist him.

"Okay," Quinn said, relieved. "Good. So just stay there and relax for a few minutes. Don't get up," he commanded. He grabbed the garbage can, brought it over to the coffee table, and dumped the dessert containers inside. He then proceeded to clean up the rest of the evidence of our culinary experience, which was just a matter of dumping a few more containers in the trash and sticking the rest in the fridge to be consumed by him another day. I felt silly just sitting there watching him, so I grabbed a clean napkin that had fallen on the floor and started to wipe down the coffee table.

"Nuh-uh. *I'll* take care of it," Quinn insisted.

Amused, I put the napkin down, sat down in my chair, and pulled my knees into my chest. Quinn walked over to his computer bag, grabbed his laptop, and brought it over to me. He proceeded to open up his iTunes music library.

"Here," he said, handing me the laptop. "Why don't you scroll down this list and see if you recognize any songs." He smiled mischievously at me, and I recognized it as the same smile he had flashed me during our walk earlier that afternoon when he'd initially concocted my surprise.

The candlelight danced across Quinn's face. He really was breathtaking—and amazing. At that moment, I became painfully aware of just how much I had fallen in love with him.

"What?" Quinn asked, suddenly looking a little sheepish. "Is there something wrong? Is there something in my teeth?" He covered his mouth with his hand.

"No, quite the opposite actually. As far as I can tell, there is absolutely *nothing* wrong with you." Even in the candlelight, I could tell he was beginning to blush. His pulse began to speed up a little too. He ran his hand through his hair and looked down as a nervous little chuckle escaped his lips. He smiled, but he couldn't look at me. I couldn't believe it—I actually had embarrassed him.

"At a loss for words?" I teased. It wasn't like Quinn to be left speechless, and I didn't know when another opportunity like this would present itself. He took a deep breath, and I felt his pulse regulate itself. I could see his cheeks returning to their normal pigment.

"No. I'm just not used to you being so direct," he remarked calmly.

"Well, I could always go back to being more ambiguous—if you would prefer," I offered, knowing full well that was the last thing he would have wanted.

"No, no. Direct is good." He bent down so his face was barely an inch from mine and smiled. His eyes were blazing. My body began to tremble with excitement. His smile grew wider, and instantly I knew he had noticed my body's reaction. He brushed my cheek with his own as he closed the distance between us. "Direct is *very* good," he whispered in my ear.

Oh, please let me have the strength to get through this, I pleaded silently with myself as a surge of electricity shot through my body like lightning. I cleared my throat and shifted in my seat to create a few inches of space between us. I looked down at the computer sitting in my lap.

"So … same idea as the food?" I asked hoarsely.

"Yup," he said smugly, looking thoroughly pleased with himself for turning the tables on me. Whatever upper hand I may have gained a moment ago was now long gone. He stood back up and walked into the kitchen to clean up the rest of the mess.

I did as Quinn asked for no better reason than to get my mind off of him—and to ignore my body's reaction to him. I quickly began scrolling through the list of songs.

It was so odd—I couldn't recognize the name of a single song, but I was familiar with using a laptop and with iTunes generally. How could I be so comfortable using a computer and a particular computer program but not remember ever learning how to do so? And what was the deal with music? Maybe specific songs or types of music were too personal, too culturally specific, to be able to retain knowledge of in the afterlife without giving away too many hints as to who the Shepherd was when human or where he or she was from. I also wondered how Peter was able to extract only specific contextual and experiential memories of my life, while leaving behind the knowledge and technological know-how I had acquired while alive.

"Do you recognize any songs?" Quinn asked.

"No," I replied, frustrated.

"Well, then we'll have to just go through them one by one."

"All of them?" I exclaimed. There must have been thousands of songs downloaded onto his computer; it would take all night—*at least!*

"I think it'll be easier if we sample different genres first and go from there." Quinn plopped down onto the couch and patted the open spot just to the left of him. I stood up and gave him the laptop as I sat down next to him. He double-clicked on a song and it started to play.

"What do you think?" he asked after a minute or two.

"It's good." We listened to the whole song.

"Recognize this one?" Quinn asked after he chose another.

"No, but I like it," I noted.

We went on like this for the rest of the evening. He would pick songs and wait for me to rate them. We listened to everything from classical to country to alternative. If I liked a song, Quinn would copy it into a playlist he had created for me named "Evie's Faves."

By the wee hours, Quinn had copied a couple hundred songs into my playlist. He also gave me a pair of earphones.

"Here, these are for you. You can just come out here and play these songs—or add more if you want. You know, just in case you're ever bored hanging around here ... Oh, you'll need this too." He wrote down the password to his computer and handed it to me.

"Oh ... thanks." I didn't know what to say. Of course, I had already memorized Quinn's password from watching him enter it into his laptop time and time again. Initially, I had every intention of snooping around his computer to find out more about him while he slept, but I could never bring myself to actually do it. It just felt wrong—a huge violation of his privacy. And, in any case, I didn't really need to snoop anymore. Since I had revealed myself to Quinn, I was able to find out a lot about him just by asking. Yet, here he was giving me his password, trusting that I would not abuse it.

"It's nice to know you trust me enough to give me this," I remarked, holding up the paper with his password.

"Don't be silly," Quinn replied. "I trust you with my *life*. Giving you the password to my computer seems like child's play in comparison." The expression on his face suddenly changed; he looked more sullen. "Besides, I don't want to keep any secrets from you."

I believed he meant what he said. But I also knew he had yet to volunteer certain information to me—like information about his brother Brady ... or about Ashley. I reminded myself that Quinn was human, and keeping secrets was part of human nature.

But wasn't I doing the same thing? Hadn't I been withholding information from Quinn? Didn't I justify such omissions as being necessary to carry out my assignment? Didn't I make the conscious choice to feed Quinn information on a need-to-know basis only? As I understood it, I was incapable of *speaking* untruths, but that didn't mean I couldn't withhold information at times. As a Shepherd, I couldn't lie, but I could keep secrets.

I thought about what Agnes had said earlier, and I was beginning to see how our ways necessarily allowed for a certain amount of give in order to meet the demands of a particular assignment. I contemplated what kind of loopholes in the Rules might exist and how I could use them to my advantage.

I was so distracted I hadn't noticed the music stop. I didn't notice the change in Quinn's breathing, each breath growing deeper and heavier. I didn't even notice that my pulse—his pulse—had started racing.

What I finally did notice, however, was that Quinn's left hand, which had been resting on the back of the couch behind me, was now playing with my hair. I noticed the subtle ripple of energy coursing through me from my head to my toes. And I noticed the butterflies fluttering wildly about in my belly from my budding nervousness. I was afraid to look at Quinn; I knew I wouldn't be able to handle seeing his brilliant blue eyes, his charming smile ... his soft lips.

His hand traveled to the nape of my neck, which he then started to massage gently. My body instinctively moved towards him. My butterflies soon gave way to something else. I felt like my body temperature was rising, if that was at all possible, and it wasn't long before his touch ignited a smoldering fire within me. I wanted Quinn—badly. I knew I wouldn't be able to control myself much longer. He started to lean in closer towards me. I could feel the electrified air dancing wildly around us.

Please don't do this! I begged silently. Agnes's words rang loudly through my head like warning bells. *"Acts of love and acts of passion are not the same thing ... To have any fighting chance of success, you will have to find a way to separate the two."*

The weight of her words was enough to snap me out of my momentary lapse of reason. I knew kissing Quinn would cross a very dangerous line—for both of us. I couldn't let this happen. I had to think of something fast. And, unfortunately, I did.

"Speaking of secrets, Quinn, are you sure *Ashley* would approve of me being here with you right now?" My voice was laced with undue venom; my words were like acid. I regretted uttering them the second they came out of my mouth.

From the look on his face, it instantly became clear he had no idea I was aware of her. He pulled away from me, ran his hands through his hair, and sat there quietly for a second before he stood up and walked into the kitchen.

Talk about ruining the moment—mission accomplished: a kiss was no longer in the stars this evening. That said, it was unfair of me to hit Quinn so far below the belt. Unable to keep my emotions in check, and I had lashed out. And Quinn was paying the price yet again for my failure. He had worked so hard to create the perfect evening, and I had single-handedly destroyed it with one cheap shot. I was beginning to think any kind of "relationship" with him was nearly impossible.

"Look ..." he mumbled as he was searching for the right words—for some explanation. He couldn't even face me.

"Quinn, I'm sorry," I interjected. "It wasn't my place to say that. It's none of my business. You don't have to try to explain anything. In fact, you have nothing to explain. I shouldn't have thrown her name in your face … I'm sorry." My voice was riddled with remorse. "I should go." I headed towards the front door and opened it.

If I had been smart, I would have used this moment to distance myself from Quinn before I hurt him any further. Having driven this wedge between him and me, I should have used it as an opportunity to end things with him. I knew the right thing to do was to walk through his front door and not look back.

But I didn't walk through the door. I couldn't. Rather, I glanced back at Quinn. When I saw the distraught look on his face, I no longer thought about the smart thing or the right thing to do. I couldn't let this evening end on such a nasty note. I wanted him to remember this night as being the fairy tale he had created for me. *I* wanted to remember it that way.

I closed the door and walked over to him. I reached up and cradled his face with my hands. The passion that had consumed me only moments before was nowhere to be found. I felt only great sadness for hurting the one person I cared for so deeply. I gently lifted up Quinn's head a little, hoping he would meet my eyes, but he refused to do so.

"Quinn, it was a stupid thing to say … Please, forget it," I begged. "I'm really sorry. I don't know what came over me. The last thing I wanted to do was ruin this amazing evening with you." I took him by the arms and turned his body to face mine, but he still wouldn't yield. He simply cast his gaze to the floor beside me.

"Quinn, I only said what I did because I'm scared and confused … Whatever it is that we're doing is destined to fail. Being with you would mean breaking Rules I can't break. It would mean trying to have a *life* with you that simply cannot exist for me. I don't have the right to ask you to turn your back on what's in front of you or what lies ahead in your future. I mean, I don't even know how much longer I can stay here—"

"Evie, I'm in love with you," Quinn blurted out as his eyes met mine.

I was speechless, my mouth still hanging open in mid-sentence, my eyes wide with surprise. Did he just say what I thought he said? I couldn't be sure. I could see Quinn searching my face, looking for some sign, some clue, as to my reaction to his statement.

I felt so naked and transparent—as if he could see everything I had tried so desperately to hide. As if he knew the three little words I had wanted to tell him but was too terrified to utter. I was afraid to move or even breathe for fear that those very same words would spill out of my mouth at any second.

"Evie, did you hear me?" Quinn asked. "*I love you.*"

There was no mistaking his words this time. I couldn't imagine any feeling that could rival how I felt at that moment. Pure bliss. Pure exhilaration. I was completely lost in the moment. Suddenly, I didn't care about the consequences for what I was about to do. I didn't want to care. I took a deep breath and leaped.

"I love you too." As I heard myself say the words. Fireworks went off inside me, the aftershocks of which radiated warmly through me, leaving me floating in a state of perfect serenity. I was consumed by feelings of love, devotion, tenderness, and adoration for the person standing before me. I wanted to give myself over to Quinn wholly and unselfishly, needing nothing in return.

Quinn grabbed me and pulled me into him, embracing me while he buried his face in my hair.

I wrapped my arms around him, returning his embrace. I pressed my face against his chest and let myself drink in his intoxicating scent. We stood there holding each other for what seemed like eternity.

"I love you too," I repeated.

* * *

We stayed up until sunrise cuddling under a blanket on the couch and talking the night away. Quinn fell asleep just as the sun breached the horizon. But the sun didn't stick around for long. He woke up later to stormy skies.

"Well, I guess going outside is not in the game plan for today," he said groggily, rubbing his eyes.

"You can always go back to sleep," I mumbled. I was so busy playing around with iTunes on his laptop that I barely glanced at him.

"Hey, are you trying to get rid of me?" Quinn feigned being upset. "If I had known you'd be more interested in my laptop than in me, I would have seriously reconsidered the second half of my surprise last night," he teased.

Getting the picture, I closed the laptop and put it on the coffee table. "Okay, then," I said, looking at him. "Just what do you have in mind for us on this rainy Sunday afternoon?"

He paused for a moment and then smiled as he had his "aha" moment.

"Movies," he announced.

"Movies," I repeated, my mind buzzing with curiosity.

"Yes. Let's figure out what kind of movies you like."

"Okay. Sounds harmless enough." It seemed like a fairly innocent way to spend the day—depending on the type of movie. I would be certain to stay clear of any movies with romantic plots; I was already treading water, and the last thing I needed was to test how much more I could withstand before I drowned.

"For some reason, I think I like action movies," I quickly added in order to circumvent any discussions about movie genres. And it was the truth. After all, I couldn't lie.

25. Life With Quinn

Over the next couple of weeks, Quinn and I maintained our regular routines. He still didn't know I ghosted him at work, so he always raced back to his place at the end of each day to find me sitting in my chair waiting for him. We spent most evenings talking. He was obsessed with trying to figure out my likes and dislikes—and just about anything he could about my new existence.

One evening, we strolled down Michigan Avenue and then Oak Street, peering through the storefront windows. I paid attention to the types of women's clothes and shoes Quinn liked, so I could tailor my look accordingly when I was in an especially flirtatious mood.

Another afternoon, Quinn left work early so we could stroll through Lincoln Park Zoo together in an effort to figure out which animals I liked best. We were at the underwater viewing window at the polar bear exhibit when Quinn recognized someone he knew—a man roughly his father's age, who was there visiting the zoo with a young boy. Before Quinn had a chance to introduce me, I disappeared, ducking behind a few other zoo-goers who were headed to the upper level of the exhibit. I waited there for Quinn as I watched the polar bears frolic in the water from above.

Even though I was a fair distance away, I could zero in on the conversation between Quinn and the acquaintance, Mr. Adams, who I quickly discovered was a long-time friend of the Harrison family. He was visiting his daughter, who lived in the city with her husband and their three-year-old son, Mason. Apparently, Mason wanted to go to the zoo with his Grandpa, and Mr. Adams couldn't refuse such a grand invitation. After a couple of minutes of small talk and a wicked temper tantrum from Mason, who wanted to see the "ree-luhs," which apparently was three-year-old code for "gorillas," Mr. Adams bid farewell and asked Quinn to extend his greetings to the rest of the Harrison clan. Quinn politely asked Mr. Adams to return the favor to the entire Adams clan.

Quinn found me lurking about on the upper deck, trying to look as relaxed as possible but failing miserably. The run-in with Mr. Adams had shaken me up; it made me realize how careless I had been acting. I should have been watching out for Quinn's safety rather than paying attention to a polar bear that had managed to pick up a few goofy tricks after years of calling the zoo its home. I should've seen, or at the very least sensed, Mr. Adams's presence well before he walked directly up to him. Quinn was fortunate that a friend approached him. He might not be so lucky next time. I shuddered thinking about how truly vulnerable Quinn was to an attack—even in broad daylight.

"Enjoying the view from up here?" Quinn asked curtly.

"Yes. Very much, thanks." I was just as short.

"Well, I don't know why you felt the need to run away from an old family friend and his three-year-old grandson."

"You know why, Quinn. It's the reason why I was reluctant to go on these little outings with you in the first place. It's why I continue to wear the hat and glasses. Nothing has changed on that front."

"So I can't *ever* introduce you to *anyone*? Not even to someone who doesn't know you? Or to someone you'll never even see again?"

"*Never* is a promise you can't make, Quinn. It's too absolute."

"So your answer is '*no*.'" He looked at me for confirmation.

"That's correct."

He sighed in frustration as he kicked a few pebbles by his feet.

"Look, don't forget I've got a job to do—and a very important one at that," I said with raised eyebrows. "And that job is my first priority, period. But, sometimes, when I'm walking around with you, I get distracted. I start forgetting who and what I really am and why I'm here. I end up lowering my defenses and am no longer on full alert. Having you show me off by introducing me to people, even people who don't know me, will only distract me further. I need to stay focused. I need to be ready to act at a moment's notice. I don't think I need to remind you that it can mean the difference between life and death."

I reached up and touched Quinn's scar just above his left temple. He flashed me an exaggerated pout.

"Don't you understand? I *can't* let something happen to you. I would never forgive myself if I did."

"Well, we certainly can't have that now, can we," he said softly as he pulled me into his arms. "Never is so *absolute*."

I stood there in his embrace, rolling my eyes at how easily Quinn had once again turned my own words against me.

* * *

That night, we strolled by the convenience store near Quinn's, only to find Ronald in front selling the current edition of *Streetwise*. I had taken off the sunglasses, but my hair was still pulled back underneath the Cubs hat. Nevertheless, Ronald recognized me immediately.

"There's my favorite angel!" Ronald sang out as Quinn and I walked past. I winked at him and flashed him a smile. Puzzled, Quinn looked at Ronald and then at me. I merely shrugged my shoulders.

"You take care of that one now, you hear?" Ronald called out to Quinn. "She's one in a million."

"Yes, sir," Quinn said respectfully and flashed me another curious look.

"Have a good night, Ronald," I called out to him.

"She speaks to me at last! You know I am blessed to-night!" Ronald exclaimed in his deep baritone voice and then chuckled and clapped his hands together.

"You know Ronald?" Quinn asked me, astonished.

"Let's just say we're both night owls," I responded. As Quinn and I continued to walk away, I turned my head back towards Ronald, who tipped his hat to me and then winked. I couldn't put my finger on it, but there was something about him—something otherworldly. I began to wonder in what ways Ronald and I really were similar.

* * *

Quinn and I spent the rest of the evening discussing sports. We talked about Quinn's swimming background, mainly—how he got his college scholarship, the IU swim team, and which races he enjoyed swimming most.

Oddly enough, I had no idea if I could swim—although I guess it didn't really matter anymore. I presumed I could survive under water for … well, for forever … if need be.

When I told Quinn I was familiar with several of the martial arts, he just laughed at me in utter disbelief. Insulted, I smugly informed him I easily could beat him in hand-to-hand combat. He challenged me to a test of skills on the spot, and I pinned him within seconds—*twice*.

"That's not fair—you have superhero powers or something," Quinn complained, after getting a taste of my immortal strength.

"Hey, you'll get no sympathy from me over this one," I teased. "Need I remind you that *you* were the one laughing at *me*? Not to mention that *you* were the one who challenged *me* … It serves you right that I kicked your butt."

Without warning, he leaped on top of me, pinning me down. In an attempt to nurse his bruised ego, I let him. He had a twinkle of victory in his eye, which made me giggle under my breath despite my best efforts not to do so.

"You're not even trying, are you?" he asked, disappointed.

"What do you think?" I said between fits of laughter.

"Damn those superpowers!" he exclaimed as he joined me laughing. Rather than get up, however, Quinn lingered on top of me. I recognized the look in his eyes that soon followed. I felt his pulse change as his chest heaved up and down on top of mine. I felt his breath on my face. Knowing I could flip him over at any moment, I just lay there, curious to see if he would try to cross any unspoken boundaries.

The truth was that I, too, had grown increasingly more inquisitive about the boundaries. While Quinn slept, I spent countless hours pondering the nuances of Agnes's explanation of the differences between acts of love and acts of passion. True love was selfless and altruistic in intent, while passion stemmed from more selfish and hedonistic desires. It sounded simple in theory; yet, it was anything but cut-and-dried in reality. I loved Quinn. And I wanted him. Often at the same time. In fact, when we were physically close, it was nearly impossible for me to separate the two. I was beginning to understand what Agnes meant by it being a fine line. Now, I just had to learn how to walk the tightrope without hanging myself with it.

It wasn't merely the act of touching Quinn that triggered how much I wanted him. Sometimes, I could hold his hand, embrace him, or even cuddle up with him without feeling any physical desire for him. Other times, we would do the same even when the passion was already sparked and I could still maintain complete power over it. But the mere thought of his lips on mine sent me reeling out of control. So kissing him was out of the question—at least for now. Thankfully, Quinn seemed to understand and accept this rule without me ever having to state it outright.

And then there were the sticky grey areas—like right now. Quinn and I were flirting dangerously with each other. The sexual tension between us was reaching a breaking point. Our eyes were expressing all of the things we *wished* we could do with each other, making our bodies buzz with excitement.

We were not only testing our own self-restraint, we were testing each other's. We teased each other, pushing each other to the absolute brink of what we were capable of withstanding to see who would give in first. And at the same time, we were hoping that one of us would have enough willpower to resist temptation and enough fortitude to prevent things from going too far should one of us falter.

Tonight, neither one of us moved; neither one of us surrendered.

26. Homeward Bound

One Saturday morning in early July, Quinn announced he had another surprise for me. His parents had gone out of town for the weekend, and he wanted to take me home. He stuffed a handful of CDs inside a backpack along with a few other things, and we were ready to go. After his half-hearted and unsuccessful attempt to protest my decision to ghost him until we reached the house, we left the apartment. Quinn hopped onto the Metra and headed north. A short while later, we arrived at his parents' house in Winnetka. Walking up the driveway, I was greeted by a large, beautiful Tudor-style home framed by a huge yard.

"Wow!" I gasped. "You grew up here?"

"Yup—all six of us," Quinn responded. "A few years after my parents bought this house, they bought the one next door and demolished it so we could build the indoor pool over there. So my brothers and I had a lot of room to run around when we were young. And then, of course, there's the beach."

"There's more?" I was stunned.

"C'mon," he said with a chuckle. "I'll give you the grand tour."

I followed Quinn inside his parents' home. Each room was decorated in a style consistent with the architectural design of the house—well, each room but one. Quinn's bedroom differed considerably in that his walls were navy blue and his bedroom furniture was light in color and much more contemporary in style.

"Because I'm still in college, my parents haven't redecorated my room … *yet*. But I know my mom is itching to get her hands dirty in here." Quinn smiled affectionately. "She never liked my taste in furniture." He dumped his backpack on his desk and pulled a bathing suit out of his dresser.

"Um, you might want to turn around ... or not." He smiled mischievously, barely giving me a second to close my eyes before he dropped his pants.

"What am I going to do with you?" I exclaimed, turning my back towards him, my eyes still closed as he changed. I could feel the heat rush into my cheeks.

"I can think of a few things," Quinn said as he picked me up from behind and carried me over to his bed. He spun me around to face him before dropping me onto his mattress only to follow suit right on top of me. He pretended he was going to kiss my lips, but kissed the tip of my nose instead. I sighed both in relief and disappointment.

"But first," he announced, "I want you to go swimming with me." He jumped off of me. "I'm assuming you can do whatever it is that you do and come up with some sort of bathing suit situation?" he asked, wiggling his index finger around at me.

"Yes, I think I can manage ... But, I don't want to reveal my tricks of the trade, and I don't trust that you'll keep your eyes closed. So I'm changing in your bathroom." Laughing, I flipped my legs over the other side of his bed and made a beeline for the bathroom with Quinn chasing me. When I saw him within arms' reach, I playfully screamed, slammed the door shut, and locked it just before he crashed into it. A few seconds later, I appeared in a white bikini.

"That'll do," he said hoarsely when he saw me. If his voice didn't give him away, his eyes surely did; I knew Quinn liked what he saw.

I followed Quinn to the pool house, which was equipped with a lap pool, a hot tub, mini-kitchen, a changing room, patio furniture, a television, a stereo, and a retractable glass ceiling. To say that I was impressed was an understatement. He walked over to the CD player and popped in the handful of CDs he'd brought with him from the loft.

"I think I've spent more time in this pool house than in the main one ... my home away from home," Quinn mused as he walked back over to where I was standing.

"Well, I can see why. This place is amazing," I said in awe.

"Well, I know my angel can fly—now let's see if she can swim." Quinn scooped me up and jumped into the pool, holding me. I shrieked in delight as we both plunged into the water.

* * *

Just before sunset, Quinn led me down to the beach with a bundle of firewood in his arms. It was a small stretch of beach that backed up to several private homes. Each nearby property line was marked by metal break walls that extended several yards out into the water. We just sat there in the sand as the sun-filled sky began to fade and the moon waited patiently on the sidelines until it was time for it to shine. For as far as my eyes could see and my ears could hear, there was no one on the beach but us. It was so quiet and beautiful.

Despite the perfect backdrop, there still was something bothering me. My mind struggled to figure out what it could be, but no matter how hard I tried, I just couldn't pin down what was causing the nagging feeling inside my head.

"Quinn, I've never been here before with you, have I?" I asked out of the blue.

"No," he responded uneasily. "Why do you ask?"

"It just seems like I've been here, or somewhere like here, before. But something about it is different this time."

"What?" He sat up and looked at me curiously.

"It feels like ... like I'm on the wrong side of the water."

"What?" he asked, confused.

"It just feels like I should be watching the sun set *over* the water ... like I should be on the other side of the lake." I looked at Quinn, hoping he had the answer, but he just stared at me, equally perplexed.

"Quinn … do you know where I was from?" I knew I shouldn't have asked the question, but I couldn't help myself. There was something about this beach, the smell of the water, and the feel of the sand on my toes, that seemed so familiar to me. Perhaps the source of my uneasiness stemmed from being homesick. Perhaps going to Quinn's house and seeing all the pictures of him growing up with his family made me long to know where I was from—to connect somehow with my home … with my parents.

"I thought we weren't allowed to talk about your past." He looked at me inquisitively, like he couldn't figure out what I was doing.

"I know, I know. You're right," I said, shaking my head. "It's just that sometimes I have fleeting moments of *déjà vu*— nothing concrete, just random flashes. But this … being here right now … this is different. It's like something is bugging me, itching for me to remember some part of my past. I don't know what it is, but I can't get it out of my head. So please just answer me this one thing," I implored: "Do you know where I was from?"

"I'm sorry, Evie. I wish I did, but I don't." Quinn looked at me and frowned.

I looked out at the lake again—still nothing. I knew I wasn't going to find any answers tonight, so I pushed the nagging feelings aside as best I could and focused on enjoying the rest of the evening.

I helped Quinn collect twigs, brush, and small branches to create kindling for our bonfire. Once everything was set to go, he lit the fire and we sat back waiting for the flames to catch. A brisk lake breeze swept over us, and he shivered slightly and goose bumps formed on his arms. I rearranged myself so that I was sitting behind Quinn and I began to rub his arms. I focused on warming up my hands a bit, hoping they would not begin to glow. It worked; his body temperature started to rise. He chuckled.

"What is it?" I asked, partly amused and partly nervous that I had just given away yet another one of my secrets.

"Nothing … It's just that I'm sure you're a lot better at this than I was last winter outside in the courtyard at …" Quinn's voice trailed off. He looked out at the disappearing horizon, lost in a memory. From his silence, I knew it was a memory about us. He was respecting my request not to say anything about my past—a request that I myself had reneged on earlier that evening.

"Should I stop?" I asked, pausing my hands.

"No, it feels good," he said, half-dazed. I continued to rub his arms for a few more minutes, thinking about how tough all of this had to be on him. How could I be so selfish and insensitive as to ask Quinn for information about my past that *I* wanted to know, but order a moratorium on all the information about us that *he* wanted to share with me? I felt miserable. I leaned into him and rested my cheek on his back.

"Quinn, thanks for honoring my request to keep my past in the past. I can't believe how inconsiderate I was to ask you to go back on the very promise I asked you to make."

"It's fine … really." Quinn turned towards me so he could see my face. "I mean, I can't imagine how difficult it must be for you to resist asking the questions. I would be going insane trying to figure out who I was."

"I don't really have a choice. If the price of knowing about my past is putting your life in jeopardy, then it's not an option."

Quinn turned his body towards mine and quickly swept me up so I was sitting in his lap facing him. I wrapped my legs around his waist. Even in the firelight, I could see his deep blue eyes twinkling. His face softened as he drew me in even closer. He leaned his forehead against mine.

"I love you, Evie. I will always love you," he whispered.

"And I will love you ... always."

27. Family Matters

The phone rang shortly after we returned from Quinn's parents' house late Sunday night. Quinn picked up his cell phone to see who was calling and immediately grimaced.

My first reaction was that it was Ashley. To my good fortune, she had been out of town for the majority of the last month on back-to-back projects. And the few days Ashley had been back in the office, she was so busy playing catch-up that she only had time to send Quinn a few cursory emails here and there, nothing of any substance. My guess was that Ashley's emails were simply her way of reminding Quinn she was still around—and still interested.

Quinn let the call go to voice mail. A minute later, his phone rang again. He didn't have to look at the caller ID to know that it was the same person calling again.

"Damn it!" He grabbed the phone and walked into the bedroom. I did my best not to listen to the conversation, but I could still hear Quinn's voice clearly, despite the fact that he was trying to be quiet.

"What do you want, Brady?" Quinn demanded in a hushed tone. "You've got to be out of your mind ... You know, Mom and Dad warned me that you would be calling to ask me for money ... Hey, don't rag on them. All they've ever done is try to be there for you and bail you out of trouble time and time again—and this is how you repay them? ... How can you keep on doing this to them—to all of us? ... Oh grow up, Brady ... Yeah, well, you're a sorry excuse for a son and a brother! ... Fine. Great. I don't want you to call me again—not until you've gotten some help." When Quinn walked out of his bedroom, he looked annoyed and emotionally exhausted.

"I guess you heard that?" he asked. I frowned and nodded my head affirmatively.

"That was Brady—the brother I don't really talk about." He walked over to the couch and collapsed down on it. I sat down next to him.

"He's a complete mess," Quinn continued. "To make a long story short, Brady's what you would call the black sheep of the family. He's only a year-and-a-half older than me, but he's a compulsive gambler with who-knows-how-much debt right now. He dropped out of school a couple of years ago, and now he jumps around from city to city, usually because some big-time bookies are after him.

Needless to say, my family and I are not happy about Brady's situation. I went out to dinner with my parents last month; they warned me that he might call and ask me for money. I didn't want to believe them, but they were right." Quinn sighed heavily. "My parents cut Brady off, and they made me promise them not to give him any money—but he's my brother; he's my family ... I don't know what to do. I know that giving him money won't help him, but I don't want to leave him high-and-dry either. He could really get hurt. I mean, the types of guys Brady owes money to don't mess around."

"So what are you going to do?" I asked.

"Sleep on it," Quinn said wearily. "I'm too tired and too angry to make any decisions right now." I could tell this situation with Brady was really upsetting him.

"If you let me, maybe we could figure out some way to help your brother together," I offered as I walked over and wrapped my arms around him; Quinn returned my embrace. The anger in his eyes seemed to vanish, revealing the beautiful sapphire hues hiding underneath. All I could see was love. All I could feel was love.

Quinn lowered his head towards mine and kissed me gently. I didn't stop him. His lips felt so soft. He pulled back slightly and let his mouth linger for a moment. His breath was sweet and warm on my face. I wanted to stay in this moment forever.

Out of nowhere, a crippling spasm ran through my chest. I felt my pulse stop suddenly, skip a few beats, and then start again as another spasm hit me. I winced. Something was wrong. I grabbed my chest and then realized that it couldn't be *my* heart I was feeling. Stunned, I looked at Quinn. Surely, he had to have felt that. Surely, he would have reacted somehow to these searing chest pains. But he looked fine—completely unharmed. A second later, the pain subsided and the rhythm in my chest returned to normal.

"Evie, are you okay?" Quinn asked, alarmed.

"Are you?" I asked, equally alarmed.

"Yeah," he responded nervously. "Why are you grabbing your chest like that?" He pulled my hands away from my chest to examine what was wrong.

"I'm not sure," I mumbled, utterly confused. I looked Quinn up and down—nothing. I ran my hands over his chest to check for any internal injuries or damage—nothing. I didn't get it. If Quinn and I were linked by his heartbeat, if his pulse echoed in my chest, then how could my pulse have stopped and skipped a few beats while his didn't? My mind was whirring, trying to come up with an explanation.

I seriously doubted the spasm was a result of Quinn's kiss; the kiss could not have been a more pure expression of love. There wasn't an ounce of heat stirring inside of me. But even if there had been, how could it have affected only me when I didn't even have a pulse to begin with?

No—something else was going on. As I understood it, my pulse was connected to only two things—Quinn's heartbeat and the Time Keeper.

Oh crap! Something must be wrong with the Time Keeper! I remembered Peter telling me that time as we knew it would stop if the Time Keeper broke—that everything would go haywire. I looked at my watch. Sure enough, the Incident Timer marking Quinn's next scheduled brush with death was spinning out of control. *What in the world was happening?*

"Quinn, I have to leave for a minute. Do me a favor and don't go anywhere tonight, okay? Just stay here until I return. I'll be back as soon as I can."

"Another late-night meeting?" he asked, concerned.

"Afraid so."

"Is something wrong? … Should I be worried?" He looked at me uneasily.

"I'm sure I'm just overreacting," I said in an effort to calm his nerves. "But to be on the safe side, *promise me* you'll be extra careful while I'm gone."

"So you mean I have to cancel my evening plans to learn how to juggle steak knives," Quinn joked, but I could tell he was anxious.

"Yes. And no sticking them in the toaster either," I threw in, also trying to lighten the mood.

"Oh come on, now, you're spoiling all my fun."

"Sorry to rain on your parade," I said as I quickly hugged him and kissed him on the cheek. "I'll be back soon. However, should you end up causing yourself any knife-related flesh wounds while I'm gone, just call out my name. I'll hear you," I said as I walked out the door.

As soon as I left his apartment, I teleported myself up to the roof and called out for Peter. But he didn't come. After a few more minutes of calling for him without success, I started to get really scared. I decided to go find him.

The Archives were empty, but I could tell Peter had been there recently judging from the open books and files scattered all over one of the reading tables. I looked up at the frescoed ceiling. It was dawn, and streaks of midnight blue, purple, red, and pink hovered above.

"Bo Peep!" I heard my name shouted jovially from across the Archives.

Startled, I whipped around to see Teddy standing right behind me.

"Teddy!" I exclaimed. "You almost gave me a heart attack!"

He roared with laughter at my words. It was only when I repeated them in my mind that I chuckled slightly too.

"Where's Peter?" I asked.

"I'm not sure. He's not up here though. I can tell you that much. But I wouldn't worry that pretty little head of yours; he does that from time to time."

"Oh," I sighed in disappointment.

"Maybe I can be of some help. What's up?"

Acutely aware that my thoughts were probably an open book to anyone in the Archives who was interested in hearing them, I tried to focus only on the issues at hand. The first issue being that I had to get Teddy to leave the Archives with me and come back down to Earth. For one thing, Teddy couldn't read my mind down there. For another thing, I hated the idea of leaving Quinn alone and unprotected in his apartment—even if just for a short while.

"Teddy, look at my watch—the Incident Timer." I practically shoved my watch in his face. "It's freaking out. I think my charge is in real danger, but I don't know what's going on. Can you come down there with me so you can help me figure it out? Please? I don't want to leave him unguarded any longer than I already have."

"Sugar, for you I'd visit the moon!" Teddy smiled.

"Can we do that?" I asked in disbelief, momentarily allowing myself to get sidetracked.

"Bo Peep, there's so much you have yet to learn." Teddy sighed exaggeratedly and gave me a hardy pat on the back. "Take the lead, honey. Let's go find your sheep."

We arrived on Quinn's rooftop and materialized.

"Teddy, wait right here a minute. I'm going to go check on Quinn."

"Spoken like a true Shepherd." Teddy chuckled.

I teleported myself into Quinn's apartment, but remained invisible. True to his word, he was taking it easy. He was snacking on some chips while watching TV.

"Teddy, thanks for coming down here with me," I said when I returned. "I hate to bother you with all of this."

"Anytime, love. Anytime … Nice view," he noted, nodding towards the skyline. "But I'm more partial to the great outdoors."

"Yeah, there's nothing like a big hole in the ground to make you feel right at home," I teased.

"Hey, now. Don't go poking fun at one of the world's natural wonders." Teddy pretended to be upset with me, but it wasn't long before a smile crept across his face.

So … let's take a look at this here watch of yours, darlin.'" He picked up my wrist and inspected it. "Hmm. Pretty interesting. When was the next Incident scheduled to occur, you know, before it started spinning out of control?"

"Late November of this year," I responded anxiously.

"Hmm." Teddy looked at his watch and did the mental calculations. "Okay, so that was still over four months away. I must say, it's very strange that your watch should react this way. Did anything else happen in conjunction with your watch going wacky?"

My mind replayed the events of the evening just minutes before my watch acted up. The kiss popped into my head, and I was relieved Teddy couldn't read my mind. Leaving that part out, I told him about the chest spasms and my concerns regarding the same.

Teddy assured me that the Time Keeper was running like a well-oiled machine. He also explained that, while unusual, it was possible that Quinn had a heart arrhythmia but didn't feel it because it was so minor. He added that our heightened senses and our ability to diagnose and heal injuries and illnesses made us much more sensitive to the human condition. That said, because the arrhythmia happened so close in time to my so-called "watch malfunction," Teddy wasn't ready to write them off as totally unrelated random acts of chance.

"Bo Peep, I don't know what to say to reassure you. Petey's the expert in this area—not me. But it seems to me that we can't predict when your sheep's next Incident will occur with any degree of certainty right now. So my advice to you would be to stick to him like glue. Never let him out of your sight—not even for a minute. And stay on your toes. Always be aware of your surroundings. And be prepared for anything. Any sign of possible danger, you get your sheep back home to pasture. Capiche?"

"Capiche." Teddy's words did reassure me. There was something I could still do—if I stayed close to Quinn, I had a good chance of being able to protect him. "Thanks, Teddy. You're the best!" I threw my arms around him and gave him a big hug.

"Like I said, any time, little lady." Teddy returned the hug, lifting me clear off my feet. When he put me down, he looked at me seriously. "Eve, I think it's safe to say that there's something very strange going on here with your guy. I don't know what's going to happen—or when—but I can tell you that this is not the usual way our assignments work."

"I'm beginning to realize that," I agreed.

Teddy hugged me one more time and then left. I stood there for a moment, thinking about what he had said. I looked at my watch again; the Incident Timer was still going nuts. Before returning to the apartment, I rotated my watch on my arm, making sure the Timer was on the inside of my wrist so that it wouldn't catch Quinn's attention.

* * *

Quinn was already sleeping by the time I got back, having crashed on the couch with the bag of chips still in hand. I turned off the TV and put the half-empty bag of chips on the coffee table, which made him stir.

"Sorry. I didn't mean to wake you," I whispered.

"No, that's okay." He slowly sat up. "I was just resting my eyes." His voice sounded so groggy. He was visibly exhausted and his hair was all over the place, but he still looked amazing.

He's perfect even when he's not perfect, I said to myself, smiling.

"So is everything okay?" he asked, rubbing his eyes.

"Yes. I just have to keep an even closer eye on you for a while." I smiled in anticipation of his reaction to my having to spend more time with him.

"You won't hear me complaining." He flashed me a goofy, sleepy grin.

"We'll see," I said, still smiling. "C'mon, let's get you to bed." I pulled him up by both hands and led him into his bedroom. After pulling back the blankets, he crawled into bed. I covered him up and turned to leave.

"Evie ... stay," Quinn murmured. Half asleep, he rolled to the right side of the bed to make room for me. Without thinking twice, I crawled into bed and lay down next to him. He turned to face me. I watched him breathe as he drifted back to sleep. I focused on my pulse; it was perfectly in sync with his heartbeat.

My borrowed heart, I thought. I cherished the close connection I had with Quinn, and I dreaded the day I would have to let it go.

From that point forward, Quinn always fell asleep on the right side of the bed, leaving room for me to lie down next to him on the left. And I always did.

* * *

The next morning, I was perched in my usual spot while Quinn got ready for work. I knew I had put him on edge last night, and I didn't want to unnerve him any more than I already had, so I decided to downplay everything today and act as casually and nonchalantly as possible.

My plan backfired as soon as Quinn walked out of the bathroom with only a towel wrapped around his waist, his wet skin still glistening. Sparks flew through me. I took a deep breath and averted my eyes.

Usually, Quinn would have made some quip about my reaction to his body. In fact, he would have orchestrated coming out of the bathroom half-naked to evoke such a reaction from me. I was half-surprised he didn't threaten to drop the towel right then and there—or better yet, actually drop it. But he didn't do any of these things. His mind was somewhere else.

"A penny for your thoughts," I said.

"Last night," Quinn began slowly, "I called my brother, Tommy, while you were out. I'm going to meet him for dinner tonight ... to discuss Brady."

"That's great," I said enthusiastically. "You can tell me all about it when you get back." Of course, I would ghost him the entire time he was out to dinner, but I would give him and his brother as much privacy as I could and try not to eavesdrop on their conversation.

"I want you to come with me," Quinn stated.

"You want me to do what?" I had a sneaking suspicion that Quinn wasn't asking me merely to ghost him at dinner.

"I want you to go with me ... to dinner with my brother tonight," he said calmly, looking directly at me without even blinking an eye.

"You mean, you want me to *meet* your brother tonight."

"Yes," Quinn said, keeping his cool. I, on the other hand, was now far from cool and collected. I was flabbergasted. What could he possibly be thinking?

"Why?"

"I want you to be there when we talk about Brady. I want you to hear the discussion firsthand ... and I'll feel better knowing you're there." Quinn paused. "This isn't going to be the easiest of conversations."

"Quinn, you do realize I can be there with you at dinner, listening the entire time, without actually having to *be* there ... *in person*. I can shadow you."

"Yeah, I know, but it's just not the same." Quinn sighed.

"You mean, it's just not good enough."

"Yeah, it's just not good enough this time around ... Evie, it's just ... we don't seem *real*. Hell, I still can't be sure that we are real. All I know is that I wake up every day wondering if this was all a dream. Every morning, I walk out here holding my breath until I see you sitting in that chair ... I can't tell anyone about you. I can't introduce anyone to you. You won't go out in public unless you're in disguise. I mean, you practically run and hide each time I *think* I see someone I know.

"And tonight, I really need you to be there *with* me. I want you by my side ... And, yes, I want Tommy to meet you ... Think of it as independent proof that you're not a figment of my imagination."

"Well, what about Ronald?" I countered. "He's seen me with you."

"Ronald?" Quinn chuckled wryly. "Ronald is not exactly who I would call the pillar of sanity. My God, Evie, he calls you *angel* right to your face!"

"Well, maybe that actually makes him the sanest character judge of all," I replied.

"Evie, I'm not going to use Ronald as the barometer against which I gauge my own mental health," Quinn said curtly. He took a deep breath. "Look," he continued, dropping the edge in his voice, "Tommy is my big brother. I trust him completely. I know I'm asking a lot, but it would mean the world to me. We don't even have to tell him anything about who you are—"

"You mean *what*," I corrected.

"Fine—*what* you are." Quinn rolled his eyes.

"I can't help you make up some story about me," I replied. "I'm incapable of lying."

"Really? You can't lie? Not ever?" Quinn's newfound intrigue in my latest concession distracted him for a moment.

"No. Apparently not ever," I said matter-of-factly.

"*Interesting.*" His eyes twinkled as he tried to fight the grin that was forming in the corners of his mouth. I could see his mind coming up with a slew of questions to ask me now that he knew I was bound by honesty.

"Can we get back to the real issue at hand here please?" I asked, hoping to get his mind off of the latest cat I had just let out of the bag.

"Uh, yeah. So fine ... *we* won't lie. *I'll* tell Tommy we met at IU, we lost touch, and we happened to run into each other this summer while here in Chicago." Quinn seemed rather pleased with his abbreviated, albeit fairly accurate, account of our story. With every passing minute, I could tell that he was convincing himself of the brilliance of his plan. I had to try a new tactic.

"Quinn, don't you think that your brother might be uncomfortable talking about Brady in front of a complete stranger?"

He sat there for a few minutes, trying to punch a hole in my argument, but he knew it was airtight. He knew I was right; Tommy wouldn't talk about Brady openly in front of me. When Quinn came up empty-handed, he just looked at me with pleading eyes.

"Evie, just do this one favor for me … please."

"I'm sorry, Quinn. We've been down this road before, and my answer is still no." I felt horrible letting him down. "Look," I offered in consolation, "if you want, I can be there the entire time … just not at the table with you."

"Great." Quinn stormed off to his bedroom. He slammed the door shut and got ready for work without saying another word. A few minutes later, he left without even saying good-bye.

* * *

Quinn was in a foul mood all day; even his office mate Kyle stayed clear of him. Quinn only cheered up when he saw his brother, Tommy, waiting for him at Marché. Tommy looked like a younger version of their father, only with dark brown hair and a smaller belly.

"Quinny!" he announced as Quinn approached him at the bar. "I'm starving! Let's go grab a table," Tommy suggested.

The two spent the first half of dinner catching up on summer events. Tommy busted Quinn's chops for not telling the family about the mugging incident sooner and for missing the Cubs game with him and their brother Doug. Quinn told Tommy about his summer internship, and Tommy mentioned he had gotten a new job downtown and would be starting in a couple of weeks. Tommy also mentioned that he and Sam were getting ready to move into the new house, which would be ready well before the arrival of their baby *girl*. Quinn congratulated Tommy upon hearing the news. He seemed genuinely happy at the thought of having a niece.

The conversation took on a more somber note when they discussed what to do about Brady. Apparently, he had also hit Tommy up for money, but Tommy wasn't in a position to give him a loan even if he had wanted to do so. Tommy then stressed that he *didn't* want to give Brady a dollar. Quinn fidgeted in his seat.

"Look, Quinny. I know you. I know you want to help him out. And I do too—trust me, I do. But the best way to do that right now is to do *nothing*. If you give Brady money, you know he's just going to piss it all away and get even deeper in the hole."

"I know," Quinn said reluctantly. "Hey," he said more optimistically, "what do you think about me asking Brady to crash with me for a couple of weeks ... just until he can get his act together and figure a few things out?"

I was mortified by Quinn's idea. He knew he was in danger, and he wanted to invite *more* trouble into his life? What was he thinking? I almost smacked him on the back of the head right then and there.

"No way, Quinny. That's a *really* bad idea," Tommy cautioned. "You know the type of guys that are always after Brady. If he owes them enough, and it sounds like he does this time, they'll follow him right to your doorstep. There's no telling what they'll do to *you* to get Brady to pay up. And, in the meantime, Brady's just going to rob you blind. Quinny, *promise* me you will *not* invite Brady to stay with you." Tommy waited for a response, but it was slow to come.

"Quinn, I'm serious. Do you want to get killed over Brady's gambling debts?" Tommy snapped. He was on the edge of his seat, waiting to hear Quinn's response—and so was I.

"No, of course not," Quinn barked. "I promise I won't invite Brady to Chicago ... but then what am I supposed to do?"

"Nothing." Tommy sighed. "Look, I wish there was something we could do for him. But for as many times as Brady has gotten himself into these messes, he's always managed to get himself out of them. He's resilient that way. Sam says Brady's like a cat with nine lives."

"How many lives do you think Brady has left?" Quinn scoffed.

"Just be patient, Quinny. It'll work itself out—it always does," Tommy said reassuringly.

I could tell that Quinn wasn't satisfied with Tommy's chosen course of action with their brother. I could also tell that Quinn's course of action had yet to be determined. That said, I was fairly confident he had abandoned his idea of inviting Brady to stay with him in Chicago. And if he hadn't given up on the idea, I would find a way to quash such a ludicrous notion as soon as we got back to his apartment.

Quinn and Tommy wrapped up the evening discussing their parents. Tommy had heard through the grapevine that Quinn had gone home the past weekend.

"Who told you?" Quinn seemed surprised.

"Who else? Mom and Dad. You know they practically call us every day to find out how Sam is doing. And a few days ago they mentioned you were planning to spend the weekend up at the house while they were out of town." Tommy raised his eyebrows.

"What?" Quinn asked, but he looked like he already knew where Tommy was going with this.

"What do you mean '*what*'? I know you, Quinny. I know your MO—you brought a girl up to Mom and Dad's." Tommy was smiling from ear to ear and nodding his head up and down slowly in approval.

"I don't know what you're talking about."

"Dude, you suck at lying—you always have. So who was it? That Alyssa chick I saw you out with that one night?"

"Ashley," Quinn corrected. "And, no."

Ugh. I winced at the sound of her name.

"Right, *Ashley*. She was *hot!*" Tommy remarked.

"Does Sam know you talk like this about other women?" Quinn teased.

"Oh come on, Quinny. You know I love Sam more than life itself … but a man can still look once he's married—he just can't touch. And Ashley is worth looking at!" Tommy made some gross gesture with his hands.

Yuck! My stomach turned over.

"You're a sick bastard, you know that?" Quinn shook his head back and forth, chuckling. "Sometimes I can't believe we're related."

His brother just laughed.

"Seriously, though," Tommy continued. "What happened to that chick? She was all over you."

"Ashley was all right," Quinn said indifferently, picking at the food on his plate with his fork."

"Don't tell me she's out of the picture already. Man, Quinny, you go through women faster than most guys go through underwear."

Tommy's interrogation was bothering Quinn—not because of his brother's line of questioning, but because of Quinn's guarded responses. I knew he wanted to tell Tommy he had met someone else. He wanted to tell him that he had met *me*. He wanted to tell Tommy that *I* was with him at their parents' place this past weekend. And I knew Quinn wanted me to be there, sitting next to him at the table.

Guilt got the better of me as I began to suspect that I should have agreed to go to dinner with Quinn. I mean, Quinn had gone out of his way to reach out to me, to help me rediscover who I was … to find a way to love me. He had bent over backwards to meet the conditions of our relationship—conditions that I instituted and forced upon him. And in return, I had done nothing but constantly shut him down. I refused to go out in public with him unless I went incognito. I refused to let him tell anyone about me. I refused to let him introduce me to anybody. I refused to let him touch me the way he wanted to—the way I wished he could. And I was refusing him right now. At the end of the day, what Quinn wanted didn't really matter because exactly which lines were crossed, and how and when they were crossed, were always unilaterally my decisions.

Suddenly, I was so angry with myself. I already had opened Pandora's Box by revealing myself to Quinn and falling in love with him, and we were able to get by relatively unscathed thus far. So what really would have been the harm in my saying 'yes' to Quinn's request to meet his brother?

"Quinn!" Tommy exclaimed. "If Ashley's just *all right*, then your standards are way too high. I mean, if that hottie wasn't good enough for you, then who the hell is? What's next—a supermodel?"

"An angel," Quinn muttered under his breath, chuckling dryly. "You finished with this?" he asked his brother as he picked up Tommy's half-empty glass of beer. Quinn didn't even wait for his brother's response.

"Sláinte." Quinn brought the drink up to his mouth. I couldn't sit back and watch another second. Making sure no one was in the bathroom, I quickly materialized in one of the stalls and morphed into one of Quinn's favorite outfits on me. One quick check in the mirror, and I walked out of the bathroom and over to their table around the corner.

"Quinn!" I said cheerfully as he was just about to take another drink.

The expression on Quinn's face was indescribable. He just sat there, frozen, with the glass just about to touch his mouth, which was hanging open. His blue eyes were opened wide in disbelief. I smiled and winked at him as I walked over to the table.

"It's amazing how we just keep seeing each other." I was still smiling.

"Uh ... yeah," Quinn barely managed. He looked at me and then at the glass of beer, which he summarily set down on the table. "Um ... Tommy, this is—"

"Evie," I said, finishing Quinn's sentence. I didn't know if, out of respect for protecting my anonymity, Quinn would have used my real name, but I didn't want him to lie for me either. I extended my hand out to Tommy; he reciprocated with a handshake.

"Evie," Tommy said, "it's very nice to meet you." He flashed a rascally grin at his little brother, which Quinn ignored.

"Do you have time to join us for a minute?" Quinn asked me hesitantly.

"Sure—that is, as long as I'm not interrupting anything," I responded.

"No, not at all." Quinn jumped to his feet and pulled out the chair next to him for me. I sat down as he pushed it in courteously. When he sat down next to me, he grabbed my hand under the table and gave it a little squeeze. I knew it was his way of thanking me for being there.

"So," Tommy began, "how do you two know each other?"

I turned to Quinn to take the lead on this one.

"Well," he began, clearing his throat, "Evie and I met last semester at IU, but, unfortunately, we lost touch ... that is, until we recently reconnected here in Chicago this summer."

"Oh, how fortunate," Tommy responded, grinning at his brother like a gossipy schoolboy. I could almost see the wheels turning in Tommy's head as he was putting two and two together about Ashley, about me, and about this past weekend at their parents' house.

"So, Evie, what brings you to Chicago?" Tommy asked.

"I'm on assignment, actually," I responded calmly.

325

"Are you working as a journalist for the summer?" he asked.

"Um," Quinn jumped in, "actually Tommy, Evie is not at liberty to discuss her assignments."

"Oh ... government job," Tommy hastily concluded. "The benefits are good, but the pay sucks—just remember that."

"I will, thanks," I said sincerely.

"Evie," Quinn asked, grinning, "what brings you to Marché this evening? Friends?"

"Something like that," I squeezed his thigh under the table and flashed him a playful smirk out of the corner of my mouth. Quinn was playing games; but I could play too. He picked up his glass of water and while he was mid-sip I couldn't resist adding. "And I heard this place has great French onion soup."

Quinn coughed, spraying water out of his mouth everywhere. Tommy and I couldn't help but laugh as he cleaned himself up. When the laughter subsided, Quinn explained that I had an aversion to onions, which he only discovered when he had made me dinner, well *ordered* it, one night at his place and French onion soup was on the menu. As Quinn told the story, he draped his arm around my chair and affectionately rubbed my arm with his fingers.

Tommy glanced at Quinn, then at me, and back to Quinn again. He was watching us. Suddenly, he flashed a knowing smile to himself—like he'd noticed something different about his little brother when he was around me. It made me nervous; I didn't want to stay on Tommy's radar after this evening.

"Tommy," I said when Quinn's story was over, "Quinn tells me that you and your wife are expecting your first child. Congratulations."

"Yes, we are. Thank you." He didn't seem all that surprised that I knew this, like it just further confirmed what he had suspected—that Quinn and I were a couple.

"And ... you're having a girl?" I asked, volunteering that piece of information mainly for Quinn's benefit. I wanted him to know I had been there the entire evening—that I had listened to Tommy and Quinn's discussion about Brady.

"That's right. How did you know? We just found out ourselves," Tommy said, amused and surprised.

I wanted to say "lucky guess," but I literally couldn't get the words out of my mouth. It hadn't been a guess; I had overheard the news. What Peter had told me was right—we really *couldn't* lie. *Crap.*

"I guess you could say Evie has a sixth sense about things," Quinn offered, rescuing me.

"Hey, that reminds me of a story about Quinn." Tommy started chuckling.

"Oh, please tell me you're not really going to tell Evie that one," Quinn begged. I looked at his face; it was getting redder by the second.

"Oh, you know I am. Sorry, Quinny, but she has a right to know who she's getting involved with." Tommy turned towards me. "So, Evie, when Quinn was about five or six, he truly believed he had superpowers; his main one being ESP." Tommy glanced at Quinn. "What was it that you called yourself?"

"I was the Mystery Mind Invader," Quinn admitted reluctantly.

"That's right, the Mystery Mind Invader," Tommy chuckled. "Anyway, Quinn was always running around the neighborhood trying to read people's minds—he even set up an ESP booth one weekend and offered to read people's minds for the bargain price of ten cents." Tommy chuckled again. "The sad thing, of course, was that he'd *always* get it wrong."

"Wait a minute," Quinn piped in, "that's not true. I mean, what about that one day when I read Mr. Green's mind—remember? I knew he wanted a PB & J and chocolate milk for lunch."

Tommy started laughing uncontrollably.

"What?" Quinn asked uneasily, like he knew he was about to be the butt of the joke.

"Quinny, you only ever believed that people were thinking one of three things—they either wanted a puppy; they had to go to the bathroom; or they wanted a PB & J and a glass of chocolate milk. Doug, Brady, and I felt so bad for you we walked over to Mr. Green's house and gave him ten cents to visit your booth and let you guess that's what he wanted for lunch."

"You didn't!" Quinn exclaimed, sounding truly astonished. Tommy was laughing so hard that tears were streaming down his face. I couldn't help but crack up laughing too.

"How could you?" Quinn continued. "My own brothers: traitors! And you dragged poor, unsuspecting Mr. Green into it. Shame on you." Quinn could barely spit out the last few words before he burst out laughing too.

Quinn and Tommy took turns sharing Harrison family stories with me until we were interrupted by the waitress dropping off the check.

"Well," I said, clearing my throat. "That's my cue. It's getting late, and I really should be going." I stood up to leave. Tommy and Quinn followed suit, rising to their feet as well. "I'm sorry if I interrupted the rest of your evening, but it was really nice to meet you. I loved hearing stories about Quinn and the rest of your family."

"No interruption at all, Evie. It was a pleasure meeting you too," Tommy said. I turned to Quinn.

"With the way things have been going, I'm sure I'll see you soon." I winked at him.

"I can't wait," Quinn said, smiling at me as he hugged me.

"Thank you," he whispered in my ear. "This meant more to me than you'll ever know."

I looked up at Quinn and squeezed his hand reassuringly once more before I let go.

"Well, good night, then."

"Good night," Quinn and Tommy said in unison.

I smiled, turned around, and walked away. I phased out of sight the first chance I got and returned to the table just in time to see Quinn and his brother getting up to leave. I ghosted them to the front door of the restaurant, where Tommy refused to let Quinn find his own way back to his apartment.

"Are you kidding me? You know I'll never hear the end of it from Mom if I don't make sure you get to your place safe and sound," Tommy stated. Quinn had no choice but to accept a ride home from his big brother.

"Thanks again for dinner, Tommy," Quinn said, patting his brother on the shoulder when he pulled up to the front of Quinn's building.

"No problem. And, hey, when you see that pretty little lady of yours later on tonight, tell her again that it was great to meet her," Tommy remarked as Quinn got out of the car and shut the door.

"Tommy, I have absolutely no idea what you're talking about," Quinn stated, grinning from ear to ear.

"Go get her, tiger!" Tommy yelled from his window as Quinn entered the lobby.

I watched Tommy for a moment longer as he pulled away. So he had figured it out ... well, not all of it, but the gist of it. He knew Quinn was smitten. I'm sure he probably guessed I was too. I smiled to myself and then looked up at the windows of Quinn's loft just as he turned on the lights.

I teleported myself outside of Quinn's apartment, phased into view, and knocked on the front door.

"Hey, Mystery Mind Invader," I called out to Quinn through the door, "I wonder if you can tell what I'm thinking right now."

A huge smile spread across my lips when I heard Quinn run across the room to unlock the door.

28. The Winds of Change

The night I met Tommy marked another turning point in Quinn's and my relationship. After work, Quinn would come back to his apartment and we would stay up until the wee hours. One evening we went up to Quinn's rooftop, and I explained the history behind many of the skyscrapers downtown. He was surprised at how much I knew about Chicago architecture—that was until I showed him one of the books on his bookshelf about the subject. Still, he couldn't believe I actually had read the book cover to cover.

Most nights we stayed in, perfectly content talking over candlelight, laughing at each other's jokes, watching old movies, and listening to music. Sometimes, we would just cuddle up on the couch and enjoy the comfortable silence between us. Other times, I would prod Quinn to tell me more stories about his childhood and his family. And, of course, we always managed to find ways to push the envelope of our physical attraction for each other.

Quinn never tried to kiss me again, much to my dismay and relief. Even though the love we felt for one another seemed to get stronger with each passing day, so did our desire for each other. It was to the point where I seriously questioned whether either one of us would be able to control ourselves if we crossed that line again.

Brady hadn't tried to contact Quinn again, which I suspected helped him unwind enough to enjoy the moment without the distraction of his brother. In fact, if he was worrying about Brady, I certainly couldn't tell. Quinn seemed as relaxed as I had ever remembered seeing him.

I wished I could say the same thing about me. My watch was still going haywire, and I hadn't the slightest indication of when Quinn's Second Incident would occur. I never left his side, even when he was sleeping, for fear of what might happen to him while I was gone.

That Saturday night, Quinn and I decided to see a movie in the park. We strolled the entire way home from Grant Park. It felt like a real, official date, and I loved every minute of it.

Quinn was about to unlock the front door to his loft when I heard a strange noise coming from inside. Someone was in his apartment. I immediately grabbed Quinn's hand to prevent him from inserting the key into the lock.

"Quinn," I whispered, "are you expecting someone?"

"No," he replied softly. "Why?"

"Because you have a visitor."

"What? Who?" Quinn whispered in alarm.

"I don't know. The only thing I can tell you for sure is that the intruder is a human." I squeezed his hand so he would look at me, "I want you to wait at the bottom of the stairs while I go inside and check things out."

"No way," he whispered sharply. "You're crazy if you think I'm letting you go in there alone. You could get hurt."

"Quinn," I whispered, "I'll be fine." I loved that he felt the need to be so overprotective of me, but now was not the time for heroics on his part. "It's my job to worry about *your* safety, remember? I'm here to protect you—not the other way around. And right now, I need to find out what I'm up against in there without worrying about you. So, please, go downstairs and wait for me."

He was about to object again, but I didn't give him the chance.

"Quinn, I'm not asking you to do this."

He crossed his arms and firmly planted his feet on the landing in protest. We didn't have time to debate this. I had to find out who the intruder was and what he wanted.

"Fine," I said reluctantly. "But can you at least stay here while I take an initial look around?"

"Evie—"

"Quinn," I interjected, "we're wasting valuable time standing out here arguing."

"Fine. I'll stay here … for a minute."

"Ugh!" I sighed. "Why do you have to be so stubborn?"

"Because it's my job to worry about *your* safety." He flashed me his incredible smile. Instantly, images of Quinn brushing his lips against mine popped into my head. I still couldn't get over how vulnerable I was to his charms; it worried me. I quickly re-focused my complete attention on the intruder.

With Quinn standing right there, phasing out of view and teleporting myself inside his apartment was not a desirable option, which left me with one other viable choice. Using Quinn's key, I slowly and quietly unlocked the door. Maybe I would have time enough to close the door behind me and immediately dematerialize so as to maintain some element of surprise.

As usual, luck was not on my side. I opened the door to see the intruder sitting on Quinn's couch with his legs propped up on the coffee table. He had the remote in one hand, about to turn on the TV, while holding a container of leftover Thai food in the other. I was confused. What kind of intruder would make himself feel right at home in a stranger's apartment?

It wasn't until I looked at the intruder's face that I realized that he was not in a stranger's apartment. His black hair and deep blue eyes gave him away immediately. I knew I was staring at Brady. The similarities in the two brothers' appearances were freaky; in fact, they could easily have passed for twins. But I soon discovered that's where their likeness ended.

Brady was very different from Quinn on the inside. Quinn's aura shone clearly and brightly, full of the energy that life had to offer those who were decent and honorable, whereas Brady's aura was dark and overcast. At the young age of twenty-two, Brady's soul was already tarnished. I could tell that his gambling addiction and the lifestyle that went along with it had caught up with him and were now suffocating the life from him—literally. Where Quinn's eyes twinkled with exuberance and optimism, Brady's were dull and lackluster, no doubt scarred from his entanglements with countless numbers of corrupt and wayward souls over the past couple of years.

"Damn it, Brady. How the hell did you get in here?" Quinn demanded from over my shoulder. He pushed the front door open and marched past me.

"Well, that wasn't exactly the greeting I was hoping for. It's nice to see you, too, little brother." Brady didn't even flinch. Instead, he took another bite of leftovers. "Relax, Quinny," he mumbled with a mouthful of food. "I didn't break in if that's what you're wondering. I simply told your super that I was your brother, and that I was visiting you from out of town and arrived a little earlier than expected. So he let me in."

"I'll have to talk to him about that," Quinn said coldly. Every muscle in Quinn's body was tense. His heart was beating loudly. He looked like he was ready to pounce on his brother at any minute.

Brady peered around Quinn and eyed me.

"Quinny, aren't you going to introduce me to your guest?"

"She's just a friend," Quinn replied offhandedly, causing Brady to cast a dubious glance in my direction.

"Yeah, well, um, *friend*," Brady began, "I hate to be rude, but it's been awhile since I've seen my baby brother here, and as I'm sure you've guessed, we have a lot to talk about. So is there any way that we can have a little privacy?"

I looked at Quinn for his cue as to whether or not I should leave ... well, *disappear* at any rate. When our eyes locked, I knew he wanted me to stay.

"What—you two tied at the hip or something?" Brady asked snidely. "She makin' the calls for you these days, Quinny?"

"Hey," Quinn snapped. "*You* interrupted *our* evening—not the other way around. So she isn't going anywhere." He took my hand in his. "Besides, it doesn't really matter anyway—she already knows all about you."

"It's not your style to air the Harrison dirty laundry. Aren't you the one always preaching about how blood is thicker than water?"

Quinn didn't respond.

"So, what, you've suddenly abandoned that platitude?"

"No, not at all," Quinn responded calmly, giving my hand an obvious squeeze. Before Brady could react verbally to what he'd just witnessed, Quinn jumped right back in.

"Why are you here, Brady? What do you want from me?"

Brady sighed heavily, as if in final protest about my being there; Quinn ignored it. "Look, I thought about what you said during our last conversation. You know, how Mom and Dad always bailed me out of trouble ... that I was ... what did you call me? Oh yeah, I think it was 'a sorry excuse for a son and a brother.' And I realized you were right.

"I know I've burned bridges with Tommy and Dougie, and I know I messed things up with Mom and Dad and you. I want to fix the mess I made, but I can't do it on my own. Quinny, I need your help. I don't want to talk to Mom and Dad—not right now anyway. I've made them a lot of empty promises, and I don't want to try to convince them that I can change this time—I want to *prove* it to them. And I know I can ... With your help, Quinny, I know I can change."

Brady was lying. I could see his heat signature, his aura, move around him in frenetic patterns while he spoke. I wasn't sure how far he was stretching the truth, but it was far enough to concern me.

Quinn broke his gaze from Brady and glanced at me. I could see the tortured look in his eyes. I knew he was struggling to find some way to believe what his brother was saying. The one thing I was certain of about Thayer McQuinn Harrison was that it was his nature to stand up for his family and to support them even if it meant doing so at the lowest points in their lives. And I was sure that Brady knew this about his brother too.

I would have given anything to be able to communicate telepathically with Quinn at that moment, but I couldn't. Besides, what would I have said? That Brady was being dishonest? That his motives were insincere? How could I tell Quinn that about his own brother? And, as far as I could tell, Brady meant Quinn no physical harm. Still, I feared that the emotional betrayal Quinn might suffer at Brady's hands would outweigh any physical pain Brady might cause him.

"You still haven't told me where or how I fit into all of this," Quinn pressed, turning his attention back towards his brother.

"I just need a place to crash for a few nights while I figure out my next move. I had to get out of Atlantic City so I could clear my head."

"Running from your bookies again?"

"No," Brady replied snidely. "I'm all squared away. That's why I left. It was now or never. I knew I had to leave the life to be able to get my act together. I want a chance at a fresh start."

"So let me get this straight," Quinn said with a strained face. "You're telling me that you settled *all* your debts and you left Atlantic City of your own accord because you want to make things right with our family?" The disbelief in his voice was audible.

"Yes—but not just with our family. I want to make things right for me too. I want to wipe the slate clean."

Brady's aura was still in flux, which meant he still wasn't being straight with Quinn. Unfortunately, I couldn't parcel out the lies from the truth. And I couldn't shake the feeling that it was all a lie. I squeezed Quinn's hand gently, hoping that he would interpret my gesture as a warning.

"Okay, Brady," Quinn sighed. "It's late, so I'm not going to kick you out. But this is *not* an invitation for you to stay either. We'll talk about this tomorrow. In the meantime, you can couch it." Quinn let go of my hand, walked over to the linen closet, grabbed a blanket and a pillow, and tossed them to his brother.

"Thanks," Brady said.

"C'mon, let's go to bed." Quinn took my hand and started leading me down the hall.

"Oh, and Brady," Quinn called out to his brother before we walked into the bedroom, "if you really are serious about this desire to turn a new leaf, then first thing in the morning we're finding a Gamblers Anonymous meeting somewhere in this city and we're going—*together*."

"Fine. Absolutely. Good idea," Brady responded. "Oh, hey, I hope you don't mind, but I took a quick shower and borrowed some of your clothes when I first got here."

"So I noticed," Quinn said dryly. "Good night, Brady."

"Good night, Quinn … and Quinn's *friend*."

"Good night," I responded as I followed Quinn into his room.

A ton of questions ran through my head, but they would have to wait since Quinn fell asleep almost immediately. I just lay there silently, wrapped up in his arms, listening to the nocturnal sounds of the city. I wondered what Quinn was planning to do with Brady. I contemplated what I would do if I were in Quinn's shoes.

I also thought about the monkey wrench that would be hurled into Quinn's life if Brady were to stick around for a while. Selfishly speaking, my relationship with Quinn inevitably would change for the worse. We would no longer be alone in the apartment because there would always be someone else there.

More importantly, though, Brady's resurgence in Quinn's life would only prove to make my job of guarding Quinn more difficult. Brady was a dangerous distraction for both Quinn and me. I knew Quinn would focus his efforts more on Brady's welfare than on his own. Quinn would watch his brother like a hawk, doing everything he could to keep him on the road to redemption, even if it meant putting himself in precarious situations and environments.

And for what? Based on what I had just witnessed and what I previously had heard about Brady, I doubted that even Quinn's best efforts to help his brother would be successful.

Not to mention there was a good chance Brady was lying about settling his debts. What if his bookies tracked him to Quinn's apartment? I sighed, knowing this was not going to end well. It was just a matter of time before Brady would disappoint his brother, his entire family, again. I just hoped he didn't endanger Quinn in the process.

My thoughts were interrupted by rustling sounds coming from the living room. Brady was up and moving about. I slowly got up out of bed, dematerialized, and wandered into the living area. The loft was dark. The only trace of light in the apartment came from the nearby streetlamps, which Brady was using to help him rummage quietly through Quinn's files, desk drawers, closets … everything. He crept over to the linen closet, reached up to the top shelf, and found a small metal lockbox. He carefully jimmied the lock open with a pocketknife and found a wad of cash inside.

"Good old, Quinny. Always following Dad's advice. Well, here's to emergency cash." Brady kissed the wad of money before stuffing it into his beat-up duffle bag.

I knew that Brady would screw Quinn over, I just didn't think it would happen overnight. I was right; Brady knew exactly how to play his brother. He had come here with one purpose in mind—to steal from Quinn. How could Brady abuse his brother's trust like that?

I was enraged. There was no way I was going to let him get away with this. Still invisible, I walked up behind Brady as he was replacing the empty lockbox in its hiding place and materialized.

"Looking for something?" I asked. Brady nearly jumped out of his skin when he heard my voice right behind him. He whipped around and saw me standing there.

"Are you going to return the money you just took from your brother?" I said a little more boldly.

Still on edge, Brady scanned the room. He looked like he was weighing his options.

"I'm only going to say this once: *Put the money back*," I said sternly.

But Brady didn't put the money back. Instead, he shoved me aside and bolted towards the front door with his duffle bag in hand.

Son of a bitch! There was no way I was letting him leave with that money. I refused to believe that the pain I was supposed to protect Quinn from was solely physical; and I had no doubt Quinn would be crushed by his brother's betrayal.

I caught Brady by the arm, stopping him dead in his tracks before he reached the door.

"What the—" Brady exclaimed, apparently startled by my strength.

I grabbed Brady's duffle bag from his hand and ripped it open, letting the contents fall onto the couch. I couldn't believe it. Not only had Brady taken the wad of cash from Quinn's lockbox, but he'd also snatched his laptop, cell phone, and a document from Quinn's summer firm that identified his Social Security number.

"I don't think you'll be needing these," I said as I shoved the empty, torn duffel bag into Brady's arms and started pushing him towards the door.

"Look, I'm not playing games here, *friend*," Brady said in a threatening tone of voice. His pupils were so dark they were almost black. Instantly, I closed the distance between us so that we were mere inches apart.

"Neither am I," I said calmly. I reached behind him and opened the front door for him. "I think you should leave before your brother wakes up and sees your true colors."

Brady hesitated for a moment, so I grabbed his shirt and escorted him out the door, causing him to trip over his own shoes and stumble into the hallway. When Brady regained his balance, he sized me up. I could tell he was baffled by how easily I'd moved his six-foot frame.

"I would *not* come back here if I were you," I warned him as I closed the door and locked it behind me. From the window, I watched Brady run out of Quinn's building and down the street.

"What an evil little prick," I muttered under my breath when he was no longer in my line of sight. I wanted to clean up all evidence of Brady's transgressions before Quinn woke up. Hopefully, he would buy whatever vague version of the truth I came up with to explain Brady's rash departure.

I put Quinn's money back into the lockbox and made a mental note to suggest that he find another place to stash his emergency cash in the future. I put Quinn's laptop back on the dining room table and straightened up his papers as best I could. Then I put Quinn's phone back on the kitchen counter next to his wallet and his—

Crap! Brady had taken Quinn's keys. There was no way of hiding this from Quinn; he would have to get the locks changed in the morning. On a hunch, I opened Quinn's wallet to discover it was devoid of all cash and credit cards. Unfortunately, I hadn't thought to check Brady's pockets before I threw him out. Now I was going to have to be up front with Quinn about what Brady had done.

Great. Just great, I said to myself as I went to go wake up Quinn so he could report his credit cards stolen.

* * *

"Damn it! Why does Brady always have to pull this kind of shit?" I could see the anger of his brother's betrayal building in Quinn's eyes. They grew so dark and cold that they reminded me of Brady's eyes when I'd confronted him.

"So am I to assume you caught him red-handed?" Quinn asked me as he slumped down onto the couch next to me.

I nodded affirmatively.

"And you threw him out?"

"I'm sorry. I just didn't know what else to do. He tried to run out ..." I paused, debating whether I should volunteer any additional information.

"You did the right thing, Evie. I shouldn't have let him stay the night. I guess everyone was right about him but me. Brady is a lost cause." Quinn sighed. "It's just ... we used to be so close." He ran his hand through his hair as he leaned backwards. "I still can't believe Brady would actually *steal* from me."

"Well, at least all he took were your keys, some cash, and a handful of canceled credit cards," I said with a glass-half-full kind of enthusiasm.

"That's not all he took, Evie," he said solemnly.

341

"I know," I said as I caressed his hair. "I know."

* * *

Quinn was in a somber mood the entire next day. That morning, he called the building superintendent, who promptly came over and changed the locks on Quinn's front door. Quinn explained to him that Brady had stolen some money from him and instructed the guy to call the cops if he ever saw Brady again.

Quinn had zero interest in going outside. So we stayed in all day. We drew all the blinds, shut out the rest of the world, and watched movies.

I gave Quinn his space. He barely spoke, and I didn't push him to open up either. He would talk to me if and when he was ready. Until then, I planted myself in my chair and flipped through magazines to catch up on the latest Hollywood gossip, stopping occasionally to watch a scene or two from a movie or to make sure Quinn had something to eat and drink.

Around midnight, Quinn began to crash on the couch. I didn't want him to sleep there all night, so I coaxed him to bed. I lay down next to him, trying to digest the events that had occurred over the last twenty-four-or-so hours. I thought about how much I would have missed had I been up in the Archives when Brady showed up. It was the first time I truly understood how important it was to remain on Earth while on assignment.

I looked up at the sky through Quinn's bedroom windows; it was a beautiful star-filled evening. Instantly, I felt claustrophobic. I had been inside all day, and the thought of being cooped up in the apartment for another minute was insufferable. I checked my watch. In all of the excitement, I hadn't realized the date of the Second Incident had reset itself to the twenty-fourth of November of this year. *Interesting.*

Feeling some relief to have a "firm" Incident date, and knowing that Brady would not be returning tonight, at least not using Quinn's old set of keys, I felt it was safe to go to the rooftop deck for a minute or two to breathe in the summer air.

From my vantage point above, I could see a few people wandering the streets, either heading home for the evening or walking their dogs. I even saw one guy out for a run, the sight of which made me laugh. But it also made me want to take a walk. I needed to stretch my legs. *Just a short walk,* I told myself.

The next thing I knew, I was walking around the block. It felt so good to be outside on my own. I realized I enjoyed the alone time; it helped me unwind and think things through. I was deep in thought when I heard a familiar voice call out to me.

"There's my favorite angel," Ronald sang. I looked up, surprised to see Ronald perched in his usual spot right outside the convenience store. I hadn't realized I had wandered this far from Quinn's apartment.

"Good evening, Ronald," I replied, smiling.

"Interesting night for a stroll, don't you think?" he asked.

"Cabin fever," I replied absentmindedly, my head still lingering in the fog of my own thoughts.

"Well, you best be careful now. The winds of change are fast upon us." Ronald's tone of voice changed; it sounded like he was trying to tell me something. I looked at him and immediately noticed the unnerving look in his eyes.

"What do you mean?" I asked apprehensively.

"Angel, do you know what time it is?" he asked me, ignoring my question. I looked down at my watch.

"Oh crap!" I gasped in horror. The Incident Timer was flashing red with an *Exitus* countdown of only seconds to spare. I had to leave immediately. But how? I didn't even have enough time to run around the corner to inconspicuously teleport myself back to Quinn's. I looked at Ronald with dread-filled eyes.

How could I have been so *stupid* as to leave Quinn's side? I had risked his life for what—the proverbial walk in the park? Waves of anxiety, panic, and nausea were crashing over me; I felt like I was drowning. I didn't know what I would do if anything happened to Quinn—if *I let* anything happen to him. I looked around me; Ronald was the only soul in sight. I looked hopelessly back at him.

"It's time to go, angel!" Ronald said urgently. "Do it! Now!" he commanded.

Instantly, I teleported myself back to Quinn's loft right before Ronald's eyes. I didn't have time to think about the repercussions of teleporting in front of him. In truth, right now I really didn't care. I couldn't get to Quinn's apartment fast enough.

I phased into Quinn's bedroom and turned on the lights. He stirred but remained fast asleep. My head was pounding so fiercely that I couldn't even focus on the rhythm beating in my chest. I ran over to Quinn and listened to his heartbeat; it was fine. Still terrified, I raced through the apartment, turning on every light switch and looking for anything out of place. Nothing was out of the ordinary.

Confused, I stopped in my tracks and looked down at my watch. It was still flashing, but the countdown had run out. I was at ground zero; the Second Incident should have occurred by now.

Just then I heard screeching tires outside of Quinn's apartment. I teleported myself outside onto the street only to see the taillights of a black Mercedes limousine turn sharply around the corner and keep going.

Still invisible, I followed the limo. I could only catch glimpses of the driver as the car raced underneath the fluorescent streetlamps that lit the path down the empty road. He was dressed like a professional limousine driver, right down to the brimmed cap that concealed most of his face. I hung back a bit and tried to look at the passengers, but all of the windows were tinted as black as the night sky. The only way I could find out who was riding in back of the car would be to go inside.

What if this was a trap? For the first time, I was nervous about my own welfare. Afraid, I stopped dead in my tracks and watched the car speed away.

"Damn it!" I muttered under my breath as I materialized on the sidewalk. It was only then that I realized my watch was beeping. The Incident Timer was scrolling at an unbelievably rapid pace—again.

"What the—" Terrified, I transported myself back inside Quinn's bedroom. He was still fine. I sat down on the edge of his bed. I didn't know what to think about the last sixty seconds. A million questions ran through my mind.

What possessed me to take a walk tonight of all nights? I knew better than to leave Quinn's side. Whatever the reason, my actions this evening were downright stupid and reckless, and they could have cost Quinn his life.

And how in the world was Ronald able to warn me? It was like he knew what I was—what I was capable of doing. And how was it that I found myself wandering near him just in the knick of time for him to warn me? Would I have even caught the countdown without Ronald's help? I shuddered, fearing the worst.

Yet, there had been no attack on Quinn's life. As far as I could tell, there hadn't been an overt threat of any kind. That couldn't have been the Second Incident, could it? Or was it just another inexplicable watch malfunction? But, then, what was the deal with the black limousine? I sincerely doubted that Brady's visit, the limo, Ronald—any of it—was all just a coincidence.

I walked around the apartment and turned off all the lights before curling up next to Quinn's slumbering body. I watched him sleep the rest of the night, silently apologizing to him over and over again.

* * *

Quinn entered the apartment with a huge smile stretched across his face after work the next day. He walked over to where I was standing by the stereo and kissed me on the cheek.

"What has you in such a good mood?" I asked, eyeing him strangely. I had ghosted him the entire way home from the office and hadn't observed anything that would spark this unexpected show of happiness.

"I just realized something," Quinn called out as he walked into his room, retrieved his iPod docking station, and set it up on the dining room table. "Today is our anniversary."

"Our *anniversary*?" I asked, bewildered as I took a few steps towards the kitchen, curious to see what he was doing.

"Yup. It was exactly one month ago today that we had our first *date*," Quinn explained as he searched for a song on his iPod. "And to celebrate, I thought I'd play you a song."

He hit play, and the music started. I didn't recognize the song, but I liked it. The rhythm was slow and sexy, the words were sultry … lustful. I wasn't sure where Quinn was going with this, but I started to feel a little on edge as he peeled off his clothes layer by layer until he was wearing nothing but his boxers.

"And why would our one-month anniversary warrant a celebration with this particular song?" I asked nervously as Quinn began to walk across the room to where I was standing. There was a sparkle in his eye and a look on his face that screamed nothing but trouble. He flashed me a smile that would have taken my breath away were I alive, and I wondered if it ever did. I took a few steps backwards until I inadvertently bumped up against the front door. Quinn remained steadfast in his approach, stopping only when he was within an inch of me.

"Because," he said as he leaned in, pressing his body against mine as he brushed his lips against my neck, "*this* is the song that was playing the first time we *ever* kissed." He pulled back his head and looked at me; his eyes were blazing—they looked like blue flames. "A while ago."

"Oh," I barely managed.

He smiled at me again as he reached up and caressed my hair, drawing it gently behind me. His fingers lightly traced the contours of my neck, making me quiver slightly. I held my breath and shut my eyes.

"And," Quinn said as he bent back down to kiss the nape of my neck, "it got me thinking," he paused to kiss my neck again, "about how we never had a chance to have an anniversary." I could hear the desire in his voice. My knees felt weak. I took a deep breath and exhaled slowly to try to calm myself down, but it was of no use. I had wanted Quinn so desperately, so completely, and for so long that I couldn't fight it anymore. I tilted my head back and he kissed me from my neck down to my collarbone. His tongue danced on my skin until his mouth found its way back up near my ear. I felt like I was about to explode.

"So I couldn't think of a better way to celebrate this one," Quinn whispered hoarsely in my ear, "this being our first anniversary and all," he paused to nip playfully at my earlobe, "than by giving you a taste of what we were like ... *before.*"

Quinn pressed his body into me, pinning me up against the door. I gasped when I felt every muscle in his body tense up. I could feel his heart pounding. I could hear him moaning

347

softly. I dared to open my eyes in time to see Quinn looking at me just before he brushed his lips against mine, sending a tingling sensation rippling through every inch of me. He nuzzled my neck and kissed it again. I knew I should stop him, but I had no intention of doing so. I was at his mercy. I closed my eyes again, surrendering my body to him.

And then, out of blue, he stopped. Quinn let up and took a step backwards. Shocked, I opened my eyes and looked at him.

"What's wrong?" I asked, alarmed.

"Nothing," he said calmly, smiling wickedly at me. "I said I would only give you a *taste* of what we were like. Now," he sighed, "if you'll excuse me, I need to go take a cold shower." And with that, Quinn turned around and headed off to the bathroom.

Stunned, I just stood there wide-eyed and with my mouth hanging open as he walked away. I couldn't believe he would tease me like that. Moreover, I couldn't believe Quinn had the restraint to stop. My knees were still shaking and my head was spinning from the vortex that he had just sucked me into and then so abruptly spit me out of. All I could do was sink to the ground and listen to the rest of the song as it continued to play.

* * *

Several lighthearted apologies later, Quinn was back in my good graces again. We decided to celebrate the rest of our anniversary by taking an evening stroll. Wanting to avoid Ronald, I suggested that we try a new route, and Quinn agreed without hesitation. We held hands as we walked through the streets of the West Loop, pausing for a moment when we reached Marché. I couldn't help but tease Quinn a little bit by referring to him as the Mystery Mind Invader.

"You're never going to let me live that one down, are you?" he asked, laughing. "Just remember, I was five when I made up that name."

"Don't worry," I said, laughing. "If you only knew what they called me up there, you wouldn't feel so silly."

"Who are *they*?" Quinn asked, intrigued. "And what do they call you?"

I stopped laughing, realizing I had unintentionally slipped up, again. I cleared my throat and looked away.

"I know ... you *can't* tell me who *they* are or what they call you, right?" he said bluntly.

"Quinn ..." I didn't know what else to say other than I was sorry—and he certainly didn't need to hear that line pass through my lips anymore.

"Don't worry about it." His tone was sincere. "I know this is hard for you too. Come on, let's go."

"Go where?" I asked.

"Home," Quinn said. "Back to our place."

Home ... to our place, I repeated in my head. The words had rolled off Quinn's tongue so naturally I didn't think he even realized the impact of what he had just said. Or perhaps he did. Maybe he had thought of his summer apartment as *our* place all along. Oddly enough, the notion had never crossed my mind. I had always thought of it as *his* apartment, although I guess I had adopted *my* chair. But I certainly hadn't expected him to think that he had been "sharing" his place with me. I liked the sound of it, nevertheless. *Our place*, I repeated again to myself and smiled.

Engrossed with the idea of officially being considered Quinn's roommate, I hadn't noticed I had stepped off the curb and out into the nearby intersection without so much as glancing in either direction. I hadn't noticed the headlights of the car parked a block or so away, or even that it had pulled out into the street and begun accelerating towards the intersection ... towards me.

"Evie, look out!" Quinn shouted as he grabbed my arm and yanked me back onto the sidewalk. A black Mercedes limousine careened past us, just barely missing me, and whipped around the next corner. I recognized the limousine as the same one that had been parked outside of Quinn's apartment building the other night.

"Are you okay?" Quinn asked in alarm.

"Yeah ... I'm fine ... perfectly fine," I answered in a daze.

"What the hell was *that* about?" Quinn exclaimed.

"I ... I don't know," I said numbly. I quickly snapped out of my state of shock and looked at Quinn. "Are you okay?" I asked, examining him for any visible signs of injury.

"Yeah ... Evie, I wasn't even in the street. I was standing here on the sidewalk."

"You—you weren't standing in the street?"

"No," Quinn responded uneasily.

"How can that be?" I asked in disbelief as I glanced down at my watch. Nothing had changed. The day and month numbers were still scrolling, which meant the next Incident could occur any time within the year ... but, as far as I could tell, it *wasn't* scheduled to occur now.

This wasn't a random accident—the limo had been waiting for us. It had been a premeditated strike. Could it have been an impromptu follow-up to the botched surprise attack last night? Is that why it didn't register on my watch? Was Quinn even the target tonight? ... Or was *I*?

"Evie," Quinn asked anxiously, "is everything all right?"

Everything was *not* all right. Everything was far from all right, and this was not the time to sugarcoat things for Quinn.

"No. We need to get you out of here *now*. We have to get you back to *your* place," I said harshly. I thought about teleporting us back to his apartment, but I didn't know if it was even possible for me to do that. I knew I could teleport with smaller objects, but I'd never tried to teleport anything of considerable size, much less anything living. Instead, I grabbed Quinn's hand and began to run, with him literally tagging along.

"Evie, tell me what's going on," he demanded, pulling back on my hand, but I didn't slow down.

"Wait a damn minute!" he yelled as he tried to free his hand from my grip for the next block. "Evie! Stop!" He yanked himself free from me and refused to take another step. "I'm not going anywhere with you until you tell me why you're freaking out like this ... What was up with that limo?"

I looked around and saw no sign of the car, but I could sense it was still lurking about nearby—like a lion crouched down in the grass, waiting for the right time to pounce on its prey. We were so naked and exposed just standing there on the street corner. I looked down at my watch—no change. My stomach turned over as anxiety welled up inside of me.

"Quinn, we can't stay here. Please. Listen to me on this one. I'll explain when we get back to the loft. I promise." I had hoped the urgency in my voice—in my eyes—was enough to convince him to follow me, but I was wrong.

"You promise?" Quinn scoffed. "How can you promise to tell me what's going on when you can't even tell me your nickname up in ... wherever it is you're from? What are you going to do? Give me some half-assed explanation of what went down tonight and then expect me to be grateful for the breadcrumbs you toss my way? Do you really think I'm just going to settle for that after tonight?"

Two blocks away, I saw the limo creep slowly around the corner and come to a stop.

"No. But I *do* think the only way you're going to stay alive long enough for me to explain what's going on is by listening to me *right now.*"

Quinn turned around at the sound of the limo peeling out. It was heading straight for us, gaining speed the entire way.

"Oh shit," Quinn mumbled in his frozen state.

"C'mon!" I practically dragged him by the arm as we ran down the block. The undercarriage of the limo scraped against the cement as it jumped up onto the curb behind us. I pulled Quinn into a nearby alley as the long, black missile just barely passed us by and came screeching to a halt. We didn't have much time before it would be on us again.

"Great," Quinn moaned. "You had to pick an alley, didn't you?"

Humor? At a time like this? Really? I thought.

"Just look for a door!" I ordered.

"Over there!" Quinn yelled as he pointed across the way to what looked like the back entrance of a deserted warehouse. There was a huge, rusty metal door on a sliding track that was bolted shut by a huge padlock.

"Great." I sighed heavily, feeling the need to create a little comic relief of my own. "You had to pick the door to a psycho's lair, didn't you?"

The mouth of the dark alley lit up. It was the limo.

"Here goes nothing." I broke the lock with my bare hands and slid the door ajar just enough for Quinn and me to slip inside. I shut the door behind us and warped the metal sliding track, making it nearly impossible to reopen.

My eyes quickly adjusted to the darkness. Old steel scraps, machines, and random parts and tools were scattered everywhere, creating a maze of obstacles for us to clear. I led Quinn behind a large, rusted-out machine. As soon as we crouched down behind it, a rat squeaked and ran by my foot. I almost screamed.

"What is this place?" I asked, horrified.

"I have no idea," Quinn replied, his eyes also having now adjusted enough to make out the metal wasteland all around us.

A loud scraping noise echoed throughout the warehouse as the door to the alley was slowly pushed open a few minutes later. The driver had parked the limousine such that its headlights cast some light into the opening of our dark hideout.

"They gotta be in here!" someone cried. Instinctively, I sidled up closer to Quinn.

"You really wanna go lookin' around in this craphole?" a grittier male voice asked.

"No," the first voice responded. "But we don't got no choice, now do we?"

"C'mon. Let's just get this over with."

I heard the door crank open even wider.

"Come out, come out wherever you are," one of the creeps called out in a sinister voice. "There's nowhere for you to run."

He was right. I scanned the warehouse; there was only one other door at the opposite end of where Quinn and I were hiding, and we'd never make it there undetected. I had to come up with another plan—fast.

"Wait here," I barely whispered to Quinn. He nodded in agreement. I carefully inched around the corner, hoping I could draw the thugs away from Quinn if they saw me; but, as far as I could tell, they didn't. I phased out of view and located the two men near the entrance. I found a couple small, heavy pieces of metal hardware. As much as I wanted to throw them at the two guys, I didn't want to break yet another Rule unless I had to. Injuring them would be a last resort, I decided.

I teleported myself into the alley and threw one of the metal pieces towards the entrance about fifty feet away. I was hoping to trick the guys into thinking we had escaped out another door to the warehouse. No such luck. They didn't even stop to check out what had made that noise. For all I knew, they didn't even hear it.

That's when I spotted the brand new Bentley convertible parked across the street from the mouth of the alley. *Sorry*, I wanted to say to the owner of the car, as I chucked the second metal chunk through the car windshield. The car's alarm blared. *That should draw their attention.*

I teleported myself inside the warehouse and waited for the goons' reactions. Sure enough, they were not very happy to hear the nearby alarm. They were even less pleased to hear the sirens off in the distance heading this way.

"Damn it!" one of them snarled.

"C'mon, we gotta to get outta here before the cops come," the other urged. "They'll trace the car back to Chloe—and then we'll have *real* hell to pay."

"She's such a kiss-ass. I would take her out if I could." As the words left the thug's mouth, I swore I saw a flash of red in his eyes. But that couldn't be right, could it?

The other one chuckled. "I'd like to see you try. She's second in command."

"Yeah, well, I'll give ya one guess as to how she *earned* that position. You see that body? I bet he's all over that!" When I saw the red flash again, I knew my eyes weren't playing tricks on me. I was suddenly nervous. It was too dark to make out their auras, but I no longer suspected that I was dealing with ordinary thugs. I had a sinking feeling that these two weren't human.

"Ya know the boss is gonna be pissed off when he finds out we didn't do what we were s'posed to."

"We'll get another chance to finish the job soon enough."

"If you say so—but you're the one doing the explaining."

I watched them walk out of the warehouse. Then I heard the car doors slam shut. The engine roared, and the limo sped away. I materialized and returned to Quinn's side.

"Okay, now are you going to tell me what's going on?" he asked.

"I honestly have no idea." I was just as confused and nervous as he was—especially since those two thugs ... demons ... whatever they were ... were planning to attack again *soon*.

Quinn and I ran all the way back to his loft—this time without any protest on his part. Before he even opened his front door, I sensed the presence of someone, or something, already inside. *Déjà vu* all over again. I grabbed his hand and stopped him from opening the door.

"What? They found us?" he whispered nervously.

"I'm not sure," I said quietly. "But something's not right."

Quinn moved aside without hesitation. I opened the door just wide enough for me to see Peter standing near Quinn's sofa in the dark.

"Rooftop, now," Peter said sternly, but in a voice that was barely audible even for me. I nodded my head slightly in confirmation and held up two fingers letting Peter know it would take a couple of minutes. I knew the conversation to be had with Peter would be unpleasant to say the least. He phased out, and I assumed he transported himself to Quinn's rooftop to wait for me.

I opened the door wide, turned on the lights, and looked around to confirm that no other beings, human or otherwise, were lingering about. Once satisfied we were alone, I motioned that it was all right for Quinn to enter. I could tell he was still shaken by tonight's events—and he should've been. I was.

"Listen to me, Quinn," I said as I took both his hands in

mine and led him to the couch. "Stay here—don't go any-where. And don't open the door for anyone either. Okay?"

"Yeah, okay," Quinn responded.

"If you feel like anything—and I mean *anything*—isn't sit-ting well, like the slightest thing's not right, you shout out my name immediately. I don't care if it's a false alarm. Got it?"

"Got it," Quinn said, nodding.

"Good. I have to go check on something, but I'll be back soon." I had made it a personal rule to never phase or tele-port in front of Quinn. I did so because I never wanted to draw attention to what I truly was—an immortal, a ghost ... a Shepherd. Yet that didn't change the fact that I was all of these things. At the end of the day, I was Quinn's guardian, and he was my charge. But I'd become so preoccupied with pretending to be human that the tables had turned, and he ended up being my guardian tonight; he had saved me from being hit by the limo.

Well, playtime was over. It had to be. I phased out of sight right in front of him.

29. Forget Me Not

"Would you mind explaining just what happened to-night?" Peter demanded without first saying as much as a "hello."

"Well, it's nice to see you too," I snapped. I was still a lit-tle annoyed with him for not being there for me the last time I needed help. Luckily, Teddy had been there to fill in.

"Eve, I don't have time for small talk—*we* don't have time. Mr. Harrison's fate is all but untraceable, and your sig-nature ... well, it ... flickered."

"*Flickered?*"

"Yes, like a candle flame struggling to stay lit in a gust of wind. And I, for one, am having trouble making sense of it all. So I'm going to ask you one more time—*what happened tonight?*" I'd never seen Peter so flustered.

"I'm not really sure," I said, shaking my head in confu-sion. "There was this limo ... and these two thugs ..." I pro-ceeded to explain the details of the supposed incident involv-ing Quinn the night before—including Ronald's part in the matter and the limousine parked on the street just outside Quinn's loft—and the near hit-and-run involving the same car just minutes ago, followed by the guys chasing us into the abandoned warehouse. Peter looked especially concerned when I mentioned that I thought one of creeps had red eyes.

"So the Incident Timer didn't register the near hit-and-run tonight?"

"Or being chased in the warehouse afterwards," I replied.

"But your watch *did* register the Incident with the limo the other night?"

"Yes, but that's the strange part—there *was* no Incident the other night," I said. "Quinn was sleeping soundly the en-tire time. No one tried to attack him or break into his apart-ment."

"And you say this Ronald character was the one who tipped you off about the Incident the other night?"

I nodded affirmatively.

"And he *told* you to teleport?"

"Not in so many words," I clarified.

"Did he tip you off tonight?" Peter asked curiously.

"I didn't see him tonight."

"Hmm." Peter paused for a moment as if to collect his thoughts. "Well, it's possible that tonight's events were a carryover from last night's—that perhaps your actions the night before forced the Servants to delay or alter their plans to attack Mr. Harrison until tonight ... And if that's the case," he continued his train of thought, "it seems likely that the Sisters wouldn't have been able to detect such a sudden change in plans. That could explain why the Incident didn't register on your watch tonight.

"Well," Peter said on a more cheerful note, "based on the past two nights, I think it's safe to say your charge survived the Second Incident. Thankfully, the next Incident should be the third and last one."

"So my assignment with Quinn is almost over?" I tried to sound indifferent, but I could hear my voice shake slightly.

"Hopefully, yes." Peter sighed with relief. "Eve, we need to get you through this assignment and onto a new one as soon as possible. It's truly for the best."

"Yes ... for the best." There was no masking the disappointment in my voice this time. I couldn't bear the thought of leaving Quinn. Then another thought crossed my mind, one that had entered my mind while I was chasing the limo the night before and then surfaced to the forefront of my mind again after the near hit-and-run tonight.

"Peter," I said hesitantly, "what if the guys in the limo weren't after Quinn? What if ... what if they were after me?"

"Why would they be after you?" Peter's tone was nothing if not dismissive.

"Because Quinn wasn't in the street when the limo came careening down the street tonight—only I was."

"Excuse me?" Peter asked sharply, narrowing his eyes.

"Quinn was standing on the curb. He pulled me out of harm's way ... " My voice trailed off as I saw the rage build in Peter's eyes.

"Eve, are you telling me that you have been so foolish as to actually walk around *with* your charge? In broad daylight for everyone to see?" Peter looked like he was ready to explode.

"Well ...," I began sheepishly, "actually we go for walks together mostly at night ... when it's dark." I knew my explanation wasn't going to get me off the hook; I was in serious trouble. Sure enough, Peter threw his arms up in the air and stormed away from me.

"Eve, *what* were you thinking? Just how many of these *walks* have you taken with your charge? Exactly how much time are you spending with him?" he asked, flustered.

"Enough," was my response to both questions. Peter didn't have to read my mind to know I was being purposefully evasive. Still angry, he began pacing back and forth.

"And Ronald has seen the two of you?"

I nodded affirmatively.

"All right, Eve, answer this for me—has anyone *besides* Ronald seen you two together?"

I mentally ran through all of the walks Quinn and I had taken. Countless numbers of people had *seen* Quinn and me together, but they weren't really paying attention to us— surely they wouldn't remember us. Mr. Adams may have seen me that day at the zoo, but I doubted it. *Oh ... yikes!* There was Tommy. And Brady. *Crap.* But seeing that I was in enough hot water at the moment, I decided not to volunteer any information about either encounter if I could help it.

"That depends on how you define '*seen*,'" I said, trying to dodge the question.

"*Eve!*" Peter seethed furiously.

"Well," I said, trying to justify my actions, "it wasn't like I advertised who I was or anything like that. I always wore a hat and sunglasses during the day."

"Oh, Eve," Peter's sighed, his anger seeming to give way to sheer dismay. "This changes things. I think maybe you're right. I think the limo tonight *was* aiming for you."

"Why? Why would someone go after me when I'm already dead?"

"The Servants can recognize you by your signature alone. It wouldn't matter if you were in disguise from head-to-toe and they had their eyes closed; they would have known what you were from miles away. And now they've had ample opportunity to observe you with Mr. Harrison. I'm sure they know he's been marked."

"Marked?" I didn't know what Peter was talking about.

"Yes, marked." He slammed the railing on the edge of the deck with his fist, splitting the wood down the middle. "I *warned* the Council this was the risk we were taking by letting you go on assignment before you were ready ... before you had been given all of the information. Now look at the mess we're in," he grumbled.

"What information?" I asked.

"Eve," Peter turned to face me. "Unfortunately, there are more humans in trouble than there are Shepherds; and we can't protect them all. So we do the best we can by selecting, or *marking*, which humans need our help the most, and dole out our assignments accordingly.

"One reason for our distance and anonymity is that we don't want the Servants to figure out which humans have been marked and which ones haven't," Peter explained in a somewhat less annoyed, more instructive tone. "It keeps the Servants guessing who is under our protection and who isn't, which ideally buys all targeted humans more time while also giving us a greater opportunity to catch the Servants in the act when they get sloppy.

"Another reason we don't parade around in the open is so the Servants can't identify us. They are dangerous. They want nothing more than to destroy us, and we don't want to make it any easier for them by giving them our names and faces.

"But with you walking around out in the open with Mr. Harrison, the Servants undoubtedly know he's been marked—and they know that *you* are his Shepherd. So my guess is that they've changed their game plan. They're probably monitoring his every move—*your* every move—so they can be ready to strike at a moment's notice when given the opportunity."

I gasped. "Are you serious?"

"Absolutely," Peter said dismally.

"I ... I had no idea."

"How could you?" His eyes suddenly clouded over and he dropped his head as a pensive look crossed his face. "I wasn't given sufficient time to explain it to you. You were sent into the field too early. I should have fought the Council's decision harder, and that was my mistake. I'm sorry, Eve."

Here I was the one who had knowingly and willingly broken the Rules, and yet Peter was the one left feeling responsible, chalking up my selfish and reckless behavior to a lack of adequate training on his part.

"Peter, this is *my* fault. You told me to stay out of sight. You told me not to get involved with Quinn. But ... I didn't listen," I said apologetically.

"Yes, well, if I had explained *why* our Rules are in place, if

I had told you how important it was to obey them, I doubt you would have been so willing to test them," Peter replied.

"Your behavior does, however, give rise to an alternate, but equally viable, explanation as to why your watch has been so unpredictable—why the Incident dates keep changing," he continued. "Chances are the Servants are after *both* of you, and the Sisters are having trouble deciphering when your charge is meant to be the sole target."

"Why would the Servants be after both of us? They already killed me."

"I'm sure the Servants believe you pose too great of a threat for them to successfully execute their plans for Mr. Harrison. Don't you see? Eve, you're a thorn in their side. If you really have been that visible, if you're always right there by his side ... ready to defend him, how are the Servants going to eliminate him?

"Hmm," Peter paused momentarily, "now that I think about it, the other night with your charge may have been nothing more than a test to see how quickly you would react at the first sign your charge was in danger. When you reacted so swiftly, the Servants probably realized they had to change their tactics and remove you from the equation first before they attacked Mr. Harrison." Peter looked up at me like he had just solved the riddle.

"My guess, Eve, is that you both were targets tonight," he concluded.

I had made a huge mess out of things. I had unwittingly put the Servants on red alert about my existence and risked Quinn's safety—as well as my own.

"Peter, I can't change what I've done, but I can change what I do going forward. Please ... tell me how to clean up the mess I've made."

"That is what I'm here for, right?" Peter sighed heavily and smirked.

"So what do I do now? And what about Ronald? Who is he?" I asked anxiously. I felt an urgent need to undo as much damage as I could. "And what about those creeps from the limo? I overheard one of them saying that there would be another opportunity to finish the job soon."

"The goons from the limo are just par for the course—a work hazard. You may run into them again or other ones just like them. Keep your wits about you—for both Mr. Harrison's and your sakes."

"Do you think they were demons?" I asked.

"I doubt it. Servants recruit humans to do most of their dirty work. I bet you got caught up in the moment and only *thought* you saw red eyes. You said it yourself—it was dark."

Peter was probably right. Still, I didn't like the look on his face. It was as if he was hiding something from me. I wish I could have read his mind so I knew what he was really thinking.

"And as for Ronald," Peter continued, "I don't know who he is, but I can tell you that he's *not* a Shepherd. Though, judging from your interactions with him, I don't think he's a Servant either. Nevertheless, I don't like how closely he was tied to the timing of the limo Incident the other night. And I really don't like how he seems to know certain things about you. I'm going to have to do some research to see if I can find out more about his background. In the meantime, however, I would steer clear of him. I'm not sure he's on our side."

"Okay, right. Stay clear of Ronald. Done." I marked it as item number one on my mental checklist.

"And for Heaven's sake, Eve, do *not* go on any more excursions with Mr. Harrison." Peter paused to take a deep breath. "I hate to tell you this, Eve, but you have been putting your charge's life at even greater risk without realizing it."

363

"Well, I realize it now," I asserted. "And don't worry, there won't be any more walks with Quinn—there won't be anymore *anything* with him."

I had to end things with Quinn. Things had to go back to the way they were before I revealed myself to him. It was the last thing in the world I wanted to do, but it was the only thing I could do to ensure his safety.

The thought of never speaking to Quinn again, of never laughing with him again … of never touching him again caused a gut-wrenching pain in my abdomen. The back of my throat began to ache, and my mind throbbed. It felt like my soul and my spirit were being ripped apart. As it was, I could barely withstand the agony, and I hadn't even talked to Quinn about it yet. My feelings must have been transparent because Peter put his hand on my shoulder.

"Peter," I managed, "I know I broke the Rules. I know I got too close … I realize now that I made a lot of stupid mistakes. I … I know I have to change things … dramatically." My words were barely audible—I felt like my throat was closing up.

"Eve, trust me when I say this … it's the only way." Peter's eyes clouded over, and I thought of Madeleine and the pain he must have endured when ended their relationship. Then I thought of the pain that I was about to go through … And Quinn. What about him? Was there any way to spare him the pain I was about to inflict upon him?

"How do I—I mean, how should I—?" No matter how hard I tried, I couldn't force the words out of my mouth. Hearing them out loud would only make this all too real.

"End things with him?" Peter asked.

I nodded my head affirmatively, unable to utter the words … unable to even look at Peter.

"If it helps, Eve, think of it this way. You're going to have to leave him at some point anyway. Your assignment is only temporary, remember?" Peter picked up my wrist and looked at my watch. "And from the looks of things, you may only have a few more months anyway."

I looked down at my watch. The next Incident—probably the last Incident—had settled once again on the twenty-fourth of November of this year.

"There is no way for you to stay with Mr. Harrison after your assignment is complete. Soon, you'll have no other choice but to break all ties with him."

No other choice. The words rang hollowly inside me. I knew Peter was right. I knew the day would come when I would have to say good-bye, I had just hoped it wouldn't have arrived so quickly.

"What will happen to Quinn? I got him into this mess. I can't just break his heart and then abandon him."

"Eve, there is a way to break it off with him—a *nontraditional* way, so to speak, where your charge won't have to feel any pain whatsoever."

"How?" I asked nervously.

"You can make Mr. Harrison *forget.* You can make it so he never even has to experience the pain of you ending your relationship. You can erase yourself and all the events involving you from his mind."

Make him forget me? Forget us? A rush of emotions erupted inside of me. I was horrified at the thought of Quinn forgetting about me. The very idea of erasing myself from his memory was devastating. I was horrified that Peter would even suggest something so wicked. But, at the same time, another part of me was intrigued, almost relieved, by Peter's suggestion. There actually was a way to spare Quinn the suffering that ending our relationship would cause him. It would be as if we had never happened—at least in his mind.

"Isn't that breaking the Rules?"

"It's part of that grey area I mentioned to you before. We

365

all have the power to heal *emotional* suffering as well as physical. It's a technique we occasionally use on humans who have been through a particularly traumatic or painful experience. We can isolate the memories of a specific experience and erase all traces of it from a human's mind … It's also proven to be quite an effective method of protecting our kind if we've been exposed in the mortal realm," Peter added.

"Is that what you did to Madeleine?" I asked cautiously. I knew it was none of my business. Peter probably didn't even know I was aware of Madeleine; yet I still had to ask. I needed to know what to expect from someone who had been through this before. I needed to hear it from someone who had experienced it firsthand.

"Yes," Peter replied flatly.

"And it worked?"

"Better than you would ever imagine." His eyes clouded over again. He volunteered no other information, and I knew better than to press for more details.

"So you can erase all memories of me from Quinn's mind? You can make it as if this … as if *I* … never happened?" I asked somewhat optimistically.

"Not me, Eve … *You. You* must do it."

"*Me?*" I whispered faintly as my anxiety began to reach peak levels.

"Yes. You know your charge better than any of us, so only you know which memories will trigger his grief when you leave," he explained. "Therefore, you are the only one capable of erasing his mind and healing him in this way."

Overwhelmed, I walked over to the edge of the rooftop and ran my fingers across the splintered wood of the railing Peter had broken.

"I can see you need time to think this through," he said. "You *should* think this through; but don't take too long. The clock is ticking, and your charge is waiting for you." With that Peter phased out of view.

I just stood there for a while … my mind buzzing. I tried to imagine every possible scenario for Quinn and me—even ones in which we could stay together. Ultimately, however, I knew it would be impossible to continue our relationship. Peter was right. It was only a matter of time before my assignment would be over and I would have to leave Quinn. I knew the sooner I ended things with him, the better it would be for the both of us.

The only thing left to consider was whether I should take the easy way out and erase Quinn's memory while he slept or whether I should sit down with him first and try to explain to him why we could no longer be together. I didn't want to hurt Quinn, but stealing his memories of me—of us— without so much as an explanation didn't seem right either. I felt like I owed him more than that—he deserved to hear why I had to go. And, selfishly, I wanted to say good-bye. Besides, if he handled it okay, then maybe I wouldn't have to erase his memory at all. If, on the other hand, he didn't take the news well, I could always erase his mind after the fact.

I thought for a moment of what it would be like if Quinn suddenly had no memory of me from this summer—of what it would be like for me alone to have memories of us. I forced a laugh as sadness swept over me. This must have been how Quinn felt all along.

I looked up at the stars and took a long, deep breath. Never in my wildest dreams could I have imagined this day— the day that marked our one-month anniversary—would be the last day Quinn and I would spend together.

30. Breaking Up Sucks

I found Quinn asleep on the right side of the bed, *his* side, with the lights on and an open book across his chest. I'm sure he had tried to wait up for me. I wanted to crawl into bed and lay there with him one last time, but I didn't dare. I knew it would only make tomorrow more difficult than it was already going to be.

I walked into the living area, grabbed Quinn's laptop, my earphones, and a couple of magazines. I wanted to lose myself—distract myself with anything that would help me forget about my own problems for the time being.

That's when I saw the piece of paper on the seat of my chair. It was a note from Quinn:

> E – Glad you're home safe and sound. I just wanted to wish you happy Anniversary once more. Don't stay up all night listening to music and reading hollywood gossip. Come to bed—*our* bed … and feel free to wake me. All my love – Q

"All my love," I whispered aloud. My throat burned and my head began to throb again. I felt like my world was spinning out of control. How was I going to find the strength to break up with Quinn? I began to wonder if I shouldn't just erase his memory tonight while he slept. I quickly shoved the thought aside—I wanted him to see me, to remember me, one more time.

* * *

It was the first time Quinn woke up without me visibly

there in his apartment since I had intentionally revealed myself to him. I wasn't ready to face him just yet. I knew that the look on my face would instantly tip him off that something wasn't right, and I didn't want him to worry all day while at work, so I wrote him a note on the backside of his and left it in the same place. Quinn walked out his bedroom, looked for me in my chair, and saw the note instead.

"Evie?" Quinn called out. "Evie, are you here?"

I remained silent—an invisible ghost. Quinn picked up my note and read it.

> Quinn, sorry. I returned later than expected, and you were sleeping so peacefully I couldn't bring myself to wake you. I'll be back by the time you return from work. Oh, and thanks for being _my_ guardian angel last night.
> All my love, Evie

Quinn looked around the living area one more time to see if I was there. Then he just shrugged his shoulders, tossed the note on the nearby shelf, and got ready for work.

* * *

I was perched in my chair by the time Quinn unlocked his front door. I took a few deep breaths, trying to calm the butterflies in my stomach, but they were fluttering around at a maddening pace. I didn't think it was possible for me to be any more nervous than I was at that moment.

"Hey," Quinn said, smiling as he walked through the door, "I missed you this morning. Where did you go?" He put his bag down and emptied his pockets onto the kitchen counter. Then he walked over to me and kissed me on the cheek before going into his bedroom to change.

"Nowhere special," I replied, trying to sound relaxed. I took a few more deep breaths.

I would have given anything not to have to go through with what I was about to do. I wanted to run into Quinn's arms. I wanted to tell him that I'd found a way for us to be together always, but that would be a lie.

"Oh, hey," Quinn shouted from his bedroom, "before I forget, someone from the office said there's some special on the Discovery Channel tonight about super cells and tornadoes."

"Oh, cool. Thanks," I replied. My anxiety level was now bordering on full-blown panic proportions.

"So did you find out what happened last night?"

"Yeah," I mumbled.

"And?"

"And it was yet another attempt on your life," I blurted out.

"Really?" he asked as he walked out of his room and into the kitchen. "So who were those two guys? Why are they after me?"

"Two very good questions without good answers at this point," I replied. "But, needless to say, I have managed to complicate matters even more." I took a deep breath and exhaled slowly. This was it—it was now or never.

"Um, Quinn … we need to talk."

"Uh oh," he said as he sat down on the couch with a bottle of water. "Nothing good has ever come from a girl telling a guy 'we need to talk.'" Quinn was joking until he saw the look on my face. "And I see that this time will be no different … What's going on, Evie?"

"Quinn, the limo from last night … there's a good chance it was after me—not you," I told him.

"What do you mean? You just said last night was an attempt on *my* life," he said, confused.

370

"It ended up being an attack on both of us. Whoever wants to harm you has figured out that I'm here and, more importantly, *why* I'm here. It seems our little *outings* have stirred the pot some, and now they want me out of the way so that you'll be an easier target."

"No joke?" Quinn asked.

"No joke."

"Well, what do we do?" His voice was so full of concern I would have smiled under different circumstances.

"*We* don't do anything ... *I* do." I paused and took another breath. I fought the ache that was creeping up into the back of my throat. "Quinn ... I have to leave."

"You have to *what?*" he exclaimed. "No," Quinn said, shaking his head from side to side. "No way. I'm not losing you twice, Evie." Quinn jumped off the couch and crouched down in front of me. He grabbed both my hands. "There has to be another answer—another way."

"I've been racking my brain all night and all day to find one, but there isn't."

"Then you didn't think of everything." Quinn stood up and began pacing, running his hands through his hair. "I refuse to believe that we can't stop whatever is going on together."

"Quinn, it's not that simple—"

"The hell it isn't!" He was all worked up. "I want to be with you, and you want to be with me. It doesn't get any more simple than that!"

"You don't understand," I told him. "It has to be this way. Eventually, it *will* be this way, regardless of what either you or I want."

"So this is what you want." Quinn challenged me. "You *want* to leave."

"What I want is of no consequence."

"You didn't answer my question," he pressed.

371

"No! Of course I don't want to leave! How can you ask me such a ridiculous question?" I exclaimed angrily. "Quinn ... I *love* you. I will *always* love you. But at the end of the day, it's not enough. My leaving is the only way to protect you.

"I mean, what did you think would happen eventually?" I continued. "You think that we can just go on playing house forever in some apartment you subleased for the summer in some city you don't even live in. *None of this is real*," I explained as I held my hands out and looked around his place.

"Tell me, Quinn, what happens when you go back to IU? We couldn't ever be able to go anywhere together again—not in a town I used to live in. I mean, what in the world are you going to tell your roommates when they think you're talking to yourself in the middle of the night?"

"We'll figure it out," he said, his eyes pleading with me to change my mind.

"For how long?" I shot back.

"For as long as we have to. For forever if we need to."

"It doesn't work that way," I said, flustered. "I don't get to stay forever. You don't understand ... we're living out some fantasy that was doomed from the start. When my assignment is over, when I know you're safe, I have to *leave*. I'll be transferred to a new case ... a new charge ... I'll be reassigned to watch over another human. I will spend every minute of every day guarding *that* human's life."

Quinn cringed, like he had just pictured me with another man.

"Well ... when will that be?" Quinn spit out, flustered.

"Sooner than you think."

"Fine, I'll take whatever time with you I can get."

"Quinn, do you even hear yourself? It's insane for you to choose me over any living, breathing human. I can't ask you to make that kind of sacrifice."

"You're *not* a sacrifice, Evie."

"You say that now, but there is no future with me," I replied. "If I stay, you'll only get more hurt."

"So that's it, then?" Quinn asked in disgusted disbelief. "You can just walk away … just like that … and leave me in the hands of someone else who has come to take your place?"

"It won't be quite like that," I responded.

"What *will* it be like then, Evie? Don't you think I have a right to know? I mean, you are talking about *my* life—right?" He was infuriated. "Or are you not allowed to tell me that either?"

"I will still protect you … just not in the same way. You won't see me anymore. You won't hear me. You won't be able to—"

"To what? Talk to you? Touch you?" Quinn blurted out.

I just stared at Quinn silently.

"Well, that's absolute crap! I don't believe for one damn minute that you're okay with this!"

"I have to be okay with it—*we* have to be okay with it," I said.

"*We*," Quinn sneered. "Well, I'm so glad I was consulted on *any* of this." He laughed contemptuously. "I'm so glad this wasn't just some decision made on my behalf." He slammed his fist into the kitchen counter and I flinched. Then he just stood there with his back to me.

"Evie, do I really have no say in what happens?" His voice had softened. "What about what I want? What I need?"

"Quinn, this decision is based solely on what you need. This is about saving your life."

"Yeah, well, maybe my life isn't worth saving if I can't be with you," he said flippantly.

"I know you didn't mean that, Quinn. Don't ever say anything like that," I said in a reprimanding tone.

"You just told me that the best thing in my life is going to be taken away from me—*again*. What the hell else do you expect me to say?"

I sat there for a moment debating whether I should dare mention Peter's solution to Quinn's pain. I decided to bite the bullet and go for it.

"Quinn … there is a way to make this easier on you," I said hesitantly.

"If it doesn't involve you staying here with me, then I'm not interested."

"Just hear me out." I took a deep breath and exhaled. "I … I could erase all memory of me from your mind."

"You could do *what?*" Quinn flew off the handle. "Don't you even dare!"

I suspected my offer might upset him, but I had no idea he would be this offended.

"You would actually *want* me to forget about you?" he roared. "You would actually *let* me forget about you and this past summer together?

"Evie, don't you get it? You are a part of my life—a part of me." Quinn looked at me like I had just tried to double-cross him. "I don't understand how you would want to take that part of me away."

"I'm sorry. Quinn, I just don't want you to suffer. You have to know that the last thing I'd ever want to do is hurt you … So I just thought … if this could help you move on with your life without me …"

"Yeah, well I'll take the pain of missing you over the loss of all memory of you any day of the week and twice on Sunday." He looked at me apprehensively. "Evie, *promise* me that you will *not* erase my memory."

I just looked at him.

"Promise me," he demanded.

"Quinn …"

"*Promise me*," Quinn demanded again.

"I promise." As soon as I said the words, I knew I would come to regret them.

"So when do you have to leave?" he asked numbly.

I knew if I stayed, Quinn would only try to change my mind by night's end. I knew if I stayed, there was a chance he would succeed.

"Now," I whispered.

31. On the Rebound

The next week was pure torture for both of us. I had no idea it would be so hard to ghost Quinn twenty-four-seven and not be able to communicate with him in any way. And he didn't make it any easier. He would speak to me on a daily basis. Sometimes he'd reminisce out loud about some of the things we'd done during our time together. Other times he'd tell me he knew I was there … that he could feel me; and I suspected he could.

And, each day, Quinn would buy me a new magazine, letting them pile up to collect dust on the seat of my chair. And every night, he would wish me good night and tell me he loved me before falling asleep on his side of the bed. He even played the song he had used to tease me on our anniversary.

He would purposely leave his laptop on overnight, with my playlist open and my earphones plugged in, only to scan the number of times the songs had been played the next morning to see if I had listened to any music while he was asleep. Of course, I never did; I couldn't string him along like that.

I had to stay strong. I had to fight how much I missed him. I constantly reminded myself that this was for the best. I reminded myself of why I was here. I had to focus all of my attention and energy on keeping Quinn alive and safe.

It was of little relief that the Incident Timer on my watch had remained steady. The next Incident was still scheduled to occur in late November. That said, I still didn't know if this would be the second or third, and last, time I was officially expected to save his life. As miserable as I was at the moment, I knew I'd feel even worse when my assignment ended.

To add insult to injury, Ashley had returned from being out of town on her latest project. She stopped by Quinn's office one afternoon when Kyle wasn't there.

"So, Quinn, you've been a little distant lately. Everything okay with you?" she asked demurely.

"Yeah. No, I'm fine," he responded absentmindedly as he continued to pour through a pile of documents on his desk. "I've just been busy. Jones has me doing some research."

"Well, let me know if he's expecting too much from you. I can easily see to it that someone else helps you out."

"Thanks, Ashley." Quinn looked up at her and his face softened. "I appreciate the offer, but it's okay—really. You know what they say ... an idle mind—"

"Is the devil's workshop," Ashley finished his sentence and smiled flirtatiously as she walked over and sat on the corner of Quinn's desk where she pretended to rifle through some of his papers.

Ugh. Quinn would have to pick that proverb, I thought to myself.

"Well, you know what else they say about all work and no play," Ashley said playfully.

"No, what?" Quinn said, now flashing a little smile of his own. I could detect a hint of a twinkle in his eye. I couldn't believe it—he was flirting back!

"It makes for rather *lonely* little boys and girls," she said as she leaned in closer towards Quinn.

You've got to be kidding me! I screamed in my mind.

Just then, Kyle walked into the office, and, for the first time, I was thrilled to see him. She backed off immediately.

"Oh, hi, Ashley," Kyle said, practically drooling.

"Hi, Kyle," Ashley replied, flashing him a big smile. She stood up and straightened her skirt. Kyle was watching her so intently, he practically tripped over his own shoes as he went to sit down at his desk.

"Well, Quinn, I just wanted to check in with you to see how you were doing. Why don't you let me know when you're free in the next day or so and we'll grab a bite to eat. I may have a last minute assignment for you." Ashley winked at Quinn slyly.

"Yeah, sure," Quinn replied. I clenched my teeth.

"Bye, Kyle," Ashley said flirtatiously.

"Bye," Kyle managed. His eyes were still glued to Ashley's body as she walked out of the office.

"Dude," he said, "you are *so* lucky to have Ashley as a mentor. She is smoking hot, and I heard she gives out really cushy assignments."

Oh Kyle, I thought, *you have* no *idea*.

* * *

That night, Tommy called Quinn. Curious to see whether Tommy would mention me, I listened in on their entire conversation.

"Quinny, how's it going?" Tommy asked cheerily.

"Fine. And you? Hey, how's Sam doing?"

"I'm good—Sam is just big and fat." Tommy chuckled. I could hear Tommy's wife cursing him out affectionately in the background.

"Hey, we're having a barbeque this Sunday and I wanted to invite you."

"Sounds great. Sure," Quinn replied flatly.

"Well, don't sound *too* excited on my account, Quinny," Tommy said sarcastically. "I don't want to twist your arm or anything."

"Sorry, Tommy. I'm just tired. It's just been a really long day," Quinn explained.

"Well, the barbeque should help you relax some. And, hey, why don't you bring that girl I met the other week at Marché," Tommy suggested. "What's her name? Evie?"

"Um, yeah … about her. Did you happen to tell Sam about her? Or anyone else in the family?"

"No, why?"

"Because I'm not seeing her anymore."

"Oh, that's too bad." Tommy sounded a bit disappointed. "I liked her. I really thought you two might have had something."

"Yeah, so did I … but apparently she wasn't convinced of the same. She ran at the first sign of trouble."

Ouch—that stung, I said to myself.

"Wait a minute—are you telling me that *you got dumped?*" Tommy burst out laughing. "That's a first!"

"Great, Tommy. Go ahead and rub salt in the wounds."

"Sorry, dude. It's just that it's about time someone else did the heart breaking in your relationships," he replied, still chuckling. "Hey, why don't you call that Amy chick?"

"Ashley," Quinn corrected his brother.

"Yeah, sure, whatever—you know … the super hot one."

"I don't know, Tommy. It just seems a little soon."

"Look, the way I see it, there's no point in just sitting around and moping. Get back in the saddle and call her."

Quinn paused for a moment to ponder his brother's advice.

"You know what?" Quinn said with a little more enthusiasm. "You're right." He shifted his posture and stood up a little straighter. "Why should I just sit around? *It's not like I'm waiting for anyone.* It's time for me to *move on.*" As Quinn said the words, he looked up at the ceiling. He was talking to me. "In fact, I think I'll give Ashley a call right now. Thanks, Tommy."

"Hey, what are big brothers for?" Tommy chuckled. "Giddy up!" He threw in before hanging up the phone.

Quinn scrolled through the address book in his phone and found Ashley's number.

"Okay, Evie. You win. If this is *really* the way it has to be," Quinn said aloud before dialing Ashley's number. "If this is *really* what you want … you got it. I'll move on."

This is not *what I want!* my mind screamed.

Quinn called Ashley and asked if she was free Thursday evening.

She was.

* * *

Late Thursday night, I watched the cab pull up to Ashley's place. Once she reached the top of the steps to her brownstone, she unlocked her door and turned back to the cab.

"You coming, Quinn?" Ashley called out.

"Yeah, just give me a minute," Quinn replied. He got out of the cab and gave the driver a twenty. As Quinn waited for change, he glanced up to the sky.

"Evie?" Quinn muttered under his breath. "If you're here, please let me know."

"What? You say something?" the cab driver asked as he waved Quinn's change out the driver's window.

"Oh, uh … no. Thanks," Quinn responded as he took the change and tipped the driver. The cab pulled away, leaving Quinn standing there alone. He took his time putting his money back in his wallet.

"I need to know if you're here," he pleaded.

"Everything all right out there?" Ashley called from inside her foyer.

"Evie?"

I didn't say anything.

"Fine, have it your way," he said under his breath. "I just want you to know that once I walk through that door, there's no turning back." He waited another minute for me to say something, but I couldn't—despite the fact that I knew exactly what would happen if he went inside. All I could do was stand invisibly there and watch the nightmare unfold.

I'd never forget the sound of the heavy wood door shutting and locking behind him. I materialized and stood there on the sidewalk for a moment while rage, jealousy, and anguish consumed me. I took a few deeps breaths to try to calm down. I knew I had no right to feel these emotions. I no longer had any claim on Quinn. He was doing exactly what I had told him to do, and now I was suffering in spades because of it. Still, I couldn't believe that he was capable of professing his love for me just days earlier only to then turn around and fall into the arms of another.

I wanted to cry. I wanted to scream and pound my fists into Quinn's chest for doing this to me … for making me witness even the smallest part of this sordid liaison. The thought of Quinn's hands on her body, his mouth kissing her, his body pressed up against hers …

Ugh! It made my skin crawl, and I shuddered in disgust. I tried to force the nauseating images from my head, but I just couldn't. The harder I tried to block out the revolting thoughts, the faster my mind seemed to conjure them. It was intolerable. My stomach churned over and over until I literally thought I would be physically ill—impossible as that would have been.

I was losing it fast. The emotions being bottled up inside were trying to fight their way out; they were irrepressible. I was mere seconds away from exploding. I knew I was supposed to remain by Quinn's side, but this was too much to bear. I couldn't stay there. I couldn't be anywhere near there. I had to leave. I checked my watch—nothing was stopping me. I immediately teleported myself back to Quinn's apartment and waited in the dark for him to return.

I thought that night would never end.

* * *

381

Quinn walked through the door a couple hours before sunrise. It was dark, but I could see his disheveled appearance. He reeked of her perfume ... of her scent. Instantly, I was overwhelmed with so much rage that I began shaking uncontrollably, and I couldn't dematerialize before he flipped on the lights.

"Evie—" Quinn gasped. He stopped, frozen in his tracks, stunned, not knowing what to do or say. His face drained of all color right before my very eyes.

I couldn't respond. I was so incensed I didn't trust what I would say—or what I would do. I just looked at him with daggers in my eyes for the few seconds it took me to regain enough self-control to phase out of sight.

"Evie!" Quinn cried out. "Wait!" he begged as I faded from view. "Look, I'm sorry ... but I had to do something to try to get you out of my head."

I remained silent.

"I know you're here. Evie, please say something. Please *do* something—yell at me, slap me—anything." The remorse in his voice was unmistakable.

"Damn it!" Quinn exclaimed when I still didn't answer him. He picked up a tall glass sitting on the counter next to him and threw it against the brick wall. The glass shattered on impact. Then he dragged himself into the bathroom and took a shower.

* * *

Quinn had hurt me more than I ever thought he could. I felt so betrayed. I knew I'd told him to move on, but, in a million years, I never thought he'd do it with the snap of his fingers. I mean, if what we had together was real to him, then it didn't make any sense. And, quite frankly, I didn't want it to make any sense. All I wanted to do was run away, but I couldn't. I needed to cry, but no tears would come. I felt exhausted, but there was no way for me to sleep.

Determined to do something to try to make myself feel better, I transported myself deep within the Grand Canyon. I checked for any signs of life. I detected various nocturnal animals scattered hundreds of yards in either direction, but no human life. So I screamed. I screamed with such vengeance and wrath the ground beneath me shook. I kept screaming until I thought I would lose my voice. I didn't want to talk anymore. I didn't want to *feel* anymore.

It was still dark when I returned. I could hear Quinn sleeping. I sat down in my chair, welcoming the darkness. Unlike earlier that evening, this time the black of night felt comforting—almost safe—like I was tucked beneath a warm blanket on a cold winter's night. The worst was over, or so I hoped, and I had endured.

As the sun began to rise, I noticed Quinn had picked up the glass—well, most of it anyway. I swept up the remaining shards sprinkled across the floor and noticed a few drops of blood on the nearby area rug. He must have cut himself while cleaning up the mess he had made.

I walked into his bedroom. He was still asleep, sprawled out in the middle of the bed on top of the covers. He had taped one of the gauze pads the hospital had given him to the bottom of his foot where the glass had cut him.

I smiled smugly. At least Quinn had also felt *some* kind of pain tonight. Guilt immediately followed my mean-spirited sentiment. As much as I hated to admit it, I still loved him. And it was still my job to protect him from harm—not wish it upon him. I slowly and carefully removed the gauze pad and healed his foot.

In the end, I had to accept that *I* was the one who'd ended our relationship. *I* was the one who'd pushed Quinn away. *I* had told him to forget about me and move forward with his life. And *I* was the one who'd abandoned him, leaving him to deal with losing me in whichever way he saw fit.

That said, I'd never forget this evening; it was burned in my brain forever. I also doubted I would ever be able to forgive Quinn for sleeping with Ashley. I certainly had no intention of ever giving him the opportunity to try to apologize to me face-to-face again. Healing him was the best I could do to make what little peace I could with him.

* * *

An hour later, Quinn's alarm sounded. He walked into the living area looking for me but didn't seem at all surprised when I wasn't there. He got ready for work and was about to walk out the front door when he paused to glance back into the living area.

"Evie?" he asked hopefully. He sighed heavily when I didn't respond. "Evie ... I am so sorry." He walked out of the apartment, closing the front door behind him.

Quinn's apology only confirmed the message he had sent with his actions—I was no longer a part of his life. He had moved on and, in so doing, he knew he had hurt me.

I couldn't handle being near him, so I sat outside on the rooftop of his office building. It was raining, but I didn't mind; in fact, it felt good. I imagined that the raindrops falling on my face were like tears streaming down my cheeks—they were the tears I wished I could cry.

I spent the next few days praying for more rain.

32. Redemption

That Tuesday, Quinn worked late. A cab dropped him off at the convenience store a few blocks from his apartment. Ronald was perched in his usual spot outside peddling *Street-wise* to passersby. A nervous feeling rippled through my mind as I remembered Peter's warning to stay clear of him. Invisible, I stood across the street and watched Quinn enter the store. Except for Ronald and me, no one else was outside for several blocks.

"My angel! Oh, my angel!" Ronald sang out in his bluesy voice as he pulled a dirty handkerchief from his pants pocket and used it to wipe away a smudge on one of his tattered brown leather shoes.

I stood there, frozen like a statue, and said nothing, assuming Ronald was only reminiscing about the last time he saw me.

"Well, well. A bit on the quiet side tonight, are we?" he sang out again, although this time he gazed unmistakably in my direction.

Does he know that I'm here? Can he see me?

"Come now, angel, you have no reason to hide from me," Ronald sang. *"Did I not warn you the other night?"*

Hold it, did Ronald just communicate with me telepathically? Or did he actually speak the words I just heard? I couldn't be sure.

"Surprised?"

I was surprised when I realized that Ronald's lips hadn't moved—extremely surprised. He had communicated with me using only his mind. I was more than a little confused too. I thought Shepherds couldn't hear each other's thoughts while on Earth.

"They can't."

Okay, so not only could I hear Ronald's thoughts, but apparently he could hear mine as well. Paranoia began to fill me. How was this possible?

"Who are you?" I asked Ronald telepathically.

"Someone you should listen to, Evie."

"How ... how do you know my name?"

"Interesting. I was sure the first question you were going to ask me was how I knew you were standing over there despite the fact that you're invisible? Or how I knew that you had certain abilities? Or even how I knew about your watch?"

I did want answers to each of Ronald's questions—and to several others.

"You still haven't told me who you are?"

"In due time."

"You tell me that you're someone I should listen to, but then you won't tell me anything about you. If you won't even tell me who you are, then how can you expect me to trust what you have to say?" I paused for a moment, unsure if I should ask the one question that was plaguing me the most. I had to ask. I had to know. *"Are you a demon?"*

Ronald threw his head back and roared with laughter, startling a young woman who had just rounded the corner with her dog. He paid no attention to her or her dog, which was now on full alert, ready to attack anyone who dared approach its owner. Instinctively, I quickly double-checked the rhythm beating in my chest; it was normal.

"Your charge is fine."

"You didn't answer my question. Are you a demon?"

"Tell me, do I project something dark and sinister?" Ronald said, still chuckling slightly.

I took a moment and studied Ronald's heat signature. A hazy, unassuming aura radiated closely around him, curling off of him like cigarette smoke. The aura was not indicative of whether Ronald was good or evil. In fact, his aura seemed oddly ... neutral.

"*No,*" I responded, wondering why I had never noticed his aura before tonight. "*But you could be masking your true self; you could have fabricated some type of signature to try to deceive me.*"

"*I have no intention of deceiving you, Evie. You see, much like you, I am forbidden to lie. And there are certain things about me that I cannot share with you at this time.*"

"*So are you like some sort of high-ranking Shepherd? Like a member of the Council?*" I persisted, attempting to bypass his runaround.

"*No. I am not a member of the Shepherd's Council. I am not a Shepherd at all. I am a higher authority.*"

"*A higher authority? So, what, the Council answers to you?*" I half-joked.

"*Something like that,*" Ronald responded vaguely.

"Hey, Ronald. Here you go buddy." Quinn unknowingly interrupted my conversation with Ronald by walking out of the convenience store and offering him a five-dollar bill and a bottle of water.

"Thank you, friend," Ronald responded in his baritone voice. "And here you go." He handed Quinn the latest edition of the local newspaper and then began rifling through his pockets for change.

"I don't need any change. You keep it."

"You sure?"

"Yeah," Quinn responded in a somber tone of voice.

"You sound a little glum this evening, my friend. Might I ask what is bothering you so?" Ronald asked.

"Women," Quinn said matter-of-factly.

"Ah yes, the bearers of forbidden fruit."

"You could say that again."

"I'm afraid I don't have much sound advice to offer you in this particular area."

"I'm beginning to believe that not many do, Ronald," Quinn sighed. "Besides, you don't want to hear the details.

All I know is that things are all screwed up, and I have no idea how to fix them."

"Well, I have been told that a sincere apology often helps—even if a man knows not what he has done to offend his female friend."

"Yeah, well, I went down that road already, and it didn't help. Ronald, I can honestly say that I think it's over—for good."

"For good, hmm? That sounds so final—so absolute."

"Huh." Quinn chuckled to himself and shook his head in mild amusement. "That sounds like something she would say." He paused for a moment. "Well, thanks for listening to me. It's late, and I have an early morning tomorrow. I'm gonna head home and try to get some sleep. Night, Ronald." Quinn saluted him and then turned and walked away.

"*Au contraire,*" he muttered under his breath, "the night is still young for you, my friend. The night is still young." Ronald watched Quinn walk away. Then he turned towards me.

"*True love is a difficult thing to surrender, isn't it?*" Ronald asked me.

"*Apparently it's easier for some than for others,*" I replied coldly.

"*We shall see about that, angel. We shall see.*"

Before I could ask Ronald any more questions, another patron walked out of the convenience store and struck up a conversation with him about the weather.

"*Good night, Ronald.*"

"*Same to you, angel.*"

* * *

When Quinn walked into his apartment, he dumped the plastic bags on the counter without even bothering to put away anything he had just purchased. He grabbed some leftover takeout from the fridge and poked at it for a bit until he eventually put it back. He grabbed a bottle of water, sat down on the couch, and began flipping through cable channels, pausing when he got to the Discovery Channel. The special Quinn had mentioned the night we broke up was being rerun, and he turned off the television.

Quinn walked over to the bookshelf, flipped through a pile of CDs until he found one with a song he wanted to hear, and popped it in. When he set the CDs back down on the shelf, he noticed a scrap of paper sitting there next to them. I recognized it as the notes we had left each other the night before our relationship had ended. He quickly read both sides and then crumpled it up before tossing it into the garbage bin near his computer. He ran his hands through his hair and began pacing the room.

A few minutes later, he walked over to his laptop and sat down. He sat there typing for well over an hour. He was so focused I just assumed he was working from home; I didn't even bother to see what he was writing. It wasn't until he was finished that I began to suspect Quinn hadn't been doing anything work-related at all. There was something in his eyes … he looked troubled. I got the feeling that whatever he had been doing was very personal.

He shut down his computer, walked over to his coat closet, and grabbed the Cubs hat I'd worn whenever we went outside together. He looked at it for a moment before readjusting the cap's strap and putting it on.

"Good night, Evie," Quinn said out loud as he turned off the lights and headed to bed.

What had he just spent the last hour-and-a-half doing? In hindsight, I wished I would have peeked. I sat invisibly in my chair, glancing back at his laptop every so often. I knew I had no right to pry, but I couldn't help myself; curiosity got the best of me. Against my better judgment, I materialized and slowly made my way across the room.

Linda Lamberson

I felt like a thief skulking about his apartment in the middle of the night as I turned on his laptop and entered his password—a spy about to steal top-secret information. I went to his Documents folder and found one file with today's date; it was simply titled "E."

I inhaled deeply as I opened the document, not knowing what to expect; but no amount of breathing could have prepared me for what I read—

> You appeared like a flash of light,
> As bright as the sun.
> You were the air that I breathed;
> The water that quenched my thirst;
> The healer of my wounds.
> You were the girl of my dreams.
> Because you were the one that I loved.
>
> You vanished deep into the night,
> To the other side of the moon.
> You were the toxin that choked me;
> And the rain that drowned me
> As you ripped my heart apart.
> Your desertion became my nightmare
> Because you were the one that I loved.
>
> I'm falling.
> Where is my guardian angel?
> Who will catch me now?

I felt like the wind had been knocked out of me. I tried to catch my breath, but it hurt way too much, so I just stopped breathing altogether. I thought I was the only one who was suffering miserably, but I was wrong.

The anger I was harboring towards Quinn began to dissipate into thin air, replaced by anger towards myself. I never should have made that promise to Quinn; it was a stupid mistake. It would have been better for the both of us if I had erased all memory of me this summer from his mind.

"Did you find what you were looking for?"

The sound of Quinn's voice startled me, and I jumped up out of the chair. I looked at him, unable to say anything. He walked over to his laptop and saw his poem up on the screen.

"Figures," he snapped. "You refuse to talk to me anymore, so you resort to snooping around to find out what's going on with my life. Is that it?"

"That's not fair," I said, trying to defend myself.

"Well, what do you call this?" Quinn practically shouted.

"I could ask you the same thing!" I pointed to his laptop.

"It's none of your damn business." Quinn slammed the laptop shut. The silence that followed could not have been any louder or more uncomfortable.

"Look," I said apologetically. "I didn't mean to snoop. I'm sorry. I just ..." My voice trailed off.

"You just what, Evie?" he snapped.

I was at a loss for words. Being here, standing in front of him, both thrilled and frightened me. I was overwhelmed with guilt for hurting him, but I couldn't see past how badly he had hurt me. I missed him so much, and at the same time I wished I never had to see him again.

"I was just so *furious* with you the other night—I'm still furious with you," I muttered.

"Evie, *you're* the one who told me to move on. I didn't want to—remember? You can't turn around now and be mad at me because I tried to let you go. You can't have it both ways."

"I know, I know," I readily conceded. "But I can't help the way I feel. I just ... I didn't expect you to move on so quickly ... and in that way. I didn't expect to react the way I did when I saw you with her."

"You *saw* me? ... *With* her?" Quinn asked, horrified.

"*No!*" I shrieked, equally horrified. "I couldn't bear the *thought* of you two together much less the sight of it." My body shuddered involuntarily. I walked towards the windows and looked outside.

"I don't know what to say other than 'I'm sorry,'" he said regretfully, "I've never been more sorry."

I refused to turn around and look at him.

"Evie," Quinn said longingly as he walked towards me, stopping a few feet away. "The last thing I ever wanted to do was hurt you. And I definitely never meant to throw it in your face like that. But when I came home the other night and saw you sitting here, when I saw you look at me like that, I knew I had.

"The weirdest thing about it," he continued in the wake of my silence, "is that even though you looked at me like you hated me, part of me was just so happy to see you." He put his hand on my shoulder.

"Quinn, please ... don't," I said as I took a step to the side, away from him, while keeping my back to him.

"What difference does any of this make now?" I asked.

"I don't want things between us to end like this," he replied.

"You know we can't be together." I took a deep breath and sighed heavily. "And even if we could, we could never go back to the way things were. Too much has changed." My mind flashed to an image of Quinn as he walked through his front door, disheveled and reeking of Ashley's perfume. Nausea washed over me, and I shuddered again.

"Quinn," I said, turning around and facing him. A new sense of conviction to be strong coursed through my body. "You were doing the right thing—you were moving forward with your life … and you would've continued to do so if I hadn't slipped up and let you see me the other night."

"Yeah, right," he said snidely. "I would love for you to explain which part of me was moving forward. Was it the part where I would've given anything to have been with *you* the other night instead of her? Was it the part where I prayed that you would answer me—that you would stop me from walking up the stairs into her place? Or was it the part where I pictured your face … your body the entire time I was with her?" Quinn paused in frustration.

"Evie, the look on your face as I walked through that door," Quinn pointed to his front door, "is nothing compared to the guilt that has consumed me every minute of every day since that night I walked out of hers.

"If that's moving forward, then I'm at a total loss as to how to do it because the way I see it, if I had a choice between you and any other woman in the world—I would pick you, hands down. I would *always* pick you."

"Quinn," I said cautiously, "I know I promised you that I wouldn't erase your memory, but I really think you should reconsider. You wouldn't have to suffer anymore. You would be able to forget about me … You'd be able to fall in love."

"I already fell in love," he countered. "And I'm still in love with you."

"But you know we're on borrowed time."

"So? Tell me, what other time is there? Life is all about being on borrowed time. Just say the word, and I'll be with you for as long as I can—for as long as you'll have me."

Even if Quinn still loved me, he had to know he shouldn't. He had to realize that this was not the natural order of things … that we made no sense. And I loved Quinn, despite the fact that I knew I couldn't. I had already broken the Rules I was obliged to uphold. To make matters worse, I knew my love for him was putting him at even greater risk of harm. Yet here we were, standing on our respective sides of an impassable abyss.

"Quinn, we obviously were never meant to be together."

"How do you know what we were meant to be when you can't even remember who you were six months ago?" he exclaimed. "You know what—you need to know. Screw the Rules; I'm sick of them.

"Evie, I think I started falling in love with you the first week I saw you in Swain's psych class … And I only got more hooked when I asked for your notes after class one morning, when I followed you to your next class like a stray dog, when I ran into you at the Union … And at the party, when we kissed—that was all it took for me. That's when I knew there was something between us—"

"Quinn, please stop—"

"Why should I? You've broken the Rules before and look where that's gotten us? It's completely idiotic, and I'm sick and tired of playing games. If we can't be together, then at the very least, you should know what you're missing—what you could have had."

"You don't think I know how idiotic this is? … I'm *dead*, Quinn! You are standing there pledging your love to a *dead* girl! A ghost!" I shouted. "I'm not real. I can never be real in the way you need me to be. I can never give you what Ashley or any other *human* girl can." Sorrow flooded me, drowning out the echo of my words reverberating within the shell of the body I now inhabited.

"Evie, you are the *most* real, the *most* alive, person I've ever known." He closed the distance between us. "The other night was a mistake … the worst mistake of my life. But it made me realize how much I love you. I don't want to be with another girl. I want to be with you."

"Quinn … we can't ever *be* together … like that," I said, choking back the ache in my throat.

"I don't care. If we can't act on our feelings for each other in that way, so be it; I'll live without it. But what I can't live without is *you*. Evie, I know I messed things up royally, but please don't push me away. Please tell me how to fix this," Quinn begged. "Tell me how to make it right again between us."

I could feel my defenses slipping. I was afraid to trust what Quinn was saying, but that didn't stop me from hanging on his every word. I wanted to believe he loved me as much as I loved him.

"Evie, I've missed you so much," he whispered hoarsely. "Please don't tell me that this is the end of the line for us." He cradled my face with the palm of his hand. I looked into Quinn's eyes; they looked like peaceful, calm blue ocean waters.

I knew that I should resist him, but I was too tired of arguing with Quinn and fighting my feelings for him. And I was tired of trying to play by the damn Rules that prevented us from being together. And, regardless of whether I obeyed them or broke them, I was convinced, now more than ever, that this moment would have played itself out sooner or later. This was more than Quinn and I just wanting to be together—we didn't know how to be apart from each other.

Quinn gently tilted my head up towards his. He leaned in and kissed me tenderly. My love for Quinn welled up inside of me like water behind a dam about to burst. Suddenly, the last two weeks didn't matter anymore. All that mattered was that I was exactly where I wanted to be—in Quinn's arms.

He pulled me in closer and kissed me again. Sparks flew the second our lips met. I reveled in the way my body reacted to his. We kissed each other like this would be the first and last time we would ever be together—for all I knew, maybe it would be. We embraced each other so tightly we couldn't physically get any closer, and yet we still weren't close enough. The heat emanating off his body was like gasoline to the fire raging inside of me. His breathing got heavier and deeper. I could feel his pulse begin to race. He started maneuvering me across the room and down the hallway towards his bedroom, kissing me the entire way. I followed him blindly.

"Evie, we better stop," he whispered in between kisses, "before things go too far."

"Shh," I whispered as I teased his lips with mine. "You said it yourself ... some Rules are meant to be broken."

Quinn took a deep breath and sighed. "I did say that, didn't I?" The serenity I had seen in his eyes now was replaced by a smoldering blue storm. He kissed me again, and I welcomed the heat that spread through my body at lightning speed.

He began pulling at my T-shirt. As if on cue, I lifted my arms up to help him. Then he reached for his T-shirt, but I simply ripped it off, not wanting to wait another second to feel the warmth of his skin against mine. Before I knew it, I was sitting on the edge of his bed with him standing over me. He paused for a moment to look at me. His eyes flickered wildly, revealing exactly how he felt ... and what he wanted.

He said nothing and neither did I. There was nothing left to say. I pulled Quinn down on top of me, feeling the full weight of his body on mine. My head started spinning out of control as he began to explore my body. I wanted to give myself to him completely.

Then, without warning, a searing pain hit me as an image flashed in my head—the headlights of a pickup truck barreling towards me. I tried my best to ignore it, not wanting anything to interrupt this moment. But another sharp pain tore through me as a second image infiltrated my mind—a man and a woman both in their late-forties. They were ... *my parents*. I immediately pushed Quinn off of me and sat up.

"What's wrong?" He sounded confused and worried.

I couldn't answer him. I was being ambushed by snapshots of my former life. My mind felt like it was being ripped apart. The pain was so excruciating that I couldn't even scream. I grabbed my head with both hands just before my body began seizing.

"Evie, what's happening to you?" Quinn asked in alarm. He scooped me up in his arms, but it wasn't long before I began phasing uncontrollably in and out of my human form. I felt like my head would explode from the pain of thousands of memories of my life bombarding me simultaneously.

"There are some things worse than death." Agnes's words haunted me.

This is the end, I thought. This was the price to be paid for indulging myself—for acting on the passion I had felt for Quinn. I had hung myself with the tightrope I'd tried to walk.

"Quinn," I gasped. I struggled to regain some control over my body, but it was of no use. My physical form was no match for whatever was attacking my mind and shredding it to pieces.

"My God! Evie?"

I tried to grab his hand, but my fingers passed right through his. I could no longer hold on to anything tangible.

"Evie!" Quinn screamed ... and then I was gone.

33. Hark! The Herald Council Calls

"Eve?" I heard my name being called. I opened my eyes to find myself in an unfamiliar room.

"Where … where am I?" I asked hazily.

"You're in the Council's quarters," Peter answered.

"What am I doing here?" I was confused. I looked around to discover I was laying on a chaise lounge. I had no idea how I had gotten there.

"That's a good question," Peter replied.

"You mean … you don't know?" I asked.

"No … none of us do," Peter paused. "Something happened to you. Your signature—it flickered again. Only this time, you managed to teleport yourself to the Archives … right at my feet. One minute you seemed to be in so much agony, and the next, you slipped into a state of unconsciousness, only to awaken now. It was the strangest occurrence I've ever witnessed." Peter's voice broke off again. "I was truly worried about you … I'm still worried about you."

My mind struggled to remember the events that led me back here. I remembered being with Quinn, talking to him … And I remembered kissing him—

"Oh no!" I gasped. I immediately glanced down at myself. Somehow, I was wearing a white T-shirt and jeans. I could only hope that my "default" outfit magically appeared while I involuntarily phased up here before Peter, or anyone else for that matter, saw me dressed as I was while in Quinn's arms.

Oh no! Quinn! I looked up at Peter, my eyes wide with terror.

"Peter! Where's Quinn? Who's watching him?" I asked, panic-stricken.

"Another Shepherd," Peter responded.

"How long have I been out?"

"Just over six hours in *Aura* time."

I had been away from Quinn for more than six days.

"Have ... have I been transferred off the case?" I asked hesitantly.

"For now," Peter replied.

"What does that mean?" I squeaked.

"It means that the Council is reviewing your case. It means, Eve, that depending on the outcome of the Council Tribunal's Inquiry, you may or may not go back to being Mr. Harrison's Shepherd."

I couldn't grasp the idea of never seeing Quinn again ... not now—not after everything we'd been through.

"Eve," Peter said softly, "tell me what happened."

"I remembered," I said, looking up at Peter. "I remembered *everything* ... Peter, I know who I am ... I know who I *was* before I became a Shepherd."

* * *

I followed Peter into the Council's conference room, which could only be described as a makeshift courtroom. In the middle of the room was a single podium. About ten feet in front of the podium was a wooden table, similar to the ones located in the Archives, only longer, with seven chairs tucked underneath, each of which faced the room. Several yards behind the podium were a few rows of pews. The room was stark and cold. In fact, it was devoid of any artwork save for a large tapestry hanging up on the back wall of the room for all to see. I looked more closely at the tapestry and saw the Rules had been intricately and expertly embroidered within the fabric. I wondered if the Three Sisters had created this artful masterpiece. I read the Rules and shivered.

Judgment day, I thought to myself.

Just then seven figures materialized in front of me; four in the form of women and three in the form of men. I correctly assumed that they were members of the Council Tribunal as I watched them take their respective seats at the long table in the back of the room. Each Tribunal member was wearing the same robe, which looked like it had been woven from gold. But when I looked more closely, I realized each of the Tribunal members was emanating a golden hue—an aura— that made him or her glow slightly. Six of the Tribunal members were wearing matching white turbans, while the seventh, a woman who sat in the middle seat, wore nothing on top of her head.

The seventh woman had an exotic look about her, much like Madame Sasha did. She, too, had dark, olive skin and dark brown eyes that were framed by long, black eyelashes. But unlike the psychic gypsy, the Tribunal member was wearing no makeup, and she had thick, white, flowing hair that fell down to the small of her back.

"Council Member Tara," Peter said. I jumped a little at the sound of Peter's voice; I hadn't realized he had still been standing next to me.

"Peter," the woman with the white, flowing hair responded cordially; her voice was incredibly soothing. "It's good to see you again. I hope all is well with you."

"Yes, thank you. I extend the same warm greetings and wishes to you and the rest of the Tribunal members."

"Thank you, Peter," Tara said, speaking on behalf of the panel. She then turned her attention to me and sighed. "Eve, my dear, I had hoped we could have met under different circumstances. Please approach the podium."

Peter took me by the arm and escorted me to the podium.

"Thank you, Peter. That will be all."

"If I may, Council Member Tara, new facts have just been brought to my attention, and I believe they are pertinent to this Inquiry."

"Very well," Tara said with a hint of curiosity. "You may

stay—for now. Have a seat please." Peter did as Tara requested and sat down in the first pew directly behind me.

"Typically," Tara continued as she turned her attention back towards me, "our Inquiries are conducted in an open forum for all Shepherds to witness if they so choose. However, because of the ... *unusual* circumstances that surround your case, Eve, the Council has decided it would be best to handle this matter behind closed doors." Tara cleared her throat before continuing.

"Tribunal members, are we ready to begin the proceedings?" Tara asked the other members without so much as glancing to her left or her right.

"We are," the other six said in perfect unison.

"Good, then begin we shall," Tara announced. "Eve, certain of your activities have been called to our attention. In fact, you stand before us now, accused of violating three of our Rules."

Anxiety and fear spread through me. I locked my knees so they wouldn't buckle right out from under me.

"We will now examine each alleged violation. You will be given an opportunity to explain and defend your actions should you feel the need," Tara explained. She paused, waiting for me to acknowledge that I understood her instructions, and I did so with a brief nod of my head.

"With respect to Rule One," Tara began the interrogation, "did you indeed knowingly seek out information about your past?"

"If I may, Tribunal members," Peter interjected before I could answer Tara's question. I turned around to see Peter standing up, waiting for permission to speak further.

"You may," Tara answered, speaking on behalf of the rest of the panel.

"The situation between Eve and her charge is complicated ... Mr. Harrison *knew* Eve prior to her death."

"We already were aware of this information, Peter," Tara remarked calmly.

"Yes, well," Peter continued, "Mr. Harrison volunteered certain information about Eve's past despite her request that he not do so."

Tara paused for a moment and looked at me.

"Is this true?" she asked me.

"Yes," I managed to say, despite my parched mouth. "But I should mention that I once asked Qui—uh, Mr. Harrison, if he knew where I was from, but he said he didn't."

"I see. Well, we will take Mr. Harrison's role with respect to your violation of this Rule into consideration," Tara said as she made a note in what I assumed was my file.

"With Respect to Rule Three, did you indeed reveal your-self to your charge in a context that did not involve his safety?" Tara questioned.

"Yes," I responded. My head started to spin. This was it. I could see the writing on the wall. I would never see Quinn again. I felt like all of the oxygen had been sucked out of the room.

"And, finally, with respect to Rule Five, did you indeed get personally and emotionally involved with your charge?"

"Again, if I may," Peter offered, this time walking up to the podium next to me.

"Yes, Peter," Tara said calmly, her face expressionless.

"It would also seem that Mr. Harrison and Eve had a re-lationship of a romantic nature at some point while Eve was alive," he stated.

"Peter, we also were aware of this information prior to Eve being assigned to his case," Tara offered.

Peter looked confused and flabbergasted. I, too, was floored. *They knew about Quinn and me, and they assigned me to him anyway? Why would they do that?*

"Is that all of the *new* information you have to offer?" Tara asked.

"No. No, it's not," Peter said somewhat arrogantly. He looked at me and then back at Tara. "It would seem the situation between Mr. Harrison and Eve has been complicated further. Just moments ago, Eve told me she remembers her past ... she knows who she was before she became a Shepherd."

With the exception of Tara, all the other Tribunal members gasped and mumbled amongst themselves. Tara, however, kept her eyes on me like I was her target. She didn't even blink an eye.

"Is this true, Eve?" she asked with a strange curiosity.

"Yes," I replied.

"And just how much do you remember?" she followed up.

"All of it," I said bluntly. "Every memory I have as a child, growing up in Michigan, going to IU—everything."

The panel mumbled again—all but Tara, who now cocked her head slightly to one side while she continued to stare at me.

"My, this does complicate things further, doesn't it?" Tara asked rhetorically.

"It does," Peter offered, unsolicited, "particularly in light of the other information I already provided you ... and the Servants' attack on Eve," he said with more confidence.

The other *information Peter already provided to them?* I repeated to myself. I felt like I had been sucker-punched. Peter had been feeding the Council information about me. He had been *spying* on me. How could he have done that to me? I was overwhelmed with anger, and it took all my strength not to lash out at him right then and there. I shot Peter a look out of the corner of my eye that screamed "traitor." If he saw my expression, he ignored it and continued making his point.

"Tribunal members, I have done some research, and I believe Mr. Harrison and Eve's destinies were entangled for quite some time," Peter remarked.

"We agree with your assessment," Tara conceded. "This is a most extraordinary case. It is unheard of for a Shepherd to be assigned to protect a human who knew the Shepherd while alive—much less to a human with whom the Shepherd had been involved."

"Then how did it happen?" I blurted out. "Why was I assigned to his case?"

"We had our reasons, my dear," Tara said calmly.

"Well, what were they?" I demanded. "What possibly could have led you to believe this was a good idea?"

Peter immediately grabbed my hand and squeezed it hard. "Eve, the Council does not have to explain the bases of its decisions to you," he stated in an admonishing tone.

"No, of course it doesn't," I said bitterly. I didn't care how I was supposed to act before the Council Tribunal members. I was furious. "The Council doesn't have to answer to me, to you—to any of us. But they can go ahead and twist the threads of fate just enough to destroy a young man's life under the perverted guise of *saving* him. The Council can go ahead and assign him a Shepherd with whom he had already fallen in love and then sit back and laugh, knowing that despite the inevitable, the Rules would prohibit any sort of reunion between the two."

"Eve!" Peter reprimanded.

"Are you quite finished?" Tara inquired curtly. Anger flashed in her eyes and the golden aura around her flickered red.

"Yes," I muttered. I knew I had to back off.

"Eve, we need neither explain our actions to you nor provide you with the underlying reasons for our decisions … even as they relate to you," Tara said sharply.

"However," she went on, regaining her composure, "given the unusual nature of your assignment, I do believe it would be prudent for me to share certain information with you. Eve, we did not play a significant role in assigning you to Mr. Harrison's case. To the contrary, your assignment came directly from the Order of the Realms. Needless to say, we were aware of your prior involvement with Mr. Harrison, as well as the potential for a reunion between you two, but we had no authority to circumvent your assignment."

"I ... I don't understand," Peter mumbled. "That goes against everything we do ... everything we stand for. Why would the Order set Eve up to break the Rules? Why set her up to fail?"

"I can assure you that failure was not the intent in this matter. The *complications* you raised, Peter, are of much greater significance than you could have surmised. In life, Eve was no ordinary threat to the Servants."

"I was an eighteen-year-old college student from a small town in Michigan," I interjected. "I wasn't a threat to anyone."

"Not yet," Tara clarified. "And it wasn't you alone that posed the threat."

"I don't follow," I said, confused.

"Eve," Tara sighed, "your fate had been inexplicably tied to Mr. Harrison's well before you two ever met. You see, you alone did not make the Servants nervous. You needed a partner to set the wheels in motion and accomplish whatever it was that would have threatened the Servants. Mr. Harrison was that partner."

"But there is nothing extraordinary about that," Peter jumped in to say. "We've seen this type of scenario before ... where a perceived threat is the result of a combined effort based on human strength, will, and intellect. And just as the Servants have done in the past, they easily could've quashed

405

any such alleged threat posed by Mr. Harrison and Eve simply by manipulating their destinies, thereby preventing them from ever meeting and forming an alliance. The Three Sisters do the same thing when they need to prevent certain disasters."

"Unfortunately, Peter," Tara responded. "This situation is different than the others we have dealt with or seen in the past. The circumstances here are extraordinary because Mr. Harrison and Eve are *true* soul mates."

"*True soul mates,*" a voice in my head repeated. Suddenly, a searing pain ripped through my chest, much like the one I had experienced weeks ago in Quinn's apartment. I couldn't help but grab my chest. I looked at Peter for an answer, but his eyes were clearly full of pain. Could it be that he felt my pain too? Was the connection between mentor and mentee that strong?

"Peter," Tara continued, completely disregarding what she had no doubt witnessed right before her eyes, "you know as well as I that in the case of true soul mates, it would have been nearly impossible to stop, or even slow down, the forces destined to bring Mr. Harrison and Eve together. Thus, the Servants devised an alternative strategy … they sought to eliminate one of the soul mates."

"Me," I said numbly.

"You," Tara confirmed.

"Wait a minute!" I exclaimed. "Are you saying that *I died* so Quinn could *live*?" Tara didn't have to answer—I knew it was true from the look on her face.

"But," Tara continued, "it is also said that the connection between true soul mates is often so powerful that it can transcend even death. The odds of this transcendence occurring increase exponentially when the soul mate who died becomes an immortal with a living soul. We believe the Servants knew of your connection with Mr. Harrison before you died and somehow discovered you had become a Shepherd upon your death. Realizing that ending your mortal life was insufficient to eradicate the threat posed against them by Mr. Harrison and you, they then targeted Mr. Harrison, manipulating his fate and making him their newest target.

"The Order of the Realms believed that if you were assigned to Mr. Harrison," Tara went on to say, "the ongoing connection between you two would provide the stimulus to revitalize the threat the Servants so hoped to foil. And judging from their recent attack on you, I believe the Order was correct in its hypothesis."

"You *used* us ... as *bait!*" I exclaimed. "So in this supposed 'master plan' to foil the Servants, was I always supposed to die? Did you *let* me die?"

"No, my dear. It would seem your death was unavoidable. Your Shepherd used all of his strength to save you in the initial car accident. But the Servants changed their tactics and immediately executed a back-up plan, one which we did not foresee."

"The pickup truck," I whispered out loud.

"The pickup truck," Tara confirmed again. "After your Shepherd used his strength to shield you from the injuries you would have sustained in the car accident, he was too weak to prevent you from being hit by the oncoming vehicle only moments later. Your body died instantly."

"It was mere chance that you were targeted by the Servants first; it could have just as easily been Mr. Harrison. Nevertheless, you were always destined to become a Shepherd, Eve. In that respect, it is unfortunate that your fate triggered Mr. Harrison's own fate and made him a subsequent target."

"You've got to be kidding me," I chuckled cynically. "I died for nothing?"

"Eve, I wouldn't interpret what happened to you that way

at all. You died so you could *save* Mr. Harrison's life," Tara clarified. "And, so far, you have done just that."

"So … does that mean I'm still Quinn's Shepherd?" I asked timidly.

"You two may be true soul mates, but be that as it may, you still broke the Rules and there are consequences for doing so," Tara replied. The monster lurking in the pit of my stomach growled as I began to drown in my own anxiety.

"Yet," Tara continued, "the Tribunal believes there are mitigating circumstances that must be taken into consideration when determining the consequences in this matter. I feel it is necessary that we take a recess from our examination at this time so we can best decide what is most appropriate in light of all of the facts before us.

"Eve, before we end the Inquiry, is there anything you would like to share with us?" Tara's eyes narrowed, like she was looking for something, like she was trying to get inside my head. "Is there anything else we should know about your actions under investigation?"

I tried to wipe my mind clean. I didn't want to the Tribunal members to know about the extent of my relationship with, and my feelings for, Quinn, but it was useless. It was like telling someone not to smile. The more I tried to purge these thoughts from of my head, the more they fought to stay close to the forefront of my mind. Images of Quinn and me together were racing through my head. I was certain the panel was reading every private thought and seeing every intimate image I tried to conceal.

When I scanned the Tribunal members' faces, however, I saw nothing indicating that my secrets had been divulged. How could that be? If they had glimpsed one iota of how much I wanted Quinn, if they had seen any one of the images of Quinn and I together popping into my head, then surely they would've asked me about them. Surely they at least would have raised an eyebrow. But they didn't. I looked at their faces again, and it suddenly dawned on me that maybe they *hadn't* read my thoughts. I didn't understand. Peter told me it would take time for me to develop the skills to shield my thoughts. In fact, Peter hadn't even taught me how to keep my private thoughts private and that's why he ...

Peter. I gasped. I cleared my throat softly and looked at Peter out of the corner of my eye. When he refused to acknowledge me, I knew I was right. He was still shielding my thoughts for me. He was risking being subject to his own Inquiry to help me.

"Fine," Tara announced, "then without further ado, we'll leave you now to confer in our chambers. We will reconvene once we have made our final decision."

"Wait!" I cried out, my mind having snapped back to the heart of what was happening.

"Yes?" Tara said serenely, seemingly unaffected by yet another one of my outbursts.

"You said I could say something ... in my defense."

"Yes, I did."

"Well, I would like to ... say something, that is."

"Go on," Tara said, intrigued.

"First, I want to apologize for breaking the Rules. But the truth is, if I had to do it all over again, if I went back in time knowing my future actions would lead me here, standing before you now, I wouldn't have changed anything. I wouldn't trade a single minute of my time with my charge, even if it means having to face dire consequences for my actions.

"I will resign from being Mr. Harrison's Shepherd without hesitation," I continued. "I'll voluntarily sacrifice my existence as a Shepherd, if it means that Mr. Harrison will be safe ... if my doing so *ensures* that he will survive and that he will be free to live a complete and full life."

"Are you so deeply in love with this mortal that you would so selflessly sacrifice yourself—your *soul*—for him?" asked another female Tribunal member.

"Yes," I said unequivocally. "But the thing is," I continued, "I think it would be a huge mistake to remove me from my assignment. No other Shepherd will be as invested in Mr. Harrison's safety as I am. No other Shepherd will be able to protect him as well as I can. I *know* him. I know how he thinks, how he acts, and how he reacts to things. And he knows me. He trusts me. He will listen to me if I tell him he's in danger.

"Besides," I added, "the Order of the Realms must have been aware of the risks that came along with assigning me to Mr. Harrison's case, but they still assigned me to watch over him anyway. You said it yourself," I said, looking directly at Tara, "they wanted Mr. Harrison and me to be together so we could stop the Servants. So I'm asking that you please let us do what we were originally destined to do."

"We will discuss your case and make a decision," Tara said calmly. "In the meantime, Sergei will escort you to a more comfortable space.

"Peter," Tara turned to look at him, "I think your insight may be of some added benefit to us. Could you please accompany us to our private chambers for a moment?"

"Yes, certainly," Peter responded. He didn't so much as glance at me once as he followed the Tribunal members out of the room.

* * *

Sergei took me to a small waiting room that was just as stark and cold as the courtroom. He closed the door behind me without saying a word. I tried to open the door, but it was locked. *Figures.*

I looked down at my watch; eight days had now passed on Earth since I had last seen Quinn. I couldn't even imagine what my absence was doing to him. I tried to listen for his pulse, but I could no longer hear it ... I could no longer find it. I only heard the ticking of the Time Keeper resonating within me. I didn't know if my inability to connect with Quinn was because I had been away from him for so long or because he had been assigned a new Shepherd. All I knew was that I felt so empty. I hadn't realized how much I had come to rely on the sound of his heart beating inside of me ... how much I had come to treat it like it was my own.

I hoped he was safe. I hoped he didn't blame himself for my disappearing act. I couldn't help but think about how backwards our relationship was: I was his protector, but somehow he always ended up worrying about my well-being.

I wanted to see Quinn, if only for a minute, and tell him I was okay. I tried to teleport myself out of the room, but I couldn't. The room was Shepherd-proof; it was a holding cell of sorts.

I sat there for the next three hours in *Aura* time, during which I thought about what Tara had said, about how Quinn and I were true soul mates, about how we had a connection that transcended death. That would explain why we were so drawn to each other ... so taken by each other when we first met at IU and why we fell so hard for each other so quickly— so completely.

I thought about how Quinn and I were destined to be a team, how we were supposed to stop the Servants' demonic plans. I wondered what we would have done—what we would do if given another chance.

Then I thought about what would happen if the Council denied us a second chance. What if I would never be allowed to see Quinn again? Not even to say good-bye? Chills ran down my spine, leaving me numb. I tried to push the thought from my mind, refusing to entertain the notion. The Council couldn't be that cruel. They had to realize Quinn and I were meant to be together. They just had to see it my way because I was terrified of the alternative.

Suddenly, I thought of my parents and of all of our family debates. I argued with them over whatever personal strife I believed they were causing me at any given moment. But even the sum of all my past familial arguments paled in comparison to the case I was struggling to make for myself, for Quinn, right now.

Just then Sergei opened the door.

"The Council Tribunal is ready to see you now," he announced, his voice almost completely devoid of any intonation.

I took a deep breath and exhaled slowly, forging an invisible trail that seemed to pave the way for anxiety and panic to find me as I followed him to the Council's conference room. I knew I wasn't going to like this very much.

* * *

"We have reached a decision," Tara said as I approached the podium.

All eyes were on me—all eyes except for Peter's; he was nowhere to be found. I looked into the faces of each of the seven Council members to try to get a read on their decision, but their faces were cold as stone and their eyes were boring into me. The tension in the room was so thick I could feel it closing in on me—suffocating me—causing me to clear my throat nervously. My knees began to quiver slightly as I stood there in front of the panel. I gripped the podium for support.

"Quite frankly, I am not convinced that you have what it takes to be one of us, Eve. And I am not alone in my opinion," Tara began. My empty chest quickly filled with an overwhelming aching sensation and my stomach twisted itself in knots. This was definitely not going to be good.

"You have been a Shepherd for mere months," she continued, "and, during that time, you have managed to make more blunders than Shepherds who have been around for centuries." A few mumbles of agreement rippled amongst the Council Tribunal, and another wave of nausea passed through me.

"Moreover, you have disrupted what was considered to be a fluid and peaceful existence for our kind," Tara said sternly. "You have made a mockery of our culture, our history, and our traditions, which have existed for several centuries. You have willingly disregarded the Rules we abide by, you often ignore the wisdom and advice of your mentor, and you have recklessly performed the duties as a guardian of your charge.

"Your disobedience and irresponsible behavior warrant severe consequences—unusually severe. Indeed, Shepherds have been stripped of their positions for lesser offenses than you have committed ... Others have received far worse punishment."

I felt like all the strength of my body was seeping out through my toes and into the floor. I was doing my best to appear calm despite the fact that, inside, I was preparing to hear the worst.

"However," Tara sighed heavily, "regardless of what we decide today, a situation still remains—a situation that is larger than any of us. It is a situation that you and Mr. Harrison are uniquely tied to in some inexplicable way.

"There is a war brewing, Eve; one that inevitably will shift the balance between good and evil. The Servants have wanted this war for quite some time. It is not yet clear exactly how you and Mr. Harrison will be involved in this fight, but it is believed that you two have the ability to fan the flames of this battle or extinguish them.

"Whether the two of you succeed in defeating the Servants—or even *try* to defeat them—is another question altogether. And while some of us doubt your abilities, we are not prepared to abandon all hope. *We simply cannot afford to.*" Tara looked to the colleagues on her left and her right.

"Regrettably," Tara directed her attention back towards me, "we have no choice but to trust that you will do what's right, what's necessary, to stop evil from prevailing. You are an immortal, trained by the best of the best to fight on our side, after all. So," she sighed again, "the question before us now is what we should do with you in light of your recent infractions."

Tara indulged herself in an exceedingly long pause, leaving me to hold my breath while I waited for the gauntlet to drop.

"Eve, we have decided to offer you a choice." Her voice was now as smooth and serene as when I had first heard her speak. "I will be the first to admit this is a most unusual course of action for us, but it is one I believe is advisable at this juncture. As it was, six of us reached a deadlock between two very different consequences, leaving me in the unfortunate position of casting the deciding vote.

"In light of your words earlier, however, I thought it would be best to let you cast the final vote as to which of the consequences we will enforce. A few of my colleagues do not agree with my decision. Nonetheless, I firmly believe a remarkable case of this nature requires a more creative and remarkable response."

"What are my choices?" I allowed myself to feel a glimmer of hope that I could go back to Quinn … that I could choose to remain with him.

"There are two options, the first of which is that you would be removed from your current assignment and reassigned to a new charge, never to see Mr. Harrison again."

I cringed inside.

"The second option," Tara continued, "would be for you to resume your current assignment and see it through to its conclusion *on one condition.*" Tara paused. I was on pins and needles waiting to hear the condition of my return. "You must erase *all* of Mr. Harrison's memories of you since you began your assignment."

I couldn't ignore the wicked twist of fate that now greeted me. It wasn't that long ago that I had wanted to erase Quinn's memory of me—that I had wanted him to forget about me. But things were different now. Quinn and I had made up; we had rekindled our relationship. Moreover, I finally remembered my past … *our* past, brief as it may have been. So to be told now that I could only return to him if I pledged to strip all memories of myself from his mind was a crippling blow.

"If I chose the latter, if I returned to Mr. Harrison, how much time would I be given with him before I was expected to fulfill the condition?" I asked hesitantly.

"None at all," chimed in a male Tribunal member. "You would be expected to erase his memory immediately."

"So I would be denied the opportunity to say good-bye to him?" I tried to keep my anxiety and sorrow at bay. I couldn't afford to be overwhelmed with emotion; I had to think clearly.

"We see no benefit in allowing you to drag out your current relationship with Mr. Harrison any longer than you have already," the same Tribunal member responded coldly.

"And what about *my* memories … of this summer … of my life?"

"They are yours to keep regardless of your choice," Tara

replied. "We do not erase memories twice as we have good cause to believe it would result in permanent damage."

I now understood what Tara had meant when she said she had heard me. I had set myself up to prove how selflessly I loved Quinn. I had professed that his safety was all that truly mattered to me. Knowing I didn't trust another to guard him from harm, the Council really had given me only one viable option—to erase Quinn's memories of me from his mind and remain invisibly chained to his side as his Shepherd until his fate was sorted out. In the end, I really had no choice at all.

I just hoped I was strong enough to follow through with my decision. I *had* to be strong enough. I knew the Council would never give me another chance. But to have any chance of succeeding, I knew I needed to see Quinn one more time. I needed to say the things still left unsaid. I needed to finish our story.

"Tribunal members, I know I am in no position to make a request," I said humbly, "but I would like to ask for one thing." I paused, waiting for the objections to fly from the panel. They remained silent, so I continued. "If I agree to your condition, if I agree to erase all recent memory of me from his mind, I ask that you please give me a day—one *Mora* day—to be with Mr. Harrison before I fulfill my end of the bargain.

"I realize my request may not make sense to you, particularly because my charge will no longer remember me or the extra time we would share together, but *I* still will—I will remember every experience I've ever had with him … as well as every experience of my entire life. It's a lot to come to terms with, and I don't want to risk making any more mistakes. So I am respectfully requesting that you please let me say goodbye to him … let me close this chapter so *I* can move forward. So I can focus all of my energy and attention on doing my job."

"I don't think we need to remind you that this is a *consequence* for your violation of the Rules." A second male Tribunal member stated tersely.

"I'm only asking for one day. Trust me, even if you granted me a lifetime of days with Mr. Harrison before I had to erase his memory, it still wouldn't be enough time with him," I responded.

"And if we refuse your request, will you choose the first option and be reassigned?" a third female Tribunal member inquired.

"No," I responded bluntly. "As I said before, I believe I'm the one who can best protect Mr. Harrison from harm, and I am not prepared to risk his life. I am his Shepherd.

"Besides," I said, looking Tara directly in the eyes, "if what you have said today is true, if Mr. Harrison and I are true soul mates ... if our love can transcend death, then I'm not sure the first option would even work. Somehow, I think I knew we were soul mates all along. Somewhere deep down, I believe Mr. Harrison and I *both* knew it. In fact, I revealed myself to him because *he felt me*—he actually felt my presence. He knew I was there, and he couldn't let that go.

"So, no offense, but if the Servants couldn't keep us apart while I was alive, and the Rules couldn't keep us apart after I died, what makes you so sure that Mr. Harrison and I won't find each other again if you separate us now? If I get reassigned and abandon Mr. Harrison without ever saying good-bye, without ever letting him know I'm okay, I'm certain he'll just keep looking for me until he finds me—or until he finds some logical explanation of what happened to me."

"We could simply reassign you and erase all memories of you from Mr. Harrison's mind," piped in the same female member.

"Which ones?" I asked. My voice was laced with a hint of arrogance now bubbling inside of me.

"Excuse me?" she asked, baffled.

"Which memories would you erase?" I asked again, point blank.

The entire panel fell silent.

"The truth is I'm the only one who knows which memories to erase. And, now, I've just learned it's unsafe to erase a mind twice. So I don't see any reason to refuse my request when I'm the only one who can be entrusted with the task of erasing all recent memories of me from Mr. Harrison's mind."

"This is sounding dangerously close to a threat," Tara said, the warning tone in her voice was clear. Without Tara on my side, I knew I didn't have the slightest chance of getting more time with Quinn.

"It's not," I said apologetically. "I certainly don't want it to be. I just want to do this the right way—the only way I know how. Look, if I can just be given a chance to say what needs to be said ... to see him one more time as *him*, then I'll agree to erase all memory of me as a Shepherd from his mind, and I'll do nothing intentional to contact my charge unless it is absolutely essential to save his life. Please, it's just one day. What's one day?"

Tara sighed. "We will grant you *eight hours*, Eve," she declared. "Eight hours in *Mora* time in which to get your ... *closure* and erase his memory," she quickly clarified. "Don't make us regret giving you this gratuitous gift," she added.

"Thank you," I said respectfully, looking at Tara. It wasn't an entire day, but it was something—it was a gift. And, in return, I would do the Council's bidding—after all, I had no other choice ... for now.

My heart began pounding loudly, and I realized that it wasn't the Time Keeper I was feeling ... it was Quinn. Not wanting to waste another second without him, I teleported myself back down to Earth.

Quinn, I'm on my way home.

Excerpt From Book Two: Peace of Mind

"Quinn," I said softly.

He stirred slightly in his bed.

"Quinn, it's me … Evie."

Slowly, he opened his eyes and looked over at me, bewildered. He blinked a few times to make sure he wasn't dreaming. He didn't say anything. He didn't move.

"Quinn, I'm here. I'm home."

"Evie?" he barely managed, his voice trembling slightly.

"Yes," I whispered. I caressed his face with my hand and felt the wet trail of a tear that had rolled from the corner of his eye down the side of his face. I wanted to embrace him. I wanted to nestle my face into the small of his neck. But I didn't—not yet anyway.

He reached over to his bedside table and turned on the light, never taking his eyes off of me. He cautiously reached out his hand and caressed my cheek, moving down my neck to my bare shoulder.

"I thought you … I mean … I thought I would never see you again," Quinn uttered. "That night … I didn't know what to do. I thought I had … well, I didn't know what could happen to you, but I thought that I had … hurt you somehow." He rested his head back on his pillow, put his hand on his forehead, looked up at the ceiling, and paused for a moment before continuing. "You know, I actually consulted a priest about what bad things could happen to angels."

"You did *what?*" I asked, unable to hold back a giggle.

"Don't mock me," he said sternly, turning his head towards me. "Evie, it's been almost two weeks since I've seen you … You should have seen yourself that night … You were in so much pain, and I couldn't do anything to stop it. And then … just like that, you were gone."

"Quinn, I'm so sorry you had to go through all of that. You have to believe me when I tell you that none of what happened to me that night was your fault."

"How can you say that?" Quinn replied. "None of it would have happened if I hadn't kissed you ... if I hadn't tried to—"

"You weren't the only one who wanted to take things further that night, you know," I interjected. "I was kissing you too."

"Yeah, but I should've been stronger. I should've stopped things before they got that far. I knew there were Rules, Evie, and I *wanted* you to break them. I was hoping you would. I was selfish, and *you* ended up paying the price."

"Shh," I purred as I put my finger on Quinn's lips. His full lips were so warm and soft—so inviting. I pictured myself kissing them and a ripple of energy passed through me. "Quinn, you actually helped me that night." I flashed him a flirtatious little smile. "Besides, do you *really* think you would have had the restraint to stop yourself?" I sat up slightly, just enough for the covers to fall away from me and expose the top half of my naked body.

Quinn took a deep breath and exhaled slowly, taking me in with his eyes. I began to draw little circles on his chest, my fingers gradually making their way down towards his stomach.

"Well," he cleared his throat and closed his eyes, trying to focus on his answer. "I certainly ... would've tried." A slight groan escaped his lips as my index finger traced the rim of his navel. I smiled even wider.

With his eyes still closed, I leaned forward and kissed him. He kissed me back, and fireworks went off inside me. I kissed him harder, deeper, as I began to maneuver myself on top of him. Quinn didn't resist—at first. But then he stopped me abruptly, pushing me off of him. He looked more worried than I'd ever seen him.

"It's okay," I tried to reassure him. "Everything will be fine."

"Fine?" Quinn asked in disbelief. He sat up, propping his back up against his headboard. "After what happened to you the last time we tried this, how can you risk breaking the Rules again?"

"You don't understand," I said softly. "Tonight, there are no Rules." I leaned in to kiss him again.

"What do you mean?" Quinn asked, avoiding my kiss and shifting his body to put a few more inches of space between us. I could almost hear the questions running through his mind. I knew it was unfair of me to deny him an explanation as to why it was okay for us to be with each other tonight, but I didn't want to talk about it. We had this one night together, and I didn't want to waste what little time we had left dodging questions I wasn't permitted to answer anyway. I sighed, trying to come up with something that would end this conversation as quickly as possible.

"Quinn, I'm so tired of explaining myself and having to justify my actions. Right now, I just want to be with you. I *need* to be with you."

Denying Quinn the opportunity to protest further, I leaned over and teased his earlobe with my tongue. He inhaled slowly and held his breath. My lips traveled to his neck, nipping it tenderly with my teeth. I could feel his body reacting to my touch. Another groan escaped his lips; I kissed him again, but he still hesitated. Not giving up, I playfully brushed my lips against his as my hand wandered down his chest and his stomach until I reached the waistband of his boxers.

Instantly, Quinn grabbed my hand to stop me. I jumped back slightly, stunned by his quick response. We both froze and stared into each other's eyes, waiting to see who would make the next move. He chuckled suddenly.

"What?" I asked, unaware there was any humor to be had in this moment.

"Never in a million years would I have imagined myself as being the responsible one in this type of situation," he said, still chuckling. "Especially with you."

"Well, I'm asking you to be irresponsible tonight." I kissed him, never breaking my gaze. "Please don't fight me on this," I begged. "Not tonight."

He closed his eyes momentarily as if to mentally weigh the pros and cons of what I was asking him to do. I leaned over and kissed him again. In one swift motion, he maneuvered me onto my back. I could feel the full weight of his body bearing down on me. His face was barely an inch from mine. I could feel his breath on my face, and it made me crave him even more.

He stared at me with such intensity I almost had to look away, but I was too mesmerized by the blue flames dancing within his eyes. I had seen that look before; I knew it meant Quinn wanted me.

Linda Lamberson is a Chicago-area native, an author, and a devoted mother and wife. After studying at Indiana University in Bloomington, she attended graduate school at The University of Chicago, where she received her Master's degree in Social Service Administration and then her Juris Doctor degree, and worked as an intellectual property attorney. In 2009, Linda was inspired to create the Evie Sanders series while on a flight home. A conversation with a neighboring passenger made Linda think about a car accident she'd been in while a freshman in college—an accident she was lucky enough to walk away from unscathed, much to the surprise and shock of witnesses. For the remainder of the flight she couldn't shake the thought, "What if I hadn't survived? Would that have been the end of my story?" That same night, Linda started writing.

Look for *Peace of Mind*, the next installment of the Evie Sanders series, in 2012.

For more information about Linda and her book series, visit her website:
www.lindalamberson.com